A Sword Among Ravens

Book Three of the Long-Hair Saga

Cynthia Ripley Miller

D1224704

BookLocker

Print ISBN: 978-1-64719-001-9
Epub ISBN: 978-1-64719-002-6
Mobi ISBN: 978-1-64719-003-3

Published by BookLocker.com, Inc., St. Petersburg, Florida.

Printed on acid-free paper.

BookLocker.com, Inc.
2020

First Edition

Library of Congress Cataloguing in Publication Data
Miller, Cynthia Ripley
A Sword Among Ravens by Cynthia Ripley Miller
Library of Congress Control Number: 2020918587

Praise for the Long-Hair Saga Novels
by
Cynthia Ripley-Miller

On the Edge of Sunrise; The Quest for the Crown of Thorns; A Sword Among Ravens

"From cover to cover a gripping read – in all senses of the word! Grips your interest and imagination, your held breath and your pounding heart! A thumping good novel!"

> \- Helen Hollick USA Today bestselling author of the *Sea Witch Voyages*

"Forbidden love, a turbulent time period, and world-changing events combine to produce a real page-turner."

> \- India Edghill, author of *Queenmaker*, *Wisdom's Daughter*, and *Delilah*.

"A passionate and intriguing take on the often-overlooked clash of three brutal and powerful empires: the Romans, Franks, and Huns. A Compelling read!"

> \- Stephanie Thornton, author of *The Secret History* and *The Tiger Queens*

"Readers will be absorbed by a setting of barbarian Gaul and the constancy of Arria's and Garic's destined love amid the strife of a dying Roman Empire."

> \- Albert Noyer, author of *The Getorius and Arcadia Mysteries*

"In this thriller, set in fifth-century Rome, rivals race to possess Christ's crown of thorns. Ripley Miller (On the Edge of Sunrise 2015) astutely brings to life a Rome teetering precariously on the brink of collapse … The plot advances energetically, and the combination of political and romantic drama—spiritual as well—is rousing. The reader should be glad to have read this volume and eager for a third. Intelligent and artfully crafted historical fiction … ."

- Kirkus Reviews ~ *The Quest for the Crown of Thorns: Book Two of the Long-Hair Saga*

"Miller writes (A Sword Among Ravens) with not only a great deal of elegance but also authority, which brought this era back to life in all of its splendour . . . she sweeps them away in a narrative that can only be described as enthralling."

- Mary Anne Yarde author of the *Du Lac Chronicles*

For my parents, Ariano and Lillian Niccoli;
and my forever friend, Dede Sayadian Frank

AUTHOR'S NOTE

I often feel like a detective searching for the facts true to the 5th century, and I enjoy it. In my previous two books and this one, I researched many items and customs that the modern person might be unaware of or take for granted. For example: Which gems were known and used in the time of King David of Israel (ruled 1035-970 BC)? Was the size, metal, and shape of a sword used in King David's time the same as a sword used in the 5th century AD? How many miles could a traveler on foot, on a horse, or in a wagon cover in one day? What materials were used to stitch and treat a variety of wounds? What were the burial practices? Did sutures dissolve, and did they shake hands? In this note, I would like to offer the reader a bit of background to help broaden the setting and customs of the time in the Roman Empire and late antiquity (AD 395-800).

Roman Months: Januarius, Februarius, Martius, Aprilis, Maius, Junius, Julius (originally Quinctilis, changed later to honor Julius Caesar), Augustus (originally Sextilis, changed to honor Caesar Augustus), September, October, November, December.

Roman Days (The seven day week introduced by Emperor Constantine AD 306-337): Monday-*dies lunae* (moon's day); Tuesday-*dies martis* (Mars); Wednesday-*dies mercurii* (Mercury); Thursday-*dies jovis* (Jupiter); Friday-*dies veneris* (Venus); Saturday-*dies saturni* (Saturn); Sunday-*dies solis* (sun's day).

Transportation and Accommodations: I used Lionel Casson's books *Travel in the Ancient World* and *The Ancient Mariners* and the 'Pilgrim of Jerusalem's' account as prime sources. People traveled primarily on foot or horseback; by carts, coaches, and wagons; and by ship.

Hospitium, stabulum, and mansio were terms used for 'respectable' lodging in ancient Rome. They provided everything travelers might need: 'meals and sleeping quarters; change of clothing for the drivers and postilions; change of animals; carriages and drivers; grooms; escorts for bringing back vehicles and teams to the previous station; porters; veterinarians to put to right animals in trouble; cartwrights to put to rights equipment in trouble.' (Casson 1994)

Although actual passenger ships did not exist in the 5th century, people traveled on trading vessels and freighters. In Lionel Casson's book *The Ancient Mariners*, I discovered that passenger lists and manifests were used. 'Travelers booked deck passage, sleeping either in the open or under little tent-like shelters.' The average amount of time it took to travel by sea was 5-6 days, depending on the destination, and 8-10 days in poor weather.

PLACES

Constantinople: The capital city of the Eastern Roman Empire from the years AD 330-1204 and 1261-1453, and as the capital of the Latin Empire (1204-1261). Later it served as the capital of the Ottoman Empire from 1453-1921. In the 1920s, the Turkish variation Istanbul became the preferred name of this historic city.

In AD 330, the Roman emperor Constantine moved the capital from Rome to Byzantium and renamed the city *Constantinopolis*, meaning 'City of Constantine.' In AD 395, the Roman Empire was divided into two parts. Constantinople remained the center of the Eastern Empire until 1453, whereas the Western Empire and Rome fell in AD 476. Constantinople was the largest and wealthiest city in the empire from the fifth century into the thirteenth century. In Roman times, the government advanced Christianity and the city as the home of the Patriarch of Constantinople and the 'guardian of Christendom's holiest relics such as the Crown of Thorns and the True Cross.' (newadvent.org, ancientcivilizations-ushistory.org, wikipedia.org)

Jerusalem: In AD 324–25, Emperor Constantine reunited the empire after winning the Civil Wars of the Tetrarchy. Within a few months, the First Council of Nicaea (first worldwide Christian council) confirmed the status of Aelia Capitolina, (the name given to Jerusalem by the emperor Hadrian in AD 130) as a residence of a patriarch. This was when a significant wave of Christian pilgrims and immigration to the city began. The city is believed to have been renamed Jerusalem in 324. In 325, the ban on Jews entering the city remained in force (first enforced by Emperor Hadrian after the Simon Bar Kokhba revolt) but were allowed to enter at different periods once a year to pray at the Western Wall on 'the ninth of Ab' (Asali, K.J., Jerusalem in History, 2000).

Damascus Gate: "Emperor Hadrian's Neapolis gate . . . now became St. Stephen's Gate for some centuries [Byzantine period] until the Arabs named it the Gate of the Column, and later the Nablus Gate; Jews called it the Shechem Gate; Ottoman's called it today's name, Damascus Gate. (Today's St. Stephen's Gate is on the eastern side of the city.)" (Montefiore, 2011)

The Tower of David: Herod the Great built three towers named Phaesal, Hippicus, and Mariamne. With time, however, only one survived. During the Byzantine era, the remaining tower, 'and by extension the Citadel as a whole, acquired its alternative name—the Tower of David.' In error, the Byzantines identified the hill on which it sat as Mount Zion and assumed it to be David's palace mentioned in 2 Samuel. The Tower of David, known to the Byzantines (this story's time period), is not the minaret built by the Muslims that is seen today and called the Tower of David. David's Road and St. John's Street are fictitious names I created for lack of data for the time.

Garic's fictional farm is called *Wilder Honig* (I used German to represent the ancient Frankish language) and *Wild Honey* in English. It's in the province of Belgica Secunda in northeastern Gaul (France).

Arria's villa is located in *Tuscia*, the Roman name for Etruria, the territories in central Italy originally under ancient Etruscan influence. In the past, it equated with the modern-day region of Tuscany.

POINTS OF INTEREST

Flavius Valerius Marcian: The emperor of the Eastern Roman Empire, Flavius Marcian, ruled from AD 450-457. He spent his early years as a soldier but rose to a position in the Roman guard, an elite unit that served as household members and bodyguards to the emperor. In time, Flavius Marcian was made captain of the guard and later raised to the position of senator. When Theodosius II died in

450, the deceased emperor's sister, Pulcheria, chose Marcian as her consort to rule the Eastern Roman Empire in Constantinople (Istanbul, Turkey).

Patriarch: In AD 451, the Council of Chalcedon raised the bishop of Jerusalem to the position of patriarch. Juvenal was the first patriarch from AD 451-458.

The Latin endearment Mellitula used by Garic for Arria means 'little honey.' The German endearment Krieger used by Arria for Garic means 'warrior.'

David's sword is a fictitious creation.

Lastly, I've endeavored to represent the events, places, and beliefs as near to the historical record as possible. However, I've also added my interpretation to the lives of all the characters, real and imagined.

The Cast of Characters

Arria Felix: A Roman Senator's daughter and a Roman envoy
Garic the Frank: A Frank barbarian noble and First Counsel to his tribe and Arria's husband
Lucius Valerius Marcian: A tribune and Arria's first husband killed in battle in AD 448
Darius: A Roman centurion under Lucius Marcian and Goth barbarian
Emperor Flavius Valerius Marcian: A senator, later emperor of Constantinople; Tribune Lucius Marcian's father
Samuel Ben Zechariah: Arria's former slave and manservant
Licia: Arria and Garic's adopted daughter, age 7
Vodamir & Basina: Garic's cousin and his wife, a Hun healer
Catalina: Arria's handmaiden
Brother Bruno: A monk from the monastery of San Petrus in Brundisium (Brindisi, Italy)
Justus &Telemachus: Emperor Marcian's royal bodyguards

Marcella: Arria's half-sister
Nerian: A Saxon mercenary and Marcella's lover companion
Accipiter: An Egyptian merchant in Jerusalem
Corvus & Jax: Mercenaries for hire
Valeria Azarian: An Armenian merchant and trader in artifacts
Kalev Ben Jonah aka Goliath & Alexander Kronus: A Jewish merchant from Constantinople
Milvus: An Armenian merchant in Jerusalem and Valeria's brother
Anna: Milvus' cousin and widow
Porcius Festus: A Roman procurator and Anna's lover

He/Nemesis: Psychopath and villain
Leo: Centurion under Tribune Lucius Marcian
Seneca & Sharpie: Soldiers under Lucius Marcian
Leah: Kalev's wife
Joshua: Kalev's son
Atticus: Valeria's bodyguard
Tygran: Caravan master

Babajan: Accipiter's servant
Rachel: A Jerusalem wine maiden
Urban: Swordsmith in Caesarea
Father Audric aka Father Prior: Prior of the Monastery of the Cross
Brother Evander and Brother Primus: Monks at the Monastery of the Cross
Patriarch Juvenal: The Patriarch of the Church of Jerusalem
Bishop Anastasius: Bishop of the Church of Jerusalem
Father Isaac: Secretary to the bishops and patriarch in Jerusalem
Erasmus: Emperor's older servant
Zoran: Milvus' servant boy

BYZANTINE JERUSALEM
A.D. 326–638

St. Stephen's
Gate
(Damascus Gate)

Sheeps
Pools

Forum

Cardo Maximus

Golden
Gate

Church of the
Holy Sepluchre

Church of
John the
Baptist

St. John's Street

David's
Gate

David's
Tower

David's Road

Red
Torch
Inn

Sion
Basilica

Sion
Gate

Prologue

A Husband, a Sword, and a Curse

AD 447: Roman Province of Dacia Ripensis (Bulgaria)—Month of Julius

Waves of burnt grass fell away as Lucius Valerius Marcian stomped through the battlefield. Behind him, his surviving cavalry soldiers—the Roman VIII Augusta Equites—found their horses abandoned when the fighting went to foot. Marcian stopped and looked around.

Toward the west, bold yellow rays stretched from the late afternoon sun across gray clouds gathering overhead. They shined with an ominous brightness that rattled through him, making him uneasy—on guard. The battle against the Huns had been fierce. Both sides suffered heavy losses, but their Roman general had died on the field, a brutal blow for the Romans. Shouting victory, the Huns had moved east toward a nearby city, and greater plunders.

A mild breeze swept past him. He winced. A stench floated from the barbarian and Roman corpses around them. The smell of death wasn't new to him. But even now, after many battles and bodies at his feet, the foul odor, the sight of bloated flesh, and gaping wounds were still difficult to ignore.

Marcian swallowed hard and turned from the wind. He searched the distance. On a small hill, he spied Apollo. The horse grazed beside a cluster of bushes that circled a large oak tree. Sweat dripped from Marcian's curls and onto his brow while splatters of blood and skin stuck to his tunic, helmet, and leather armor. The summer heat had laughed at the slaughter, adding a cruel torment to the battle, but they had persevered, fought tight, outmaneuvered—and lived. He would see Arria again.

The other horses stood farther away, and the men fanned in that direction. Marcian grinned. It was just like Apollo to go in his own direction and very similar to his master, who often struggled with his own independent nature. Even the girl he chose to marry was not the average Roman woman. Arria had been raised unconventionally. Her father had provided her with a man's education, not just the domestic arts taught to women. As a result, many in Rome respected her for her sharp wit, powers of deduction, and diplomacy. Marcian's friends warned that she might be a difficult wife to control, but he had no desire to rule over her; he just wanted to live with and lay beside her. He loved her tenacity, her keen mind, and most important to him, they laughed together.

Marcian ran up the hill while Apollo continued to graze. Suddenly, he stumbled and went sprawling face down onto the ground. Something solid had tripped him. He rose to his knees and shook his head. Running his fingers over his forehead, he glanced behind him. A small black object jutted out from the grass at an angle.

Scrambling to his feet, he went and crouched over it. To the eye and touch, it looked and felt like an iron ring pushing through the earth, eroded by weather and time. Marcian drew his knife and scratched the exterior. Hardened dirt stuck to the surface, forcing him to chip it away. The more he scraped, the larger the object grew. After several more attempts, the ring appeared attached to a metal slab. Marcian looked around. The field was quiet. Most of his men had retrieved their horses and returned to the field camp. Roman bodies needed to be stripped and buried. Not far from him, he spotted his centurion riding in his direction. He waved, and the Roman soldier trotted his horse toward him. A barbarian by birth, the tall, husky blond Goth, Darius, wore only a tunic with a thick leather belt, boots, and no helmet. He lent a sharp contrast to Marcian's shorter, rugged build and dark coloring.

"Darius, help me!" Marcian stood and shouted. "I've found something odd buried in the grass."

The centurion rode up the hill and jumped from his horse. "What is it, sir?" he asked.

"An iron ring attached to a lid or door, but I want to know what's inside. Tie up my horse. Then go to the camp and bring back two shovels."

Marcian returned to his knees while Darius tethered Apollo and then rode away. Thunder pealed in the distance. He looked toward the sky. A few sun rays still pierced the clouds, but the moving layers looked darker, heavier. He raked his knife faster. With a strong hand, he brushed away the earth. Marcian sat back on his haunches, gazed at the ring, and waited. Soon, Darius arrived with the shovels. They dug along the perimeter in opposite directions. Within minutes, they uncovered two hinges on what was clearly a bronze frame. Whatever lay beneath the earth was larger than Marcian had imagined.

In unison, they fought feverishly to unearth the mysterious object and beat the threatening rain. With the last layer of dirt gone, both men stopped to rest. Embedded in the hill's grassy slope, a three by six-foot rusted iron door shone dark brown in the light. Darius sat on a nearby rock. Marcian took a breath, removed his helmet, and dropped it on the ground.

"How strange," Marcian commented, pulling a short scarf from around his neck. He wiped his brow and then tied it around his forehead.

Darius nodded, then pursed his lips and scratched his jaw. "Looks heavy, I wonder if it can be opened?" With a quick laugh, he added. "I brought some mead to strengthen us."

"Good man!"

Darius retrieved a pouch hanging on his saddle and tossed it to Marcian, who took a swig and handed the pouch back to the centurion. Darius took a long drink.

Marcian looked at the sky. "The sun is hidden now. Let's open this door—to the devil knows what—and be done before the rain falls." He grabbed the handle, and Darius used the shovel to pry open the door from its frame.

The first attempt proved futile. Their breath labored, they heaved and groaned as thunder rolled over them.

"Balls! This is stubborn," Darius hissed between clenched teeth.

Marcian tugged at the handle. Darius wedged the shovel's blade between the door and the frame. The door hinges creaked, giving them hope. Their muscles straining, they braced their legs, bent forward, and yanked. The door screeched like a warning owl. "Harder," Marcian gasped. Darius bellowed a curse.

The door suddenly gave way, almost knocking Marcian backward. He steadied himself, took a step, and looked down. A dark hole leading into a tunnel gaped back at him.

"*Shit!* What's that?" Darius spat.

"How the hell do I know," Marcian replied gruffly, but I'm going to find out."

Darius nodded, swiped the pouch from the ground, and took another drink. "Will you go first, Tribune?"

Marcian laughed. "Centurion, I won't let my rank trump your lack of courage." With a last look into the pit, he jumped in. The edge of the earth came to his waist, and he knelt to crawl in deeper. A few feet ahead of him, he saw bone fragments, a partial jaw with several teeth, and a bundle of deteriorated leather. A shield rested nearby.

Marcian's heart beat faster. He looked closer. A metal box poked through the bones and animal skin. A sudden rush of dread washed over him. Sweat trickled from beneath the scarf covering his brow. He paused but spied a metal grip. Marcian quickly yanked the box and scurried backward, dragging the case to the opening. Darius gave him a hand, and Marcian jumped out. Together, they reached into the hole and lifted the box onto the ground.

They stood beside it and stared. The box looked about three feet long, a foot wide and half as deep. Marcian tore away the decomposed leather clinging to the outside. On closer inspection, the case proved to be silver, heavily tarnished. A lock secured the lid. Marcian snatched a remnant of the aged leather and rubbed the top of the metal. A short row of engraved and unrecognizable letters or symbols, dulled by time, appeared. He frowned. The case seemed quite old, perhaps ancient.

"Shall we open it?" Darius asked, his eyes shining.

"Better to open it here than in camp with many around us. Use the shovel."

Darius nodded and swung the blade down against the lock. Yielding to the force of the clanging iron tool, the lock snapped open. Marcian planted his feet firmly behind the box, at the base, and clamped his fingers on the lid's edge. Darius pressed one foot on the front side and used his knife to pry at it while Marcian pulled from behind. The rusted lid budged a little but groaned its refusal.

"Lift!" Marcian barked, and his jaw tightened. The lid creaked one more time—then gave in and opened.

A *whoosh* escaped the box trailed by a faint odor of eucalyptus. Both men flinched with the sensation and glanced at one another. Inside, an object wrapped in grayed linen cloth fit snugly into the container.

"This gets more mysterious by the moment," Marcian said softly.

Darius scratched his head. "What is it?"

"Let's find out; the day is dying, and a raindrop just brushed my cheek." Marcian kneeled and lifted the bundle from its case. With a pivot and his arms extended, he gently placed it on the ground. As Marcian unwrapped the object, pieces of the linen crumbled. A soft flash of light burst through the fabric and struck his eyes; he blinked. When he looked again, a sword, simple in form but strangely beautiful lay nestled in the cloth. Gazing at it, he knew it must be an ancient weapon. The gray metal harbored slight flakes of rust and held a matted gloss. The sword was short, more like an old *gladius,* and not as long as the standard *spatha.* The round ivory grip was carved with circular lines. The silver pommel held small, bright-red rubies that sparkled in the light from their tiny recesses. Just below the blunted cross-guard, etched down the center of the blade, gold symbols—similar to those on the surface of the box—flowed in a line.

Darius let out a whistle.

Marcian took a breath and picked it up. "It's lighter than I thought it would be." He ran his finger over the flat surface, then gently pressed his thumb to a surprisingly sharp edge just below the tip. "This must be the sword of a king or nobleman, but from where or when?"

"Wherever the sword is from, it could be of great value," Darius added. "Why else would it be so carefully preserved and hidden?"

Marcian frowned. "Say not a word to anyone in the camp." Placing the sword back into the silver casket, he closed the box. He slipped the scarf from his brow to his neck, replaced his helmet resting near his feet, stood, and thought, *I'll take this to father in Constantinople. With his power as a senator, he may be able to help me unravel the mystery surrounding this weapon.*

Marcian ordered Darius to shut the outer door and cover the site with dirt to protect the grave. Regardless if the bony remnants came from a servant, guardian, or nobleman, they would show respect for the dead, even if they kept the sword. Then Marcian folded the pieces of cloth on top of the sword and closed the lid of the box. He carried it to his horse and, with leather straps, secured it to the backboard of his saddle. Both men mounted and proceeded down the hill.

At the base, Darius took the lead and gave Marcian a sly look. "I'd wager the sword is worth something. Or maybe . . . it carries bad luck—the evil eye."

"I'll never wager this sword, not for anything, but I bet it's more valuable than damned." Marcian grinned.

The centurion let out a hearty laugh. "Are you sure you'll never wager?" He put the pouch to his lips. Marcian swore. As he watched Darius drink, a swift and sudden *zip* pierced the air and careened past him, almost grazing his ear. A chilling horror gripped him. An arrow struck Darius in the neck, and the centurion slumped over.

Marcian slid frantically from his horse using Apollo as a barrier. Twenty feet away, a wounded Hun rested on his knees, his body hunched, a bow resting in his hand. Marcian grabbed his spear from its case and hurled it with all his strength into the warrior's chest. The impaled barbarian grunted and fell backward. Marcian ran to Darius. The centurion had survived the battle, but now he sat lifeless in his saddle—bled to death.

Marcian kicked the ground and went to the dead Hun. "Son of a bitch!" he swore, yanking the spear from the Hun's body and stabbing him again. He circled around, letting out an angry cry, ripped out the spear, and threw it down. Darius the Goth had ridden by his side from Marcian's first days with the cavalry.

Rain started to fall. Marcian pushed Darius' body forward and tied him to his saddle. Mounting Apollo, he grabbed the reins of Darius' horse. His soldier and friend had fought the Huns bravely and lived. But now, by an unexpected twist of fate, he was dead.

Marcian stared at the dark clouds as a brooding premonition shook him. He prayed the sword carried no curse.

I

Call on Me and I Will Answer

EASTERN ROMAN EMPIRE: Constantinople—AD 455
The Imperial Palace, The 25th day of Aprilis

ARRIA

Morning sunlight radiated through Emperor Flavius Valerius Marcian's office chamber. Called to a private meeting, Arria Felix and her husband, Garic the Frank, sat across from Arria's former father-in law, and now emperor, in plush red chairs with golden claws curled over the armrests. Three slaves stood behind them and another beside the emperor. The month warmer than usual, servants waved tall fans, feathered and shaped in half-moons, to cool them.

Their quest for the Crown of Thorns completed, and the Crown safely enshrined in the Great Church in Constantinople, they were ready to return to Italia. But to their surprise, the emperor approached them about another task that he felt only they could carry out.

Emperor Marcian's eyes shined intensely at Arria. "I have prayed for guidance to know whom to choose for this mission. On the day you arrived with the Crown, I realized my prayers had been answered. You—and Noble Garic—can fulfill my hopes. I possess another artifact known only to me and the one who gave it to me—my son, Lucius."

Arria winced. Had her deceased husband, Lucius Marcian, retrieved, found, or looted an artifact of value and not confided in her? A strange feeling rose inside of her, and she raised her chin a bit higher. Lucius always told her everything. Why not about this artifact? "May I know the artifact and what this mission entails before we accept?"

"In honor of my son and the supreme trust I have in you, yes. But you must decide by tomorrow before the end of the day. Agreed?"

Arria glanced at Garic, who glanced back and said, "Please tell us the nature of this undertaking. Arria and I have endured a lot in these last months and adopted a child who waits for us in Italia at Brundisium. We'll take the time given to reflect. We traveled here with Vodamir and Basina and should consider their feelings as well. I know my cousin. If we accept, he'll most likely want to join us, but his wife, Basina, may not."

Arria nodded her agreement and addressed the emperor. "Garic is a counselor to his tribe and known to speak wisely." She slid Garic a proud grin, then continued, "We will hear you and consider your petition as you have asked."

Emperor Marcian picked up his goblet, from the cups set earlier before them, drank, and replaced it on the table before them. "Excellent." He sat back in his chair. "Years ago . . ." the emperor paused as if recollecting something, cleared his throat and began again, "Before my beloved Lucius married you, Arria, he came to me with an unusual artifact. He and a soldier named Darius found a sword in a strange burial site while fighting in the east. Oddly, after they removed this ancient weapon from its coffin and took possession of it, his centurion was killed in an unexpected attack from a wounded Hun. Lucius carried the sword back to Constantinople and told me, a senator at the time, this strange account."

The emperor's face glowed with intensity, and his voice rang deep and strong. "My son showed a mild obsession concerning the weapon. Lucius never let the sword out of his sight. He packed it among his things and sometimes even wore it at his side. If anyone commented, he would laugh and say it was an old weapon found on the battlefield. When politics called us to Rome, the sword went with Lucius. In Rome, he met and married you."

The emperor paused, a painful expression on his face. Sunlight streaked the columns behind him, and in the garden, just beyond the portico entrance, newborn spring and the bright sky above seemed a cruel contrast to her father-in-law's pain.

"When Lucius died two years later on that wretched field in Germania, and sadly in your arms, you were fortunate that his comrade, Severus, helped to bring him home." The emperor's brow wrinkled. "But afterward, Severus brought me this strange artifact. He claimed that just before the battle, Lucius propped his own sword against a supply wagon that accidentally lurched, snapping his weapon in two."

Emperor Marcian spoke as if he needed to believe his own explanation. "My son had no choice. It was only natural that he would fight that day with a weapon familiar and available to him, this unusual sword. Right before the battle, he made Severus pledge to bring me the weapon if he should die. Lucius wanted to protect it. And now, even Severus is gone, killed by that mongrel dog Attila and his Huns at Catalaunum. At times, I wonder if Severus ever used that sword?"

A lump rose in Arria's throat. Both Lucius and Severus had died horribly. Drawn to this puzzling dilemma, she walked through their former home in her mind, their private chamber, dining area, the atrium, and even the stable. She could not recall ever seeing this particular sword among his weapons.

People in Tuscia and even some in Rome referred to her as *La Precipienda*—the one who perceives—after she solved the murder of a local magistrate's daughter. How could she be unaware, blind to the fact that her husband kept a mysterious weapon hidden from her? She had loved and trusted Lucius and thought only of their time spent together. When he died, Arria believed she'd never recover from losing him. Each night she lay in bed, feeling as though she lay in the tomb beside him. Each morning when she woke, she dreaded another day, but she forced herself to rise and live, even if all the color had left her world.

One afternoon, two years after his death, a messenger came to her country estate. *Emperor Valentinian requests your presence,* the missive read. She left immediately for Rome.

Emperor Valentinian, aware of Arria's negotiating abilities as well as her perceptive talents, had good reason to send for her. For years she had traveled with her widowed, senator father, and from him learned the art of diplomacy. As an only child, her father raised her unconventionally, requiring she be educated like a son in mathematics, philosophy, Latin, and Greek. She kept company with other elite young women recognized for their acumen. Through her studies, she came to admire noted women: Porcia, daughter of Cato known for her thinking and philosophical understandings. Julia Domna, who like Arria, had traveled to the battlefield with her husband. And even the powerful, Galla Placidia, Valentinian's mother, and regent until he came of age. Their lives gave her hope and a greater sense of courage in a patriarchal world. When her father became infirmed and unable to travel, Emperor Valentinian recognized her ability to take her father's place.

Arria's loneliness and desire for a purpose had pushed her to accept the position as political envoy to the Assembly of Warriors in Gaul. She would ask the barbarians to join the empire in a stand against Attila's Huns. But before she reached the assembly, destiny drove her into Garic's arms. He saved her from an enemy attack and won her heart.

Now she stood before her dead husband's father, emperor of the Great City, Constantinople. Her life had moved forward, and although Lucius had never mentioned the sword, the existence of the artifact appeared to be real.

Emperor Marcian sighed but continued, his face grim. "It may sound incredulous, but the sword belonged to King David of Israel. My most educated priests and Jewish leaders in Constantinople have validated the weapon's period, and lineage by its style and the language engraved on its blade. The inscription reads, *A curse on the one who wields David's Sword and not be chosen.*"

Marcian stopped and glanced away. His face fought for composure, but after a moment, he returned his attention to them. "These holy men claim the legend behind this ancient weapon is based on an act of betrayal and hypocrisy." The emperor reached for his goblet and drank the wine down. A servant promptly refilled his cup and came to them. Arria waved him away, but Garic raised his goblet, drank, and in unison, the men rested their cups on the table.

"Are you familiar with the story of David and Bathsheba?" Emperor Marcian asked, placing his hands on his knees.

Arria replied, "I am. King David lusted over the married woman Bathsheba, and he caused her husband's death. As you know, Garic is a new Christian and unfamiliar with the stories from the bible."

The emperor's eyebrow raised. "Ah, yes. A pagan convert. Then your husband may find this story most interesting." With a pensive tone, he began, "One day, David saw a beautiful woman named Bathsheba bathing, and he was filled with desire for her. But she had a husband, Uriah, a soldier who was away fighting. David summoned Bathsheba to him and seduced her, and she became pregnant. David despaired. To save her from death for adultery, he decided to bring Uriah home to lie with his wife."

The emperor reached for his cup and drank. Handing it to his servant, he raised a palm but pointed to them. They both shook their heads. As the young man backed away, he continued, "Uriah being a loyal soldier, and true to the code of warriors still fighting, refused to return to the comfort of his wife and stayed with the palace soldiers. This was when David plotted to make Bathsheba a widow. He ordered his general to place Uriah in the front of his army and sent him to battle where he died. Later, David married Uriah's widow, but Israel's prophet, Nathan, came and reprimanded him for his deception and murder. Out of guilt for his sin and loss of honor, it's thought that David had his favorite sword inscribed with this warning and buried, along with Uriah's body, in a land where it might never be found." The emperor became quiet. "Those who know the legend of the sword believe this inscription foretells that, if discovered, the sword will choose a mighty and righteous owner. One who is strong and virtuous of heart. Only he can wield it in combat and not be cursed. Anyone else must suffer a tragic or untimely death."

Emperor Marcian bowed his head and gripped his chair's gilded armrests. He looked up. His eyes brimmed with conviction, and his voice grew solemn, "I do not know why, but I believe that Lucius fell victim to this curse. Right now, very few know of the sword's existence, but in time, more men—some who are mercenary—may become aware."

The emperor raised his hand and commanded all but one slave, a slight man with thin grey hair and round eyes, to leave the room. Then, he ordered the servant, "Erasmus, bring me the artifact."

Erasmus shuffled over to a large wooden trunk set in an alcove, undid the lock, and pulled out a metal box about three feet in length and six inches high. He brought it to the emperor. Emperor Marcian rose from his chair and placed it on a nearby table. Arria and Garic followed and stood over it.

"When Severus brought me the sword, it was in the bronze sheath Lucius had made for it, but my son told me that he found it encased in a silver box, which I think he might have left at your villa in Tuscia."

Arria frowned. "I have never seen this box," she replied grimly. Why had Lucius chosen to be secretive? Had he felt he was protecting her? These questions filled and confused her.

The emperor unhooked the latch and lifted the lid. Arria looked inside. She was struck by an odd luminescence that emanated from the weapon, even in the sunlit room. She glanced at Garic, who appeared transfixed. Arria reached out and touched the smooth, cold metal. "How strangely beautiful. The stones in the pommel still shine a brilliant red."

"*Ja.*" Garic agreed. He looked at the emperor. "May I hold it?"

Emperor Marcian nodded his consent.

Garic lifted it from the blue linen folds lining the box, drew it from its sheath and held it vertically tip to the ceiling. Admiration filled his eyes.

"The weapon is priceless," the emperor said. "King David lived more than a thousand years ago, and from him, Christus was descended. The artistry, silver, and rubies also add to its value." The emperor shook his head and continued, "I could try and protect it here in Constantinople, but when I look at it, I feel only a bitter hatred. Besides, my holy men believe that if the sword carries a curse, it must be returned to its source and home, to break the spell."

Garic slipped the sword into its sheath and placed it in the box. He wrapped his arm around Arria's shoulder. She knew Garic understood the emperor was about to reveal the destination of this mission.

Emperor Marcian sat down and waved them toward their chairs. "I've considered the right of the Jews to claim this relic, but they are banned from Jerusalem and cannot worship there. The Patriarch Anatolius and I agree. There is only one place where the sword will be safe and its curse arrested—in the Church of the Holy Sepulchre in Jerusalem, the Holy City. Emperor Constantine directed his mother, Helena, to build this church over the tomb where Christus was buried."

Arria watched as Garic's admiration shifted to an intense curiosity. A tremble ran through her and stirred her feelings as well. She turned toward the emperor who, in the past, insisted she call him 'father.'

He waited for their response, as still as the marble statues surrounding them.

"Father," Arria said in a soft voice, "What you propose would be a great undertaking. We have only just finished one mission, and there are other people to consider." She reached out for Garic's hand.

Emperor Marcian smiled. "Contemplate carefully, but I trust in you and Garic. You're the most reliable envoys to represent my decision to the church fathers in Jerusalem, concerning the artifact. I believe a supernatural force lies hidden in the sword. It needs a home … protection from anyone who might try to steal it for power or fortune."

The emperor stood, and they as well. He grasped the fold of his toga; the purple cloth draped from his left shoulder to his right thigh. "If you accept—this task must be handled with the utmost discretion. I think traveling with others can disguise the true nature of the mission. I'll also provide you with two soldiers from my royal guard. They'll attend you but be dressed as ordinary citizens on a pilgrimage to Jerusalem." The emperor nodded toward his servant, who opened the chamber doors.

"Father, we'll return with an answer as soon as we can." She and Garic bowed and left the room. The massive wood doors closed behind them with a hollow thud. They walked toward the palace atrium where Garic's cousin and his wife, Vodamir and Basina, awaited them.

THE NEXT DAY

GARIC

Arria and Garic sat with Vodamir and Basina in the antechamber of one of the palace guest rooms provided for them. Sunlight poured through a wide wrought-iron door and spread a fiery glow across the mosaic tiles. Just beyond the twisted black rails, a veranda melted into a lush spring garden.

Garic's cousin, Vodamir, leaned forward from his chair, folded his hands, and rested his elbows on his knees. Strands of copper hair fell forward from his shoulders. "We've considered your request to join you on this mission. You know I'm willing to follow you and Arria anywhere, but Basina is reluctant," he said and glanced at his wife.

"*Ja,*" Garic answered, nodding his understanding. After all, their recent trip to Constantinople from Rome had been difficult and dangerous. While waiting for their ship to sail from Brundisium to the Great City, Basina had been attacked by a vengeful assailant in the monastery that lodged them. Later in Constantinople, Arria was nearly killed trying to safely deliver the relic, the Crown of Thorns, to

Emperor Marcian. A duty thrust on them by her father and General Aetius' wife, Pelagia, a few years after the Roman war with Attila. "Arria and I have decided we cannot refuse her former father-in-law and now emperor. We'll take on one last mission."

Basina stood and knelt before Arria. Basina's sweet round face and ink-black bangs framed cat-like eyes. "I was trained by the Huns as a healer. My heart wants to be with you both to help protect, but my soul longs for Gaul and *Silbereiche*, Silver Oaks. I want to live on Vodamir's farm, have children, and watch them grow."

"I'm torn, Cousin," Vodamir interjected. "From the time we were boys, we've had many adventures. We fought and became men together. Basina and I were with you at the Battle of Catalaunum, and you and I helped chase that bastard Attila out of Gaul. But now, I feel drawn to the life that Basina wants."

Arria hugged Basina and then rose and hugged Vodamir. "We love you both and want you to be happy," she said. "Go with our blessing. When we've completed the emperor's task, we'll return to Gaul and," she flashed Garic a sweet grin, "*Vildeer Hoeneeg*, Wild Honey. We'll make it our home. Garic's brothers will welcome his return and our help on the farm as well."

Garic chuckled and said, "Arria, you still pronounce *Wilder Honig* like a Roman."

"Does it matter?" she replied, an eyebrow arched, wisps of chestnut brown hair clinging to the sides of her cheeks. "Besides, I am a Roman," she snapped pertly.

Vodamir and Basina laughed at their banter. Garic shook his head, but the sharp gaze from Arria's sea-green eyes suppressed his laughter.

After a few seconds, they all grew quiet, realizing that their journey together was at an end.

Garic broke the silence. "It's been decided." He looked at Vodamir. "Will you carry a letter for us to the monastery at San Petrus and give it to Brother Bruno?"

"Without question," Vodamir replied.

"Then come," Garic said, standing. "Let's spend our few remaining nights enjoying our time together."

When they left the palace, the stars shone brilliantly in the night sky. Tonight, they would spend the evening dining and drinking in the grandest city in the eastern empire.

CONSTANTINOPLE: The 29th day of Aprilis

ARRIA

Arria and Garic stood on the pier and watched Vodamir and Basina step onto the ship. Garic wrapped an arm around Arria as she lifted a cloth to her eyes and wiped away tears. Seagulls screamed overhead. The briny scents of seawater and silvery fish ferried across the breeze. Once onboard, Vodamir and Basina came to the railing. They lifted their hands and waved. The ship slipped away from the harbor toward the Sea of Marmara. On its journey to the eastern shore of Italia and the port city of Brundisium.

Arria turned her head into Garic's shoulder.

"Arria, don't cry, we'll see them again," Garic reassured as he stroked her hair.

Arria sobbed, "I'll miss them terribly. Basina is like a sister to me, and even Vodamir's cocky humor made some of the most trying times bearable."

"Mellitula, dry your eyes." Garic grasped her shoulders and smiled at her.

Arria dabbed away her tears but struggled with her words and feelings. "The night we weighed our choices for this mission and considered our daughter's involvement—could she withstand a rigorous journey and possible danger . . . we decided she must be with us and learn to travel by our sides. After all, the years I spent traveling with my father as a young girl, I learned so much. And yet, to be sure, I want to ask again. Do you still agree we should take Licia with us?"

"I do," Garic nodded. His blue eyes gazed at her intently, and he grasped her shoulders tighter.

Arria sighed with relief and wiped away a few more tears. "Good. I believe this too. Out of respect for the emperor, we've accepted his mission. We'll deliver this unusual weapon to the Church of the Holy Sepulchre and lay it to rest." She tucked a curl behind her ear and shook her head. "I just hope we've made the right decision regarding the sword. I feel a bit uneasy. This weapon might have brought about Lucius' death."

Garic hugged her close. "Do not worry. I, and the emperor's guards, will see to it that we all get there safely." He cupped her chin, gently kissed her, and then smiled. "Besides, destiny seems to propel us in the most adventurous directions."

"It's amazing indeed," Arria whispered and then gave him an anxious glance. "Do you believe the sword is cursed or has mystical powers?" she asked.

Garic tilted his head. "I imagine it's possible. The world is filled with things we cannot explain or understand. Like the striped bow that colors the sky. Is it really a bridge that my people believe stretches to the home of the gods? Or, is it like you once told me, the reminder of a promise made by my new god to never flood and destroy the creatures of the earth again as he did long ago?"

Arria nodded. "Yes. There are many things that mystify. If the sword has special powers, then I pray it'll help us to deliver it safely!"

Garic laughed and gave her another hug. Noisy seagulls circled above, and he looked up.

"Krieger," Arria said, using his pet name and tugging on his vest. He was a *warrior* in the true meaning of the Frankish word, a wise counselor to his people, and a member of the tribe's elite fighting force, the *Wespe*—Wasp. When she looked upon him, his rugged stance and blond hair, which fell against the golden stubble on his cheeks and touched his shoulders, always brought her pleasure. "Let's walk a bit. The fresh air feels good, and we should begin to make plans for our journey." She looped her arm through his. Together they looked one more time at the fading ship while Arria whispered a prayer for her friends' safety.

Garic turned them toward the path that led away from the port and toward the *Mesê*, the market street of Constantinople. "I feel relieved that Vodamir will carry the letter to Brother Bruno in Brundisium."

"I agree," Arria answered. She thought about their adopted daughter, Licia, every day and felt confident that she was safe with the monks at San Petrus who had cared for Licia after the tragic death of her parents. When Arria and Garic asked to adopt her, the brothers had consented. "If Brother Bruno accepts our request and brings our daughter, I hope he'll join us on this sacred mission."

"The brother is a good man and was pleased that we adopted Licia. You've certainly provided him with enough *solidi* to pay their passage and travel comfortably. Besides, I think he might have a nose for adventure."

"If he agrees, they should arrive here within seventeen to twenty-one days, if all goes well with their journey—I pray that it does. If he refuses our request, I asked him to write to us. Then, we must reconsider our plans." Could they leave Licia in Brundisium a bit longer, or should they go and get her themselves? These questions weighed on Arria's mind. An answer, either way, was sure to arrive in the coming weeks. In the meantime, they would make provisions for a journey, no matter which direction they chose—Brundisium or Jerusalem.

II

Hidden Desires

CONSTANTINOPLE: The White Flower Tavern—The 15th day of Maius

CORVUS

Corvus wrinkled his nose. The room reeked worse than ever before. Most likely from rotting garbage, waste dumped on the city streets and the sewer a few doors down, or the owner—cheap bastard—was trying to slip the drunks some soured wine or mead. Corvus stretched, then crossed his long legs under the table to avoid scraping his knees. He frowned as his partner, Jax, hiccupped and swept a leathery hand across his brown beard and over his balding head. He sat hunched over his cup across from Corvus. "Hold your breath, man!" Corvus barked over the room's chatter, then shook his head.

Jax mumbled and inhaled; his face turned red. He snorted and grabbed his cup, gulping down more wine.

"Attila's ass! It stinks in here—like vinegar." Corvus grumbled.

"You can say that again," slurred Jax.

Corvus swallowed the rest of his mead and dropped his cup with a thud. "Don't know why they call this place the White Flower, there's nothing clean or sweet about it."

Jax hiccupped again and knocked a fist to his chest. "That's the truth!"

"I'd never be so drunk that I'd drink sour wine—I think." Both men burst out laughing, and Corvus slouched closer to the table. His broad back always got in the way of a passerby whenever he was in a crowded room. It made him nervous at times. He liked knowing what was coming his way, but it wasn't always possible to get a chair or bench against a tavern wall.

"Yeah, this shit is swill, but I'll have another," Jax added.

Corvus raised his cup in agreement and glanced around like a lost traveler. He was pleased when a barmaid broke through a crowd of men, circling some dice players, and approached them.

"A person is looking for a tall man, black hair with a white streak. Someone named Corvus. That you?" the barmaid asked, looking at him.

Corvus gave a brief nod. "Who's asking?"

"Across the room. The lady near the door. Says she wants to talk to you—in private. Will you meet her in the storeroom?"

He stood and turned toward the entrance. A woman, of medium height and build, with grey-streaked auburn waves clinging to the edge of her hood, looked in their direction. Strange, a lady in this place and alone, he thought, but shrugged. "Why not? It must be important."

The barmaid snipped, "Wouldn't know. She paid the owner for a private meeting with you and said to include the brawny one too. Follow me."

The barmaid stepped ahead while Corvus and Jax followed. As they drew near the front door, the cloaked woman came alongside them with a nod but swept in front of him and Jax without stopping. The barmaid led them to a storeroom lined with shelves stacked with jars of wine, ale, and supplies. Once inside, the barmaid left, and they faced each other. The woman dropped her hood. Corvus felt a rush of curiosity. A comely woman for her middle years, her striking hazel eyes fell first on him.

"The only introduction I can make is that I represent a benefactor and collector of antiquities. He'll go by the name Goliath. It has come to his attention that you're men for hire for most any job. Is this true?"

"Any job that pays well." Corvus raised a quizzical brow. "What does he have in mind?"

"There's an item, a sword, that he desires. He'll pay a handsome price if you can recover it *intact* in a reasonable amount of time."

"How much?" Corvus looked at Jax, silent, hiccup gone, his eyes somewhat cleared.

"Nine gold solidi. A soldier's pay for six months."

"But there're two of us." Corvus waited, his expression blank.

The woman stared at him and drawled, "There are indeed." She cast a scrutinizing look at Jax. "Fifteen solidi. There are *others* for hire in the Great City."

"Twenty solidi, and you'll have your sword in perfect condition. You came to us first, didn't you? We're Goths from Pannonia, the best mercenaries around."

She didn't hesitate. "Eighteen solidi but no more."

Corvus thought a moment, then nodded and slapped Jax on the back. "What do you say, Jax? Up for adventure and half a year's pay?"

Jax grinned. "Count me in."

The woman raised her hood, her face half-hidden. "Good. Meet me here tomorrow at the same time. I'll come with the particulars and money for your expenses. The full amount will be paid upon delivery of the sword, which my employer trusts can be completed within the month."

"Please assure *Goliath* that he'll have his prize."

The woman's lips broke into a thin smile. "Goliath hates to be disappointed."

CONSTANTINOPLE: A Townhouse on the Second Hill

VALERIA

Valeria stepped from the White Flower Tavern onto a poorly lit stone street. In the distance, she knew her bodyguard, Atticus, hid in a shadow. As she reached the end of the street, he appeared before her. "My lady, your carriage waits around the corner," he said and led the way. With an extended hand, he helped her into the covered coach and jumped beside the driver.

"*Ha!*" the driver shouted and yanked the reins. The two small front wheels slipped on the pavement. Still, the larger back wheels spun forward, and the *Carruca* clattered toward a wealthier quarter of Constantinople.

Once inside her townhouse, Valeria dropped her hood and trembled under her cloak. The mild drizzle, slippery streets, and chilly night made her happy to be home. She never liked risking an outing to a portside tavern or a shop in a run-down district, but there were times when a *venture* required her to step beyond her comfort. Yet, in a strange way, she relished the danger. She felt most alive when traversing a dark street in a squalid part of the city. It mattered little that her bodyguard followed not far behind once she left the relative safety of her coach. Her vehicle would never stop at the door. Being recognized might prove embarrassing or compromising in the future. Of course, Atticus blended into the tavern crowd to be there if needed, but he provided her the illusion that she navigated her business on her own, which pleased her very much. Atticus had proven himself to be an excellent protector and one who came highly praised by Goliath.

A servant quickly removed her cloak and said that she had a visitor. Valeria tensed, but hurried toward the salon and entered. Fires burned in several braziers situated in the middle of the room. A welcome glow bounced off the walls and across the blue mosaic floor. Several couches and two tall-backed chairs surrounded the burning coals. Kalev Ben Jonah sat with his eyes closed on one of the couches. His solid frame, which gave him the appearance of strength, was relaxed. Valeria approached him.

Round, brown eyes beneath a black mop of curls sprang open. "Ah, Valeria. I'm happy you've made it safely home."

Valeria smiled. "Thank you. I am too." She bit her lip but asked, "Can you stay awhile?"

He gave her a patient look like a man who had explained before. "I want to . . . but I must leave soon."

"Of course," she replied, feeling foolish. Valeria shifted her gaze to the fire.

Kalev waved a quick hand in her direction. "Please, sit down. It's your home, after all."

Valeria took a seat on the edge of a couch beside his chair. A long vest covered Kalev's ankle-length tunic, and soft brown boots jutted from beneath the folds of his clothing.

Flames danced from the braziers behind his head, casting a faint shadow across his face and close-trimmed beard. His gaze penetrated and held her. "Were you successful?" he asked.

She nodded. "They've agreed to work for you."

"Good. At what price?"

"I had to offer more because Corvus will not work without his mercenary companion."

"How much?"

"*Eighteen* solidi."

Kalev tilted his head, a slight frown on his lips and a keen look in his eyes. "A bit more than expected, but acceptable. I'm counting on my brother-in-law's information being dependable. He visits the emperor's court on business frequently. His jewels and silks are quite popular, and at times, he may even provide a loan to a loyal customer."

"Nonetheless, through one of the courtiers, he learned that several of them believe the emperor has acquired a sword, belonging to King David of Israel."

"Are you sure about this?" Valeria interjected.

"My best spy is convinced the sword is genuine and on its way to a shrine in Jerusalem. In truth, to me, the sword is real and worth more to me than anyone might believe." He looked pensive for a moment, and then, with an even sharper look, he asked, "Did they inquire about me?"

"Briefly. Naturally, I used your black-market name."

"No doubt," he said and stretched his legs. "You're the best private liaison and merchant in Constantinople and Jerusalem—along with your brother, Milvus, of course. Your ability as a Gentile to enter easily and work in the Holy City has benefited us in many ways." His smile was sure. "I trust you."

"I hope so," she answered, and her thoughts ran to the first time they met in her brother's shop. The attraction was immediate, despite it being forbidden. He a married Jew; she a widowed Armenian Christian. "I'm as determined as you to acquire this sword— especially if it's as valuable, *mystical* as the rumors claim."

"I believe this sword holds great power, which can mean great wealth. If these men prove reliable, we'll know one way or another."

Valeria reached for Kalev's hand and ran a thumb over his slender fingers. "I've missed you." She looked up at him and smiled.

Kalev's sharp brown eyes softened. "I feel the same," he whispered, "but I must go. Leah waits for me."

Valeria put his hand to her cheek. "I know," she said.

KALEV BEN JONAH

Kalev Ben Jonah walked out of Valeria's home and into the carriage. He was grateful the night protected him from preying eyes, from those who would know even a morsel of his business. He lowered his hood and pulled his cloak tighter as his covered carriage rolled away from her door.

Valeria was the love he longed for if he were to love any woman. She was a beauty who admired and loved him and would do anything he asked. Their attraction had been immediate the first time they met. Her hazel eyes, and auburn waves with wisps of grey, unusual for most Armenian women, had captivated him. In time, their relationship growing deeper, she had sought comfort in his arms and he in hers. A widow for several years, she refused to marry again because of him. He had confided to her what Milvus already knew that he was Goliath. She had accepted him for who and all he was, and both siblings were loyal and trustworthy.

Valeria helped her brother operate a trade, dealing in rugs, amphoras, and rare objects in Constantinople and Jerusalem. Kalev believed she possessed a sharp eye and ability for shrewd negotiation. Her only deficit was being a woman in her early thirties in a man's world, but her brother's partnership offered her an acceptable façade. Those who often dealt with the siblings knew that Valeria ran the business.

Kalev respected that she thought like him in many instances, calm and fearless, elated over a well-profited deal. Her only flaw found itself in the root of her nature, and like a woman, her heart beat much kinder than his, and this worried him. He gazed past the coach's open frame and gripped the wooden seat. He watched walls, windows, and pathways roll by. Clattering hooves echoed across cobblestones in the background, and the painful tragedy of just a year ago, gnawed on his heart, fresh and raw.

Valeria had come to him as soon as she heard about his son, Joshua, wanting to comfort him. Would her opinion of him have changed knowing the revenge he had taken on his son's murderer? His beloved boy cut down in youth by a filthy beggar—stabbed to death for a few coins while shopping for his mother's medicinal to alleviate her sad spirits. Now, Leah was lost, inconsolable, worse than before.

A few acquaintances had witnessed Valeria's indiscretion, her show of affection toward a married man and Jew, even though he took her quickly by the arm and escorted her from his shop. "Not here, Valeria, not now," he had whispered, cautioning her innocent indiscretion. A part of him found it difficult to forgive her. A part loved her a bit more.

Kalev sat further back into his seat and closed his eyes. He relived the night of his vengeful satisfaction—the few hours after Joshua had been buried. The beggar's screams rang in his ears like beautiful music when his henchmen first took the beggar's eyes, then his nose from his foul and dirty face. But to Kalev's dismay, the murderer's cries hadn't lasted long enough. Blood pooled on the ground in the wooded patch of land a few miles from the city. The beggar pleaded for mercy as Kalev ranted and shouted over the beggar's face and into the night—until his rage, at a pinnacle, ignited a strange, icy calm that ran through his veins, and he ordered the men to *finish* it.

He'd never seen a man castrated before. In the torchlight, it appeared as an ancient ritual to the Roman gods, savage and strong. The beggar choked and coughed blood. Believing the murderer had ceased to feel, an infuriated Kalev kicked him again and again. The beggar groaned and clawed at the air. Kalev watched him take one last shallow gasp, then die.

"Do you want we shove his prick in his mouth?" A henchman asked.

Kalev nodded. "Dump him on the *Mesé* in the center of the market. Leave a sign that says, 'murderer and thief' on him."

The henchmen had rolled the beggar in a blanket and gone. Kalev followed behind. He would go to a bath and cleanse himself, and then go home to sleep. The next day he would observe Shiva, the days of mourning—weeping and lament—and try to console his wife. As for himself, a darker rage now burned deeper within him. Kalev opened his eyes. He was forever changed.

III

Stumble and Fall

CONSTANTINOPLE: The Imperial Palace—The 19th day of Maius

ARRIA

Late afternoon bristled with an uncommon heat that began weeks ago. Emperor Marcian leaned from his seat over his desk and swiped at the air with his parchment. "Damn flies," the emperor grumbled as an insect avoided the blow and flew away. He grimaced and wiped his brow with a wet cloth.

Arria and Garic sat before the emperor in his office. A servant approached them with a silver platter and bowed. They each helped themselves to a moist hand cloth.

"I cannot be without my cooling towels," Emperor Marcian admitted with a smile.

Arria dabbed her cheeks. "Quite refreshing, thank you." Garic patted his forehead and dropped his towel into the basket; another servant swept in front of him. Arria added hers as well.

"These warm winds are sure to get you safely to Caesarea. You'll glide over the water."

"Your optimism is encouraging, Father," Arria replied.

The emperor smiled at them. "I'm grateful that you've accepted this task. I do not anticipate any problems, and with the help of my soldiers, I believe it will go smoothly. Anything you need at all, I'll provide. Just ask."

Arria nodded. "Your generosity is appreciated, but we're here to serve you."

"You have in so many ways." The emperor wiped his brow again. "And since the arrival of your newly adopted daughter and Brother Bruno, I've found it a pleasure getting to know her. She seemed excited about sailing here on a ship for the first time and told me she's seven but will be eight on the ninth day of *Junius*. I think she's counting."

"Licia is precocious." Pride welled in Arria's heart. "We were told she's a natural-born sailor, and she insisted on watching at the rail. Brother Bruno had to attentively keep her from climbing the boxes stacked on the deck. She wanted a better view. Licia is quite the monkey. The sailors aboard the ship viewed her exuberance for the sea as a good omen and spoiled her with all sorts of treats."

"How fortunate that she's this way, Arria. The journey will be strenuous, but a child with a disposition for travel and adventure will make it so much easier."

Arria smiled at Garic. "We are indeed blessed."

Emperor Marcian slid a scrolled parchment toward a stack on his desk and folded his hands. "When will you leave tomorrow?"

"Our ship's captain hopes to cast off at the latest midmorning," Garic replied.

"Most of our luggage and provisions are ready, and thank you for arranging our passage on a ship with a cabin that can accommodate the three of us," Arria added. "Brother Bruno met with the two guards who will accompany us. He reported that they've pitched their deck tents in a good spot close to the stern. They'll sleep on board tonight."

"Good. Justus and Telemachus are the best men for this job. You have yet to meet them." The emperor summoned his attendant. "They may enter now."

The servant bowed and left the room. Seconds later, he returned with two soldiers. They wore brass breastplates strapped over white tunics and soft brown leather ankle boots. Both men bowed.

"Let me present two of my finest guards." The emperor swept his hand in the direction of the taller man. "Lady Arria and Noble Garic, Tribune Justus."

Shiny, chestnut waves flowed from a side-part and hung past the tribune's brow and around his ears. Brown eyes warmed a crisp and polite manner. He replied with a nod, "My lady and lord."

The emperor nodded toward the second soldier. "Tribune Telemachus."

Arria thought Telemachus appeared to be a Greek, and his namesake, the son of the famous Odysseus, the hero of the Trojan War, supported this impression. Sandy curls, inching down his neck to his collar, added a handsome contrast to his tanned complexion and bright hazel eyes. "My lady and lord," he said with a perfect smile.

The emperor sat back in his chair. "I do not wish to bring undue notice to your travels. These men will provide added protection, but for greater anonymity, will shed their uniforms and dress plainly. They have pledged to help deliver the artifact safely to Jerusalem, but they have not seen or held the weapon. Patriarch Anatolius and his priests have hidden the sword in a large oil amphora filled with barley to approximate the weight of several jars being transported in its company. This special amphora bears a secret mark, a star, for your identification."

"May we see them, or have the jars been loaded onto the ship?"

The emperor's sudden grin expressed his mild satisfaction. "Your attentiveness always pleases me, Arria. They are crated for sea travel and stored among the other provisions needed for your journey. Early in the morning, all the supplies will be brought to the ship and loaded. My tribunes will make sure the crates are safe and secure. Once you're on board, they'll show you the special jar."

Arria nodded and then asked, "Father, will we see you in the morning before we depart?"

The emperor rose and came around the desk. "I could never let you leave without saying goodbye." He hugged her and nodded toward Garic. "Once you get to Caesarea, Telemachus and Justus will hire a coach, horses, and a wagon. With the Lord's blessing, you should all make it easily to the church in Jerusalem."

Arria took the emperor's hand and kissed his ring. Garic and the tribunes did the same. The servant opened the door while Justus and Telemachus stood at attention, each with an arm across his chest. Arria and Garic left the room, and the soldiers followed. Her heart surged with anticipation as she and Garic headed for their quarters. This journey was just beginning.

CONSTANTINOPLE: The Harbor Road—The 20th day of Maius, Early Morning

ARRIA

Wings—soft flapping wings—flitted before Arria's eyes as they opened. A hawk ascended across the bright blue sky and glided in a circle on the wind. She rested her head against the coach's awning post and squeezed the small hand nestled warmly in hers. Her daughter, Licia, rode between her and the new servant, Catalina; Garic sat across from them and Brother Bruno beside him. The coach clipped its way to the ship from the palace over the crowded streets. It was only a few miles, but the rocking motion and the warm sun streaming through the window had lulled Arria to dose.

She straightened and stretched her limbs. Throughout the night, a combination of nervous excitement and some worry had kept her mind racing, keeping her awake. What if this mission wasn't as simple as the emperor believed? Would Licia travel easily—adjust to her new life with them? Had they put themselves and their daughter in possible danger? She hoped not but knew the world could be perilous and unpredictable. Yet, she had traveled with her father across some rugged and less civilized parts of the empire on diplomatic missions, and from this, she had learned amazing things. Many religious pilgrims and people, seeking a better life, had taken their families and traveled to foreign lands. Should fear keep them from helping the emperor and experiencing new places? She must trust her instincts. Once they reached Jerusalem, they would leave Licia and Brother Bruno at one of the monasteries surrounding the Holy City, and then proceed with the sword's delivery.

As the coach rolled past two warehouses, Arria admired a lonely patch of golden-topped grasses, splattered with poppies and caught between the buildings. She smiled. But her thoughts returned. She also wanted to be sure she had included everything necessary for their travel comfort. The proper clothing, soaps and towels, preserved foods, games to pass the hours, reading scrolls, parchment and writing tools, and all pressed into four satchels. It was a task she did not find enjoyable, simply because she had the tendency to overpack. It often took her several attempts to decide what was most important. Did she really need to bring extra shoes? A pair of sandals and walking boots should suffice. And now that her friend Basina was gone, Arria had decided it was time to find a handmaiden to help her with domestic chores and Licia's care.

Her previous handmaiden, a kind, devoted woman named Karas, had died years back while defending Arria's life. A small fragment of Arria's heart had been torn away with Karas' death. Could she find a woman to replace such a fine person?

Arria had told the emperor of her need. He informed her she could choose from any of his orphaned servants as a gift from him. The last few days had been spent searching for the right girl. In the end, she selected a young woman named Catalina, brought to the palace as a child from the territories to the east. She thought she had chosen wisely, but this change also added to her worries. She hoped the girl would complement her family.

Licia wiggled beside Arria. "Mama, you look pretty when you sleep."

Arria laughed, and Garic chuckled even harder. Arria shot him a look.

"Your Mama is indeed pretty—even when she snores." Garic returned a mischievous grin.

"Licia, that's not true, I do not snore!"

"I heard Papa snoring the other night when you sent me to wake him for dinner."

"Ha! There's the truth. It cannot be denied. Licia is the witness." Arria laughed.

Still smiling, Garic shook his head and motioned to Brother Bruno. "What about the good brother, Licia? Did you ever catch him snoring on your journey?"

Licia giggled, her berry red plaits bright against her creamy skin. "Yes! He snored a lot!" She giggled again.

Brother Bruno swung his head from right to left. "Who me?" he said, pointing to himself. "No, not me!"

They all laughed, but their merriment was cut short when the coach lurched to a sudden stop.

Garic quickly jumped from the *carruca*. Arria leaned out to see what might be the problem.

A man dressed in tattered clothes lay on his back at the feet of the horses. His brown hair was long and tangled, his beard untamed. As he fought to sit up, Arria noticed his withered hand and a scorched cheek. An odd sensation rippled through her. She stepped out of the coach and walked behind Garic, who went to help him up. Once the man stood, she noticed the leather strap across his tunic, belonging to a Roman soldier's uniform. She peered closer and recognized the emblem of the VIII Augusta Equites, her dead husband's legion. This man might have been a soldier.

Standing beside Garic, the coach's driver scowled at the man. "I might have run you down!" he yelled.

"That's what I wanted, you stupid ass," he growled. The odor of wine clung to him, and he belched. "Can't a man die when he wants?" His eyes narrowed as his lips spread in a grimace. He belched again and made an attempt to brush himself off. Looking up, he caught sight of Arria.

They stared at one another.

"Leo?" fell from Arria's mouth. She knew him. It had been years since she'd seen him. He was in a bedraggled state, but she had met him on several occasions after Lucius had returned from Dacia Ripensis. Back then, he had the look of a seasoned soldier, broad chest with muscled arms, no scarring burn, and his large jaw and high cheekbones were not easily forgotten.

"Lady Arria, . . . is that you?"

"It is." Arria approached the man cautiously. "Leo, how did you come to be here? What has happened?"

"Your husband did not tell you?"

Arria cringed inside; she knew Leo meant Lucius. She glanced at Garic. Now was not the time for explanations. "I'm not sure I know what you mean."

"The legion bounced me. I'd been with the army since I was seventeen. Now, look at me."

Leo tried to stand but wobbled and slumped to the ground. He crossed his legs and stared at Arria.

She quickly moved Garic to one side. "We must take him to the dock and on the ship with us."

Garic's blue eyes grew wide. "Mellitula, why? The man is drunk and unkempt—not in his right mind. He threw himself in the path of our coach. He wanted to die."

"Can we turn our backs on a person in need, especially one I know?" Arria said, pursing her lips.

"How *do* you know him? Does this have anything to do with Lucius?" Garic asked, his tone gruff.

Arria's cheeks grew warm. "Must you speak like that, my lord? Leo served under Lucius, and he's in distress. It's a Christian duty to help those in need."

"Christian duty?" Garic responded, running his hand through his hair. "What are you thinking? The man appears disturbed and unable to care for himself. He may cause us problems."

Arria squared her shoulders and stood taller. "We must help him." She gave Garic her most leveled gaze.

He stared back, sighed, but raised a finger. "Just this one time will I relent against my better judgment … but I'm going to keep my eye on him." Garic placed his hands on his hips. "He cannot ride inside the coach. Oh, wait, does he want to come? Have you asked him?"

Arria crouched beside Leo. "We would like you to travel with us to the dock and perhaps even farther if you like? We'll give you food. You can sit next to the coachman. Will you come, and after you've eaten, tell me what happened to you?"

"If my lady is so kind, I'm willing to tell you how I came to be here." Leo leaned toward her and whispered, "It's because of Marcian."

"The emperor?" Arria asked softly.

"No, the son—your Lucius."

CONSTANTINOPLE: The Harbor of Eleutherius

ARRIA

They sat on the dock, each on a barrel cut in half for seating. Several ships lined the wharf, but the gangplank of the *Ventus* jutted onto land only a few feet from them. Arria handed Leo a water pouch and bread, then stared at him. What did Leo mean? But before she could question him, the old soldier's attention shifted. "Is the tall barbarian your bodyguard?" he asked, his eyes narrowing.

"No. Garic is my husband. Lucius Marcian was killed in battle in Germania almost seven years ago. I was there. Severus and I found him, gravely wounded beneath his horse. He died in my arms." Arria sighed. She gazed at her hands, resting in her lap and the gold ring on her finger. She lifted her eyes to Leo's. "I came to know Garic when Attila invaded Gaul, and I was an envoy to the Assembly of Warriors—a group of barbarian allies—that Garic helped lead. He

fought for Rome and left his home for me. He was my brave
protector—then and now."

Leo nodded, but anger puckered at the corners of his mouth. His
brooding eyes made Arria uneasy. Should she be wary? Leo shoveled
a hunk of bread into his mouth from the broken loaf in his hand. Little
grunts of satisfaction fell from his lips as he rapidly chewed the
mouthful with a dim awareness of his surroundings.

Garic, standing beside them earlier, had soon lost patience with
Leo's grunting and mumblings, which he conveyed to Arria with a
roll of his eyes. He voiced his desire to complete their travel
arrangements and boarded the ship. Leaning against the rail, Garic
spoke with the accompanying soldiers but occasionally glanced over
his shoulder toward her and Leo.

Father Bruno, Catalina, and Licia played marbles under a shade
tree close to the pier.

Arria continued to watch Leo eat. She couldn't forget what he had
whispered to her earlier. How had her deceased husband caused his
former centurion to be in Constantinople and in such a damaged and
ragged state? "Leo," Arria prompted. "What did you mean when you
said you are here because of Lucius?"

Leo wiped at his mouth with his withered arm and then raised it.
"My curiosity cost me everything." His eyes glazed over. "That
damned sword," he muttered and looked nervously around.

Arria leaned closer. "Which sword do you mean—the ancient
one?" she ventured.

"Do you know of it?" he asked.

Arria nodded.

"I fear it might be cursed—evil," he whispered.

An icy chill rushed through Arria, and she bit her lip. She thought
a moment and pulled a gold necklace from beneath her bodice.

During the mission, involving the Crown of Thorns, a locket
precious to her was stolen. Afterward, Garic gave her a gold chain,
dangling a slender cross. Much like the cross he wore now and gifted
to him by Arria on a night, not so long ago in Gaul, when they
declared their love for each other. She let the cross rest in her palm.
"I'll say a silent prayer for protection."

Leo mumbled his agreement.

Seagulls sang overhead as she closed her eyes. A minute later, she
spoke, "Leo. Tell me what you know."

Leo nodded but stole another glance around. Moisture shined faintly in the corner of his eyes. "Lucius Marcian seldom carried the blade, but when he did, he protected it like it was a treasure and not, as most of us around him believed, some antique piece of rubbish. I worried about him." Leo looked at his arm again and slid his fingers over his burnt cheek. "Drunk!" he said belligerently. "My friend, Seneca, and I got drunk the night the officers were meeting. I got the idea to see the sword up close while Marcian was occupied. He seemed obsessed with it—like it owned him. We snuck into his quarters. Not hard to find. It lay wrapped in a blanket beneath his bed. We took it outside to the firelight. I held it up and pulled the sword from its sheath. Didn't look sturdy, but I was surprised. Small rubies, set in its handle, glowed in the light. Never noticed them before. Some strange letters ran down the blade."

Leo took a breath and scowled. "Like a drunken imbecile, I waved it about as if I were fighting. Seneca demanded a turn, but I refused him and kept wielding it high—low. When I turned my back, Seneca grabbed me from behind and tried to wrestle it from my hand. We fought. I tripped and crashed into the scalding rocks lining the fire's edge. Leo jutted his cheek toward her. "As you see, I burned my face." He thrust out his arm toward her. Arria recoiled. Leo snickered. "Broke my hand in many places. Never healed properly. Just withered as the army physician said it would from lack of use."

Leo's face grew still like the harbor's water. He reached for the pouch at his feet and took a drink. "Marcian heard the commotion and ran toward us. 'Stupid fools!' he shouted when he saw his sword in Seneca's hand and me on the ground, twisting in pain. 'It's not your sword to wield! See what you've done!' Marcian grabbed the weapon from Seneca and walked away. He never spoke to me again." Leo leaned the elbow of his good arm on a knee and cupped his cheek. "Do you have any wine, my lady?"

Arria shook her head.

A puff of breath shot through his nostrils, and he straightened. "I was released from duty. And Seneca … sent to the next barbarian skirmish where he died."

Leo looked at Arria this time with lost eyes, and she felt herself choke up.

"Are you sure you got no wine?"

Arria touched his arm. "Let's see if I can find you some."

Leo grunted his approval but hung his head. He gave Arria a sideways glance and said, "My lady—there's one more thing."

IV

The Root of All Evil

EASTERN ROMAN EMPIRE: AD 455 Constantinople—Harbor of Eleutherius

ARRIA

Arria lifted a defiant curl behind her ear and braced herself. Her stomach churned. Should she fear what Leo might confess? Perhaps it was nothing. Did he desire more food or a place to sleep? "Go ahead, Leo. I'm listening."

"You may not like it, my lady, but I swear it's the truth—every word."

Arria tried to smile.

"I didn't expect Tribune Marcian to be so angry with me, especially when I knew his secret." Leo shot Arria a dark look. "He made me promise never to tell soldiers under his command or anyone, and never a slip of the tongue, especially with you, whenever we might meet."

Leo paused, reached for the water pouch at his feet, and drank.

"Go on," Arria urged. Leo seemed to pale, and she held her breath. What would tumble from the soldier's lips?

"I swear, my lady, Lucius Marcian wasn't one to run with the men on drunken brawls or sleep with camp followers or barbarian women, like most soldiers and officers. His need for release came with gambling and the games. He liked playing dice. Some nights, as his losses grew, he'd turn to drink, making matters worse. Yet, there were times when *Fortuna* smiled on him, and he'd walk away with a pouch full of *denarii* all satisfied and confident—but not very often."

Arria's brow tightened. "He gambled?" She had never seen him play dice with anyone or even refer to it. His interests leaned toward riding horses and practicing with sword and shield.

Leo took another gulp of water. He wiped his mouth on his good arm and scowled. "I'm not a gambler . . . but one of the officers—called Sharpie by the men—was a sly fox and the best at dice and knucklebones. When he wasn't taking everyone's money, he'd be sharpening his weapons and barking orders." Leo scowled, and his eyes grew grim. "He would challenge Marcian to a *friendly* game of dice, and the tribune would always take the bait. Sharpie made sure that Marcian's wine cup was never empty, and Marcian would gamble into the night, unable to stop." Leo hunched his shoulders and shook his head. "I tried to warn him that Sharpie was a clever bastard and knew how to cheat, but he wouldn't listen. He couldn't give it up.

"In time, Marcian owed Sharpie, and a few other officers, a good deal of money. Most soldiers carry enough coin to pay off small losses, but being in a field camp, there was no way for him to make good on his larger debts. He promised these men on his return home, he would pay them."

Arria jumped up, paced back and forth, then stopped. She faced Leo. "He never showed a desire to gamble around me. Are you speaking honestly?"

Leo met her gaze and nodded. "I swear it's true, every word."

Belief and disbelief wrestled inside of Arria. "Continue," she said through clenched teeth.

The crippled soldier took another swig from the pouch and smirked. "They assumed Marcian could pay, or at the worst, get it either from you or his father, so they trusted his word. Afraid that you and his father would learn of his weakness and debts, he decided when he returned home, he'd sell that damn sword." Leo belched and scratched his beard. "Those rubies alone offered a good value. He secretly confided to me—before my accident—he believed the sword was worth much more. A rare artifact and valuable to the right buyer.

"When Seneca and I foolishly snatched it and put it at some risk, Marcian went crazy. It ended for Seneca and me like I said. A year ago, . . . ran into Sharpie . . . seems Marcian's father, while still a senator, heard of his son's gambling debts and paid them off."

Leo drew a deep breath and looked at Arria with sad eyes. "I never heard Marcian was killed. Sorry about his death—even though he had no mercy for me." A sunray broke through a passing cloud and sailed over their feet. Leo tilted his head to the side, and the shadows captured his sun-toughened face. "I wonder what happened to that damn sword?" he snarled.

AEGEAN SEA: The Ship Ventus—Day 1, The 20th day of Maius

ARRIA

"Mama, are you well?"

Arria took a breath but gave Licia a reassuring smile. "I'm fine, just a bit seasick. I'll get over it soon enough."

"I feel good," Licia chirped, standing before Arria seated on a chair. Their servant Catalina, also not well, rested on the cabin's top bunk.

"Well, I believe you're a natural sailor. Some of us are made for the land, but others are drawn to the sea as if they're part fish."

Licia grinned. "I want to be a fish or maybe a mermaid. When I sailed from the monastery to you, the sailors called me *Syreni*. They told me these are girls and ladies who are half fish and live in the water. But some days they called me monkey because I asked if I could climb the sails and look out over the sea from the topmast. I just wanted to see far and feel like a bird." A small pout spread across her lips. "They'd always say no; it was too dangerous."

"Oh, my. Fish, mermaid, monkey, and bird. Can you be all these? Perhaps we should start with *fish*. Do you know how to swim?" Arria smiled as Licia nodded, yes. It occurred to her that there were so many things she didn't know about Licia. She never experienced her learning to walk or speak, breaking the first tooth, or feeding herself. This little, red-haired girl with blue eyes and a sweet smile appeared accomplished and vibrant. Arria was glad for Licia's abilities, they would certainly help to make the trip easier, but she wondered how it would feel to guide an infant through the milestones of growth. A second wave of nausea rolled through her. "Shall we walk the deck a bit for some fresh air? Maybe we'll see a mermaid."

"If we see a mermaid, I will name her. Then maybe she'll hear me and follow the ship."

"That would be wonderful, Licia. And what will you call her?"

"*Soror*, Sister. Then she's sure to follow me."

Arria laughed. "How exciting to have a mermaid for a sister! Let's go look for her."

They climbed the stairs to the deck, leaving Catalina in the cabin to rest.

Arria saw Garic up at the rail with Brother Bruno. Beside them, the soldiers, Telemachus and Justus, sat on some crates eating pears. Leo rested his back against a couple of sacks of grain pulled from a stack. His arms were folded across his stomach, his eyes closed. Garic didn't trust the crippled centurion and wasn't pleased Leo now worked for them. Arria felt differently. Something urged her in his direction. A part of her allowed her to perceive things, see a problem from different perspectives. At times, an inner feeling or intuition about a person, place, or situation would nag her. She made her case for Leo's hire to Garic. She asked him to—just trust her. Having a big heart and respect for her, he had agreed.

THE SHIP VENTUS: Day 2—The 21st day of Maius

GARIC

"In the back of the hold, behind the provisions," Justus directed. A metal lamp in his hand, he opened the door leading to the merchant ship's storeroom.

Garic nodded and followed the guard down the steps. They walked a few feet but heard a movement and stopped. Garic touched Justus' shoulder, and they grabbed their sword hilts. From among a stack of crates, Leo emerged. A small candle in his good hand, the flickering light danced a shadow across his face, giving him an odd, shriveled appearance.

The old centurion's eyes widened when he saw them, but he swiped his crippled arm across a half-smile. "Uh, good day, sirs," he mumbled, bringing his broken fist to his chest in salute.

"Why are you down here?" Garic demanded.

Leo grinned. "Just looking for a bit of wine." He raised a small cask from behind his back.

"Are you sure you're not prowling around?" Justus barked.

"Oh, no, just thirsty and looking to calm my nerves. This rocking. It's hard on a soldier used to the land."

Garic eyed him carefully. The centurion's bloodshot eyes and dazed manner lent credibility to his words. Leo could be telling the truth, but Garic felt cautious. "Find my Lady Arria and assist her and my daughter as you were brought along to do. If you need wine in the future, ask Justus. But I warn you, do not drink yourself sick or stupid. Understood?"

"Yes, my lord. Thank you, my lord." Leo bowed, scurried past them up the stairs and onto the deck.

"Noble Garic. Do you think he was telling the truth?" Justus asked.

"I think so. Leo has no way of knowing about the sword, but before anyone else joins us, let's check the amphora to be sure it's undisturbed."

Justus nodded and raised the lamp higher. They wove their way to the clay vessel with its small six-point star. It sat behind some crates and up against a sack of grain.

Garic sighed relieved. "It looks untouched, but we'll check every day. Bring a sack of grain back with you now. Tomorrow, Telemachus can bring up some wine. I'll go the next day. No need to draw anyone's attention."

"I agree. Too much activity down here might make some sailors curious." Justus turned to leave.

Garic followed. "With fair winds and good luck, we'll be in port soon. Then I'll have a few cups myself."

They laughed and stepped out onto the deck. A sharp gust of wind surprised them and swept across the ship. Garic looked starboard. On the edge of the horizon, now a charcoal-grey, a distinct flash ripped through the sky. Sailors scrambled about as the wind grew stronger, and the vessel climbed on mounting waves. Garic turned. Arria hurried toward him, fear in her eyes and Licia in hand. A vast mist topped with angry clouds rolled across the sea. With the speed of a sea-serpent, an angry squall raced in the ship's direction.

V

Pass Through the Waters

THE SHIP VENTUS: A Squall—Day 2, The 21st day of Maius

ARRIA

Thunder boomed overhead, breaking the heavens even farther apart. A violent wind blew around them, whipping the few sails not yet furled, sending boxes and equipment skidding across the deck. A great cloud, the color of dark granite, hung in the air.

"Arria!" Garic shouted above the wind. "Take Licia! Go to our cabin below!"

"What will you do?" Arria shouted back, clutching Licia closer.

"Help the sailors . . . go now!"

Moments later, the gale rushed upon them with a blast and a shower of cold, pelting rain. Arria covered her brow with a hand and turned toward the stern. The ship held a small storage room next to the captain's quarters. The emperor had ordered it furnished for Arria and Garic's comfort. Leo ran up beside her and took her arm. She wrapped her other arm around Licia's shoulder and grabbed tighter as the centurion guided them safely toward the cabin, despite the rocking ship.

As they approached the door leading below deck, Brother Bruno sat against a water barrel curled into a ball, his hands above his head.

"Brother, come with us!" Arria shouted and shook his shoulder. The monk scrambled to his feet and followed.

Inside the cabin, Arria moved quickly to the lower bunk where she and Garic slept. Wet and dripping, she grabbed a few blankets from a nearby chest and handed one to Leo, Brother Bruno, and Catalina. She and Licia would share one. Licia had pleaded to sleep on the top berth along with Catalina when they first boarded, but now their daughter sat curled up and wrapped in her embrace while Catalina clung to the upper bunk and whimpered. Leo and Brother Bruno sat on the floor nearby. Arria noted their ashen faces and queasy frowns. She avoided closing her eyes as the rocking motion grew rougher.

"Mama, when is it going to stop?"

"I don't know, my darling. Once this nasty storm passes over us, the sun might break through and shine on us, but if not, at least the sea will calm again."

Licia trembled in Arria's arms. "I feel sick."

Leo scrambled to his knees and grabbed the empty privy bucket. "Here, child, use this," he offered kindly.

Licia quickly spewed the contents of a little girl's breakfast. Sweat beading off her forehead, she fell back into Arria's arms. Arria didn't feel well herself, even though she'd sailed through a storm before, and she could tell by Leo's sour look that he was struggling too. The good brother was curled up in a ball again. Then, clutching his stomach, he groaned and heaved into a bowl fallen from the table where he lay.

Arria glanced away from the brother to Licia. Wanting to block the monk's retching sounds and calm her daughter, she said with a soothing tone, "Come, let's try and pretend we are swaying to music. I'll sing for us."

Licia nodded and held her hand tighter. A favorite children's song popped into Arria's head. Her mother sang it to her often but mostly at night while tucking Arria into bed. It told a story about heavenly sprites that lived on the moon and made cakes from stardust.

Arria started slowly. The strength in the melody rolled with the ship and acted as a shield against the blustering wind. Her eyelids felt heavy. Rain poured down on her words and senses and the roof above their heads. Arria's song filled the air as the storm grew louder, forcing her tune to a crescendo. She pulled Licia closer and stroked her hair.

The *Ventus* arched upward toward the shrieking gale, turning the day into night, then plunged into battering waves that started the movement over again. She could feel the long swell beneath them running the sea higher and higher. Creaking and groaning, the ship pitched in the choppy sea, rocking them back and forth. Licia started to cry.

"Mama's here," Arria said, and taking a breath, she continued to sing, but the tune slowed on her lips as the ship dove deeper into the sea and rose up. Dark as night, the cabin glowed with sharp flickers of brightness, then peels of thunder trumpeting overhead.

Earlier commands and shouts from the sailors above were drowned out. The only master of the vessel now was the furious downpour. Time stopped for Arria. The pit in her stomach clenched harder. Lightheaded, she forced herself to push through and repeat the song, although her strength was fading. Heat, humidity, nausea, and the pounding sea bore down on them all.

She wiped Licia's brow, then her own. Even in this climactic moment, it fell upon her that they were minuscule players caught in nature's fury. She shuddered as the monstrous squall swept over them—a vengeful creature run loose, thundering, booming, and wreaking havoc. Their bodies swayed from side to side. Terrified, Arria clung harder to Licia and crooned in her ear. She fought and held on to the notes, even as the storm bellowed and raged.

Arria was not sure of the time or when the gale reached its height. She had lost the measure of it. But after a while, the wind lost its roar and receded to a moan. The ship rose on top of a huge watery billow and then slowly fell. The waves began to calm. Like a bored and impatient warrior in search of new vessels to torment or destroy, the storm sailed away—its anger peaked—the battle won.

An eerie quiet surrounded them. Light ebbed through the cracks in the cabin door. Arria stopped humming and kissed Licia's cheek. "It's over, my sweet. The storm is gone."

Leo sighed and ran his good hand over his face. "Apollo's balls, I need a drink," he grumbled. "Excuse me, my lady." His penitent glance veered toward Licia. "Sorry."

Licia appeared puzzled.

Arria gave him a stern look but added, "It falls on innocent ears, but say no more."

Sudden footfalls sounded on the stairs outside the cabin. The door swung open.

Garic stood there, his hair and clothes soaked to the bone, but a tremendous relief shone on his face. "Thank Christus. It's over. Are you, Licia, and the girl all right?" he directed toward Arria. She nodded, her smile weak. "Brother?" he added. The monk uncurled himself and took a breath. Garic gave Leo a sideways glance. "And you?" The centurion nodded, his face grim.

Arria stood, unwrapping her arms from Licia. "I'm so grateful we're safe. I need some air."

"Come, I'll help you and the girls to the deck. We can all dry out there."

Garic led Licia and Catalina up the stairs with Arria behind them. Leo and Brother Bruno followed. Once on deck, they raised their faces to the sun and breathed deeply. Catalina found a place to sit. Arria wiped Licia's brow again and then her own. "Shall we go to the railing and look for some dolphins?" Licia nodded, and they walked to the port side of the ship. A mild breeze floated past them. It seemed hard to believe that just a few minutes past, they huddled in the cabin in fear for their lives.

Their eyes scanned the water when Arria spied a rope hooked farther down the railing toward the stern and thrown over the side. Her eyes followed the line. A man dangled at the end, a hangman's knot around his neck. His body bumped against the ship's timbers. Arria covered her mouth. She grabbed Licia's hand and turned her away. "Sweetheart, come and sit on this box and rest."

"Can't we see the dolphins, Mama?"

"Perhaps later. I'll send Leo to fetch your doll. Play with her for a bit while Mama works with Papa to get things ready for dinner and the night. Can you do this for me?"

"Yes."

"Good girl."

Arria called Leo over and whispered what she had seen. He looked surprised. "Tell Garic, and please bring Licia her doll," she said. The soldier scampered off.

Garic returned and rushed to the railing. Several sailors had also seen the body and were attempting to lift it onto the deck. The guards, Telemachus and Justus, were close by. They had helped in the effort to save the ship as well. Arria brought Licia to Brother Bruno's deck tent and settled her inside. Once her daughter had her doll and was engaged in play, she moved to the crowd of men surrounding the body and stood beside Garic.

The sailors called him Paolino, a seaman from Hispania. Garic whispered to her that a sailor told him that Paolino had no family and sailed when it suited him or when he needed additional *denarii* for drinking and whoring. The crew only valued him because, on occasion, he carried drugs, made from juices and powders that brought on euphoria and helped with pain.

Several bruises covered his face, and a bloody patch over his heart implied a stab wound, but what shocked Arria, even more, was the rough cross, carved on his forehead.

A few sailors scratched their heads. Some scowled while others mumbled prayerful words of protection. The ship's captain looked dark.

Arria understood that the captain knew it would not help their voyage if the men felt fear or let their superstitious minds run wild.

The captain barked, "Get going! Wrap him up!" Finding the monk in the circle of onlookers, he added, "Brother, will you say a short prayer for our shipmate?"

Brother Bruno nodded, stepped forward, and clasped his hands. The seamen followed and bowed their heads. "Lord, may Paolino's soul find its way to Heaven and rest in eternal peace." A moment of silence filled the crew, and in the ancient custom, the men repeated the word *Vale*, farewell, three times.

The captain shouted, "Commit Paolino to the sea!" Two sailors slid him overboard. Afterward, the crew looked toward the captain, who placed his hands on his hips. With a stern gaze and gruff voice, he commanded, "Hear me—I'll have no vengeance or disputes on my ship. One or maybe more of you murdered him. If anyone knows anything, come to me when you think it's right. We just fought our way through a storm, and as long as I'm captain, there will be no dissension. Now get back to sailing, and God help you, don't try anything else. We should arrive in four days in the morning — the 25th. A bit later than expected, but at least we're here, and we have the wind behind us. When we reach Caesarea, there will be questions for all before anyone disembarks. Got it, you dirty dogs?"

The men grumbled but nodded and went back to their duties.

Arria grabbed Garic's arm. "The cross carved in Paolino's forehead seems like a message or warning. Perhaps, that's why he wasn't thrown overboard. Do you think this murder connects to our mission?"

"It's hard to say, but I want to go and check on the sword."

"I agree, but don't go alone."

"After what just happened, I'll bring Telemachus with me and leave Justus with you for your safety," Garic replied. Just then, the soldiers approached them. "Telemachus, come with me to the hold, I want to check on our *possessions*. Justus, you'll stay to protect Lady Arria and our daughter."

Both soldiers acknowledged the order with a curt nod. Telemachus appeared pleased, but a slight speck of disappointment showed in Justus' eyes. Of course, he would want to join the men. A healthy rivalry never hurt, but orders were orders, Arria thought. "Follow me to my cabin, Justus," she said. "We'll gather the girls to the railing to look for dolphins." This time, the soldier stood taller and nodded with a smile.

GARIC

The air smelled dank, and the boards creaked as Garic led Telemachus down the stairs into the cargo hold. He raised the candle lamp in his hand higher. Stormwater, mixed with wine and floating oil, coated the wooden timbers as they scampered over toppled crates and shattered amphoras. Wet shards from the broken vessels lay strewn across the floor, and a cluster of fractured jars sat toppled with the grain poured out. Among the rows of wooden crates, a few had fallen and rested on the planks, their lids torn open. They worked their way back to the supplies, heaving several boxes out of their path to reach the amphoras.

Garic saw the jar with David's star first. A thick crack ran from top to bottom, and the glint of the sword's handle shone through the grain sliding through the gap. "Telemachus, find me a blanket or a bag. The amphora that holds the sword is ruined."

Telemachus scrambled through the ship's hold and returned with a square bolt of linen cloth he found spilled from a broken crate. "Will this work?" he asked.

Garic nodded and took the cloth from the soldier. "Go now," he instructed, "and search for a small, unbroken crate, perhaps one carrying arrows, with the emperor's logo to signal our property. Empty it. We'll place the sword in the box and carry it to my cabin. Hurry!"

He glanced toward the stairs. Soon the first mate would arrive to assess the damage. Sailors would accompany the ship's officer and mop the water beneath their feet.

Garic unwrapped the bolt, took his knife, and cut several feet of cloth. Then he laid the fabric onto an undamaged box and pulled the sword from the jar. Its gemstones twinkled in the dingy light of the ship's storage. He felt a sudden reverence run through him as he placed the sword on the cloth while Telemachus, having returned with a box, lifted the linen and wrapped it tightly. Garic handed the guard a piece of rope, which he tied several times around the precious object.

Then, Garic took the covered sword, laid it in the wooden case, and closed the lid. Telemachus gathered the box to his side, and Garic led the way. Once on deck, they walked with a casual air. No one seemed to notice, and only one sailor asked, "Is it very bad down there?"

"Bad enough," Garic answered, but they kept walking as the first mate, and his men passed them, headed for the hold.

Once in the cabin, Garic stowed the case under their bed.

Arria sat folding clothes and watched him. "What does this mean?" she asked.

"We now have to carry the sword ourselves." Garic placed his hands on his hips and shook his head. "This feels strangely familiar."

Arria sighed. "I'm afraid I had the same thought. Just a simple mission, right?"

⟡⟡⟡

THE PORT AT CAESAREA: An Egyptian ship—The 22nd day of Maius

NERIAN

Nerian stood on the deck at the rail. Stars stretched across night's hollow dome, immeasurable and grand. He heard Marcella's footstep and the rustle of her dress as she came beside him.

She glided her hand down his back. "Should I be jealous of the stars? Do they captivate you more?" she purred.

Nerian wrapped his arm around her waist and kissed her temple. "They should be envious of you," he said and took a breath. The scent of myrrh, fragrant and soft, floated through her long, black hair, and gold twisted loops dangled from her earlobes. He brushed a spiral strand from her cheek and kissed her neck. He sensed her smile even in the moonlight. "In the morning, when we reach Palaestina, I'll show you the land. You may forget your desire to live in Cairo." Nerian paused, then added, "And the past, Marcella. Can you forget what happened in Constantinople—your half-sister, Arria, her husband, Garic."

Marcella faced him and folded her arms around his neck. Her tone reflected the bitter hatred in her heart. "I do despise them," she said. "I cannot forget. We barely escaped death in Constantinople—and then—on our voyage to Egypt, Brutus, *your* pet monkey, almost poisoned me."

"That *was* close," he answered and shook his head. "Who would imagine the Lady Arria carried deadly *belladonna* in her silver locket, instead of a lock of hair . . ."

"Or a cameo likeness of *her* beloved mother or *our* father?" Marcella interjected, sarcasm dripping from her words. She placed her palms on his chest. "I warned you she could be deceptive."

Nerian pulled her closer. "For a short time, I was Arria and Garic's friend and fought beside them. But my loyalty is to you."

With a slow hand, she caressed his shoulder and looked into his eyes. "Your quick thinking and shrewd manner have saved my life twice. I'm grateful, but I'm sorry that Brutus died. I know you liked your pet, although I found his chatter insufferable."

Nerian laughed and fondled a long strand of her hair as she spoke.

"Thank the goddess Isis the monkey liked to drink! Since it appears, he opened the locket and accidentally spilled the poisoned powder into my cup of wine. The goddess must love me."

"Could she not? Any man who sees you loves you, Marcella."

"Should I feel honored?" Her words sounded bitter.

"Feel secure. A woman like you will always find her way, and your beauty is an asset." Nerian tightened his grip on her waist. "Do you know why you're attracted to me?"

Marcella drew him closer. "Tell me."

"I'm a mercenary. Strong with a weapon, quick of mind, and able to find my way rather easily." Nerian chuckled. "And the ladies love me."

Marcella tilted her head and grinned. "You're quite confident."

"If you stay by my side, I'm certain adventures will come our way. And who knows, we may even fall in love."

"I'm not sure about the love, but I am rather fond of you." Marcella went to her toes and kissed him.

Nerian pressed her closer—kissed her lips, neck, and lips again. He hugged her close, and together they gazed across the rail at the sky. Thin clouds drifted beneath a yellow moon. In the distance, on the edge of night, they saw flickers of light. The port at Caesarea waited for them.

VI

Arrivals

CAESAREA: The Port—The 23rd day of Maius, Midday

MARCELLA

Marcella sauntered down the gangplank as if the city expected her arrival. The day seemed even more glorious than the breathtaking sunrise she had witnessed when the ship sailed into port, weighed anchor, and furled its sails. The air smelled like spices and the lingering scent of lemons. People walked, ran, rode, children hopped and skipped along the wharf; women waved scarves or yelled out to grab the attention of their sailors or to sell light meals and sweets to the hungry passengers. If it were possible to fall in love from first senses, then she loved Caesarea.

"Come, Marcella, hurry," Nerian urged. "A carriage awaits us. I hailed it while you stood daydreaming."

"Must you spoil my moment?" Marcella sighed. "We'll find a way to our lodgings." She took a deep breath and let her eyes feast on the scenery before her. "This place is wonderful."

"It's just the port. You have yet to see the city." Nerian grabbed Marcella's hand. He pulled her along to a mid-sized, seated, and covered *carpentum*. The two-wheeled horse-driven cart held a driver who waited for them. Nerian helped her up and then jumped onto the bench beside her. A porter carrying their bags tossed them to Nerian, who stored them behind their seat. He turned and wrapped his arm around Marcella and tapped the driver on the shoulder who yanked the horse's reins. They moved down the road toward the center of town.

The view along the coastal road filled her with contentment. A sensation she'd not experienced since her days with Severus when they would lounge on a hill outside Fort Cambria in the warm spring sun. With food and wine to quench their appetites, and days before that accursed battle at Catalaunum. She silenced her mind as it drifted toward sadness and looked around. Patches of tall grass sprouted from golden ripples in the sand. Sprawled across the dunes, yellow, red, and white flowers nestled on the tips of plants and shrubs. Carob trees dotted the road to offer weary travelers shade, and a brilliant sun held in a vibrant, blue sky that stretched before her. Marcella felt a wave of pleasure. The sun on her face. Peace.

Nerian squeezed her shoulder. "The driver knows of a man and his wife that rent a clean room for a modest sum. We can stay there. It's not far from the market and will give us the privacy we need."

She scowled, feeling snatched from her bliss. "I am particular about my accommodations. On the trip to Constantinople, I insisted on staying at the best inn Drusus could find." She stopped abruptly. "I haven't thought of him in a while, or Arria and Garic—only my mother." Marcella fell silent. A raw emotion crawled its way to the surface, guilt, but her anger knocked it down. Her mother, the vengeful Daliza, was dead—and by Marcella's unwitting hand. Arria was to blame and Drusus too. They would pay one day if the goddess Isis was kind. She pursed her lips and wondered. Despite Drusus' betrayal, what had become of him? She would have Nerian inquire about her former master and partner among the merchants who frequented Constantinople.

"Why frown, Marcella?" Nerian asked gently. "Those are the people from your past. Reliving those memories will only smother the flame that's in your heart. Look to the future. Great things await us."

"You have no sister to reckon with—one who did me wrong." Marcella's face burned. "In the end, Arria contributed to all I lost."

Nerian gave her a doubtful look. "And what did you do?" He swung his gaze ahead. His angular jaw appeared set in resignation, but then, a grin filled his lips. He raised a pointing finger. "Look! The aqueducts of Caesarea."

Annoyed, Marcella decided to hold her tongue; there was no point in fighting over a matter Nerian couldn't understand. She looked at the structure and murmured her admiration.

"Once we get to the inn, we'll unpack, eat, drink some wine, even take a quick nap." Nerian chuckled and gave her a devilish look. "Afterward, we can explore the city. I prefer shopping the market in the late afternoon when the heat has cooled. It's more enjoyable, don't you think?"

Marcella flicked her long, black hair from her shoulder and gave him a skeptical look. "Wine sounds good, and shopping is even more appealing."

"What about the nap?"

She smiled, leaned in, and brushed his cheek with her fingers. "Did I tell you? I'm especially partial to blue silk."

CAESAREA: Thirsty Goat Tavern & Inn—The 23rd day of Maius

CORVUS

Corvus sat at a table near a window. A haggard-looking barmaid strolled up to him, a hand on her hip. Although the evening had yet to begin, the *Taberna* was filled with gamblers, hustlers, thieves, farmers from their fields, and a few well-dressed pilgrims—he assumed coming from a nearby church or shrine.

"What can I get you men?" the server asked, oily strands of hair straggling over her ears.

Corvus gave his companion, Jax, seated beside him, a broad smile, and then eyed the server. "What are you offering today?"

She frowned and cocked her head. "Mead, wine, roasted partridge, bread."

"Nothin' else?" Jax spouted and eyed her slyly.

She shot him a bored look and sighed. "For the right price, we offer *dessert* upstairs, but for no longer than half an hour. We're busy today."

Corvus interrupted, "Two cups of wine, two birds, and bread will do for now."

She strolled toward the kitchen.

"No dessert?" Jax asked, grinning like a drunken fool.

"Thought about it, but we don't need brothel lice or trouble—not now." He looked at a group of men playing a game of dice, shouting with each roll. "Our directions insist we find our contact as soon as possible, remember? We're lucky we outran that sea storm, but we've been here over a day. We need to get on to Jerusalem."

"Who do you think this Goliath is?"

"Don't know and don't care. As long as he pays us, he can be a ghost."

The barmaid returned, plopped the food and drink on the table and held out her hand. "Pay now," she barked and told him the sum.

"Before we eat?" Corvus snapped back. "What if we don't like it?"

"Your loss, I guess. The owner avoids *dodgers* and problems this way."

Corvus nodded toward Jax, who smirked, pulled a few coins from his belt purse, and dropped them in her hand.

"Enjoy," she snipped and walked away.

"She's a real charmer." Corvus shook his head and pulled a leg from the hen. Chomping on it, he thought about how they would get to Jerusalem; rented horses no doubt would be the fastest.

He looked around as he chewed the tasty bird. The din of conversations made him think about their mission. Luckily for them, he could speak Greek as well as Latin, especially when dealing with eastern merchants. This ability added another veneer to his mercenary talents and the reason his services were in demand. According to Goliath's messenger, Valeria, upon arriving in Jerusalem, they were to meet an Armenian merchant who went by the name, Milvus. An odd name, he thought. If his memory served him, it referred to a bird of prey. He laughed to himself. His own name was similar. His mother, a rugged tribeswoman from the Pannonian mountains, loved birds. She told him when he was young that on the day of his birth, a raven had perched outside her hut. Pannonian culture viewed this as a sign. She had as well and had named him such. He just used the Latin form, Corvus, to keep his life simple. It was good to blend in and not be so memorable.

A chair slid roughly on the floor at the table next to them. A strapping barbarian with sharp grey eyes, black chin-length hair, and rugged features, along with a beautiful woman, took their seats. He signaled for the barmaid while she loosened the brooch on her cloak. She resembled an Egyptian. Her long, coal-black hair hung bound at the neck, and her eyes, the color of soft brown leather, sparkled.

"What you staring at?" Jax whispered across the table.

"Are you blind? That woman." Corvus took a drink and glanced at her again. "Now, that's something a man dreams about."

"Keep dreamin', you shaggy dog," Jax answered, a doubtful look on his face.

"May a mule kick your balls for all the good they do you. Ha!" Corvus said, and watched Jax drop the last bone picked clean onto his plate. Corvus did the same and took a final swallow. His cup hit the table with a thud. The woman looked in his direction, and Corvus smiled.

Her eyes held an imperious shine, but she glanced away. The barbarian next to her scowled and shot him a warning look.

Corvus stood. "Let's get to Jerusalem and find the merchant. When we acquire what we've come for, we'll have enough money for all the women we want."

Jax flipped him a toothy grin and followed.

CAESAREA: The Seaside Inn—The 25th day of Maius, Late Morning

ARRIA

A window overlooking the street and the seawall that flanked the shore caught Arria's attention as she entered the room. The scent of freshly cut mint, resting in a bowl beside a few flowers, made a wonderful impression, especially after a long sea journey. Beneath the window, stretched a cot. A few feet away, up against the inner wall, stood a second bed. Fresh towels hung over a chair in one corner. An embroidered Byzantine rug rested between the beds.

Arria felt a surge of happiness as she looked around. After the long sea journey, it felt good to settle into a room that offered fresh air, a high measure of cleanliness, and that didn't rock and heave. The recommendation of the Seaside Inn from one of the palace ministers had proven worthy.

Garic entered with her belongings and those of Licia and Catalina now in the company of Brother Bruno, who offered them a tour of the nearby market. Some plump figs and ripe dates had captured his attention before they made the doorway of the Seaside Inn. The portly brother was known to have a fondness for sweet fruits, and Bruno's eyes glittered with eagerness. The girls expressed excitement at savoring the fruits as well. Arria laughed with pleasure and let them go, but asked they return after an hour.

Arria and Garic had agreed earlier that the women would sleep together in one room, and Brother Bruno, Leo, and Garic would share another. Still, on their arrival, they discovered a lack of accommodations for the soldiers. Telemachus and Justus, somewhat reluctant but reassured by Arria, chose to sleep at the nearby Roman barracks just for one night. They would rejoin them first thing in the morning. Leo vowed to aid Garic in case of trouble while Arria watched Garic's eyes widen on hearing Leo's pledge. The innkeeper jumped in and assured the soldiers a room for the next day, so they could all lodge in one place.

"Does the room please you?" Garic asked, placing a satchel and two bags on the floor.

"Absolutely. We have a view of the sea. I find it calming."

Garic walked past her to the window. "It is . . . beautiful. Five years ago, I never thought I would see any place but Belgica and Gaul." He stared out at the view.

"What are you thinking?" she asked tenderly and went to him. She circled her arms around his waist and rested her head on his back.

Garic covered her hands with his. "Of our farm, *Wilder Honig*— Wild Honey . . . my brothers. And the land, so familiar to me and yet different. It seems fresher—newer than this land, but Gaul is ancient as well." He turned and held her in his arms. "Life is strange. One never knows where it will take you."

Arria smiled up at him. "Once I thought I knew, until destiny jumped in and grabbed the reins." She ran a hand over his shoulder. "We certainly have had our surprises, but despite my sorrows, you and Licia are my greatest joys. For this, I'm grateful."

Garic kissed her, then cradled her chin in his hand. "And your sadness? Do you think of your father often or how he died?" He caressed her cheek.

Arria nodded. "I do, but my heart and mind see only his handsome face and kind manner. I think of all the sacrifices he made for me so that I might learn and survive in this world. I think about how respected he was in Rome ..." Arria felt tears rising in her eyes and caught her breath. "Painful thoughts sometimes grab me—how he was killed for mistakes he made as a young soldier—I won't allow myself to dwell on them. After Lucius died, Father encouraged me to find peace with the past. Move forward into the future." Sadness seeped through Arria, yet she smiled. "Bitterness and regret burden our days . . . rob our hearts of happiness."

"And this mission? Any regrets, worries?"

"I'm reassured now that we're here. But . . . ." She lay her hand on his chest. "I haven't forgotten about the murdered sailor. I hope his death has no connection to our journey. A dangerous squall seems like an odd time for someone to seek vengeance, don't you think?"

"The storm may have been the best distraction and moment for revenge. We never spoke with or knew him. Do not worry."

Arria reached for Garic's hand and held his gaze. "I know we've come here on behalf of the emperor and empire, but for me, completing this mission is in honor of my father. I've given this much thought. A contribution. The emperor wishes the sword to rest in the Church of the Holy Sepulchre. I shall work to fulfill his desire, but mine as well." Arria grasped Garic's hand tighter, excitement ran through her. "I'll offer a generous donation to ensure a splendid shrine is built, and hopefully, in my father's memory."

"And the church fathers? Will they agree with you?"

"They know we're coming, but may or may not. Jerusalem has many holy relics. Perhaps my charitable patronage of a beautiful tabernacle in their church will persuade them."

Garic grinned. "You always amaze me," he said and kissed her again.

"And one more thing . . ." Arria added but caught a breath. Was now the time to tell him she might be with child? It was still early. She'd only missed one cycle.

A sudden, thumping knock startled them.

JERUSALEM: Shop of the Egyptian merchant, Accipiter—The 25th day of Maius

MARCELLA

Marcella held the rail of the mule cart for hire as she and Nerian trundled peacefully through the market off the Cardo Maximus, the main street of Jerusalem. A hungry growl forced her hand to her stomach. She'd finally eaten a decent meal in Caesarea after days at sea with limited provisions. The Thirsty Goat Tavern—a name she found amusing—had been busy, but the service and meal proved only adequate. After this visit to the merchant, she would enjoy the reputed quality and bountiful foods Jerusalem had to offer.

She grabbed the water pouch hanging from her shoulder and quenched her thirst. The sun's bright light beat down on her head, and she squinted as she looked around. She feared the lines that might appear around her eyes and tugged her veil lower over her brow. Too much sun would parch her skin, leaving it dry and deepening the warm color of her complexion. As a child in Egypt, Marcella never thought about her beauty, but her adolescent and adult years as a Roman concubine taught her many methods and tricks to enhance her looks, to maintain a youthful appearance. Delicate, soft skin aroused her former patrons whose own skins were often weathered or aged, and they would compliment her on her thick, long hair and how it shone with an ebony luster.

Marcella also knew from the fashion of the day—a too rosy tip of the nose or sun-browned cheekbones would make her appear common. The men in her past could afford, and desired, more than ordinary. Her welfare, she had learned, depended on her beauty, and so, she never traveled without a veil. Today, she would also purchase, or rather Nerian would buy, a fragrant oil for her skin.

"Here we are," Nerian said. He sat beside Marcella and signaled the driver to stop.

The lumbering cart came to a halt. Nerian jumped out and offered her a hand as she stepped onto the stone block pavement. They stood in front of an open-air shop with a large, striped awning that shaded the owner's wares.

The store was one of a row of two-story buildings, housing a variety of businesses on the ground level. It seemed well kept and successful. A man, who appeared to be a customer, perused some rugs thrown over a rack. Two women bent over a statue of a young girl holding a bouquet of flowers in her arms. Marcella peered inside the shop. A terracotta tiled floor held an abundance of carpets of various sizes and designs, no doubt coming from Persia and the lands to the east. In the rear of the store, several low shelves against a clay-colored wall displayed brass candlesticks, ornamental boxes, and trays. Further up the row of shelves, pale green and opaque glassware, plates, and goblets glistened with a soft iridescence in the pale light.

Marcella recognized the familiar aromas of cinnamon and myrrh lingering in the air. She glanced around to see if the shop carried any of her favorite oils. To her right, a table laden with a variety of glass bottles and jars gleamed in a ray of sun.

"May I be of service, madam?" a deep, friendly voice asked behind her.

Marcella turned. A merchant—short, dark, full-bellied with a long beard, and eyes sharp as a hawk scanning a landscape—smiled at her. Remarkable white teeth covered the extent of his grin, and a woven round cap sat on top of curly hair.

"Good day," Marcella responded, returning a radiant smile. "My companion and I are looking for a few things, but I believe you're acquainted."

Nerian entered the shop, having paid the driver, and approached them. "Accipiter, my friend! How are you?" He extended his hand, and the merchant grasped it, shaking it with vigor.

"Nerian! It's been a while. I'm well. As you see, I'm still in business." Accipiter swept his arm, indicating the shop. "The last I heard from you, Princess Honoria had you in Constantinople tracking some pilgrims on a secret venture. Did it prove profitable?" Accipiter gave Nerian a sly wink.

Nerian laughed. "You're always thinking of money, but that's good for business, right?"

Accipiter slapped Nerian on the back. "Are you going to introduce me to this lovely woman?"

Nerian gave Marcella a proud look. His affection warmed her, and she returned a delighted gaze. It felt safe to be with him. Everything about him echoed the finer qualities she'd found in her lost love, Severus. A quick breeze swept into the shop, and a sudden wariness seized her. She corrected herself. No point in getting attached to Nerian or turning soft. For her entire life, she'd been someone's pawn, but she'd learned to fight back in her way, a hidden way. Now for appearance's sake, she maintained her happy demeanor. She might forgive what the men in her life had done to her, but she would never forget.

"Accipiter, may I introduce the charming Marcella." Nerian turned toward her. "Marcella, the finest merchant in Jerusalem, Accipiter."

Accipiter bowed. "It's a pleasure to meet you."

"My pleasure as well," Marcella purred. "What a wonderful shop. I'm hoping to find a rose oil."

Accipiter grinned. "I have the best oils in Jerusalem."

Before the merchant could lead Marcella to them, Nerian interrupted.

"My darling, why not browse while Accipiter and I get reacquainted and talk a little business." He pulled a leather pouch from his belt and emptied several coins into his palm. "When I paid the driver, I noticed a store across the way with cloth goods. My friend here doesn't carry materials. If you want that veil, you'll find a variety to choose from there."

Accipiter jumped in. "Absolutely, my neighbor merchant has beautiful fabrics from Egypt, Rome, Constantinople, and the far east. You're sure to find something."

Marcella started to frown but caught herself. "I can always buy a veil and would love your help," she said, smiling sweetly at Nerian. "I'd rather stay. Business talk seldom bores me. I find it stimulating." She lowered her lashes, giving Nerian a side-glance.

Nerian chuckled. "See, Accipiter, what I'm up against?"

With a wise nod, the merchant stroked his beard. "Then come. Join me in the back of my shop where we can sit and sip a sweet wine from Sicilia." He called for his servant, who came running in from a back door. "Babajan, pour us some wine, and then, help any customers that wander in."

Babajan bowed and scurried to his duty.

Accipiter raised a hand to the taller Nerian's shoulder. "Come my friends. You've arrived at a good time. I have a story to tell you."

THE ROAD TO JERUSALEM: The 25th day of Maius

VALERIA

To Valeria, the heat felt unbearable, and a fine dust sifted through the air. She pawed at the neckline of her *palla,* the linen shawl stifling, yet a necessary protection against the sandy wind. Why did so many pilgrims flock to this place? Constantinople's weather was so much more pleasant and the city sophisticated. Still, Jerusalem had grown as a place for monasteries, incredible churches, and holy sites. At the same time, businesses flourished. She and her older brother, Milvus, had expanded their enterprise to Jerusalem as well. Milvus preferred Jerusalem. His pensive manner and quiet nature aligned with the spiritual atmosphere that permeated the Christian city. He proved himself to be a loyal member of the church by attending Mass and donating money regularly. But Valeria knew her brother, above all, as a businessman. His ambition was powered by his dream of living and aging comfortably when he could no longer work. Milvus never married, and once said, he relished more, counting his coins at the end of the day. He was also a man who believed in appearances.

Although Milvus knew Kalev was more than just a wealthy merchant—that he was Goliath of the dark market—they worked well together, and their business dealings meant profit. But Milvus and society would never have approved of her love and affection for Kalev, a married Jew. And so, Valeria's deception tore at her heart. Kalev, gone from Constantinople before her, was at his home in Bethany outside of Jerusalem, and she longed to see him.

The small caravan she traveled with came to a sudden stop. They had found pleasant weather and made good time and had evaded any bandits who may have been along the way.

On this trip, she came with an array of artifacts and jewels from Constantinople and Kashmir further east. The caravan master, a tough leader the travelers called Tygran, rode his horse beside her covered cart and called to her. "My lady!"

Valeria raised the canvas flap. His heavy brows and fleshy nose contributed to his brawny, gruff exterior, which bolstered his reputation for providing swift and generally safe journeys.

"Jerusalem is in sight. I hope your trip has proven comfortable."

"As always. Thank you."

Tygran shifted in his saddle, then ventured, "A rumor floats on the wind." He pursed his lips as if calculating his words. "Have you heard it? Perhaps from the merchants you know?"

"What sort of rumor?"

His eyes narrowed, the pupils shining from beneath the lids. "An ancient artifact—quite unique. A weapon, I believe. Fallen into the emperor's possession, possibly coming to Jerusalem."

"Odd. I've heard nothing. What sort of weapon?" she asked, wanting to hide that she was aware of the artifact's existence.

"A sword."

"Of great value?"

"Not certain. Something about it belonging to a king."

"Interesting. A king is not unusual."

"True. Unless it was a king of great fame." Tygran's stare penetrated her skin.

She kept her gaze firm. "I imagine so. Strange. I've not heard anything about this. My curiosity is piqued. I might inquire about this mysterious sword." Valeria smiled. "The gates of Jerusalem beckon us, and I'm famished. Will we make it before dinner?"

"Within the hour, my lady."

Valeria nodded and hoped she had lied well enough. "What a welcome relief," she replied, her smile even, and dropped the canvas flap of her wagon.

VII

A Difference of Opinion

CAESARIA: The Seaside Inn—Arria and Garic's room, The 25th day of Maius

SAMUEL BEN ZECHARIAH

S amuel raised his fist, hesitated a moment—then knocked on his former mistress's door. His knuckles sounded strong on the wood, but he listened, waited. A board creaked, and the door swung open. Garic, tall and muscular as Samuel remembered, stood before him. Golden stubble still covered Garic's square jaw, and wheat-colored hair reached his shoulders. The cleft in his chin deepened as his smile lit up beneath intense blue eyes. Four years had passed, but it seemed like only days. "You haven't changed," spilled out of Samuel. His heart burst like a plunge into a warm sea.

Garic laughed, stepped into the hall, and embraced him with a slap on the back. "Neither have you, my friend. You still have a lion's mane of brown curls and the look of a warrior, even though I suspect you've put your sword away."

Samuel nodded. "The way of the *Wespe* is behind me. Tell me, does the elite warrior clan still thrive?"

"Very much so," Garic assured him.

From behind Garic, Arria appeared. Tears welled in Samuel's eyes, but he fought the impulse. He could barely utter, "Arria," and smiled.

She moved past Garic and wrapped her arms around him, then kissed him on the cheeks. Stepping back, her hands clutching his arms, she held him in her gaze. Her pretty green eyes glimmered, and he could see she was overwhelmed. "My dearest friend, we have missed you, but I'm so happy to see you here. Tell me, how is Angelus?"

"Very well, Arria—and grown into a man. He's fourteen years and handsome with his mother's looks."

"Karas was beautiful," Arria agreed. "And you? Have you remarried?"

Samuel thought a moment, before his years as a slave and trusted manservant to Arria in her father's house, slave traders had captured him while on his way to Capernaum to sell a horse. He was only eighteen and betrothed to a girl named Miriam. Later, in Arria's household, when the slave woman Karas and her son Angelus came to serve, Samuel fell in love. With Arria's permission, he married Karas and adopted her son. Despite the tragedy they experienced at the Battle of Catalaunum in Gaul, Arria still cared about his well-being and his family. It warmed him. They always had been more like brother and sister than mistress and servant.

Samuel shook his head, and a sad sobriety tugged at him beneath his smile. "Miriam found happiness with another man. In the town where I live, there are few unmarried women or young widows."

Arria's hopeful look faded. "I'm sad to hear this . . . perhaps one day, a stronger love will find you."

"Maybe, but I am happy."

"And what news of your parents, your sister?"

Samuel noticed she caught her breath, and he folded her hands in his. "My mother died four years ago, the year I returned. I was only able to spend a few months with her, but I'm grateful to God for this gift. My father is still strong. My sister married. She's carrying a second child, and I have a nephew who adores Angelus."

Arria hugged Samuel one more time and stepped beside Garic. "Come, let us take some refreshment and get reacquainted. I have much news."

The trio proceeded down the inn stairs to the first floor. On one side of the room, chairs sat clustered together in an open parlor for guests and private conversation. A window, behind the seating and adjacent to the entry's oak double doors, overlooked the main street. Across from the parlor, near a separate kitchen, two rectangular and several square tables stood available for communal dining.

Garic pointed the way to a table with four chairs and signaled the innkeeper's daughter his way. He requested cups of wine, fresh bread, and a bowl of figs. She scurried toward the kitchen while Samuel pulled a chair for Arria. He politely sat across from Arria as Garic seated himself beside her.

Samuel gazed at them a moment, then at Arria. "I can't believe you both are sitting before me." He leaned in. "Tell me news of

Vodamir and Basina, and what of Luthgar—Gaul and your land, Wild Honey."

Arria assured him that Vodamir and Basina were in love and married, and they had left them in Constantinople to return to Vodamir's farm, Silver Oaks.

The innkeeper's daughter arrived just then with a large tray, which she set down, placing drinks, plated bread, and a fruit bowl onto the table. "If there's anything else you require, please call me," she chirped and left.

Garic raised his cup. "To friends. Let our lives always intertwine."

Arria and Samuel raised their cups. "To friends," they repeated and drank.

Garic quickly tore a chunk of bread from the loaf and offered it to Arria, another to Samuel, and then pulled a piece for himself. Garic informed Samuel about the growing power of the Franks in Gaul and their province of Belgica Secunda, his farm, and Luthgar's tribe and how it flourished. That before he and Arria left for Rome and later Constantinople, the Wespe welcomed three young new warriors, inexperienced but exceptional in their military prowess.

Samuel marveled over the positive changes for his friends and the land where he once lived. He expressed his relief and gratitude to God that they were together, safe, and sitting before him.

He then told Arria and Garic about his return home with ten-year-old Angelus and the happiness his family felt upon his arrival in their village of Nazareth in Galilee. They had wept and welcomed them with pure joy. Their son, who disappeared on the road north of Capernaum, on his way to market, had returned after seventeen years. They had suspected foul play—robbers or an unexpected accident—but were shocked and saddened to discover he'd been kidnapped by pirates and sold into slavery. Yet, they were extremely grateful, he had survived and returned to them.

Memories filled him, and he was silent for a moment. A ripe fig caught his eye, and he popped it into his mouth in an effort to change his mood. Garic reached for one, too. Arria sipped her wine; her eyes glistened. Samuel swallowed the fruit, rested his eyes on Arria, and continued, "My family wanted to know everything. They said they wouldn't press me, though, if it was too painful to speak about. But I wanted to tell them. After all, I had returned after so many long and painful years . . . with them thinking the worst, never knowing what happened to me."

Thirst filled him, and he took a quick drink. He felt a spigot had opened a vent in his heart, allowing his emotions to pour out. "That night, we ate our first meal together in so many years. I shared that after my owner's death, his widow sold me to Senator Felix, who charged me with serving and tutoring his only daughter, Lady Arria, and assisting her with her studies. My family was amazed to hear of my good fortune—my transformation from slave to Wespe, my experiences in the Hun camp and at Catalaunum—my love for Karas and her son, her death. They comforted me, especially my mother. Their prayers had been answered. I was home."

Arria's eyes brimmed with tears. "I know your mother and father's joy was boundless. We, too, have a child, a daughter."

"A daughter?" Samuel looked from Arria to Garic. "Where is the child? How old is she?"

"Her name is Licia. She is seven years, soon to be eight—as she would tell you—and our adopted daughter. We met her at a monastery in Brundisium. She was living with the good brothers who took her into their care after thieves murdered her parents. She is precious to us."

Samuel smiled. "Fate has given the child a gift, despite her misfortune. I cannot think of a better mother and father for her."

Garic looked at Arria, whose face lit up. He clutched her hand, resting on the table. "The child is special."

"When can I meet her?"

"She will be here shortly. She is visiting the market with our servant, Catalina, and Brother Bruno, who brought her to us."

Samuel nodded. "I want you to see Angelus as well. We live in Nazareth and Caesarea. In Nazareth, we have a small olive grove where we press the oil for sale. My father builds cabinets, tables, and chairs—anything a person wants if it can be fashioned from wood. I help, but I mostly make spear and javelin shafts for a swordsmith here in Caesarea. This is why I have two homes."

Arria glanced at Garic. "Did you say a swordsmith?"

ARRIA

A sensation of clarity rippled through Arria. How perfect could this be? Samuel worked for a swordsmith, and they had a valuable sword. And more than value, it bore the tale of honor and legend.

Samuel squinted. "Yes, a swordsmith. Why the surprise? As a Wespe, I proved more than adept, especially with the javelin."

"Oh, no. It's not about your ability but more about your craft," Arria reassured him.

Samuel appeared even more confused.

"Let me explain." She looked at Garic, who nodded and glanced around. A few tables had patrons, but not within hearing distance if they spoke low. "We came to Palaestina for numerous reasons. A visit to the holy city, and to help build a shrine and create a memorial in my father's honor. But the primary reason is as emissaries for the emperor. We carry an artifact of great value and ancient myth."

The hotel's serving girl unexpectedly appeared, asking if they required more wine. They pulled back their heads, smiled, and politely declined. As soon as she moved on to a neighboring table, Samuel leaned in. "Tell me more. I'm intrigued."

Arria placed her hand on Samuel's arm. "The relic is a sword . . . very old, belonging to a king."

"How old and what king?" Samuel asked, his gaze firm and expectant.

"More than a thousand years. The story is long and complicated, but suffice it to say, my late husband discovered it in a grave in a foreign territory. After he was killed in battle, it came into his father, Emperor Marcian's possession. The emperor, the patriarchs, Christian and Jewish, believe it belonged to King David."

"King David of Israel?"

Arria and Garic nodded.

Samuel whispered, "Amazing."

"We are here to bring it to the Church of the Holy Sepulchre. If the church leaders agree, I will help finance a special shrine for it in memory of my father."

Samuel looked pensive for a moment as if some thought had invaded his former astonishment. His features and scar, acquired as a slave, above his left eye, folded into worry, and a slight frown

captured his smile. When his gaze grew serious, Arria knew that
something was wrong.

"Arria," he stuttered, "If this relic . . . sword, truly belonged to
King David, how can it remain in Christian hands? It should belong to
the Jewish people."

A knot gripped Arria's stomach. She instinctively knew it was not
the child she believed lived within her. Samuel's words, although
true, were contrary to what she felt, even believed. "My friend," she
said, releasing her hand from his arm. "Where would it be enshrined
for all to see? The Jews are forbidden to enter Jerusalem except on a
few of your holy days and only allowed to worship at the Western
Wall. There is no temple. If enshrined in a synagogue elsewhere, only
Jews could admire and revere it. Gentiles would not be allowed to
enter." Arria shook her head. "This cannot happen. The relic is far too
precious . . . and may have caused the death of many men on its
journey to return to where it was first created."

A bead of sweat trickled down the back of her neck, and a chill
filled her. She loved Samuel like an older brother. They had just
reunited. How could there be discord between them?

Samuel looked at Garic who sat, his brow furrowed. His eyes
shone with quiet alarm. "Garic, my brother, do you feel the same as
Arria? You're a warrior, but most of all, a counselor. What do you
say?"

Garic appeared unsure and pursed his lips. Silent a moment, he
directed his gaze between Arria and Samuel. "I believe the story that
lives in the sword. Created for a king who used it to fulfill his greed,
and acting on that desire, he claimed the life of an innocent man—his
soldier. But David repented and buried it with the victim of his greed
and lust. It's not by chance that the sword found its way to the shores
of its origin. I believe . . . the sword . . . belongs to its people. They
should say where it must rest." He tapped his fingers once on the
table, nodded, and looked at Samuel and then, hesitantly, at Arria.

She could not believe her ears and gasped, "My lord, surely you
cannot believe this. Are we not here on the emperor's behalf? We're
to deliver the sword—to the church—not a synagogue."

Garic rested his hand on hers. "I must tell the truth of what I know
and believe. I'll not tell you what to do, but I must confess, Samuel is
in his rights to see this matter as he does. Maybe you should give

Samuel's opinion some thought. The sword belonged to a Jewish king. It belongs with its people."

Arria withdrew her hand and frowned at him. "I'm shocked and hurt that you would take this position. Your belief will make the mission all the more difficult."

Samuel spoke up. "My friends. Now is not the time to make decisions. I have yet to lay eyes on this sword, and I want you to see Angelus . . . meet my family. Come, we've just reunited. There is no room in our hearts for a disagreement. We can discuss it later."

"You speak wisely," Garic offered, running a hand through his hair and attempting a smile for Arria.

"Indeed," Arria added, wiping away a frustrated tear. "The sword cannot come between us."

A sudden burst of laughter filled the room, and they turned to watch Licia and Brother Bruno sweep into the room, carrying several parcels. "Mama! Papa!" she cried, "We bring sweet treats."

Arria rose to greet them, clasping Licia in her arms. "Let's see what you've bought and come meet a friend who's very dear to me." She turned her daughter toward the table and gave Samuel a loving look. He smiled back. Arria cherished him with all her heart, but an uneasy premonition filled her and whispered disturbing thoughts. Was the sword's curse true? Would it divide them?

VIII

Shadows and Signs

CAESAREA: An Alley at Dusk—The 25th day of Maius

HE

(Nemesis)

A mist floated in from the sea and rolled across the dirt-trodden stones of the alley between two shops. He entered the dimly lit passage and ducked into an arched alcove used by pedestrians to relieve their bladders. Urine's pungent odor and the evening's warm humidity seeped up his nostrils. Sweat trickled down his brow. With a quick swipe of his hand, he knocked away the moisture. His eyes fixed on Leo. The drunken sod had spent the day in a wine shop filling his beak and babbling to anyone who'd listen about his campaigns as a centurion in the infantry.

Nemesis had spied on the soldier and followed him after he stumbled out of the shop in a daze, detoured into the alley, and fell back against the wall. Leo slid to the ground in a slump, legs splayed. His head rested against the wall, his face turned upward, eyes closed, mouth open.

Leo lay there, helpless. *What a worm*, Nemesis thought, and hate filled him. *How fast should I kill the drunk? A dog should die swiftly. Why play with him?* He needed to be quick. The alley led to a back entrance to the nearby shop, and he must avoid discovery.

He approached the centurion and jabbed his thigh with his boot. The soldier snorted, licked his lips, and an eyelid popped open. "Got a bit of wine, my friend," Leo mumbled and raised his good hand. A swift, slicing *whoosh* echoed in the darkening passageway. The soldier's severed hand fell with a soft thud onto the sandy gravel. Blood spurted from the suspended stump. Leo's eyes widened, and a bellow coursed from his lips. Without hesitation, Nemesis stabbed the defenseless soldier through the heart. No sound ushered from the centurion's mouth now, his head hung low.

Nemesis lifted Leo's head, dropped his sword, and pulled his knife. He carved the sign of revenge into the centurion's brow. He stepped into the recess across the way and grabbed the folded canvas he'd dropped on the ground. In minutes, he had Leo's body bundled and tied.

He would dump the drunk where he belonged—for all to see.

JERUSALEM: Shop of the Egyptian merchant, Accipiter—the 25th day of Maius

NERIAN

Accipiter waved a hand toward a cluster of blue pillows, flanking one side of a squat round table. As Marcella and Nerian seated themselves, the servant, Babajan, finished pouring their wine into thick green glasses and returned to the front of the shop.

Accipiter sat across from them on a large red pillow and raised his drink. "A toast to reunions . . ."

"And successful business ventures," Nerian added and glanced at Marcella beside him. She smiled demurely and raised her glass.

Nerian swallowed, savoring his wine, excited about what Accipiter might share with them. An opportunity, it seemed, had fallen into their laps within the first days of their arrival. He knew Marcella felt the same.

Accipiter placed his drink on the bronze tray that rested on the table. "An object of purported value has come to my attention. This may be a rumor . . . or it may be quite real. As of now, I'm not sure whether it exists or not, but I mean to find out."

"What sort of object? A jewel?" Nerian asked.

"More priceless than a jewel . . . an ancient artifact, belonging to a king." Accipiter wrapped his fleshy fingers around his glass and raised it to his lips. Over the rim, he gazed at them a moment. His hawkish black eyes glowed sharp and sure. He gulped the last of his wine.

Marcella's sideways glance showed her delight. Nerian began to chuckle and said, "A king will always have the best of things. How ancient is this object, and to which king does it belong?"

"Have you heard of King David?"

Both Nerian and Marcella shook their heads.

"David was a Jewish king who ruled well over a thousand years ago. Long before the Romans came, Palaestina was inhabited by the Jews and divided into two kingdoms—Judah and Israel. David united the kingdoms under his rule as Israel."

Nerian maintained a respectful demeanor but had already lost interest in the merchant's explanation. *Name the damn object*, he thought impatiently but smiled. "A historian as well, Accipiter. I respect that, but what could be this ancient and still have value?"

"For collectors of rare objects, this may be a most prized acquisition. After all, you were just involved in a quest surrounding an artifact—the Crown of Thorns belonging to Christus—as I've heard from a few reliable sources."

Marcella tensed beside Nerian, and a quick glance in her direction revealed a frown on her face. He rested his hand on her knee. This would not be a good time to revisit the feud with her sister, Arria, and the outcome of their prior adventure. He kept his tone neutral. "We had a slight involvement."

"Of course, the *secret venture* you mentioned in your letter from Constantinople," Accipiter replied, glancing at Marcella. "But my point, I hope, is made. This artifact will have multiple potential buyers, willing to pay a great deal of money. . . and many, like us, who'll want to possess and sell it."

Before Accipiter could say another word, Nerian jumped in. "My friend, before we can help you, we must know what it is."

The merchant folded his hands in his lap. "My sources claim the antique is either here or en route to the city. The name being whispered is the Sword of David. A beautiful sword with perhaps the dark power of a curse. Only a few have seen and held it. I was told it lay buried in a grave that may have belonged to Uriah, a soldier who died because of David's desire for Uriah's wife. But the legend behind it bears no consequence to us." Accipiter shrugged. "I see it as an artifact that can *wield* a hefty profit." He laughed at his own clever use of words.

Nerian seldom thought of history or those who came centuries before him. His thinking lived in the everyday and survival, but he wasn't stupid, he understood a quick turn of words. Nerian laughed back and gave Marcella a nudge. She played along and laughed, even though, he suspected, she might be annoyed. Reminding her about

Arria was not a good thing. "From what you've told us, the sword appears to be very rare and valuable. If others are seeking it for profit, then so will we. Marcella and I will pass ourselves as a wealthy Saxon landowner and his Egyptian bride. Of course, you'll have to advance us some money, so that we can infiltrate the market and Jerusalem's best circles of patrons, dealing with art and artifacts."

Accipiter grabbed his knees and nodded with pleasure. He called Babajan for more wine. "I'll advance you for pretense's sake. When we have the object in hand, I'll split the profit fifty-fifty, but I want the advance back. This way, you'll be cautious about your spending."

"Do you think I'd take advantage of your generous offer and this opportunity?"

"Although you've worked for me before, and I consider you a friend—I live in Jerusalem, and I'm a businessman first. I have stronger connections and I don't tolerate disappointment very well."

Nerian noted the gentle warning with a dip of his head.

Just then, Babajan appeared with a fresh flask of wine. Accipiter directed his servant to fill their glasses. Again, the merchant raised a toast. "To an ancient sword," he said. "And my lady," he added, looking at Marcella, "let me buy you that rose oil you desired and that veil, as a friendly gesture, to complement your exceptional beauty in the challenge that lies ahead."

Marcella gave him a dazzling smile and cooed her thanks.

Shadows cast by a pair of hanging lamps danced across their feet as Nerian, eager for this new opportunity, raised his glass, and nodded. Together they drank to their partnership.

CAESAREA: The Seaside Inn—the 26th day of Maius, Early Morning

ARRIA

A scream penetrated the dining room from outside the front door, alerting the few early diners, breaking their morning fast. Arria almost choked on the mulled wine she was sipping while Garic rose to his feet.

"My word, what has happened? It sounds like the innkeeper's wife." Arria wiped her mouth on her napkin and rose beside Garic.

"Stay here, Arria," Garic said as the innkeeper ran past them and out the door. Garic followed the owner, his hand on his sword.

Arria followed despite Garic's order. She was concerned and interested, as were the other two diners who ran to the window, but she felt no fear. Through the door and into the morning light, they came upon the innkeeper and his wife standing over a bundle, more than five feet long. The innkeeper's wife stood beside it clutching her skirt, her face flushed and eyes filled with fear. The woman turned toward her husband, and the words tumbled from her lips. She explained that when she opened the inn's door to let in the fresh air and sweep the entry, she discovered the rolled canvas on the doorstep. She yanked open the cloth at one end, exposing the head and a chopped hand, resting on the victim's neck. That was when she cried out. Having finished her story, she covered her mouth and folded her other arm around her waist. Her husband stood beside her, his face grim.

Arria stepped beside Garic. He glanced at her and shook his head in resignation, his playful habit when she would have her way. She shot him a determined look and then addressed the innkeeper. Her tone commanded attention. "Before you notify the authorities, may I observe closer?" The innkeeper's wife had dropped the canvas over the face.

"It's not a pretty sight, but if you like, my lady," he replied, and looked puzzled by her interest.

Her curiosity stemmed from the murder on the ship of the sailor, Paolino, and felt compelled to see for herself. Another murder in such a short space of time was alarming. Crouching beside the body, she lifted the cloth. At first, the burgeoning light struck the contours of the face from the side, hiding its full features. But in an instant, the sun topped the horizon, and the victim's face came into full view. Arria gasped, and Garic muttered, "*Verdammt.*" The innkeepers had not recognized their servant, but it was unmistakably Leo. The poor man's mouth hung open, his eyes closed, and his chopped, bloodied hand appeared to grasp his own throat. His crippled hand hung at his side. Arria stared for a moment in disbelief, but her eyes quickly rose from the curled fingers to a mark, tinged with dried blood, carved on Leo's forehead. Her insides cringed. This was not a robbery—it was murder.

Garic knelt beside her. "What is it, Arria?" he asked in a hushed voice.

"Look closely. The symbol is the Star of David."

"Like the symbol on the amphora that once held the sword?"

"Yes, it's the symbol the Jews use. It represents David and Judaism."

"Arria, I'm confused. Leo wasn't a Jew, or was he?"

"No. I fear this is a warning or an act of revenge. I wonder. What secrets did Leo have? Did he hurt or betray someone? A Jew, perhaps? Or could this be a warning to us at the expense of an innocent man? Easy prey—a drunk." She shook her head and stood. Garic covered Leo's face and stood as well.

Arria pulled Garic aside and away from the innkeepers and gathering bystanders before anyone could question them about their servant. His pet name passed her lips as a whisper, "Krieger, we need to leave for Jerusalem as soon as possible. There is sure to be an inquiry from a local magistrate about this murder. Especially because the body was dumped in front of a public inn."

"I agree, Mellitula," he responded quietly with her endearment in kind. "We'll cooperate with the authorities, but we must make ready to go."

Arria pulled her shawl tighter and raised a loose curl behind her ear. "Samuel will return with Angelus this afternoon when he arrives from Nazareth. I couldn't bear to miss our meeting. It's been so long since we've seen the boy. We'll leave in two days."

"There's also the matter of Brother Bruno and Licia."

"I know. Now, more than ever, I think Licia should stay at the monastery just outside of Jerusalem. There's no need to expose her to any threat the city might bring. "Do you agree?"

"I do. She and Brother Bruno will be safer with the monks."

Feeling reassured, Arria added, "The brother told me it's known for being a peaceful sanctuary, but some of the brothers were once soldiers. They know how to use a sword if needed." Arria looked into the blue eyes she loved so much. They always seemed filled with light. "Krieger, why does death seem to follow us?"

"Because you agree to missions that are noble but carry danger. But I assure you we'll do our best to outrun it. We must, for all our sakes."

Arria grabbed his hand. "If I have to outrun danger and death, there's no one I'd rather do it with than you."

Garic grabbed her shoulders and kissed her for those gawking on the street to see, as the sound of marching feet drew closer to the inn. The word of a murder had spread.

IX

Secrets of the Heart

CAESAREA: The Seaside Inn—The 26th day of Maius,
Early Morning

GARIC

Gusty gray clouds driving toward the sea cast a pale light on the morning. The air smelled of salt and fish as Garic took a breath and waited. Around the corner, several soldiers came into view and approached the scene outside the inn. Behind the soldiers, Garic could see their escorts, Telemachus, and Justus. They were returning as promised after spending the night at the local barracks. Tonight, with a room now available, they would sleep at the inn.

Four soldiers and a centurion halted in front of the corpse. Telemachus and Justus hurried to stand beside Garic. He nodded at them, relieved they had returned in the middle of the confusion. Having skilled fighters by his side added to his sense of protection.

"My lord? What has happened here?" asked Telemachus.

"Indeed," Justus added, a sour look on his face.

"Leo. He's been murdered . . . and marked," was all Garic could offer before the centurion barked questions at the innkeeper.

The innkeeper, his hands shaking, stammered that his wife had found the disfigured body on their doorstep at daybreak.

The centurion asked the onlookers if anyone knew the man.

Garic spoke, "He was our servant traveling with us."

The centurion frowned, tugged on the canvas, and exposed the body. New onlookers in the crowd gasped.

The officer knelt and peered at the corpse. "Strange," he muttered but said no more. He rose. "Officially, this is a matter for the magistrate. He'll want to ask a few questions. It appears your servant may have infuriated someone, but I'll only present the facts to his honor. Was anything stolen from this man?"

"He had nothing to steal," Garic offered. "What money he had, he spent on drink."

"There's a cost to dispose of the body. Bring your purse to court. He's your servant."

Garic looked at Arria. She asked, "Can we purchase a single grave, rather than a common pit? Leo was a soldier who served Rome well."

The centurion's gaze swung toward Arria and lingered a moment, then shifted back to the corpse. "Looks like his service demanded a cruel price from him. It's up to the magistrate." He glanced at his men, then quickly at Arria and Garic. A slight smirk tugged at his lips. His voice lowered, and he added, "The right amount of coin won't hurt your request."

Turning from them, the centurion slipped his foot under the open flap of canvas and kicked it into place covering Leo. He ordered a soldier to disperse the crowd and the rest of his men to lift the body. One of the huskier soldiers leaned in and hoisted the body onto his shoulder. From the force of the lift, Leo's severed hand came loose from his neck, slipped through the canvas fold, and plopped onto the ground. Another gasp resonated through the crowd, and some people groaned, turning their eyes away. Arria covered her mouth to muffle her cry.

"Scheisse!" Garic uttered and watched as the soldier picked up the severed appendage grinned at it, and on the centurion's command, tossed it to another soldier who wrapped it in the apron seized from the innkeeper's wife.

As the soldiers marched away, the crowd dispersed amid some rumblings over the morning's event. The innkeeper and his wife hurried toward the building as she complained loudly that the murder had delayed their chores, hurt business, and robbed her of a favorite apron.

Garic and Arria stood there a moment, both feeling numb, and watched the soldiers move down the street with Leo.

Telemachus removed his helmet. Damp blond curls clung to his ears. "I could use a morning ale. How about it, Justus? Join me?"

Justus removed his helmet as well, allowing a chestnut wave to drop across his forehead. "Let's tip a cup in the poor beggar's memory. I'm sure he'd appreciate that," he replied and steered Telemachus toward the inn.

Arria sighed. "It's sad that Leo spent part of his life begging for drink. He once had the pride of a soldier." She grew quiet and pursed her lips. "Do you think Leo's death might be tied to the sword?" she asked. "The symbol carved on Paolino and Leo are different, but the deed appears similar. Can this be a coincidence?"

"Perhaps, but even so, it's best to stay alert." Garic took her hand. "We should check on Licia and the good brother. Hopefully, our daughter is still asleep." He thought he saw a hint of fear in her eyes. "What, Mellitula?" he asked.

"Now, more than ever, we must guard the sword."

ARRIA

Sunshine slid through the glass window at the end of the second-floor corridor, lighting their way. A torch, used at night and snuffed when the innkeeper retired, stretched from its metal sconce cold and ignored. The right side of the hallway held the rooms, whereas the left half-wall acted as a solid banister to the common area below. The brother's room, the first at the top of the stairs, showed an open door. Garic led the way, then stopped. Arria stood behind him. Brother Bruno sat on his bed, a small codex filled with prayers in his hand that Arria quickly recognized. Throughout the journey, the brother spent his time reading from it as part of his devotions.

Garic stepped into the room, and Arria followed.

"Good morning, Brother. Did you sleep well?" Garic asked.

"Well enough, thank you, considering what just happened. Soon after I woke, my prayers were interrupted by the commotion outside. I went downstairs and stepped outside the door into that crowd. I can't believe what I heard and saw. Poor Leo—dead and being carried away." Brother Bruno shook his head. "I returned to my room immediately to pray."

Arria felt her throat tighten. "I feel horrible about this. I knew him when he was healthy and strong. Back then, Leo carried himself like a proud soldier, a protector of Rome. I never imagined such a fate would befall him. I hoped that with us . . . his life . . . his future might improve."

"Lady Arria. Noble Garic," the priest began, his face calm. "The church teaches that as Christians, we are called to a path in our life that includes salvation. Although Leo led a troublesome life filled with disappointment and pain, I believe he considered himself a Christian and must surely be with the Lord in Heaven. Let this console you."

"Your words offer a new way of thinking for Garic, a recent convert, but they are a reminder for me," Arria said, feeling comforted. "You've brought me some peace." Muffled sounds filtered through the bedroom wall, and Arria tilted her head to listen. She turned toward Garic. "Licia is awake. I can hear her giggling next door. It's time we go to her."

"*Ja*. She and Catalina must be hungry," Garic replied. "One more thing, Brother," he added, "We'll go to the magistrate in the afternoon to petition our right for a private burial for Leo. Please come with us; your presence will help our request. Regardless where he's buried, you can still pray over him, the prayers for the dead."

Brother Bruno's smile was filled with assurance. "I can, and I will."

Garic nodded his gratitude and walked out of the room.

Arria thanked the monk as well and followed Garic. A sense of both relief and warmth coursed through her heart. Although she had not seen Leo in years, she truly felt a gentle connection with him. She would try her best to provide the old soldier with the honor he deserved, a safe resting place.

ARRIA

Licia quickly dressed while Arria and Catalina gathered some of the dirtier clothes and straightened their room. Licia hummed a tune as she slipped on boots and came to stand before Arria.

"You're like your mama, you like to sing," Arria said, wanting to appear happy for Licia's sake, and slipped a comb through her curls.

"I do. I like the sounds, how they go up and down. Just like the birds."

"That's true. Birds make very pretty sounds, and if you listen often, you can learn to tell which kind of bird is singing," Arria answered and gently tugged the teeth of the comb through a tangled strand.

"Why don't animals sing?"

Arria hesitated. What had she learned in school? Cows and horses couldn't sing because, unlike man, they didn't have the gift of speech. Although, maybe in a way, wolves howling was a sort of song, but a dog's bark didn't seem so melodic.

What if Licia asked her why animals didn't speak? Arria pursed her lips. She had accepted that they couldn't because they were less intelligent than man. This was a question, which could lead to more, and too challenging to ponder so early in the morning. "I'm afraid your mama cannot answer your question. At least—not today. Maybe we can ask the learned Brother Bruno if he knows anything about animals and song."

"Yes, Mama, I will," she answered sweetly.

Amused but relieved, Arria put the comb down, and Licia began to prance around. "Licia, go with Catalina now. She'll bring you downstairs for breakfast."

Catalina, holding the laundry to give to the innkeeper's wife, took Licia's hand, and they left the room. Licia's carefree innocence always raised her spirits. Standing at the door, Arria smiled and watched them go.

At the same time, Telemachus and Justus came down the hall, ready to move into the newly available room next door to them. The good brother and Garic would continue to share a room, even though Leo was gone. Arria sighed. She missed the intimate moments spent with Garic that meant so much to them. The travel and these accommodations had made their private time together impossible. Once in Jerusalem, she would make sure their lodgings allowed them the opportunity to be alone together.

Arria nodded toward the soldiers. "After what we witnessed this morning, I'm pleased you're here."

"Very happy to serve you, my lady," Telemachus answered as they stopped before her.

"We're at your service," Justus added, respectfully.

Arria smiled. "Thank you." The soldiers proceeded to their room. She stepped into the hallway, locked her door, and then hurried to Garic's room.

He sat on the bed, looking at a map.

Arria sat beside him. "Krieger, where is the priest?"

"He went to Mass. He also seemed eager to experience one of Caesarea's churches." Garic folded the map and laid it by his side.

"The Christian devotion in this land and all the pilgrims that come this way intrigue him. He informed me that afterward, he would visit the market."

"Then it's a perfect time to take a closer look at the sword—away from prying eyes and before Samuel arrives. I sense that there is more to the sword than we discovered in our brief glimpse. Curiosity compels me. Where have you hidden it?"

"Behind the wooden cabinet." Garic beamed and pointed in its direction. "I attached a canvas bag to the back panel of the wardrobe and slipped the sword inside."

"My lord, a very clever choice considering the lack of hiding places," Arria replied, knowing he basked in the compliment.

"I thought so as well," he said, grinning again and squeezed her knee. He rose and locked the bedroom door, then went to the wooden cabinet and moved it from the wall. The slim, canvas bag hugged the backboard. He pulled the wrapped sword from the bag, sat back down, and laid it on the bed between them. He untied the cord from the bundle and peeled back the cotton fabric, revealing the weapon. They gazed at it a moment. Garic slid the sword from the bronze sheath.

The sword's round ivory handle was carved with circular lines and sat above a blunted cross-guard. Just as they had seen before in Emperor Marcian's presence when Garic held it.

The silver pommel resembled a rounded half-moon cap about two inches tall, an inch wide, and three inches in diameter—large enough to keep a hand from slipping off the handle. A circle of rubies graced its center. Engraved down the center of the blade were the Hebrew letters.

Arria was amazed by the remarkable condition of the sword. If not for the ability of the earth and time to bury and protect ancient objects and relics over the centuries, there would be few artifacts for men to discover, collect, and admire. Did the spirit of redemption contribute to the sword's safe journey as well? Her dead husband, Lucius, and perhaps a few other men had carried, wielded, and protected it. The sword possessed strength and resilience. Was it determined to return home?

Garic raised a finger and examined a gold band, which wrapped the center of the ivory grip.

"I wonder if the band existed with the creation of the sword or as a later addition?" Arria asked softly, so no one outside the room might hear. "It seems more of an ornament and less practical."

"Perhaps," Garic answered but continued to eye the grip. On the band, four images were engraved: a coronet of flowers, a garland of grain, a cluster of withered grape leaves, and a naked tree branch. "I think these represent the seasons," he murmured.

"I agree." Arria tilted her head and looked closer. Garic moved it toward her. "Why would these images be on a king's sword?"

"A logical question, my love. Why?"

They continued to stare, lost in their thoughts. "What do the seasons have in common?" Garic asked aloud as he rested the weapon across his knees. Turning the sword over, he scanned the blade. He flipped it again and studied the front.

Arria stood and paced back and forth. It helped her to think and reason. She thought back to her lessons. Speaking in a low tone, she said, "The two days of solstice, one in summer and one in winter, mark the direction of the sun and *length* of the days." She stopped. "Perhaps, the band slides up and down."

Garic looked at her, nodded, then tried moving the band up and down. Nothing. It stayed in place and wouldn't move.

Arria frowned, but determined, she continued to pace. "The length of the days . . . the light . . . the sun . . . how it crosses the sky. "Movement!" Arria declared, striding a bit faster, hands on her hips. "One season moves into another. We say they . . . turn . . . Summer turns to fall . . . fall to winter."

"Maybe the band turns," Garic interjected, and with a tight grip and calculated force, he rotated the gold band.

It moved. He looked surprised and glanced at her.

A curious thrill rushed through her. She came and knelt beside him.

Now Garic appeared puzzled. "But why the four seasons? Why not the phases of the moon? Or a king's emblem?" he asked.

A sudden solution popped into Arria's head. "Because my love, you must turn it *four* times." She bit her lip. Her heart beat faster.

Garic looked at her, and his eyes danced with excitement. Fixing on the band, he took it in his fingers, and having completed one rotation, he rotated it three more times.

Arria held her breath.

Click. They heard it, ever so softly. Garic shook his head. "Mellitula, you're the cleverest woman I know."

Arria smiled inwardly. Perhaps, one day, she might rise to the *cleverest person.* Her father had warned to temper her ambitions in a world ruled by men. But with Garic, she felt there was hope. She leaned closer. "I think the pommel is unlatched now and might turn as well, but be careful in the twist."

Garic applied a bit of pressure, but nothing happened. He took a breath, gripped tighter, and turned. With a squeak and one rotation, the pommel cap budged, then stopped. A determined look on his face, he cupped the pommel tighter and turned it again. The cap came loose in his hand. He exhaled and flipped it over. Circular grooves rested on the inside of the rim.

On the sword, and jutting an inch from the center of the ivory grip was the tang. Arria knew it also as the 'tongue,' which narrowed from the blade and formed the core beneath the ivory handle. The tang also had grooves around its edge. "What a clever design," Garic observed, holding both parts of the separated sword, one in each hand. "The pieces turn to fit together. But why detach the pommel from the handle and blade?"

They peered closer inside the cap. A round piece of parchment acted as a barrier.

"What is this?" Arria whispered softly. "A covering? Can it be hollow?"

"Your fingers are smaller. Lift the parchment out," Garic encouraged, handing her the cap.

Arria used a fingernail to pick at the edge of the barrier. It lifted, and she pulled it free. Stuffed beneath the parchment cover lay a small white cloth. More curious than ever, she plucked at the fabric, which came easily into her hand. The linen, in the shape of a circle, appeared as if an object rested beneath the folds.

"Hmm," fell from Garic's lips. He had noticed the protrusion as well.

"How many more surprises will this journey provide?"

Garic chuckled. "Venture a guess, my lovely?"

"Not this time, but I am anxious to reveal this mystery," Arria replied, just as a morning shadow stretched across the floor and across their feet. Unease gripped Arria. She swallowed, cupped the cloth in her palm, and peeled back the fabric. She stared riveted, then glanced at Garic, his gaze fixed as well. Nestled in the linen sat an incredible gem that Arria recognized at once for its opaque iridescence. A diamond. The size of an almond, it lay there boldly set in a gold Star of David.

"My word," Arria uttered. "How very beautiful." The sunlight shone higher through their window, and the star shimmered rose gold. Two fused, solid triangles, one inverted on top of the other, held the raw gem embedded in its center. With an angel's touch, Arria flipped the star on its back. Engraved letters that she now recognized as Hebrew stretched across the bands. "I wonder what the letters say?"

Garic took the star between his fingers, turned it, and admired its beauty. "We'll ask Samuel," he said. He paused a moment, then raised his keen blue eyes to her. They harbored an intensity that frightened her. "Mellitula," he frowned. "This expedition has just become more valuable—and—more dangerous."

X

Birds of Prey

JERUSALEM: High Tower Tavern and Inn—The 26th day of Maius, Early Morning

MARCELLA

Sunlight broke through their guest room window. Nerian stirred in his sleep as Marcella slipped out the door to go to the market. The morning air blew, raising her skirt and caressing her legs. With a quick hand, she stifled the folds of fabric and picked up her pace. She enjoyed arriving early at the marketplace. Before her, wooden stands, newly stocked and teeming with goods, lined the street. Vendors shouted out their offerings: mullet, sturgeon, and moray, leeks, onions, and mushrooms.

Pure contentment filled her as she sampled ripe olives from large brown baskets and purchased freshly baked bread, pomegranates, and dates for their breakfast. A savory dinner came with the price of their room above the tavern, but for lighter fare, the market offered a wider variety. Satisfied she had enough food for two, she headed for their lodgings.

Marcella hoped Nerian would be awake upon her return. They needed to scour the local shops again, to make subtle inquiries into the whereabouts or any knowledge of the sword. When she entered the tavern, the innkeeper approached her and handed her a parchment. Thanking the owner, she glanced at the seal, then climbed the stairs to the second floor.

Once inside their room and finding Nerian awake, she informed him, "A message has arrived from Accipiter." She placed the bag with bread and fruit on the table and removing her shawl, she sat in a chair.

Nerian was stretched out on the bed bare-chested and wore only leggings. His tousled hair hung over his forehead and ears. Marcella gazed at him. A passionate impulse and the subtle glimmer of something deeper, emotional gripped her. Nerian radiated virility and strength. A slight vulnerability clung to him as well, making him quite appealing but also dangerous. Finding this sensation intoxicating and distracting, she glanced away, but his question demanded her attention.

"What does the wily merchant have to say?" he asked, with a provocative grin and a seductive stare.

Had he read her thoughts? Marcella feigned a bored expression as she broke the seal and silently read the note. Within seconds, she lifted her eyes to Nerian. "Accipiter will hold a private party tonight at his home in the hills. Only select merchants and city officials, a few wealthy men, and some bishops are invited. Perhaps, even the city's patriarch, Juvenal, might attend."

Nerian shyly asked, "Is he very important?"

"He's the chief bishop. Accipiter says, Juvenal often represents the ruler of Palaestina, the aged Empress Eudocia. She has long been a patron of shrines and protector of Jerusalem and is an avid collector of ancient relics and artifacts."

Nerian bolted to a sitting position his legs akimbo and ran his fingers through his hair. "Sounds to me like a perfect opportunity. We'll represent ourselves as wealthy traders interested in the artifacts that Accipiter has to offer. I would say you should make discreet inquiries among any women there, but I think you might work better among the men." He stood and reached for his tunic.

Marcella watched as he ran his arms through the sleeves to lift it over his head. "Of course, you might also prove more effective among the women as opposed to the men," she coyly replied.

A low laugh tumbled from his lips. He tossed the tunic onto the floor and stretched out his barbarian arms, chiseled and strong. "Come and kiss me. I need waking up."

"You appear awake to me." She let the words slide into the air.

Nerian dropped his arms and crawled onto the bed. Facing her, he propped up his arm and rested his head on his fist. "I'm not fully awake. A Saxon waking is . . . more complete."

"Then a Saxon waking it must be," she replied and went to him.

JERUSALEM: Moon Gold Antiquities Shop—The 26th day of Maius, Late Morning

CORVUS

Corvus chuckled aloud. Jax snorted as he followed behind. His friend often boasted about his agility and prowess, but Jax could not outrun, or like today, even out-walk him.

Corvus glanced up as he traveled the white stony street. In the blue-grey sky, two black crows circled and rode the wind while their shadows brushed the street below. Were the birds of prey following their path, he wondered? With a final flap of wings, they landed on the rooftop of a wine shop across the way and stared down at them with sharp, mean eyes. A brief unease tugged at Corvus.

He slowed and glanced briefly over his shoulder. Jax, still close, gave him a lopsided grin but wasn't one for conversation. Corvus looked around. A pretty girl stood in a nearby doorway. She gave him a seductive smile. He smiled back and kept walking. Pilgrims and shoppers, some in a hurry, some out for a stroll, passed them. Along the narrow street, merchants and vendors sold their wares from the long row of shops that led toward the Pool of Israel and the Temple Mount.

Jerusalem was different from Constantinople. A peaceful mood permeated the city. It made him want to soak it in and not rush. The heat of the day was manageable, and the atmosphere around him was languid. An impulse struck Corvus, and he took a breath. He could live here, make this city his home. Yet this unexpected notion disturbed him. It felt threatening like the birds perched overhead.

A shrill cry from a vendor barking his wares pulled Corvus from his reverie and back to his surroundings. He passed under an archway and turned off the main avenue, known as the Cardo Maximus, near St. Steven's Gate, and onto a side street. A rainbow of colored awnings, red, orange, green, and indigo stretched and fluttered over the open-air stalls before him. They blended dramatically between several Greystone buildings that traversed the narrow alley.

Corvus found the store connected to a house and stopped. Jax came beside him. The storefront had a small window and a separate entrance from the home. He'd been informed the building belonged to a merchant called Milvus. His sister was Valeria, the woman representing his employer Goliath.

"Come on now, Jax," Corvus said, turning to his partner. "Let's see about this sword. I'm hoping Milvus can describe this great prize. It would help to know what it looks like. After all, there are plenty of swords in Jerusalem. What's to keep someone from passing off an imposter?"

"Why not do something like that ourselves," Jax said with a grin.

"I suppose we could," Corvus rubbed his brow, "but that would put us up against Goliath. Word is he takes *extreme* revenge when he feels injured. Ask any poor bastard that's crossed him—if you can find one still alive. After he orders an enemy killed, he has him strung up and lets the crows feed on the body."

"I guess you're right," Jax answered, sounding a bit rattled. "Don't need an enemy like him. Just a hefty bag of coin."

"And the pleasure it will buy. Let's remember that!"

Jax laughed, his good nature shining through.

Corvus swung open the wooden door and entered the shop. A bell tinkled overhead. The bright light from the afternoon sun shone on a small atrium. In the center of the rectangular court, stood a square pool with an alabaster fountain shaped like a tree. Perched on the white limbs, multi-shaded finches—gold, brown, red—chirped and flitted about. Beside the atrium's marble columns, tall green ferns in ceramic pots glistened in golden light and stood as perfect companions to the colorful birds and the sound of bubbling water. A sense of serenity coursed through him, another sensation he seldom felt.

Responding to the bell's chime, a short, plump man appeared from a hallway door off the atrium that Corvus assumed led to the larger home. He was dressed in a linen robe striped in purple. His eyes carried a strange brightness —hazel green with a burst of gold around the pupil.

Corvus found them unnerving. A band of brown hair circled his balding crown and grey wisps feathered at his temples. A short beard hugged his chin. He seemed detached and solemn with neither a smile nor frown on his face.

"May I help you?" the man asked.

"We are looking for Milvus," Corvus replied.

"I am Milvus. And you?"

"I'm Corvus. He's Jax. We're here to meet Valeria and find an artifact."

"Ah, yes. I was informed you would arrive. Come take a seat." Milvus showed them to a small couch. "May I offer you some wine?"

Jax licked his lips, but Corvus shook his head. "We can drink later. Business first."

"Very well," Milvus said. He took a seat in a chair across from them. "Please excuse my candor, but to be sure you are who you say you are, what is the artifact in question? Can you tell me?"

Milvus' eerie gaze bored into Corvus, and he felt himself flinch. Valeria's brother provoked in him a gnawing apprehension, or was it suspicion? He cleared his throat. "We are seeking a sword, belonging to a king called David."

"When did you hear about this sword?"

"When we met your sister for a second time in Constantinople."

Milvus nodded, apparently satisfied and smiled. "Good news. My research has proven fruitful. I may have found a description of the object we seek."

"This would surely help us," Corvus replied and leaned in closer. "Where and how did you find it?"

"In a scroll . . . hidden for centuries, among other scrolls. Just last year, it was discovered in a majestic jar buried in a cave beneath the city, in a place once sacred to the Jews. I procured it from a wealthy client, a collector of antiquities, and ancient documents. It's an opportune find."

"Can we see this scroll?"

"When my sister arrives from Constantinople, which should be any day now, she'll draw an image of the sword from the description. Afterward, we'll meet."

"We are staying at this address." Corvus handed Milvus a small piece of parchment. "A widow with a room to let. Send a messenger when you and your sister are ready." Corvus signaled Jax, and they rose to leave. "I commend you, Milvus. Seeing a drawing of the sword is a worthy advantage."

Milvus nodded, "I'm confident if there are other seekers, they'll not be as fortunate." He waved a hand in the direction of the door. "Allow me to show you out. I will tell Valeria you were here. We'll summon you very soon."

CAESAREA: The Seaside Inn—The 26th day of Maius,
Early Afternoon

SAMUEL

His sandals felt light on the steps. Samuel looked forward to this meeting and could sense the excitement emanating from Angelus on the stair behind him. The boy had grown into a kind young man, strong and firm and a bit bull-headed. But as Samuel saw it, these traits, smooth and tough, stood a person well in the world of Palaestina. He had never known the boy's father, but he had loved the boy's mother. He was sure Angelus' kindness sprang from her.

Angelus even smiled like Karas, filling Samuel's heart with joy. He missed her so and believed she would have been happy and content to live in Nazareth as a family. Even now, four years after Karas' tragic death on the battlefield at Catalaunum in Gaul, he found her loss difficult to reconcile. Her memory would often surprise and take hold of him, entering on the whim of a scent floating by, gentle and sweet, or a woman's wayward laugh in the marketplace—a twinkling star at night. But he labored to shelter these thoughts for private moments spent alone when he might speak to her without intrusion.

Nonetheless, today should be about reuniting with Arria and Garic, two people whom he loved very much.

Samuel stepped onto the landing, just as two men, one lighter in appearance and the other darker, approached the stairs to descend. Graciously, they stepped aside to let him pass, but not before Samuel noted a somewhat soldierly manner about these men dressed in ordinary clothes. Excited, he sped to Arria's door and quickly looked over his shoulder. Angelus' smile resembled a bright moon, and his eyes glistened. Samuel rapped his knuckles on the wood surface with a few short bursts. The door swung open.

Arria stood before them flushed and beaming happiness. "Welcome!" she gushed, but her gaze went straight for Angelus. "My darling boy—I can't believe my eyes. You've grown so tall and handsome!"

Angelus grinned. "Lady Arria, I'm happy to see you again."

Arria gave him a warm hug despite his blushing face and awkward posture. "Come," she said, grabbing his hand. Behind her,

Garic waited with Licia, wide-eyed, beside him. Arria pulled Angelus into the room, and Samuel followed.

Chairs were positioned next to a small table with light afternoon fare, bread, and sweets. They took their seats, and Arria and Garic asked Angelus many questions as they devoured honey cakes and a mild wine blended with spring water, a popular drink in this seaport town. Samuel noticed a sweet interaction between Licia and Angelus as he teased her, and she looked up at him with slightly shy but shining eyes.

After time spent laughing over moments involving Vodamir's boyish pranks, the Frank chief Luthgar's reactions to Vodamir's mischief, and sharing fond memories of Karas, they fell into a nostalgic silence. With all the food eaten, and the sun almost to the horizon, they seemed to sigh at the same time.

Arria spoke first. "Angelus, would you be so kind and take Licia to the dining room? The innkeeper's wife keeps games for patrons to enjoy—knucklebones and your favorite, *calculi.*

"Lady Arria, you remember that I love a good game of checkers?"

"How could I forget those afternoons you played against the servants at Fort Cambria. I believe you were the champion."

Angelus proudly smiled. "No one could beat me, not even Samuel."

Samuel, listening quietly, balked, "I had other things on my mind—like your mother. She distracted me."

Angelus laughed. "A worthy excuse, which I'll accept, but only for my mother's sake."

Arria cooed, "It's such a pleasure to see you both again. Go now, Angelus. Ask the innkeeper's wife for a checkerboard. What Garic and I have to speak about is not suitable for a little girl's ears."

Angelus jumped up and stretched out his hand. "Licia, I challenge you to a game of *calculi.*"

Licia rose to her feet and smiled. She took his hand. "I will win. I'm good at games."

Angelus laughed. "We shall see *puella.*"

"I'm not a little girl. I'm almost eight."

"My apologies, my lady," Angelus answered, glancing back and winking at Arria as he led Licia out of the room.

Arria, having risen as well, shut the door behind them and returned to her seat. "Samuel, we have so much to tell you. Our companion Leo is dead. Murdered."

"When? Why did I not hear?" Samuel asked, shocked by this news.

Garic spoke up. "It happened when you went to gather Angelus from Nazareth." He then explained to Samuel how the soldier died.

"A Star of David was carved into his forehead," Arria added after Garic finished. Her eyes glowed with worry.

"How cruel," Samuel replied, shaking his head, and then looked pensively toward the ceiling. A shaft of light reached toward a corner, and several thoughts filled his mind, but he said, "A holy symbol etched on his brow and his hand severed. A crime of hatred or a warning, but definitely not a robbery."

"We agree. What's even more disconcerting . . . a sailor on our ship was found murdered . . . hanging over the rail." Arria swallowed and paled a bit. "On his head . . . was carved *a cross.*"

Samuel placed an elbow on the table and rested his chin against fisted fingers. He gazed at them and pursed his lips. "Interesting. That, too, feels like revenge or a warning. Otherwise, why not just throw the poor man overboard?"

"Our conclusion as well," Garic agreed. "We must be careful. We cannot be sure of anything. Are we being followed? Is the sword in jeopardy?"

Samuel listened. Garic's questions were justified. "And what of Leo? What has happened with his body?" Samuel felt empathy for the old soldier. A Wespe warrior, himself. He had fought Attila at Catalaunum with Garic and survived. He understood the hardships that followed a soldier and the sacrifices they made even to losing their lives. Often, more died than survived.

The heat of the day waning, a chill in the air seeped in from under the door and through its cracks. Arria reached for the shawl hanging over her chair. "After discovering Leo's corpse, we went before the magistrate to claim his body and explain our connection to him. We could not provide him with any reason for Leo's death. We expressed our desire that Leo would have more than a vagrant's grave.

"The magistrate demanded to see our papers. Garic complied and showed him the emperor's letter stating we are on official business. He asked a few questions and seemed curious. I respectfully informed him our business was confidential. His response was curt and surly, but expressing his desire to close the case, he allowed us a private grave. We buried the old soldier with a small ceremony with help from Brother Bruno."

Samuel nodded his approval, but felt compelled to ask, "And the sword? What now? Will you bring it to a Christian shrine in Jerusalem?" His throat tightened, but he continued, "Have you had time to consider my viewpoint?"

Arria pressed her lips together and raised an eyebrow.

Samuel knew that look on her face from the years he spent as her manservant, and later, a friend. She was determined. But he also sensed fear. She looked at Garic. Samuel watched their eyes lock. Garic gave a slight nod.

Turning to Samuel, she pulled her shawl tighter. A slight shudder rolled over her shoulders. "Prepare yourself," she said to him. "We have another surprise."

XI

Two Are Better Than One

CAESAREA: The Seaside Inn—The 26th day of Maius

GARIC

A low hum skimmed the air as Garic pulled the sword from its bronze sheath and laid it before Samuel on the table. They all gazed upon it, but Garic wanted to be sure. "Did you hear the sound?" he asked Arria and Samuel.

They both nodded. Unease filled their eyes. It was not the soft sliding sound of metal scraping metal as the sword left the sheath, it was a subtle vibrating sound emanating from the blade.

Garic took a breath and asked, "Samuel, is the sword as you expected?"

The once Wespe warrior leaned closer and ran his eyes from top to bottom over the weapon. Gently lifting his hand, he brushed his fingertips across the pommel's gems. Lingering there for a moment, his face reverent and quiet, he slid his fingers to the handle, over the cross-guard, and down to the letters engraved into the blade.

Garic watched Samuel's eyes glisten. Arria seemed transfixed by her friend's reaction, and her eyes betrayed a watery shine. "My friend," Garic said, breaking the silence. "Are the words clear to you?"

Samuel glanced at Garic but returned to his appraisal. "Not entirely, but enough for me to understand most of what is written. 'A curse on the one who'—does something. I don't recognize the word— 'David's sword and not be'—I believe the last word is an older form of, *chosen*." Samuel looked at them. "Do you know the exact translation?"

Arria nodded, "The sword and it's saying were validated by the emperor's most educated priests and Jewish leaders. The word your searching for is *wield*. *A curse on the one who wields David's sword and not be chosen.*"

Before Samuel could respond, Garic spoke, "There's something more." He reached for the sword and holding the hilt, he rotated the band four times and then turned the pommel. The cap came loose, and he handed it to Arria.

She removed the gold Star of David and passed it to Samuel, who took it into the palm of his hand and stared. He did not speak. He wet his lips and lightly caressed the diamond, then flipped the star over. His head reared back. He appeared amazed and able to understand the inscription.

"What does it say, Samuel?" Arria asked. Her voice was low, almost reverent.

His voice rang sure, "'My sin. Bathsheba's love. Atone and Forgive.'"

"How beautiful," Arria whispered.

An anxious beat flickered through Garic. He watched them both curiously. Where would this lead?

Samuel's face sank, his expression grim. He shook his head once and then, looking at Arria, said, "The sword and the star. David's command. Such a treasure . . . a gift. All the more reason for this artifact to live among the Jews, protected by our rabbis and religious leaders." He sat a little taller, a strength invading his manner.

Arria sighed, "My dear friend. I can understand what you believe, but I cannot agree. I promised the emperor. Do you not think all the world should know the beauty of David's sword and amulet, his redemption and honor restored?" Her loving patience but conviction clung to her words.

Samuel drew a long breath and raised an open palm. "I know your heart. And your willful *resolve* in most matters you believe important. I'll not press you further—for now. Our biggest problem, especially if the news of this relic has leaked out, will be to keep the sword safe." His hand fell to his lap. "What if we were to visit the master swordsmith on the way to Jerusalem?"

"Whatever for?" Arria's question sounded cautious.

"Would it hurt to have a replica?" Samuel tilted his head, a sheepish grin on his lips.

Garic grinned back at Samuel. "My brother-in-arms. You've risen another level in wisdom in my eyes. What a *clever* idea." He leaned forward, excited by the strategy, and shifted his attention Arria's way. He waited for her response.

Her eyes narrowed, but she remained quiet. Garic wondered if she would resist this new course of action for an already complicated mission.

Arria placed her elbows on the table and folded her hands. She glanced down. Garic could tell her mind was racing. After a moment, she lifted tenacious green eyes, but with a hint of sparkle, toward them.

Garic drew in his breath.

"Would it take long?" she asked.

CAESAREA: The Swordsmith—The 26th day of Maius, Late Afternoon

SAMUEL

Samuel led Arria and Garic into a small barn-like building on the edge of town, sheltered from the sky, but with a wide wooden door that let in the light and allowed the heat from the forge to escape. The clanging of metal could be heard as they walked through the entrance. They saw a tall, shirtless, burly man, wearing black trousers and a leather apron, and with arms as thick as the wooden posts that supported the roof. His face and body were covered with soot and beads of sweat.

"My friend, Urban," Samuel called to the swordsmith as he approached him.

Urban's face lit up. He laid the sword and hammer he was using on the anvil and wiped his hands on a cloth tucked into his belt. "Ah, Samuel. It pleases me to see you," he said and then glanced at Arria and Garic. Have you brought friends or customers to meet me?"

"Both. May I present Lady Arria Felix and her husband, Noble Garic. They are old friends of mine, but potential customers as well."

Urban gave a polite nod and replied, "Welcome. How can I help you?"

Garic spoke up. "We're looking to recreate in some simplicity an ancient sword we possess, and it should have a sheath. We need it in less than two days. We must leave the city, at the latest, on the 28th before dawn." Garic looked at Samuel and then back to Urban and waited.

Urban's brow furrowed as he shook his head. "I don't think this is possible. It would require additional help from my apprentice and Samuel as well. I also need a design. I make modern swords—not ancient ones."

Samuel interjected. "Urban, what if we refashioned one of the antique swords you've collected over the years? We need a short sword. Don't you have a gladius? I can make a box that resembles an ancient era? Within it, we'll place this altered and aged looking sword with a decorative handle in an embellished, rustic sheath. So, that at first glance, it would appear antiquated and genuine. We could recreate our own version of the original sword that we want to protect from thieves. I'll help you design and reforge the sword." Samuel took a breath and added, "Also, this project must be kept secret. Your apprentice need only know that the sword is meant as a decorative piece for a monastery shrine."

Urban shook his head again. "I have a gladius, but I don't know about this."

Samuel's mind raced. "This is a task of official importance and will benefit all the land. We just want to ensure the success of our mission."

Arria stepped in front of Urban. "Sir. My husband and I were selected for this mission by the emperor. Once our task is complete, we'll speak to him about your participation and your craftmanship. We trust Samuel's opinion, and the government is always in search of the finest weapon makers in the empire." She smiled at Urban. "We can also pay you a generous sum for your service."

The swordsmith cocked an eyebrow, shot a glance toward Samuel, and back to Arria. "My lady, you have made a convincing case." He bowed his head. "I'm at your service, but we best begin now and work through the night if completing it in a day is your goal."

OUTSIDE OF JERUSALEM: Accipiter's Party

MARCELLA

Nerian jumped from the coach and lifted his hand to help Marcella down. The evening held shades of waning light as torches, flanking the arched entrance, burned brightly in the sultry breeze. Stone steps met the gravel path where they stood. Their driver called to his horse and pulled away, leaving them alone in front of Accipiter's townhome in the hills near St. Stephen's Gate.

"Well, what do you think?" Marcella dropped her shawl off her shoulders and twirled before Nerian, the rose-colored layers of her silk gown rising and floating with the spin. "You made no comment before we left."

Nerian smiled back at her, his face even more handsome in the dusky light. "Forgive me. Our mission this evening preoccupied my thoughts. You're stunning and will turn many heads. Don't stray far from me tonight. I may become jealous."

"We are spies. I must use my charms."

"The translucent quality of your bodice alone—dazzles." His gaze dropped. "One cannot help but notice your beautiful breasts."

"Perfect. While the men are gawking, I'll be working to gather information."

"A clever diversion, my sweet. And what about me?" Nerian spun around, playfully mocking Marcella. "Will the ladies tell me their secrets?"

Marcella chuckled and came beside him. She gave his earlobe a gentle tug and brushed a kiss over his lips. "That's up to you. Which skills will you employ?"

"Like you, tonight, I'll use my charm. But if necessary, I might, in the future, have to compromise my own feelings and play the lover for the success of the mission."

Marcella stepped back a bit ruffled. She stood taller and raised her chin. "I agree," she replied. "The means do justify the end. If a brief dalliance is required, then why not?"

Nerian pulled her close. "Regardless of the choices we may have to make, I am yours, and I believe you are mine." He looked briefly over her shoulder. "Another coach approaches. Say this is true before we enter."

Marcella nodded. "This is true."

Nerian bent and kissed her, his lips lingering longer than she expected, which warmed her. Could she trust him? The vulnerable, lonely girl locked in her ironclad heart desired her freedom. She would fight her fears, try to believe him, but she needed more proof.

"Give me your hand, Marcella. It's time to go to work. Remember, we are a Saxon merchant and his Egyptian wife."

As another carriage pulled up, she gave Nerian her hand, and they walked to the door. Nerian tapped the brass knocker. An elderly manservant opened the door. They crossed the threshold together.

PALAESTINA

HE

(Nemesis)

He sat alone. On the tree branch above him, a tribe of sparrows twittered. Their lush, rust-brown feathers and freedom struck him as beautiful. He often wished he could catch a bird and keep one. When he was a boy, he once held a she-dove. The tranquil bird cooed softly. He had contemplated the dove's lucky existence but immediately felt sad. Soon his sorrow turned to envy. Anger filled him, and a sudden and powerful urge overcame him. What right did the dove have to be at peace—when as children, he and his younger brother were made slaves to a patch of farmland as fickle as the weather and the world around them? His father, mean and ornery, spending what little they had on drink. His broken mother, taking her husband's beatings, letting him beat them. Why should anyone feel happy when his life reeked of misery? *Twist the dove's neck, shut her up*, a voice whispered in his head. And Nemesis obeyed. *Snap*. An unexpected satisfaction glowed inside him. It had been so easy.

He met a girl when he grew older. She also had a beauty about her; she reminded him of the dove. Soft with milky skin, her hair smooth and fine. He first noticed her on one of his trips alone to market. She stood behind a table, filling a basket with apricots from a sack at her feet. As he pushed his cart laden with turnips and leeks past her family's fruit stand, he stole a glance and was smitten. That was a glorious summer.

Each time he returned to the market, he would look for her and nod as he passed by. A pink flush on her cheeks, she always smiled back. After selling his produce, he'd stow his cart behind a stack of boxes, not far from her father's stand. Hiding, he watched her, sometimes for hours—as he did the birds. Her fragile bones and glowing skin, the way she turned her head on a long, slender neck, her vulnerability and innocence all consumed him. He wanted to speak with her, hear the soft tones in her words.

But people and merchants surrounded and kept her from him. Bitterness found a pit in his stomach. His heart seethed in the hollow of his chest. Once, he followed the girl home and hid in a line of bushes near a window. When night settled, he peered through the lighted opening. Her parents and brothers sat around her with happy looks on their faces. Envy smoldered in him, and he hurried away. Here was not the time or place. He would wait and watch.

One sultry morning, when she tended the fruit stand alone, Nemesis stopped and spoke to her. He acted the customer and bought her figs—no point in being noticed. But when she placed the fruit in his basket, he whispered that she should meet him outside of town, later in the afternoon when most everyone rested.

She blushed, her eyes shining, and nodded her acceptance. She met him as planned, and he talked to her sweetly and held her hand. He told her he had a secret place with a view beautiful enough to melt a heart. Would she see it with him? She agreed, and he brought her to the tall juniper tree at the top of a ravine where a river ran below.

The day glimmered with light and heat. The sky reflected the blue in her eyes. He made a blanket of ferns cut with his knife from the bushes around them. They spread out like a willowy fan. "My lady?" he said, smiling, offering her a hand. She giggled and cooed, "My lord," and wrapped his fingers in hers.

They sat, and he pressed his mouth to hers. Her lips were warm and full, almost sweet to the taste, and she smelled of figs and brought him peace. She kissed him back.

But the memory of the dove rose in his mind.

His heart, a moment ago so full and open, snapped shut. Fear and desperation filled him. Nemesis grabbed the girl tighter. She squirmed against him, but he fought to hold her—to possess her and her tranquility. She twisted harder. Anger flashed through his body and throbbed at his temples. The voice inside whispered again. *What right does this farmer's daughter have to refuse you?* He frowned. Why would she deny him a moment of joy found in his brutal world? A world sunk in poverty and ruled by a cruel father.

A dark and primitive growl rose in his throat. The blood in his veins boiled. Nemesis desired the farmer's daughter, and he would have her. This time, he'd be the strong one. Dominate, possess something of his own—even if only a girl.

She clawed and fought against him. He grabbed her wrists and subdued her. The gentle dove cried out, but he pushed to his feet and pulled her fragile body with him. She almost struggled free, but he grabbed her from behind. Wrapping an arm around her neck, he locked her against his panting chest. A plaintive, agonized wail burst from her lips upward toward the sky.

He hesitated and took a breath. Resist! He thought. Stifle your anger—find mercy. Fight the voice inside. Let her fly away this time—and not die like the dove.

He dragged her to the edge of the cliff. As his arm grew tighter around her neck, she choked. He thought he heard her gasp, "Noooo . . ." It didn't matter. Her savior, he lifted her like an offering, and with all his strength, he tossed her into the air. Nemesis waited for her to soar upward and glide on the wind. Instead, she plummeted downward like a wounded bird. Her arms stroked the air, her long, brown tresses rippled behind her. He turned away.

In a few seconds, a splash vibrated on the breeze. He kicked at the ferns, destroying their nest. A brooding disappointment welling in him, he walked back toward town. He had lost another dove.

XII

Nothing Stays the Same

JERUSALEM: The Outskirts

KALEV

Kalev Ben Jonah was determined to enter Jerusalem on his own terms. Let Roman law be dammed. At first, he thought to pave the way secretly. He'd cloak himself, pay a bribe to the greedy entry guards, and slip in. But he quickly saw the flaw in this method. How long before the price of admission would increase, or he met a new and diligent guard, one who could not be trusted or bribed.

On his first merchant trip to Bethany, a town outside of Jerusalem near the Mt. of Olives, he spent the days on the road mulling over his dilemma. Jews were barred from Jerusalem. When would this oppression stop? After the destruction of the second temple and under early Roman rule, they'd been driven out. In the centuries that followed, a few emperors had allowed them to return, but soon they were expelled again on the whim of a newer emperor. Some years ago, under the Empress Eudocia, restrictions were relaxed for a while. His people were allowed to visit the Western Wall and a few holy sites for chief festivals in Jerusalem, but that had fallen away. Kalev looked at the orange sun above and gazed ahead. Jerusalem was the city of his ancestors. He deserved, as much as any man, to walk its streets. And he would—somehow.

After two days on the road, one afternoon, his caravan arrived at a water stop, a desert spring along the way. While Kalev drank from his cup, he spotted a movement on a nearby dune. Beneath a desert willow, a sand cat rested, flicking its tail. He watched the feline cloaked in half-shadow lounge complacently. A sudden idea, the notion of hiding himself but out in the open, came to him. A new persona would allow him to move freely through Jerusalem. It would be difficult and dangerous, but if his plan worked, he could establish himself comfortably in the city's elite social circles, increase his wealth, and perhaps ensure the elusive sword's safe acquisition. And if his plan failed? He could be arrested, run out of Jerusalem, or even killed. Despite these possibilities, an instinct urged him to take the risk.

Another thought occurred to him. What if his persona was compromised? His bold way in through the front gate might not be his best avenue for escape. He would need an extra and unique way out. Hezekiah's Tunnel could secret him out of the city. Although ancient and dangerous, the water tunnel beneath the city was at times used by traffickers with money and influence. These revelations filled him as he finished his last drops of water and tucked his cup into his shoulder bag. Hands on his hips, Kalev gazed again at the cat who stared back.

He'd pose as a Greek weapons merchant with the proper documents and with a side business in illegal merchandise—after all, he was the black-market boss, Goliath. He'd build trust with officials and guards at the entry gates. In his experience, bribery with coin, goods, and frowned upon pleasures, most often paved the way for what he desired, especially if one was a person of reputable status. This dangerous challenge invigorated Kalev's spirits, pushed him to the edge of risk. And it helped suppress his never-ending anguish—his son Joshua, rotting in his tomb.

JERUSALEM: Accipiter's Dinner Party—The 26th day of Maius

As soon as Kalev reached Bethany, and with this plan in mind, he began to create a new identity. He made sure that every detail felt solid and real to those he encountered. Valeria, newly arrived in Jerusalem, brought him new clothing. From a discreet forger of the highest caliber, and known in the underworld as far as Constantinople, he attained documents of identity that could pass the strongest scrutiny.

He became a new, secret person. A man behind an invisible Greek drama mask. The thrill of disclosure fueled him in an odd, new way. He longed for it. Whenever he entered Jerusalem, a city his ancestors once ruled, but now forbidden to him, he felt a sense of pride. His heart soared and pumped harder. Blood and emotion rushed through his body. This was not battle's exhilaration, but a subtle danger that enlivened him, making him feel bold and strong. Another game in his world, but one that brought him a deep sense of satisfaction. He could lead this other life, one quite different than the one he lived. Kalev Ben Jonah in Constantinople, Goliath in the black-market world—and now—Alexander Kronus in Jerusalem.

Alexander stepped from his coach and instructed his driver to wait with the others. He climbed the steps to the door of Accipiter, the Egyptian merchant, living in the hills close to Jerusalem. Accipiter's invitation had arrived at Kalev's home in Bethany. As Alexander, he had purchased a modest dwelling and built a reputation as a discreet weapons dealer who traveled often and collected antique weapons, mostly decorative knives, and daggers.

In Jerusalem, he altered his look and kept his face clean-shaven, while in Constantinople, he wore a short beard. As Kalev, his clothes were modest and plain, but as Alexander, his clothing bordered on elaborate and in-line with the current fashion. Round colorful caps covered his curls. From the far east, he painted a black dye on his gray temples that washed clean when desired. He wore knee-length tunics with embroidered sleeves and expensive leather boots. A long cloak added the finishing touch to the popular ensemble for the well-dressed man.

Although Greek and Latin were the primary languages spoken, the Greek tongue dominated at most class levels, and he spoke it fluently, having learned both languages as a child. His approach and appearance helped manifest a demeanor of quiet boldness, a manner not always true to his serious self, Kalev. He discovered that people told Alexander things about themselves, their experiences, and sometimes their inner feelings. These confessions provided him with not only useful information but advantages as well. Business soared for him, and many sought his company. Because of this, he felt secure in his Greek persona.

Only two people knew his true identity, Valeria and Milvus, and they would never betray him. Valeria loved him. Milvus needed him. As Kalev and now Alexander, he supplied their shops with goods and antiquities and opened doors to influential contacts. Theirs was a symbiotic relationship. Milvus understood that without Kalev, he'd lose money or even fail. In addition, Milvus' partnership with a Jew in Jerusalem would not be good for business.

Alexander walked through the door into Accipiter's home. He handed his cloak to the attending servant and entered into the atrium from the vestibule. Torches burned in decorative sconces throughout the pillared court. Flaming braziers, standing beside couches, marble benches, and small clusters of chairs, offered a pleasant warmth on the cool evening. In the center of the atrium, a long table held platters filled with savory and sweet-smelling delights. A roast lamb staged in the center of the table captivated at first glance, giving the sumptuous display a regal appearance. At a second table along a nearby wall, servants accessed wine for the guests. It held a collection of glass and silver cups and carafes of different shapes and sizes. Garlands of fresh flowers hung from the columns surrounding the atrium's center pool. The pleasant scent of sandalwood perfumed the air, and soft musical tones filled the room. Alexander Kronus was impressed. He must surely get to know his host, Accipiter, the Egyptian.

Gingerly he pulled the sleeve of a passing servant. "Where is your master?"

The servant looked around but shook his head and darted off before Alexander could ask another question. Alexander looked about perplexed but decided to make the best of it. He moved toward the wine table where a tall man, perhaps a Frank or Saxon by his clothing, was pouring himself a rather full glass of wine.

"Looks like a good idea," Alexander offered. The barbarian turned and offered him the glass in his hand. "Here, take this one, I'll pour another."

"My thanks," Alexander replied.

The barbarian filled another glass, took a step back from the table, and nodded. They raised a toast and drank.

"I'm Nerian, a Saxon merchant. I work with Accipiter, and you?"

"Alexander Kronus, also a merchant. I deal in weapons, and I must admit, I enjoy collecting ancient ones as well.

Nerian gave him a broad smile. "How interesting. Please, tell me more."

"What would you like to know?" Alexander replied, peering across the cup he raised to his lips.

ACCIPITER'S PARTY

MARCELLA

Marcella popped a grape into her mouth from the cluster she held and looked around. A trio of musicians, playing panpipes and a lyre, sat near a small fountain in a corner of the atrium and beside the dining room entry where she stood. Within the center of the fountain pool stood a statue of the pagan god of love, the Romans called Cupid, and the Greeks called Eros. She found the depiction of the handsome young god with wings engaging and expertly carved into the marble, a talent she admired. Her secret dream was to own a grand home filled with valuable art she could appreciate every day.

"Does my lady enjoy the beauty the fountain holds, the pleasant music, or both?"

Marcella turned to face Accipiter. "Without a doubt—both. How nice to see you and what a beautiful home you have. Nerian and I looked for you but missed you among all these guests."

"An unexpected meeting kept me from greeting everyone, which I must do now. I'm pleased to have spotted you first among so many, but then, you're quite noticeable, especially in that rose gown."

Marcella laughed. "You flatter as always, another quality shown by an excellent host."

Accipiter clasped her hand in his. "It's more truth than flattery."

Smiling demurely, she squeezed his hand. Being both Egyptian, they felt a friendly bond.

The merchant beckoned a servant carrying a tray filled with cups. "Wine?" Accipiter asked Marcella as he grasped one.

She shook her head. "No, thank you. I prefer wine with my meal and not before, but the fruit is quite delicious."

Accipiter smiled, tasted the wine, and added, "There are several new persons here tonight. In particular, a Greek weapons dealer, Alexander Kronus. Word has it that he collects ancient daggers and swords."

Marcella glanced around to be sure no one might hear and said softly, "A possible buyer—if we can find the sword?"

"He'd be worth approaching." Accipiter lowered his voice. "I met with a very interesting informant earlier this evening. Where is Nerian? We must talk later."

"He's mingling with the guests." She smiled dryly, "Most likely more with the ladies than the men. I'll inform him that we should stay after all have left."

"Excellent. Until later."

Just then, a bald-headed, portly man broke through the cluster of people gathered around the tables laden with foods to whet the appetite for dinner. He called to Accipiter, who went to greet him.

Marcella moved through the guests and looked for Nerian's black hair, knowing he would tower above most surrounding him. She spotted him conversing with a distinguished-looking man dressed in fine clothes, clean-shaven, and with short black curls. He was not as tall as Nerian, but solidly built. Marcella slipped through the guests and approached them.

Nerian smiled and extended his arm toward her as she came beside him. "Sir, allow me to introduce my wife, Marcella."

With a direct gaze, the man nodded and smiled. She observed confident brown eyes. His face placed him in his mid-thirties, but although middle-aged, there was a youthful quality about him despite the weathered wrinkles near his eyes.

"Marcella, meet my new acquaintance. Alexander Kronus, a merchant who collects antique weapons."

"What a curious hobby. It's a pleasure to meet you," she said, giving him a charming smile. Just then, bells sounded calling the guests to the main dining room where a feast awaited them. "Please join us at the table, or do you prefer a couch?" Marcella invited.

Alexander gave them a gracious smile. "I'm pleased to join you, especially if my lady prefers the table. I enjoy the modern custom, although there are those in Constantinople who still favor the couch."

"It appears we're in agreement. I imagine ours to be a remarkable friendship."

A gleam showed in Alexander's eyes, and he grinned. "Ah, once again, we're in agreement."

Marcella smiled sweetly at him as Nerian offered her an arm. Along with Alexander, they walked into the *Triclinium* together.

Marcella beamed. *How fortunate. A possible buyer or this merchant may even know about the sword—bringing us closer to the prize. Hmm,* she wondered. *What art piece should I purchase first? Perhaps, I'll buy the fountain from Accipiter.*

NERIAN

"Your party was a great success," Marcella complimented their colleague and host with a lavish smile. She sat upright on a couch, her legs tucked beneath her, in Accipiter's atrium. Nerian sat in a chair beside her. All the guests had gone, and only he and Marcella remained. A pale-yellow light stretched across the marble floor just below the open ceiling. A meadowlark could be heard welcoming the dawn. The chilly air nipped at them, and Marcella hugged her silk wrap closer.

"Thank you," Accipiter acknowledged. "I was pleased and happy to have met Alexander Kronus, a new merchant in Jerusalem. If we find the sword, he could be a potential buyer."

"Yes, we sat beside him at dinner," Nerian replied. "He's an interesting man."

"I noticed, but I have more to tell before I retire for some much-needed sleep." On a couch across from them, Accipiter rested on his side and on an elbow. He took a sip of his Valerian wine just poured for them by a servant and expressed how it was the perfect remedy after a long night of festivities—especially if one is ready for bed.

Nerian swallowed a large gulp and placed his cup on the center table.

Marcella looked at Nerian wide-eyed, took a long drink, and set her cup down as well. "Please begin," she said. "We're anxious to hear. I, too, am weary, and the wine will soon make me sleepy."

Accipiter smiled. "I met with a most interesting person, right before the party began. A man who claimed he was a courier on a ship named, *Ventus*, that left Constantinople bound for Caesarea. A murder took place during a storm. Afterward, a body of one of the sailors, a man named Paolino, was found hanging off the side of the ship."

Marcella's eyes cringed.

"Go on," Nerian urged, his pulse livened by the details.

"According to the courier, there were whispers aboard that Paolino's death seemed puzzling. Why would anyone want to kill him? He provided the desired contraband that many craved. The consensus was that perhaps Paolino owed someone money or had insulted the wrong person. But here's what's intriguing. The sailors also wondered if his murder might be connected with a secret shipment or object they believed had been brought on the ship. The captain had instructed them to avoid the deep end of the storage hold—the emperor's private business, he told them. If they felt they needed to go there, they should consult with him first.

"The sailors thought this cargo might be connected to the fact that there was a party of aristocrats traveling on the ship. A tall, blond barbarian, the courier heard addressed as Noble Garic and his wife Lady Arria, a pretty woman with a pleasant smile. They were accompanied by two men, who carried themselves like bodyguards, and a monk and child. They were not the usual passengers: the lone traveler, a couple, or transported slaves and prisoners. This group stood out as quite different."

Marcella gasped. "Isis, goddess of mercy, say it's not true!"

Accipiter seemed surprised by Marcella's outburst. Nerian calmed her with a gentle squeeze on her leg and directed his conversation toward Accipiter. "We've had some dealings with this couple while in Rome and Constantinople. It's complicated and personal is all we can say right now."

"I can respect this," Accipiter offered, but the tilt of his head implied that he was curious. "However, if this barbarian and his wife happen to play a part in this affair, I will want to know how and why."

"Of course." Nerian nodded and returned to the subject of their meeting. "The events on the *Ventus* do seem peculiar, but why did the courier come to you?"

"He heard of my inquiries into the arrival of a secret artifact. I made sure to *discreetly* express to a few that for any information concerning this matter, I would pay in coin." Accipiter laughed. "I knew it would only be a matter of time before someone would surface." He sat up, swung his feet on the floor, and finished his wine. He wiped his lips with a hand and added, "There's also a rumor that the mistress to a Roman official may know something about an artifact, but I have not spoken with the lady."

Nerian placed his hand on Marcella's elbow and stood up, bringing her along with him. "This is excellent news. Now we know that the sword is most likely real and worth pursuing. Someone may have murdered the sailor, Paolino, over this treasure. We should seek this mistress or even others with information. Perhaps, we should raise the amount of coin and see what we catch?"

Accipiter stood and yawned. "Let me sleep on this, but you're most likely right. The bigger the bait, the larger the fish."

Nerian grinned. "A worthy investment, if we find the prize."

XIII

Discovery and Disguise

JERUSALEM: Moon Gold Antiquities—The 28th day of Maius

MILVUS

"Oh, I love this Greek vase," Cousin Anna said with a young woman's excitement. "The black lions battling on the red terracotta background are quite vivid, despite its age." Wealthy and widowed, Anna smiled sweetly at Milvus. She slid a hand over one of the bow-shaped handles flanking the vase. "How old is it?"

Milvus thought a moment. "By the style . . . I believe ... hmm, two hundred years?"

"Will you give me your best price?" She tilted her chin and shot Milvus a coy glance. "I have some choice gossip that might interest you."

A soft breeze tripped through the airy shop as Milvus took Anna's arm. "You've piqued my curiosity," he replied and led her away from the wall of shelves that held a collection of antique vases and pottery. They moved past the columns and across the atrium to a couch and chair just beyond the open ceiling. The seats were arranged near the opposite wall of shelves holding sculptures, paintings, and metalwork. Milvus knew his cousin might have some valuable information. After all, she was the mistress to the Roman procurator, a man of influence, and in charge of provincial finances.

Anna sat on the couch, and Milvus sat in the chair across from her. He stroked the short beard on his chin. "Of course, Anna, I can always offer you a discount, but some *choice* gossip, especially if it helps my business, is much appreciated." He smiled and held her hand. "The vase is yours at half the cost. Do we have a sale?"

A wide smile burst across his cousin's lips, and her eyes sparkled with delight.

"Milvus, I do love the vase. What a generous price. Thank you."

"It's my pleasure to see the joy in your face." He tilted his head and held her gaze.

Anna leaned closer. "As you probably know, I'm a very good friend of the financial procurator, Porcius Festus."

Milvus feigned a mild look of surprise.

Anna raised a doubtful glance but continued, "He often confides in me. I suppose he finds me a willing ear and one to be trusted—I am, of course—but you're family. It cannot hurt to share some information you might find helpful—especially in your line of business."

"Go on," Milvus encouraged.

She leaned closer. "It seems his good friend, a magistrate in Caesarea, had an encounter with a woman and her husband on official business for the emperor. They had a manservant that was murdered. When they came before the magistrate investigating this crime, they asked for permission to purchase a respectable burial site for the victim. The magistrate was puzzled by this display of generosity for the servant but was more concerned about the murder that took place under his jurisdiction and their involvement with the crime.

"They claimed they knew nothing of why he was killed and needed to get the business of his death and burial done because they were on a discreet and important mission for the emperor. They provided the magistrate with an official letter. He was surprised to read that they carried a relic, a sword that must be brought to a holy shrine in Jerusalem where it should rest ..."

A grimace spread across her lips. "... And that this couple, a Frank noble and his Roman wife—*the daughter of a senator*—should be accommodated at all cost and allowed to travel unhindered by any restriction. They were also accompanied by two royal guards, a priest, servant, and a child who also traveled with them. The magistrate thought it all very strange, but he gave them permission to bury their servant in any manner they desired, as long as it adhered to the law, and to leave Caesarea."

"How curious. A Frank noble and a Roman senator's daughter?" Milvus replied, his mind racing.

"Yes. Can you imagine? A daughter of a senator lowering herself by marrying a barbarian? What is happening in the world? Women of the noble class marrying below their station—and with foreigners. Is he even a Roman citizen? Appalling!" Anna shook her head and scowled, then plucked a small, round silk fan from the net purse hanging at her waist and waved it before her face.

Milvus shook his head and frowned. "Sweet cousin, my sentiments agree with yours, but there seems little we can do but hold fast to our views or perhaps reevaluate. The empire is in turmoil, and changes are inevitable." He sighed and gave Anna his most fatherly look. "Transformation starts with us, but we mustn't go too far in the wrong direction. Appearances are important. They can lead to opportunities." Milvus couldn't help but allude to the fact that she was the mistress to the procurator. In truth, he sensed that she was lonely, but this dalliance with the procurator was unbecoming to her station and the notion of 'the pious widow' that many held.

A smart woman, Anna understood his subtle reference to her affair but dismissed it by dropping her fan into her purse and rising from her seat. "Thank you again, but I should be going. I have a long list of errands. I'll send you payment in the morning. Can you arrange its safe delivery?"

"Of course. This vase will definitely add to your collection." Milvus kissed Anna on both cheeks and led her to the door. A servant standing nearby ran to open it, and Milvus waved as Anna entered her carriage and drove away.

He returned to his chair and stared at the fountain. The sword was real. What a treasure, but it appeared the emperor had sanctioned its future. Acquiring the sword from this Lady and her barbarian would be difficult and dangerous. In the morning, he would send out a spy. Were they in Jerusalem? He must know their names.

THE MONASTERY OF THE CROSS: The 30th day of Maius

GARIC

They arrived in the late evening several hours before dusk in Jerusalem at the Monastery of the Cross, a few miles outside the Old City in the Western Valley of the Cross and near a central market. While traveling, Brother Bruno explained that many Christian pilgrims believed the monastery was built on ground that grew the tree used to build the cross that crucified Christus.

Samuel had heard the story as well, but more. The seed for the tree was given by Abraham to Lot who planted and fed it with waters fetched from the Jordan River. The story amazed Arria, who knew her bible stories well, and thoughts of a warm bed and fresh bread lifted their spirits and made them move faster and eager to arrive.

From the road, the monastery's square bell tower and a brown dome with a cross at the top stretched above the walls and glowed in the amber light. Once at the gate, their request for respite was granted, by the prior, Father Audric, governing in place for the abbot who was traveling.

"Follow me," the porter said, and led them down the cloister to their sleeping cells for the night.

Garic carried Licia, fallen asleep in their cart, into the monastery while Arria followed behind with the two soldiers, Brother Bruno, and Catalina.

Samuel had offered to bring the horses to the stable and join them afterward.

Just days before their departure from Caesarea, Garic had expressed his desire for Samuel to participate in the mission.

"Samuel, join us. Your skills as a warrior will ensure added protection for the sword."

"How will I enter the city? I'm a Jew, and besides, Angelus is with me and is Jewish as well," he had replied.

"We cannot bring him with us. He's still young and cannot fight if needed. He should return to Nazareth and your father's care."

Samuel nodded his agreement and said, "I want to come with you, but you haven't explained how I will enter."

Garic smiled. "You were once a Frank Wespe soldier. So, why not again? And you can truthfully say, you're my former comrade working as a swordsmith and living in Caesarea where we were reunited."

"And the others traveling with you, what do they know about me?"

"The soldiers, Telemachus and Justus, and Brother Bruno have seen you briefly at the inn, but were never introduced. I'm reasonably sure that a former soldier and comrade of mine will not be openly questioned by the soldiers or the priest. Besides, you still carry the manner and spirit of a former Wespe warrior."

"Do you really think the Wespe still lives in me?" Pride welled in Samuel's eyes.

"I believe the warrior in you will never die. Say you'll join us."

Samuel had grinned and offered Garic his hand, and they shook on their renewed partnership. All the while, Garic noticed that never once did Samuel bring up the possibility of danger to his own life. Samuel cared about them and the well-being and restoration of the sword, hoping the weapon would find its rightful home.

When Garic told Arria that Samuel was traveling with them, she was overjoyed, but she wondered if Samuel's name would give him away. Perhaps it was too biblical for a pagan Frank; although slaves were bought, sold, and grown in so many different tribes and cultures in the empire that it might go unnoticed. In the end, they agreed that Samuel should become Samrick, and if asked, he would explain that he was named after his father, a Frank from Luthgar's tribe. Samrick the Frank would travel with them and guard the replica sword in a large travel satchel among his belongings that only Garic, Arria, and Samuel knew about.

The new Samrick trimmed his beard close like Garic's, altered his clothing to appear more rugged, and tied back his hair. Once they reached the city of Jerusalem, they would enter through St. Stephen's Gate, hoping all the commotion and the desire to pass visitors through might make getting Samuel in easier. Of course, Arria would show the emperor's official document, and if needed, Garic still carried Princess Honoria's medallion. The sister of the Western Roman Emperor Valentinian, she had rewarded Garic with her amulet for winning the hunt on her estate, where he and Arria stayed while on their way to Constantinople.

This ruse and all the factors involved streamed through Garic's mind as he approached the room where Licia and Catalina would stay. It proved evident by Licia's gentle snoring and Catalina dragging behind him that they all needed sleep. Leaving Caesarea two days earlier and hours before dawn, they had pushed through their journey of nearly sixty miles to reach the monastery by dusk.

Garic entered the room, with Arria beside him, and laid Licia on the bed. He smiled as he watched Arria remove their daughter's shoes and cover her with the rolled blanket from the end of the bed. Arria whispered a few words to Catalina, who held the handle of a small clay lamp. The servant nodded, placed the light on the table, and opened a satchel. He knew Arria was reminding Catalina to snuff the flame before getting into bed.

Garic walked outside into the hall and waited. Arria soon joined him. As they left to find their room, he reached for her hand. Tonight, he would clutch Arria into the curve and warmth of his body. Folding his protective arms around her, he would rest his cheek in the soft waves of hair fallen on her back. In the morning, though, after many days filled with conflicts and interruptions, he would wake and make love to her. Garic kissed her hand and smiled again.

THE MONASTERY OF THE CROSS: The 31st day of Maius

ARRIA

Early dawn began in a bad way. Arria felt ill and rose from the bed. She laid her hands on her stomach and found the ceramic pot in the corner, knelt beside it, and lifted the lid. The odor rising from the bowl only made matters worse. Her head over the dark hole, she heaved and coughed. Sweat trickled down her temples as she emptied the bile and remaining food in her stomach. Sitting back on her haunches, she wiped her mouth. From behind her, she felt a gentle touch on her shoulder. "Arria, what's wrong? Are you ill?" Garic asked and helped her stand. He led her to the edge of the bed made for two, where she sat on the rumpled blanket with him beside her.

A few dull rays of light seeped in from a small window at the top of their cell wall. The monks kept several small rooms for married couples, for which they were both grateful. Of late, their time alone and moments of intimacy were strained and often interrupted by the demands of the journey and the events surrounding the sword unfolding around them. Yet there was little doubt in her mind. "Krieger, I'm not ill. I'm . . . pregnant." Her mouth felt dry as she waited for his response. Only an edge of queasiness lingered.

Garic's eyes shined like bright blue stones in a bubbling fountain. He placed his hand on her neck and rested his forehead against hers. "Mellitula, this news brings me great joy. How long have you known? Are you sure?"

Arria lifted her head and looked into his eyes. "As you know, my monthlies are not always predictable; however, I noticed some signs before we left Constantinople. I felt queasy at the last banquet before we left the emperor's palace and while on the ship. I thought perhaps some fruit that did not suit me—but no one else felt sick—or the ship's rocking might be to blame, but now I've missed a second monthly as well. I feel certain that I'm with child."

Garic hugged her and whispered in her ear. "This time, the child will be strong and healthy. I feel it."

"I hope you're right. I want this child more than anything."

"Believe, Arria. All will be well."

Arria nodded, and feeling thirsty asked, "Will you pour me a cup of water?"

Garic rose and poured her a cup from the pitcher on the nightstand.

Arria drank while Garic stretched out beside her. He wore a loose nightshirt, and the light patch of blond hair on his chest showed through the v-cut of the neckline. Arria placed the cup on the floor and gazed at him. She knew he desired her, but the kind and loving man he was would wait. "At this time of day, only a few monks are awake. Let's sleep an hour longer. I'm certain my nausea will be gone by then. I feel much better, even as we speak."

Garic pulled her beside him. His eyes glittering with desire and his tone flirtatious, he asked, "When the morning rays break through our window, I'll wake you up."

Arria sighed and held him tighter. "You better. It's been far too long."

ARRIA

Arria awoke to Garic's hand, sliding gently across her buttock and up her back. She lay on her stomach, her head on top of the pillow and her arms beneath it. She bit her lip and pretended to stir as if just being roused. She turned on her side, facing away from him. Part of her excitement and joy was toying with him. Making him want her.

He cupped her breast, his palm strong and warm against her skin. "Mellitula," he whispered as his lips brushed her lobe.

"Hmm," she responded.

"We have little time. The sun has fully risen."

Arria stretched out an arm, flipped onto her back, and gave him a sleepy smile. She rested her hand on his open nightshirt and fondled his blond chest hair with her fingers. His warm skin and devilish grin aroused every inch of her body.

Excitement danced in Garic's eyes as he leaned over her and greeted her with a long and urgent kiss. It had been weeks since they had made love, and she could feel the heat boiling in him. "Take off your nightgown," he commanded quietly.

"Take yours off first," she said with a mischievous smile.

He laughed and quickly removed his nightshirt and then pulled her close.

Her breasts rested against his solid, muscular chest. His handsome face and deep blue eyes still held her fascination, even after five years and all the trials they'd weathered. She loved the bronze sheen on his skin, and when he turned his head a certain way, the vision of wheat-blond stubble on his square jaw excited her. She knew, in all the years to come, she would never grow tired of looking at him. She ran her fingers delicately over his taut stomach and down to his thighs. He had a warrior's body and the heart of a lover. In her eyes, he was a lion, noble in manner—but fierce when life demanded it from him.

His hand moved between her legs and softly teased her. His tongue swept from her mouth, down to her neck, and then to a nipple that tingled from the wet softness of his lips. She arched herself, and he looped his arm beneath her waist against him. As the light crept into the room, a mild sweat covered their skin and heightened her sensation.

"I've missed loving you. I didn't realize how much until now," Garic murmured, and kissed her nipple again. His tongue slid over her bud and then across to the other.

Arria yearned for his touch. In his arms and lying beneath him, his protective warmth was all she needed at times. It revived her and made her feel whole. Garic knew her mind, her heart, her ways. She ached for him, and the world around her became dormant. "Remember when you saved me from the brawl in the Roman camp at the Assembly of Warriors?"

Garic nodded.

"Do you remember what you asked me?"

"Always. I asked if you wanted me because by Thor—god of Thunder and the old ways—I wanted you the moment I set eyes on you. I knew the path for us would be difficult, and I needed to hear you say it back."

Arria raised her lips to his with only a wisp of their breath between them. "I want you," she whispered.

Garic's eyes glowed with ardor and love. A fragile gasp escaped her as his eager lips touched her mouth, and his tongue sought hers. He mounted her and swept the damp curls from her cheek and kissed the fragile hollow of her throat.

A lingering scent of honey soap clung to him as he nuzzled the curve of her neck. She lightly bit his bicep and ran her lips across his collarbone. His moist skin held a mild taste of salt.

She dug her fingers into his shoulder, and his passion poured from him in the hard stiffness against her belly, but he hesitated. "I will not hurt you or the child, will I?" he asked in a gentle tone. They had mourned the miscarriage she'd suffered in Gaul a year before their return to her father's villa outside of Rome and six months earlier.

"No harm will come to the child. I know this from the wiser, older women in my life. Making love did not hurt our first child. Nature had its way." She rubbed his arm. "Do not worry. You can love me as always."

Garic broke into a broad smile and kissed her again. He teased her now, his lips lingering on a breast, then back to her mouth. He rolled to her side and lifted himself on an elbow.

His strong hand—the hand that wielded a sword—tenderly explored and caressed all parts of her—the rosy skin beneath her nipple, the hollow behind her knee, the inside of her thigh, while his other hand clutched the waves of her hair beneath his fingers.

Arria drew him to her and pressed herself firmly against his body. He rested his cheek on hers and whispered words that excited her. "*Krieger,*" she urged and tugged on his arms.

Garic entered her, and she was filled by the most wondrous feeling. It had been too long, and she felt her limbs stretch and melt from the wholeness of him. She held on to the soft curves of his bottom, yearning for more. Smooth and sensual, like a wave rolling toward the shore. Hot and strong, like a drumbeat searching for satisfaction. This dance bonded them together.

His breathing labored, Garic moved deeper inside of her. Arria moaned beneath him.

He caught his breath and rocked faster. He reared onto his arms, his head down. Long strands of his hair came loose from its leather knot and fell onto her breast. The hint of woodsmoke in his hair made her senses soar and tingle.

Garic held her gaze. Love filled his eyes. Arria saw his desire and believed in him. Folded in ecstasy, she clung to his naked body raw and driven. Breathless words fell from her lips, and she called him to come—climax together.

A good and loving husband, Garic obeyed.

XIV

He Who Persists Wins

JERUSALEM: A Monastery Road—The 31st day of Maius

HE

(Nemesis)

*P*aolino that rotten snitch!
    A fiery pain shot through his muscles. Sweat dripped from his nose and down his chin. He clutched his stomach. *Now's the time to overcome—win.* Ever since he'd met that damn drug runner, his plan had taken a turn. But today, he would finally be free, abandon his crutch and brave the world on his own. His escape into the world of euphoria—once a reasonable madness—had now turned sour.

    Nemesis walked several feet and rested his hand on the trunk of a palm tree along the way. He grabbed his water pouch and let the pure liquid roll down his throat and stifle the ache wrenching his gut. He had emptied his body earlier and felt oddly clean. Tomorrow, the ill effects of weaning himself from his daily dose of *daydream* elixir would diminish even more, and in a few days, be gone.

    He must be tough. There was a bigger battle to conquer. He wanted the sword—its existence revealed to him by Paolino, a seller of contraband and information—that he discovered, many desired as well. Nemesis would have it before the others. With the money from its sale, he could rebuild his family farm. He would return to their land ravished, and his parents killed by war. Reclaim his right as owner. A slave no longer, he would be his own master, find a wife—a girl, perhaps like his mother.

    Nemesis returned his water pouch to his belt and pushed away from the tree. The morning air was crisp, and golden rays peeked over the horizon. He was only a few hundred feet from the spot where he would meet the monk called Evander, an old man he met the day before at the local market, with a bad taste for the poppy. He'd placate him with the last of his elixir in exchange for his assistance. If everything went according to plan, by this afternoon, the sword would rest in his hands.

JERUSALEM: Moon Gold Antiquities—The 31st day of Maius

CORVUS

Corvus woke with a cloud over his head, or was it an anvil? His temples throbbed, and his throat was parched. To his *somewhat* surprise, a woman rested against his chest, hunched forward, and under his arm that draped over her. Her naked body and matted tresses shone from the heat stifling the room, and a pungent mixture of sweat, sour wine, and body odors permeated the air. Corvus sat up and blinked. On the cot across from him, Jax snored flat on his back, his naked belly rising above his dirty trousers.

The woman stirred while a few remnants of the night before stomped through his mind. Oh God, another night of carousing gone too far, and a big price to pay the next day—a nasty hangover. What had he been thinking? He and Jax were to meet with Valeria and Milvus before midday. A messenger had arrived yesterday afternoon, requesting their presence in the morning.

He rolled over the woman and stood on his feet. A dizzy sensation rushed between his eyes, and he had to center himself. The impulse for water grabbed him, and he looked around. Slowly he teetered to a small table under the bedroom window. On top was a water pouch, for which he was extremely grateful, and wasting no time he opened and drank from its spout. After several long gulps, he wiped his mouth and looked out the window.

Half the morning was gone. Would they make their appointment? He hurried and nudged the woman's shoulder. She raised her head and looked blindly at him, but then her gaze focused. She recognized him. "Get up! You must go," Corvus barked.

She sat up and saw she was naked and looked on the floor. A dark blue tunic lay crumpled by the bed. She grabbed it and pulled it over her head. Standing slowly, she straightened it and gave him a crooked smile. "Would you have a few coins for some bread and morning wine?"

Corvus had to glance about for his clothes as well. He found his trousers and tunic not far from the bed. He slid into them and then looked for his satchel that held his coin pouch. It rested on a nearby chair. He pulled a few coins from the small bag and placed them in her palm. He opened the door, and she hurried out of the room. As he closed the door, Jax gave out a loud snort. Corvus shouted, "Shut up, you ugly bastard!" He shook his friend. "You could wake half the city with your snoring."

Jax sat up, like a corpse rising from the dead. He blinked a few times. "I feel like a wagon and horses rolled over me."

"No wonder. We let things get out of control last night. Come on. Let's grab something to eat—if we can hold it down—and get sharp. We have to meet with Valeria and Milvus. It's time we get this sword. We're running out of money."

Corvus quickly put on his leather sandals. "Hurry, and meet me downstairs. I'll hire a *carruca*." As he hit the street, he saw an available cart to taxi them to Milvus' shop. He flagged it down as Jax came beside him. Both men jumped in. By the time they arrived, it was an hour past midday. Corvus hopped from the vehicle, and Jax followed.

Once inside the store, Corvus sighed with relief and attempted to compose himself. His eyes adjusted to the cool dimness, but his gaze was drawn to the sunny atrium and the clustered seating near a pillar in the shade.

Valeria stood, came toward them, and bristled, "You're late. Not the best way to start."

"My apologies," Corvus stuttered. Jax, beads of sweat on his brow, echoed him.

"Come, there's much to do," she ordered. Visibly irritated, she led them out of the shop into the connecting home. "We also have a weapons merchant joining us. He's interested in the sword as well."

"What about your patron, Goliath? I thought he wanted the sword."

"Goliath deals in many different ways, and multiple paths can exist that lead to a final sale. Just remember, you work for him. He'll handle the merchant if necessary."

They walked down a short corridor to an entrance that led into the house and a larger atrium than the one in the shop. Ferns and flowers were spread among the row of columns surrounding a rectangular pool decorated with marble figurines of water plants and fish. On each side of the court, there were several rooms. Valeria led them to the closest one and opened the carved double doors. Corvus and Jax followed her into a library filled with several rows of shelves holding rolled parchments, codexes, pens and bottles of ink. At a large round table with six chairs sat Milvus and the merchant.

"Welcome," Milvus said, standing. He turned to the merchant. "These men will look for the sword." He shifted his gaze back toward them. "Corvus and Jax, let me present, Alexander Kronus."

Both Corvus and Jax nodded. Alexander's smile, although polite, seemed waxen, almost vacant. Corvus dealt with thugs and thieves. His intuition told him that these two men weren't much better, only richer. He should be careful, but his advantage might be that they thought him a fool.

"Alexander, these men were hired by an associate that Valeria and I represent in the trade of antiquities."

"May I ask who they work for?"

"I'm reluctant to repeat his name because of his reputation and desire for privacy, but in your case, with your interest in possibly purchasing this sword, it seems necessary. He goes by the name Goliath."

Alexander raised his eyes and rested a finger on his lips. "Hmm. Goliath the Philistine warrior-giant? Slain with a sling-shot by David, a shepherd boy, before he became King of Israel?"

Milvus nodded and looked at them. Corvus came from a tribe of Goths. Although many were Christian, he vaguely knew the story. He learned the sword had belonged to David, a king, and had asked a priest about it. Jax, a Goth as well, openly showed his bewilderment, and Corvus shot him a glance as a warning to mask his ignorance.

Alexander continued, "How interesting and alarming. I grew up in Greece, hearing the priests tell the story of David and the giant Goliath. A name that sounded fierce to me."

Corvus thought the merchant appeared amused. Without thinking, he blurted, "Wouldn't it be ironic if David's sword got the best of Goliath in some way?" and laughed.

The room grew silent.

Like a cold wind blowing in from the sea, Alexander's expression turned icy. "If that was the case, we'd all lose. Shall we get on with business," he added, abruptly.

Corvus glanced at Jax, who shifted feet and wiped a hand across his forehead.

Valeria looked away. Milvus stifled a cough and went to a shelf. He returned with a parchment. "Let me show you the picture I've rendered from the details given by the ancient texts. Valeria created a beautiful drawing." He rolled the parchment out on the table and pinned the corners down with marble weights. "As you can see from the illustration, we were able to deduce from the written text that the sword is short, almost like a gladius. At the top is a silver pommel in the shape of a half-moon with a rounded cap and inset with rubies. There are circular lines carved into the handle, and according to the description, a gold band engraved with four images. A garland of grain, a coronet of flowers, a naked tree branch, and a cluster of withered grapes. Down the blade is an engraved inscription in ancient Hebrew." Milvus pointed to the middle of the blade. "The men who wrote this document translated the phrase into Greek. It reads: *A curse on the one who wields David's sword and not be chosen.*" Milvus said it almost in a whisper as if a sacred warning hung in the words. He sighed and looked at them, apparently finished with his explanation.

The first to speak was Alexander. "What a discovery. Valeria, you've brought the sword to life on parchment. It's amazing." His gaze carried a softness that made her blush.

Corvus watched as Valeria thanked the merchant for his compliment. A strange tension flowed between them. He also noticed that she was quieter than usual. *Maybe Kronus intimidates her.* Generally, she was more outspoken—but he was here to do a job. Valeria wasn't his concern. "So, now that we know what the sword looks like, where should we start? Any thoughts or suggestions?"

"Actually, I have a lead for you and Jax," Milvus answered and took a seat. "My sources say that a Roman senator's daughter and her barbarian husband have the sword. They're traveling with a small group and on their way to Jerusalem, or perhaps, have arrived. Your job is to find them, devise a way to steal the weapon, and return here. Upon completion of this task, you'll be paid."

Corvus rested a thumb in his belt. "Does this woman and her husband have a name?"

Milvus smiled, and his eyes shone victoriously. "Lady Arria Felix and Garic the Frank. Be careful, they're under the emperor's protection."

Before Corvus could respond, Alexander sat straighter and rested an arm on the table. His sharp gaze matched the edge of his words. "Will fear of Marcian's power stop you?"

"Not likely. The emperor always has food on his plate." Corvus tossed his head toward Jax. "Me and him need money to eat."

Jax nodded with a crooked grin.

Alexander pursed his lips. "I can't speak for Goliath; after all, I'm just a merchant and his customer. However, I think it's safe to say, 'Go then, get the prize—and return to a feast.'"

ARRIA

"Mistress Arria!"

Garic and Arria awoke again. Only this time to a knocking on their door and Catalina's urgent voice.

"Mistress Arria. I'm sorry to disturb you." The servant girl's tone held an edge of panic.

Arria jumped out of bed, pulled on her tunic, and opened the door. "What's wrong? Is Licia all right?"

"Oh, I thought she might be with you." Catalina's forehead wrinkled, and her eyes shone with fear. She began to cry.

Garic came behind Arria at the door. "Is Licia unwell?"

Arria's voice rose above her servant's tears. "She's not with us. What happened?"

Catalina shook her head, her sobs blurring her words as Arria pushed past her and ran down the hall to Licia's room. As she crossed the doorstep and entered, Garic followed on her heels. Both beds were empty, but Licia's dress and shoes were gone.

Catalina came up behind them a bit more composed. "I awoke to prepare for the day. When I sat up in bed, I noticed that she was gone. The door was slightly ajar. I dressed and came immediately to you."

"Do you have any idea how long she's been gone?" Arria asked the servant.

Catalina shook her head and wiped away more tears.

Garic spoke up, "I'll wake Samuel and the soldiers. Perhaps she is wandering the halls. You know how curious she is."

"I'm coming too," Arria replied. "We'll all look. She can't be too far, can she?" Arria swept a glance around the room. Her deductive instincts clawed their way to the surface of her sight. How long had it been since she had called on her ability to see things others might not recognize or discern? She was known for her power of perception and felt secure in her talent, but it had been some time since someone or a situation required her help.

Garic noticed her observation. "Do you see anything?"

She had detected an overturned cup with several drops of wine pooled near the rim slightly beneath Catalina's bed. The edge of the bed covering touched the floor and bottom of the cup. Arria picked it up. Anger filled her, and she turned to Catalina. "Were you drinking wine?"

The girl's face reddened, and her breath grew short as sobs escaped her, and she nodded. "An elderly monk came to the door after everyone retired. Licia was asleep and safe. He told me that it was customary for the monastery to offer visitors hospitality and to ensure a good night's rest and pleasant dreams with a nightcap. He said you would approve. I thanked him and did as I was told and drank it all but for a few drops. I did feel a warmth and sleepiness afterward. All I can remember is lifting my feet on the bed and then waking to find Licia gone."

"Did he say his name?" Arria demanded.

Catalina sniffled and looked down. She slowly shook her head and wiped her nose with a fold in her skirt.

"We should go now before more time escapes us," Garic said.

Arria frowned and answered, "You're right. This is not good. We need to hurry. Muster the men. Then meet me at the prior's workroom near the monastery's entrance. We'll inform him and make our plan there." Arria clenched her fists and fought the terror she felt rising within her.

Garic sensed her fear and grasped her by the shoulders. "Do not worry. Compose yourself and contemplate our best course. We'll find Licia. Let's believe she's just a lost little girl."

Arria nodded, gave him a trusting look, and hurried out the door. She would fight the demons of hell, if necessary, to find her little girl.

HE

(Nemesis)

Hidden behind a nearby tree, he watched the white-haired, old monk and sweet little girl walk hand-in-hand along the warm, sunny path to the open meadow. *A beautiful little girl ... almost like a tiny bird before it learns to fly* popped into his head.

When they reached a row of wildflowers, the child stopped to pick a few. The monk encouraged her to move quickly. "Hurry, Licia. The goats will wander deeper into the meadow soon. You want to see the baby goats, don't you?"

Licia nodded and took Evander's hand.

Nemesis watched them as the monk wobbled a bit, and they disappeared over the rise. His attitude took a grim turn. He banked on Evander, getting as far away from the monastery as possible. Perhaps the monk would get lost, which might be better. His sour mood dissolved, and his hope rose like a cresting wave. Confidence rushed through his veins. He lifted his water pouch to his lips and drank; it calmed his pain. He turned away. *Now, to the monastery before the little dove is found.*

GARIC

Garic found Samuel and Brother Bruno in the room they shared with Telemachus and Justus. Samuel informed Garic the two soldiers had gone off to the creek, one to bathe, the other to hunt for berries. Garic quickly explained the situation and left the men to ready themselves.

He sped down the corridor to raise the alarm from a nearby balcony overlooking an outer courtyard. The creek stretched behind the monastery, and the soldiers knew the sound of his horn meant something was wrong. It would call them back immediately. The monastery bell signaled a larger danger from attack or fire and required the abbot's or prior's permission. This would take too much time. Garic took his strongest breath and blew the horn in several directions.

Afterward, he found the path that led to the monastery's entrance and the prior's workroom off the vestibule. The door stood open. Catalina sat on a bench in the hallway outside the entrance. She looked like she might break into tears and gave him a weak nod. Garic felt bad for the girl. He knew she meant no harm, but he only responded with a stern dip of his head. His mind was on finding Licia. Garic entered the room.

The prior sat behind his desk a handbell in his hand. Brown hair circled his shaved tonsure; his robe looked freshly cleaned. His neat appearance, kind eyes, and reserved edge projected a competence that filled Garic with relief.

Arria sat on the edge of her chair with her hands clasped tightly in her lap.

The monk rose. "Ah, Noble Garic. The news about your daughter is alarming."

Arria glanced anxiously at Garic. "I informed Father Audric that we scoured the immediate area and passageway off of Licia's room without success and that we're frantic with worry."

The prior placed the bell on his desk. "As you may have heard, I've rung for assistance. A brother will arrive shortly to guide you through the corridors. I imagine a child will not get too far, but she may have become lost. Our abbot has gone to visit some of the neighboring monasteries and is not here. I stand in his place, but upon his return, I'll inform the abbot about this situation."

Garic frowned. "We hope to find Licia soon. Arria will go with the brother through the monastery, and I'll take the men and ride the property." An idea occurred to him, and he added, "Licia may have wandered outside to pick flowers or to see the animals, especially the goats. Before our arrival, she asked if there would be baby goats here for her to pet."

The prior picked up a rolled parchment and handed it to Garic. "This is a map of the monastery's estate. It will guide you."

A sudden voice spoke behind them. A young monk, lean with short waves of blond hair, stood in the doorway. "Father Audric, you requested me?"

"Brother Primas, enter and meet our guests, Lady Arria and her husband, Noble Garic."

The young monk stepped into the room and nodded his greeting.

Father Audric continued, "Their little daughter, Licia, has gone missing. Please help Lady Arria search the monastery. Check every passage and room that stands unlocked for now. Perhaps begin with the chapel, its alcoves—the well and surrounding area."

Arria gasped upon hearing the word *well* and raised a palm to her breast. Her eyes welled with tears.

Garic moved to Arria's chair. He calmed her with a gentle hand on her back and addressed Primas, "I agree, start with the well, but Licia knows we have rules against climbing on wagons, wells, and anything that might hurt her."

"As you wish," Primas responded, his eyes kind and eager. "Please follow me, my lady."

Arria rose, wiped away her tears, and took a breath. She turned to Garic. "We'll find her and return here."

"Yes," he answered, his tone firm and manner reassuring. "Go, Arria, I'll take the men and scour the estate."

Arria spun on her heel and followed the brother, who set a brisk pace down the hall. Garic watched as Catalina trailed behind them. He turned and left the building from the main entrance and headed for the stable.

Brother Bruno, determined to help, had hurried there ahead of him. He would have the attendants saddle the horses for Samuel, Justus, and Telemachus. Samuel was the first to arrive, followed by Garic. The soldiers had heard the call of alarm from Garic's horn and returned as well. From the time they discovered Licia was missing to organizing the search, almost an hour had passed. This worried Garic. He directed them, and they took their paths without delay.

One of the soldiers headed west, the other north. Samuel and Garic would go east toward the grazing pasture, and if unsuccessful, head south past the monastery. Each would survey the property in a circular fashion and then return. On orders from the prior, most of the monks were searching the grounds around the wall. If Licia had wandered outside of the abbey, hopefully, they would find her in a short amount of time.

XV

Crossroads

MONASTERY OF THE CROSS: The 31st day of Maius

HE

(Nemesis)

Bright shafts of light from the high window shone on the floor as he dropped to the ground and into a small meeting room off the cloistered courtyard. A tree near the window made his entrance easy. The monk's robe, stolen from a laundry line outside the church, clung to his legs, but he found his balance and hurried down the passageway. Soon, the brothers, the Lady, and husband, and their traveling party would return from the frantic search for the child. He must hurry.

Yesterday afternoon at the market, Evander, desperate for poppy juice, had told him many things. Nemesis believed that the sword might rest in the bag of the friend called Samuel, and stored among the few persons in a large cubical used to sleep. Evander, always looking to relieve visitors of their minor possessions—a dropped coin purse, leather shoes, clothing, and weapons to trade for some poppy, had noticed Samuel carrying two bags and a satchel, which he seldom put down. Evander had shared that he found it curious, and most likely, the satchel carried some valuables.

Nemesis found the room and slowly opened the door. It was empty, and he entered. Closing the door behind him, he scanned the room and went to a corner behind one of the beds. More than a few bags rested together in a pile. One, in particular, caught his eye, a dark brown satchel that appeared less worn, almost new.

He snatched and placed it on the bed. With a quick look inside, he spotted a silver box large enough to hold a short sword. His instinct told him this was the prize, but he must be sure. With an agile touch, he lifted the lid. Inside rested a sword with gems in the hilt, and a Star of David engraved into the pommel. Joy ran through him, and he snapped the lid shut. Glancing over his shoulder, he pulled a woven sack from beneath his robe and dropped the box inside. Then, he closed the leather satchel and flung it onto the bags resting in the corner.

There was no easy way to scale the wall back up to the window. He scanned the hallway and decided to secret his way to the nearby courtyard. There he'd hide the sack beneath a cluster of bushes, surrounding a palm tree and leave. He would return for it in the latest hour of the night when all were asleep. Then on to Jerusalem and Evander's recommendation, the antiquities shop called Moon Gold. There he would sell the sword for the money he deserved.

GARIC

Garic felt the sun on his face as he and Samuel rode east. From a small path leading away from the monastery, they rode up a hill, brought their horses to a halt, and scanned the countryside. A small meadow filled with wildflowers and a grove of trees at the southern edge seemed like a probable place to find a herd of goats. "Let's ride to the meadow," he said to Samuel. "Keep your ears open. They're noisy creatures and might be wearing bells."

Samuel nodded his agreement and added, "Do you think the girl would follow them?"

"Follow and chase them. Licia has a great imagination and a lot of energy. I'm hoping that if she found them, she'll tire quickly and try to return whichever way she came."

Garic glanced at the sun, now risen in the sky. He nudged his horse down the hill toward the sea of wildflowers. Samuel followed beside him. Garic surveyed the land to their left while Samuel surveyed to their right. Once they entered the open grasses, they walked their horses, scrutinizing the view before them. Garic sharpened his gaze and looked for a red patch of color, thinking of Licia's hair. As they moved along, a northern wind blew around them. Garic noticed a dark ribbon of clouds stretching in that direction. He pointed and asked, "What do you think? A storm headed our way?"

"I'd say yes and soon."

"Then, we need to move faster. The thought of Licia caught in a rainstorm . . . alone . . . We must find her."

Samuel pulled on his reins. "Perhaps it's best we split up."

"*Ja,*" Garic agreed and came to a stop. "You ride closer to the edge of the grove. I'll ride toward those rolling clouds." He lifted his hood. "Shout her name and search until the downpour is upon us."

Raising his hood as well, Samuel nodded. "I'll meet you back at the monastery. Most likely, once the storm breaks, the soldiers will abandon their search and return."

"I told Arria if anyone else finds Licia before we return, she must ask the abbot to ring the bell three times. This way, the surrounding neighbors will not be alarmed. In case of fire, when help is needed, the bell is rung many more times."

"God help us, Garic. We'll find your daughter." Samuel rested his palm on his chest, a Frank Wespe warrior gesture to signal determination and comradery.

Garic returned the gesture, placing his hand on his chest and watched Samuel ride away. He directed his horse and rode farther into the meadow, toward the oncoming storm. Scouring the landscape around him, he searched for any sign of Licia, perhaps following some goats or looking for a way home.

Garic watched the dark roll of clouds expand across the sky and worried. *The storm will be on us soon! Where are you, Licia? I must find you.* Soft ripples of thunder drummed behind the clouds, and a few drops of rain wet his brow. He scanned the landscape. Garic was grateful for his keen vision, especially when many of his friends and kin struggled with poor eyesight. But his eyes remained sharp. In the distance, he caught a movement. A dark figure seemed to rise above the grass and a patch of red beside it, and he urged his horse to a trot.

The wind whipped around him, and the air grew moist. Long yellow grass woven with stalks of green fell before his horse's hooves as the dark figure grew closer. He could see a man in a monk's garb with a child, a red-headed girl—Licia! A few small goats circled their legs, and he could tell that Evander and Licia had seen him and were waiting for him to arrive. Garic rode to a stop and jumped from his horse. With less than a stride, he pushed past the monk, lifted Licia in a hug, and swung her around. "My girl, you are safe!"

She cried, "Papa. I'm so happy you found me."

Garic set her gently down. He ignored the brother and tucked red strands of hair, fallen from her braid, behind her ear, and held her shoulders. "Licia, why did you leave? Your mother and I have been searching everywhere for you. When we discovered you were missing, we became frightened."

She pointed to the monk, who stood there, his eyes darting about and a slanted grin on his face. "Brother Evander came to my room and woke me up. He wanted to show me the goats. He said it would be all right, you and Mama wouldn't mind."

Garic stepped toward Evander and grabbed him by his robe's collar and growled, "Who are you that you would take our child *anywhere* without our permission?"

Evander cowered and held up the palms of his hands. "Pardon, my lord. I just thought it would be fun for the girl to play with the goats, but it was perhaps too early, and we sat for a while and fell asleep."

Garic shoved him away and looked him over. Evander looked unkempt, and a faint, sweet odor, not familiar to Garic, clung to the monk. "If I find you hurt my daughter in any way, I'll skin you alive. Or better yet, I'll carry out Frankish justice for a crime against an innocent." Garic leaned in, and his finger pointed in Evander's face. "A horse will drag you by your feet around the monastery until your face is a bloody pulp of flesh, and your body is unrecognizable."

Evander blanched and fell to his knees. His arms raised in protest, he began to sputter, "Please, my lord. I harbor no malice in my heart. I'm just an old man, who rises very early to tend the goats. I thought to make your daughter happy by letting her help with the creatures on their morning walk to the meadow."

A jagged slice of lightning interrupted them, followed in seconds by a thundering boom.

"Get up!" Garic barked. "I'll deal with you later." The long strands of hair, resting on his chest, whipped in the wind. Loose curls blew around Licia's face as he took her hand. "The storm is bearing down on us. We must hurry and leave."

The monk raised his cowl and struggled to his feet, his portly body making it difficult. "I cannot leave my goats. I need help."

"The goats will run faster than you, and Licia and I have a horse. You best get started before it rains."

Evander darted back and forth and called a few of the goats by name. Garic lifted a shivering Licia onto his saddle and mounted behind her. Stroking her hair, he whispered calming words in her ear. With a flick of his reins, he turned his horse and trotted off to the sound of Evander's plaintive cry. "Wait for me," he wailed.

Garic trotted a few feet, stopped, and brought his horse around. He shook his head, partly in disgust and slightly out of pity as the rain broke cold and hard in a torrential downpour. The water drenching them, he shouted, "Keep walking, brother. I'll send a man with another horse to help you home." Garic turned his stallion around and galloped toward the monastery with an arm clenched tightly around her waist. Now, his only enemy the storm, he would return Licia to Arria's welcoming and loving arms. Garic smiled. His little girl was safe.

GARIC

When Garic arrived at the monastery entrance, Arria, along with Father Audric, Brother Bruno, and Catalina, stood waiting under the arched portico. Arria's shawl fluttered in the rain, and her face held a cold tinge of blue and worry. Her hands appeared from beneath the folds of fabric, and she waved with joy.

Once the rain broke, Samuel had ended his search as planned and found them on the trail near the monastery. Wet like seals drenched by ocean spray, Garic jumped from his saddle, grasping Licia to his chest. She wrapped her arms around Garic's neck and held on as he ran for shelter. Samuel followed behind them.

Beneath the stone arch, Garic placed Licia on the ground. Arria waited with open arms and hugged her to her breast. "Oh, my sweet darling. I was so worried when I discovered you were gone. Papa too. Everyone. Many people have been looking for you."

Licia looked down. "Sorry," she said. "I wanted to see the goats."

"Speaking of goats. Brother Evander needs a ride back," Garic interjected.

Samuel smirked but noticed aloud, "The soldiers are arriving now." He pointed down the path. "I'll give them some reprieve and fetch the priest." He looked toward Father Audric. "May I use a covered cart from the stable?"

"Of course," the prior, standing beside Arria, agreed. "Samrick, is it?"

"Yes," Samuel replied.

Father Audric looked grim. "I'm especially eager to learn what happened from Brother Evander. Brother Primas will help you get the cart."

Primas stood by the door. He smiled when Samuel looked in his direction, then lifted his hood, and filed down the portico toward the path leading to the barn. Samuel trotted after him.

The prior turned and bent slightly toward Licia. "So, the lost girl has been found." He pressed his lips together and gave her a stern look. "We're thankful you're safe and unharmed, but you frightened your parents and the brothers as well. You cannot go off on adventures with strangers, even if they appear friendly. Do you understand?"

Licia's blue eyes shone with remorse. "I do."

Father Audric smiled at Licia, gave Arria and Garic a nod, and re-entered the monastery.

Arria grabbed Licia's hands and spoke with a soft but firm voice, "Never go anywhere with anyone again without our permission."

"Yes, Mama." Licia nodded, but no longer in his or Arria's embrace, she began to shiver again.

Arria quickly wrapped her shawl around the girl. "Now hug me, and let's get you out of those wet clothes, and bathed, then dressed for the day. Your papa and I have many things to do before we leave for the city."

Garic stroked Licia's damp hair and said, "Arria. After I change my clothes, I'll join Brother Bruno and the soldiers at the stable. We'll make preparations for our departure to the city and await Samuel's return with Brother Evander."

Perhaps the old monk, who appeared oddly senile, had just sought to perform a kind deed, Garic thought. But a strange suspicion crept through his bones, and his warrior instincts screamed within him. Something was not right.

ARRIA

Arria led the charge. She held Licia's hand, almost dragging her along while Garic and Catalina followed behind. They walked briskly down the corridor that led to her daughter's room. Even in the moist, morning heat, Licia still shivered. She needed dry clothes and a warm blanket, so she wouldn't catch a chill. Garic, a seasoned soldier, would fare better. His body knew the discomforts from nature's elements. He wasn't invincible but toughened from years of battles and hardships born from human conflicts.

Arria swept a curl behind her ear. She was mildly annoyed with Catalina, but then, how could their servant be held accountable when she'd likely been drugged? What prompted Evander's strange and dangerous behavior? She would talk with the old monk later.

When they reached the room, Garic continued to theirs while Catalina followed her and ran to Licia's suitcase. Rifling through Licia's clothing, Catalina pulled out clean clothes while Arria helped Licia off with her shoes, dress, undertunic, and briefs. She gazed up and down her daughter's body. She looked unharmed.

Arria wrapped Licia in a blanket and sat her on the bed. She held the girl's hands. It was time for a worldly talk about trust. "Licia. Listen to Mama. If any person, man or woman, that you don't know asks you to go anywhere with them or do anything for them, you must ask Mama or Papa first. Is that clear?"

Licia looked wide-eyed and serious. She nodded.

"Papa and I want you to be safe, always. Arria softened her voice, "Did Brother Evander hurt you in any way, or was he kind to you?"

"He let me feed the goats and pet them. He's nice," Licia replied with a happy smile.

A sense of relief flooded through Arria. "I know Brother Evander wanted to show you the goats, but he didn't ask our permission. We'll speak to him about this, too. Now come, give me another hug, and let's get you dressed."

Licia wrapped her arms around Arria's neck. Arria hugged her and planted a kiss on her little girl's cheek. Licia was safely home. Arria's eyes surged with tears of relief and gratitude. She had many to thank, but especially Garic, her husband, and hero.

SAMUEL

The ride to the meadow proved quicker and easier than Samuel expected. The worst part of the storm had passed, and with only a light rain falling, he found Brother Evander on the path. His shoulders hunched and head bent beneath his soaked cowl, his robe drenched as well, he looked like a drowned cat. Samuel suppressed his impulse to laugh.

"Hop on!" Samuel ordered, jumping from his driver's seat. The old man eagerly took his hand and lumbered onto the back end of the cart. "God bless you, my son," the monk stammered and sat on the small wooden bench used for passengers.

They rode back to the monastery's stable in silence. The elderly brother seemed to dose from exhaustion by the sound of his occasional grunts and snorts. Once around a small bend, the stable popped into view, its weathered grey boards streaked with dirt, random black knots, and ruddy gashes. Samuel drove the cart to a stop in front of the entrance and helped the monk down. Evander thanked him and started toward the monastery's living quarters.

From the stable door, Samuel saw the prior and heard him call, "Brother Evander."

The stout monk shuffled to a stop, turned, and sputtered, "Ah, Father Audric. So nice to see you. How's your day going?" Evander crossed his arms into his wide sleeves and rested them on his chest. He offered Audric a weak smile.

"Considering the morning events, not very well. In addition to your jaunt in the meadow, you've missed Mass as well."

Evander frowned and bowed his head. "Forgive me. I lost my sense of time and was overtaken by the storm."

Father Audric shook his head. "Report to my workroom in an hour after service. We have more than a few things to discuss."

Samuel noticed Evander's face fill with apprehension as he frantically scratched his neck and licked his lips. Was the monk not used to the grasses of the meadow? He had not expressed he had a thirst while in the cart. Samuel watched with curiosity. *Something about Evander seems odd. Is he just a helpless, aging monk, or a man with secrets?*

HE

(Nemesis)

Nemesis watched from his distant perch as Evander toddled off to the latrine, scratching his neck and mumbling to himself. After he came out, he headed toward the entrance to the chapel. No doubt, he was going there to pray for his redemption, gulp a few drops of the poppy unnoticed, and catch a few winks before the bell calling *Sext*, the fourth service of the day sounded. Perfect. Should he part ways with this old one? The monk was unreliable, and although he knew nothing of his plan or who he might be, Nemesis saw him now as a possible liability.

On the one hand, a desire for the poppy could help him control the monk's behavior. Keeping him from revealing secrets to the prior about his addiction, their meetings that morning, and in the market the day before. However, the poppy could be the old man's demise. Causing his loose tongue to ramble and reveal details that might bring Nemesis harm. The problem was how he should dispatch this fool to the ever after, as he and many believed? Today, he had accomplished one mission, but now there was another—Kill Evander and make it quick. He needed to get to the city and sell the sword.

XVI

A Matter of Choices

MONASTERY OF THE CROSS: The 31st day of Maius

ARRIA

Arria pressed her fingers to her temples. *What should we do?* She wrapped her arms around her waist and paced back and forth. The plan was good, or at least, it had been. They would leave Licia with Brother Bruno in the safe comforts of the monastery. Their journey into Jerusalem's old city in the effort to enshrine the sword could be dangerous. She would not want Licia's safety compromised in any way. Sinister characters might see the girl as their *weakness*, which she was, and a means to hurt or manipulate them.

Yet, after the day's events, Arria felt unsure. She sat on the chair in the room she shared with Garic. Just early this morning, they had spent time together, and all seemed well, wrapped in the warm sensation of love and ardor and ending in satisfaction and peace, like a warm blanket on a chilly day.

But now, after what transpired with Licia, could Arria trust Brother Bruno and Catalina to watch and protect their daughter, even with help from the prior and brothers? Arria whispered a prayer to herself for guidance as she gazed out the bedroom door standing ajar. She heard footsteps and low voices. It was almost sunset. Shadows danced across the stone floor as oncoming light, from a lamp or candle, flitted down the hall. Soon, she watched as the two soldiers, Telemachus and Justus, walked by apparently headed for their cell.

As they passed, it suddenly occurred to her. Why not leave one of the soldiers behind at the monastery? His charge would be to protect not only Licia but Brother Bruno and Catalina as well. With all the commotion centered solely around an old, eccentric monk—who appears to have meant no harm—a soldier, an attentive priest, and a servant girl would provide Licia with greater safety. It could be much more dangerous if they brought Licia into the city than if they left her doubly protected at the monastery. But which soldier should be left behind?

Telemachus had skill on the battlefield, but also an expert knowledge of languages and diplomacy that could prove beneficial as a protector, advisor, and translator if needed. Justus was known for his prowess in battle and quiet manner. The logical choice seemed Justus. Arria would talk to Garic and ask for his opinion. Perhaps this was the solution to this new and unexpected problem.

Arria rubbed her temples again. The farm in Gaul or even her estate in Tuscia seemed so appealing right now. She felt a slight flutter in her stomach and patted her belly. They needed to complete this mission. She wanted to go home, first to Tuscia and then to Wild Honey, where she was determined to have her baby.

MONASTERY OF THE CROSS: The Church

HE

(Nemesis)

He slowly opened the door leading into the church. A crisp wave of air shot past him as he slipped in and watched the outer light disappear—the vestibule fade to dark. He crept toward the sanctuary and Evander. Down the aisle, candles burned in sconces. Red chancel lamps, nestled in chains that hung from the ceiling, cast an eerie glow across the altar.

The monk sat in a pew near the altar railing; his head was bent either in prayer or sleep. Nemesis stopped a moment. Doubt seeped into his mind. Should he kill the daft old man? Perhaps, it was wiser to threaten and frighten him to near death. The core of his being smiled with delight as he danced the choice around in his head.

Killing Evander would be easy. Nemesis touched the handle of the blade stuck in his belt and took a few steps. But on second thought, the monk might prove useful in the future. Afterall, Evander could not expose him. That evening in the marketplace when he sold Evander the poppy, he had worn his hood low and partially covered his face with a scarf. Travelers often used a mask to protect against odors and the elements. Besides, the monk—trapped in his desire for the drug—had seemed uninterested in Nemesis and his appearance. Evander had extended a hand filled with coin and shuffled restlessly from foot to foot, waiting for Nemesis to drop the poppy into his waiting palm.

He stole deeper into the church. Fading behind a nearby column, he bit his lip and mused. Yes, perhaps he would keep the monk around and just intimidate and terrify him. Nemesis sailed down the aisle, quietly entered the empty pew behind Evander, and knelt on the kneeler in back of him. A low snore, followed by an occasional grunt, vibrated from the holy man's nose, filling the air around them. Nemesis grinned. If all went well, this would be amusing. He pulled his knife. Bringing it around, he slid it under Evander's chin and nudged his shoulder with his free hand. He watched as the monk's eyes popped open. Nemesis put his lips close to Evander's ear and hissed, "Be silent, and you'll live. Cry out, and I'll cut your throat!"

The old monk blinked. His body tensed, then trembled. Sweat surfaced on his cheek.

"Good," Nemesis replied, his voice low and harsh. "When questioned, by anyone, about your escapade with the little girl, you'll say nothing about the poppy and our arrangement or that we even met. If I hear that you've wagged your tongue about me, I'll return and kill you. Is that clear?"

Evander stared straight ahead and responded with a slight nod.

"My spies will inform me if you do. Beware," he growled and jabbed his shoulder again. "Now shut your eyes and count slowly to one hundred. Do not move or turn around before you're finished. My knife can fly into your back as well as slit your throat."

Nemesis watched Evander's lids close. For a moment, the old monk seemed about to swoon, but instead, uttered a low whimper, then the order of numbers: 1, 2, 3 ... .

Nemesis hurried out of the pew, glided down the aisle, and rushed out the side door toward the tree-lined walk just as he heard another door open. The acolytes had arrived to prepare for Mass. He made for the trees and his next task.

MONASTERY OF THE CROSS: The 31st day of Maius

SAMUEL

The moment Samuel stepped into the cell shared with the soldiers, his senses jabbed at him. Something was wrong. He scanned the room, and his eyes fell upon their luggage piled in a corner. The leather satchel rested oddly on top of the heap. His heart beat faster. He remembered burying it beneath a few others. Something was wrong, or had the soldiers just rifled through the pile looking for their belongings?

A lump caught in Samuel's throat as he rushed toward the head of the cot. With a swift kick, he knocked the bed out of the way, creating a wider path toward the mound of luggage and yanked the satchel toward him. He dropped it on the bed. The bag felt airy and light. Samuel held his breath, lifted the leather flap, and peered inside. The cloth that once wrapped the box laid limp in the hollow space. The silver box with the replica sword was gone.

A groan escaped his lips. His deepest fears were real. Someone, or possibly multiple persons, knew about and wanted the sword. Now, the thief or thieves would try and sell the fake weapon. Time was against them. They must get the sword to Jerusalem and to safety. Samuel cringed, and doubt tripped through him. Perhaps, the best future for the welfare of the sword was in Christian hands. They did dominate, and their power and presence backed by the empire was sure. Could even the largest synagogue in the land keep the sword safe? If it rested in Jewish hands, would it be wiser to hide the sword in an earthen jar and bury it in a holy place protected from the world, or to pass it along through time in the hands of the Jewish leaders and rabbis where it might secretly be revered?

He gazed out the door into the hallway at the ground. Rough-hewn stones, laid down in a varied pattern, basked in dusky sunlight. A few spindly shadows stretched across the surface from a barred window just out of sight. He stood, gathered the bag, and placed it back onto the pile. Regardless of where the sword would land—in the possession of the Christians or Jews—it needed protection more than ever, and the ruse of the replica proved their theory all the more. He must inform Arria and Garic immediately, and they should leave for Jerusalem at once.

Samuel stepped into the corridor and closed the door. He heard voices and the sound of footsteps in the hallway. Not wishing to be seen, he turned and ducked into another corridor he knew led to Arria and Garic's room.

Why had a mission of this proportion and significance come to him? He had no answer but felt terrified and awed at the same time. After the trials he suffered as a slave and later as a warrior at the Battle of Catalaunum, he had managed to stay alive and with Arria's help return to his family and country. He had not chosen this endeavor, but he could not walk away. An intense feeling washed over him. Had the sword chosen him? If this was true—what must he do or sacrifice to protect it from harm? He shook his head and told himself, *No time for doubt or worry, only action,* then hurried down the hall.

XVII

Trust in the Face of Deception

JERUSALEM: Moon Gold Antiquities—The 1st day of Junius

HE

(Nemesis)

The intense yellow sun shone just above the horizon as Nemesis breathed in the brisk air mixed with the scents of straw bales, horses, and mules. The stable owner stretched out his hand to him. "Pleasure doing business with you, sir. Your mount is in good hands. What's his name?"

Nemesis stared at the beaming owner. *It's too early in the morning for such happiness*, but he mumbled, "Brother," then dropped a few coins in the man's hand and inquired about lodgings. He was directed to an elderly street vendor, a widower who sold nuts and dates and who rented space in his apartment to bolster his income.

As he hurried through the market, he spied and bought a leather bag to provide the sword with greater protection. Afterward, he found the vendor at home above his shop. The old peddler, being clever, had cordoned off his room with rope and a curtain. They negotiated a price, and he quickly paid the man.

While the vendor stoked his brazier, Nemesis drew the curtain shut and removed his clothes and sword from the woven sack he used at the monastery. He placed the weapon in the leather bag and folded his few garments neatly on the blanketed cot beside a stool holding a water pitcher. After storing his items, Nemesis waved the old man a brief farewell and entered the street.

With a few inquiries, it wasn't long before Nemesis found his way to the shop of Milvus, the Armenian, located on a side street off the Cardo Maximus. He looked around. Compared to the Cardo, the street slept quietly in the fresh morning air. He cracked the door open to the antiquities shop. At the top of the door jamb, he saw the bell ready to announce the arrival of a customer. He preferred to appear unannounced. An element of surprise might provide an advantage, but the bell's chime might hopefully bring Milvus and not a servant to him.

Nemesis tugged at the knotted scarf beneath his cloak and around his neck. He brought it up over his nose, then pulled his hood lower. It would be best to hide his identity due to the nature of his work, and he would explain this when he met the merchant. He felt confident that motivated by greed and experience, Milvus would not object.

Cool darkness met him as he stepped into the shop, and the bell above the door tinkled. Ahead, rays of light beamed down onto the atrium courtyard from the open ceiling. All around, shelves displayed pottery, sculptures, and paintings. Many appeared old and delicate, and in his mind, useless. Never would he spend the money from the sword on objects such as these, but at the same time, he was pleased that some people found these artifacts of value. Just seeing the costly wares before him, he reasoned the sword should bring him a high price. Nemesis licked his lips. In due time, he'd be a wealthy man, and he'd return home to a new life. A place where he was master of his land and destiny.

The sudden appearance of a short, plump, and balding man pulled Nemesis from his thoughts. The man crossed the atrium and out of the light. He stepped past the columns into the shaded entryway.

Nemesis raised his hand as a peaceful gesture and asked, "Are you Milvus?"

The man drew closer, then suddenly stopped. He heard the question and his hazel eyes piercing, he suspiciously tilted his head. "Who's asking?"

"I do not wish to disclose my identity—the reason for my mask. I've come to sell a valuable artifact. I was told the merchant, Milvus, might be interested."

"I'm Milvus, the owner of this shop. I'm also a reputable merchant with powerful friends. This is not the place for double-dealing or pranks. Understand?" With a quick snap of his fingers, the figure of a man stepped forward into their view. He stood with his arms crossed and carried a sword in his belt. "Insurance," Milvus offered, his expression serious.

Nemesis nodded, impressed. "I cannot say how I acquired this object, but for the right amount, it's yours if you're interested. I do not have a lot of time. You can see it now if you like." He lifted the strap of the leather bag slung over his shoulder and turned sideways so Milvus could see its length.

"Very well," Milvus said, waving a hand toward the atrium. "Follow me. I have several *cubicula* past the columns. I view artifacts in a private room and away from unexpected customers."

Nemesis smiled and followed the merchant, who led the way to a small room with a curtain. This was going well and according to plan. Who knows, within the hour or less, he could be leaving with a large amount of money. He would ask for payment in gold *solidi,* sure to purchase anything in the empire. The thrill of accomplishing his goal and attaining a fortune rippled through him. This entire venture had been easier than he thought. He pursed his lips, and his hands itched to show Milvus the sword. Some said the sword was cursed, but this was his lucky day.

Milvus led the way; Nemesis and the bodyguard followed.

Once inside the cubicle, Nemesis turned and watched. The merchant stepped around him and drew a curtain across the entryway. His bodyguard positioned himself in a corner of the room. It appeared to Nemesis that Milvus operated at a superior level of business. His shop and manner were far from common, and this filled Nemesis with pride. He was no longer an underling. With the theft of the sword, he'd risen in status and wealth. A soft breath swept through his nostrils as he lifted the strap from his shoulder, over his head, and laid the leather bag, resembling a longer, wider quiver, on a small, rectangular table in the center of the room.

"All right, what have you brought me?" Milvus asked Nemesis.

"From what I've been told, a sword belonging to the great King David." Mild sweat covered his palms as he loosened the drawstrings at the top of the bag.

Milvus shifted feet and blanched. "Are you sure?"

The words had fallen from the merchant's lips as if pushed. He could not hide a ringing incredulity in his tone. Nemesis smiled and nodded. Then Milvus did something unexpected. He pointed to the only chair in the room.

"Please take a seat. I must step out. There's a document that will help me validate the appearance of the sword. I'll only be gone a few minutes."

Heat surged through Nemesis, beneath his tunic, and under his mask. Perspiration ran down his neck, and he loosened his cloak. He narrowed his eyes. "May I ask what sort of document?"

"This is quite a coincidence, but I possess a drawing based on an ancient scroll describing the very sword you claim to have brought me. If they match, I believe we can do business." Milvus gave him a broad grin. His shrewd eyes gleamed with excitement. "One moment, please." He parted the curtain and disappeared.

Nemesis glanced sideways at the bodyguard and instinctively slid his hand to the dagger tucked into his belt. Better to remain standing. Play it safe.

Just beyond the open curtain, Nemesis looked into the atrium. Random rays of golden sunlight slid downward across the gurgling fountain and onto the mosaic floor. Grapes, rabbits, fish, and deer glowed in green and brown tiles, set in a series of squares, and surrounded by a cabled pattern. The shop seemed too perfect, Milvus too smooth. Had he overstepped? Uncertainty tugged at him. An urge to leave filled him, but his fear was curbed when suddenly the merchant appeared with a document in his hand.

Milvus entered the cubicle, closed the curtain, and returned to the table. He nodded toward Nemesis.

With stiff fingers, Nemesis slid the silver box out onto the table. He looked at Milvus, whose eyes widened as he leaned closer to the case. His confidence returned, exhilaration coursed through Nemesis. He held his breath and lifted the lid, his hands steady, his mouth dry. They both peered into the box together.

The sword rested in the case and appeared shinier than yesterday when he'd taken a second look and imagined his farm built and thriving. The grip was wrapped in dark brown leather strips, and the hilt was bronze set with green and red round stones running from end to end. A smooth iron pommel, perfectly round like an apricot and engraved with a Star of David, sat at the top of the grip. The short blade ended with a sharp tip. By its length and color, it appeared old and antique.

Nemesis looked up at Milvus.

The merchant's brow was wrinkled, and his face held an odd expression. He reached for two silver candle holders on a shelf and rested them on the table. As he slowly unrolled the document, he placed one silver holder at the top and one at the bottom. The image of the sword, drawn in bold colors and specific details, was clearly different from the weapon resting before them.

The illustration showed more beauty and was far more intricate and precious than what lay on the table. The drawing showed a gold band around an ivory grip, rubies, and engraved images. An inscription ran down the center of the blade. Although the rendering appeared antique to the eye, the artist had painted a bright rose wash across the blade, giving the sword an unusual sheen, almost a glow.

Nemesis felt his stomach turn, and heat flashed through his body. His eyes burned, and his pulse throbbed. There was no doubt. The sword—his sword—was a fake.

"My friend," Milvus addressed him with a sigh and dour expression, "as you can see, your sword is a shallow attempt at a replica. A forgery. I'm sorry. We cannot do business today. What a shame."

"Are you certain your document is accurate?" Nemesis replied, leaning into the merchant. From the corner of his eye, he saw the guard take a step forward. He strained to suppress the fury rising in him.

Milvus frowned. "I'm sure this news is quite upsetting to you. However, please feel free to contact me with any other future treasures you may come across. Be aware that rare objects must come with certain validations. Many fraudulent persons and merchants are looking to deceive for gain." Milvus placed a hand on his chest. "Of course, I seek only to participate in honest business practices. This attitude reflects my beliefs." He parted the curtain and waved Nemesis out. "Let us walk you to the door. Oh, and don't forget your sword."

Nemesis stared at Milvus and managed a tight grin. He placed the sword in the box and slid it into the bag. He walked to the door; the merchant let him out and shut the door behind him. He stepped into the street and yanked the mask from his face. The light grown pale and grey, he spit his venom onto the pavement. *How did this happen?* Played over and over in his mind. His temples pounded, and he stifled a scream. There would be no mercy for those responsible for his humiliation. He heard his father's laughter from the grave.

He clutched the bag tighter. His head reeled with bloody, brutal images. After today, his path was clear—Destroy his enemies, steal the *true* sword, and capture the little girl—his farm needed a dove.

JERUSALEM: The 1st day of Junius, Night

KALEV

Kalev left Hezekiah's tunnel and worked his way to a broad, busy avenue. Buildings, made from rough and tawny stone, lined the street; their walls held burning torches set into wrought-iron sconces. Strong orange flames helped guide the nightly bustle of merchants, residents, and pilgrims, out for dinner, attending evening Mass, and shopping the late hour vendors. The busy way led to a side alley that ran uphill and crossed through a block of housing, ending on Sparrow Street, where Milvus had his home and shop. Earlier, Valeria sent word by courier that Milvus had news, concerning their ancient interest, and that he should join them as soon as possible.

Kalev wanted to protect Milvus and Valeria in case he was caught posing as a Greek to hide his being a Jew or his dubious business dealings. He, therefore, found an Armenian couple with a child, willing to rent him a cubicle in their two-room apartment on the days he was in Jerusalem and away from the home he bought outside the city. This arrangement would also allow him greater anonymity. He replied to Valeria that he would come directly to the shop, but must finish some necessary business first.

Earlier that evening, he'd arranged for some illicit goods to enter Jerusalem in secret. Having access to the city as Alexander, he discovered a way to set up a discreet chain of delivery through one of the city's neglected tunnels fallen to rubble and difficult to traverse. With some extra help from Valeria and his new acquaintance Accipiter, the Egyptian, he found a reliable crew of five men. They would smuggle in goods that were either banned—the poppy being one—or sold in the market at high prices affordable only to the rich, such as silk, richly colored textiles, silver and gold accessories, and accoutrements. This new market thrilled him, and he felt quite at home in Jerusalem, but he couldn't forget why he came to this city. He'd come for David's sword.

A wagon lumbered by him, and he stepped deeper into the shadows. From the back of the cart a young man sat, his arm thrown across a sack of grain stacked on a pile. Kalev swallowed hard. The boy's innocent face and bright cheeks reminded him of his son, Joshua, gone too early. At the beginning of this venture, he had thought to sell the sword for his personal gain and wealth, but once in the city, his mind had changed. He believed the ancient weapon, holy and blessed, not cursed like some were whispering, would fill the obsessive void in his heart if he could only possess it. Without being able to explain why, Kalev felt that to own the sword and view it at will might vindicate Joshua's murder, soften the pain of his loss, and help keep alive his son's memory as a comfort and physical reminder in his own life.

His son's image was fading, even at this moment. Some days, he fought to remember the sparkle in the boy's eyes, his light-colored skin highlighted by soft, fine golden hairs forming on his jaw. A young voice beginning to break into a man's tenor. And Joshua's frame, youthful and strong.

He would build a room, private and sacred, a place to rest and think. There he would encase the sword flanked by hanging lamps, surrounded by other fine objects worthy of the sword's company. He envisioned this secret room, and the money needed to bring the weapon home to Constantinople. He would think of Joshua and see his face and grow more determined to succeed—before the boy's image was cruelly erased by time and fading memory.

These thoughts and images filtered through him as he trod over the cobbled stones to the front step of Milvus' home. The front door entry to his home, unlike the neighboring entrance to his shop, was solid wood, and there was no flanking window. Tonight, he would enter as a guest. Kalev knocked on the door. A servant answered and led him to a salon.

"May I ask who's calling?" the servant asked.

"Inform your master that Alexander Kronus has arrived."

Kalev had instructed Valeria and her brother to refer to him only as Alexander, to help keep his secret. He would not risk anyone knowing his true identity. He even believed it a bit risky that Milvus knew he was Kalev. Valeria could be trusted completely; after all, she loved him, but her brother was still a man whose scruples, although not too rigid, could at times get in the way. Besides, if one's life or livelihood was in jeopardy, loyalty often fell quickly aside. Regardless, Milvus knew him from Constantinople and for many years. He couldn't have entered into Jerusalem without Milvus and Valeria's help and knowledge. He hoped that Milvus, loyal to Valeria and wanting to protect his sister, would feel compelled to show him loyalty, no matter what might happen.

The servant gestured he might take a seat on either a couch or one of two ornately carved ebony chairs. Kalev wasn't in his chair very long when Milvus and Valeria entered. He rose politely, and Milvus motioned him to sit. Brother and sister sat on a couch across from him.

"How has your day been and evening?" Valeria asked, her eyes gleaming with kindness.

"Profitable, and well. Thank you."

Milvus, who seemed anxious when he entered the room, blurted, "We have surprising news."

"You found the sword?" Kalev asked, leaning forward.

"Not quite, I'm sad to say, but I came across a replica. A rather strange-looking man came here early this morning, wanting to sell me what he claimed was the Sword of David, but when I compared it to Valeria's drawing, it fell short of many and precise details."

"Did he seem a trickster?"

Milvus shook his head. "Exactly the opposite. By his eyes, he appeared surprised and confounded. His face was covered with a scarf, so it was difficult to read any deeper emotions."

A stern insight gripped Kalev. "This is an interesting situation. Word must have spread throughout the street, concerning the sword. There might be more seekers . . . and cheaters entering this race."

"I will inform Corvus that he must search harder and faster," Milvus replied.

"Yes, let him know the stakes are higher, and so will be my payment if he brings us the *true* sword in the next two days."

"He'll be happy to hear, at least, about the increase in his salary if he delivers. Maybe not about the deadline."

"In the meantime, a visit to Accipiter might be in order. I'll go tomorrow. It's likely the wily merchant knows something about this

Roman woman and her barbarian husband revealed to you by, as you've assured me, a reputable source. Accipiter stays abreast of occurrences in the city and is acquainted with many people."

Valeria interjected, "A shrewd action on your part. Accipiter especially likes gold coins."

"Of course, he does. He's Egyptian, and rivaled only by the Armenians." Kalev winked in Valeria's direction.

Milvus nodded his head, a wry grin on his face. Valeria laughed. "Not only Armenians and Egyptians like gold. I believe you're a fan as well."

"As usual, you're right, my beauty." Kalev grinned, his cynicism tugging the corners of his lips. "In fact, when one considers it: find me a man or woman who doesn't desire gold. Those who don't are most likely—under the ground or in their tomb."

XVIII

A Haunted Past

MONASTERY OF THE CROSS: The 3rd day of Junius, Morning

GARIC

The walk to the horses proved difficult for Garic. He held one of Licia's hands, and Arria held the other. Her little fingers felt warm nestled in his grip, and when she smiled at him with her bright blue eyes, his heart swelled. She had awoken in him the quiet realization of what it meant to be a father. He kept his promises, but his sight was on the future. He and Arria would complete this mission, and then they would return to his farm and raise their family. But today, they must leave her behind.

Brother Bruno, Catalina, and Justus stood on the path leading to the stable, waiting to say their goodbyes. It had been decided Justus would stay behind to assist the good brother, protect Licia, and keep an eye out for any sign of trouble. The soldier had dutifully accepted this task and knew what was expected of him.

Telemachus hurried past them to join Samuel, already at the stable. After discovering that the replica sword was missing, Samuel believed they should leave the next morning for Jerusalem. In the city, they could decide the fate of the sword. Arria and Garic had disagreed with him. They needed two extra days to prepare, spend time with Licia, and ensure that secure measures were in place for her safety.

Garic hugged Licia close, told her to behave, listen to Brother Bruno, and when he and her mother returned, he would bring her a special birthday present.

"Oh, Papa," she spouted as she clapped her hands and chatted exuberantly about how much she would like another doll to be a friend to the one she already owned. "Please bring me an ivory doll like I saw in the market with a pretty dress, curls, and whose arms and legs bend."

Garic held Licia's chin tenderly. "I'll buy you the prettiest doll I can find."

Arria watched with tears in her eyes as he kissed Licia's head; then Arria said her goodbyes. "My darling, listen to your papa. Mind your manners and do as you're told. Stay by Catalina's side and no more adventures to find the goats. Do you understand?"

Licia nodded, and asked, "When will you come back?"

Arria hugged her. "We'll be back in a few days," she answered, tenderly, and the servant girl came up and took Licia by the hand.

Dreary, gray clouds stretched across the sky and mirrored the dull ache in their hearts. Arria and Garic thanked the brother and Justus, turned, and walked toward the stable. But Arria looked back and blew Licia a kiss. Garic stopped and raised his hand in farewell, too.

Licia waved at them and yelled, "Goodbye! I promise I'll be good!"

Garic's eyes met Arria's tearful gaze as they turned away from Licia for the last time and approached Samuel and Telemachus in front of the stable, holding the reins to the horses and a pack mule.

Arria wiped away her tears and took Garic's hand. "I'm praying, she'll be safe, but I feel wherever the sword is, so lies the danger."

"I believe this is true," Garic's voice was firm. "The prize is the sword, not a little girl. By leaving Licia behind, we are protecting her."

Arria sighed and looked back once more. Licia was swinging hands with Catalina but waved again. Arria fought back new tears, but a few escaped to her lashes. As she dabbed a handkerchief over her lids, she took a sharp breath and then rubbed her stomach.

Garic noticed her gesture and wrapped an arm around her. "Are you ill?"

Arria shook her head. "I felt a sudden pinch inside my belly, and I was taken by surprise. My miscarriage last year happened so early that this is a new sensation for me."

"This news brings me happiness." His eyes glowed, and he kissed her hand, but he added, "Are you able to handle this mission?"

A confident grin tugged the corners of her mouth. "This sensation is a joy and not a hindrance in any way. I am capable, but I'll miss Licia very much."

"Please, do not worry, Mellitula. Licia rests in good hands. We'll arrive at the city's main gate in the late morning. The day's heat—the crowd of merchants, travelers, and residents passing through the gates will help us. The soldiers will be busy. We must pass Samuel off as a Gentile and find a reputable place to stay. Then, we shall decide what to do with David's sword. Where it should rest."

Arria smiled at him, and he smiled back. They drew near the men, and he nodded at Telemachus and Samuel, waiting patiently for them. Three nights ago, Samuel, with a troubled look on his face, had found Arria and Garic and urgently told them, "My lady, and Garic. I've just come from my room. The replica is missing. A thief or thieves believe they've found and stolen the prize." Their fears were confirmed. Without question, the sword was coveted and in jeopardy. Arria had voiced her distress over the matter, but Garic quickly pointed out that this ruse might give them an advantage, the time necessary to safely bring the sword to Jerusalem. "We can trust no one. We'll need a plan," Garic had suggested, and so, they devised one.

Earlier in the morning, before their departure time, and in secret, Garic and Samuel pulled the sword from its case and wrapped it like a bundle for bedding. Samuel tied it to the back of Garic's saddle. He would keep watch over it until they left. At night when they slept, Garic would use the bundle as his pillow. After securing the sword, they placed the empty box in a sack and stacked it with the supplies and extra blankets strung to the mule.

Garic was determined to never let the weapon out of their sights. The success of their mission rested first on the sword's protection. If he could not watch it, Arria or Samuel would keep it in their possession. As First Counsel to his tribe and a Wespe warrior, Garic understood the importance of courage, fortitude, wisdom, and honor. He often measured a man by these traits. He, Arria, and Samuel believed in these qualities and would protect the sword to the best of their abilities.

The four mounted their horses and trotted out of the monastery yard and toward Jerusalem. As they rode through the hills, Garic wondered—*If alive, would King David have been proud of our commitment to the sword's safety and return to its home?* He smiled and believed, maybe so.

JERUSALEM: Shop of the Egyptian merchant, Accipiter—The 3rd day of Junius, Late Morning

MARCELLA

Marcella arrived with Nerian once again at the shop of Accipiter. She found a delightful comfort in the shop. The materials, oils, exotic sculptures, and wares—expensive silver spoons and plates, newly blown wine glasses—appealed to her sense of beauty and artistry. But she also enjoyed the rays of light that poured into the shop, the sweet odor, and comfortable pillows for a weary customer or visitor to sit and rest upon. All these touches proved pleasant and charming.

Earlier, the Egyptian merchant had requested they come to his shop. She and Nerian would join Accipiter for refreshment and private conversation. He had some news that might help them in the pursuit of the sword. So far, despite attending several parties and discreetly asking questions in the marketplace, their attempts to uncover information about the artifact had proven futile with no solid lead to follow. Just a few murmurings that an artifact of some reputation may have entered into Jerusalem.

The day was warm, but a fine desert dust wafted through the air, so she pulled her favorite blue silk scarf a little tighter under her chin and over her shoulder. Nerian walked beside her, his shiny black hair hung just past his chin, and his trimmed beard clung to his jaw. He looked as handsome as ever. Their day had started with his playful teasing, but in time, it ended with his vigorous seduction. Marcella sighed; she actually felt good today. It had been a while since she felt content—her resentment and anger set aside, not plaguing her thoughts. She reached for Nerian's hand and squeezed it. He smiled at her, and raising her fingers to his lips, he kissed them. They stepped into the shop and were greeted by the servant, Babajan.

"My master has been expecting you," he said and led the way to the back of the shop.

Accipiter, sitting on his customary red pillow beside the center table, greeted them. As they took their seats, Babajan swiftly poured them a glass of wine and then returned to the front of the shop. Accipiter's eyes gleamed, his brows arched higher than usual. A wide grin pasted his lips. "I have wonderful news."

"And we're anxious to hear," Nerian interjected. He leaned forward his grey eyes as intent as the merchant's hawkish gaze staring back at him.

"Well," Accipiter began, crossing his arms over his chest in a relaxed manner. "I recently ran into an acquaintance at another party and late into the night. The lady, having drunk too much hot wine infused with poppy—delectable but quite dangerous, especially, if one desires to keep secrets—found herself on a pillow beside the couch where I reclined. We spoke a little as I watched with amusement as everyone dissolved into disarray and drunkenness.

"For a while, I found my observations quite entertaining, but after some time, I grew bored and decided to leave. This is when my new friend, Anna, started rambling on about the latest gossip. Such a lovely woman, but being a widow can get lonely. I had heard rumors, she had found comfort in the arms of the Roman procurator, Porcius Festus, who seems unaware that his lovely Anna, has an appetite for gossip. With not much prodding and the right questions, I discovered that her lover, Festus, has a magistrate friend in Caesarea who presided over an unusual case in his court. It involved a woman and a man whose servant was murdered. They were on urgent business for the emperor. The woman and man asked the magistrate to expedite burial privileges for their servant and produced an official document for validation."

"Why is this gossip so important?" Marcella asked, wondering where Accipiter's story was going.

"In time, my dear, this story is well worth the wait." And as if to tease her, Accipiter reached for his wine and took a long sip. Then, placing the glass on the table, he grinned and said, "Festus told Anna that the magistrate was surprised to read the woman and man carried a relic, a sword that must be brought to a holy shrine in Jerusalem."

"That's certainly good news," Nerian said, stroking his closely cropped beard. "The sword is real and is either on its way to or already here in Jerusalem. Finding it has become a little bit easier."

Accipiter nodded his agreement but raised a silencing hand. "Wait, my friends. There's more." Devilish merriment danced in his eyes.

Marcella shifted in her seat, but held back from blurting, "Get on with it." She could see the wily shop owner enjoyed relating every detail of this chance encounter, despite her growing impatience.

"The emperor's document mandates," Accipiter continued, "that this couple should be allowed to travel unbothered by any restrictions. The magistrate described the woman as a Roman senator's daughter, brown-haired and petite; and her husband, a Frank barbarian noble, tall, with blond hair reaching past his shoulders. They shouldn't be hard to find."

"What?" Marcella gasped, resting her hand on her chest. "A Roman senator's daughter married to a barbarian Frank noble?" tumbled from her lips. "Have I fallen into Hades?" Anger swept through her in a flash of fire. Her ears burned. "Sekhmet, goddess of destruction, make it not true," she moaned, turned toward Nerian, and glared. He scowled and closed his eyes.

Accipiter gave her a puzzled look. Then, he glanced at Nerian.

Before the Egyptian merchant could say anything, she demanded, "Is there more?" Her impatience dissolved, the merchant had her full attention.

Pursing his lips, Accipiter proceeded with less glee. "Marcella, it appears, I've upset you with this information. Can you say why?"

"Finish your story, and then, I'll explain."

Accipiter continued, "The Roman woman and barbarian were also accompanied by two royal guards, a priest, servant, and a child who also traveled with them."

Marcella questioned aloud. "The guards make sense, but a child and a priest?"

"That is what Anna told me. Does this information connect to you in some way?"

Nerian, sitting beside her, turned his head toward her. "We have an advantage. We know Arria and Garic, and how they think. Tell him your story, Marcella. There's nothing to hide."

Now, it was Marcella's turn. She grabbed her wine, gulped it down, and plunked the cup on the table. She wiped the back of her hand across her lips like a peasant, but right now, she didn't give a damn. Her sister was back in her life—her realm, and from what Accipiter said, she wasn't alone. Arria was in Jerusalem with Garic, and even more painful to Marcella, she might have a child. And just like the righteous, privileged woman that Arria was, she traveled in the company of a priest. Not surprising.

Marcella took a breath. The words clashed in her throat. "The Roman senator's daughter, is my half-sister, Arria Felix. Garic is a

Frank, her husband, and First Counsel to his tribe. I was with them at the Battle of Catalaunum in Gaul." Marcella paused. Should she continue? Why should Accipiter know all her past? She turned to Nerian and reached for his hand. With her eyes, she told him she would divulge only what she felt necessary. "I can only add that she robbed me of a mother and recognition as her father's daughter and kept me from standing by her side as an equal. Due to certain events, Nerian and I were forced to leave for Egypt."

Accipiter nodded but looked grim and disappointed.

Marcella knew he was smart enough to know that she had held back information, but she didn't care. It was her life. If she wanted to keep secrets or guard the details of her past, she would. Tears began to well in her eyes. She would not let the men see her cry. She rose. "Excuse me for a moment, I need some fresh air."

Accipiter and Nerian looked at her sheepishly. It was apparent neither knew what to say, nor would they stop her. As she stormed toward the shop's entrance, she heard them mumble something about devising a plan while she was gone. She didn't care.

She reached the open air, and under the shop's canopy, she took a quick breath and then laughed between tears—she had thought today was a good day. How could she be so stupid?

JERUSALEM: Shop of the Egyptian merchant, Accipiter—The 3rd day of Junius, Late Morning

KALEV

The streets, as usual, rang out with the voices of vendors selling their wares and the musky scents of donkey, horse, and camel dung. Rather than offensive and crowded, Kalev found the market invigorating and calming at the same time. His thoughts in the last few days had even strayed to Valeria and their clandestine nights spent beneath the moon and on the rooftop of his villa outside the city walls. They had finally found a haven where they could live unjudged as lovers, confidants, and partners.

All this freedom, coupled with an atmosphere charged with excitement, danger, money, and love, whirled around him and made him feel even stronger than he felt as Goliath. The persona, Alexander Kronus, felt like his youth, which had slipped away years ago while he fought to survive, earn, build, and live day-to-day. And, as if almost in his sleep, he moved through the motions, taking his breath and heartbeat for granted. Counting his coins, doing business, then sleeping—only to rise the next morning and start again.

He stepped past wares lined and piled up in front of the numerous market stalls stretching as far as his eye could see. Before long, he spotted the striped awning hailing Accipiter's shop.

As Kalev drew closer, oddly, the woman he'd met at Accipiter's party, Marcella, stood out in front under the canopy. She appeared lost in thought. A frown graced her beautiful lips, full and inviting, and her arms were protectively wrapped around herself. Not wanting to startle her, he approached her with a greeting. "Good day, my lady. What a pleasant surprise to find you here."

Marcella turned to him. Her eyes glistened as if from tears, and her smile, too wide, struck him as forced.

"Alexander. A good day to you as well. Are you browsing or shopping?"

"A bit of both. I wondered the same about you?"

She laughed. "I assure you, I enjoy shopping, but today, I'm here with Nerian on business."

"How fortunate, I'm here to see Accipiter and make some inquiries into an artifact. You and Nerian may be able to help as well."

"They are in the rear of the shop. I needed some air and left them. Come, let us return."

Kalev raised a sweeping hand, "Lead the way, my lady."

"Alexander, formality is for strangers and mild acquaintances. I view us as friends and associates. Please, call me, Marcella."

Kalev followed her to the rear of the shop where they came upon Accipiter and Nerian in a hushed discussion. Upon seeing him, they looked surprised and stopped, but both were cordial. Accipiter pointed him to a large pillow beside the one Marcella now occupied and called Babajan to bring Alexander a cup for wine.

They randomly spoke of the unusual heat of the day while they waited for the servant who soon arrived with a fresh carafe of wine. As Babajan poured Kalev a glass and refilled theirs, they nibbled on the plump dates resting on the table.

Accipiter raised his glass in a welcoming toast, and they drank. Afterward, the Egyptian merchant asked, "Alexander, we're pleased by your visit. How can we help you?"

"Friends, I've come to enlist your help. I recently discovered that the ancient weapon I seek may be in the possession of a Roman senator's daughter known as Arria Felix and her Frank barbarian husband known as Garic. They may also have arrived in Jerusalem or will arrive soon, but neither is confirmed." Nerian shot Accipiter a look, but the Egyptian's gaze did not waver from Kalev's.

"How coincidental," Accipiter replied, pursing his lips. "I recently heard the same story. A Roman woman and her Frank husband traveling with the sword on behalf of the emperor. So, it must be true, which raises the stakes and the question. Are we stealing from them or the emperor?"

Kalev tilted his head and spoke with a pensive tone, "I believe the case can be made that the emperor is stealing from the Jews. After all, David was their king." He sighed. "I'm a man of many beliefs, and I collect religious relics as well as ancient artifacts and weapons. I'm willing to take my chances and will pay a tantalizing—but reasonable—price for the sword." He shot them a piercing look to reinforce his serious intent. "Are you still interested in working together?"

Accipiter folded his hands. "Unless my colleagues disagree, we'll scour the city to find this sword for your purchase." The merchant turned to Nerian and Marcella, who smiled at each other.

Nerian nodded approval. "We have no objections. We hope to make a sale."

"Good!" Kalev responded. "When will the hunt begin?"

Nerian spoke with enthusiasm, "Today."

Kalev beamed inwardly and lifted his cup. Accipiter, Nerian, and Marcella did likewise, and they drank to success. But Kalev drank for Joshua. With so many seekers on the trail of the weapon, he could feel the sword in his hand.

JERUSALEM: St. Stephen's Gate—The 3rd day of Junius,
Late Morning

ARRIA

St. Stephen's Gate, the principal gate into Jerusalem, loomed before
them. Telemachus and Arria traveled on their horses, side by side.
Garic rode further behind, pulling the mule carrying their supplies
with Samuel beside him. As they drew closer, Telemachus shared
with Arria that he'd been to Jerusalem some years past when he was a
new soldier. Intrigued, she urged him to tell her of the history he
might know. She found stories and details about the past fascinating
and waited with anticipation to hear him speak.

Telemachus—more talkative than Justus, his soldier companion
left behind to guard Licia and Brother Bruno—eagerly obliged Arria.
"Several centuries ago, the Roman emperor Hadrian came to rebuild
Jerusalem. At the time, it still held the ruins of the Jewish-Roman
war, a century before him. When he found himself engaged in another
Jewish revolt, he crushed it, expelled the Jews from Jerusalem, and
renamed the ancient city, Aelia Capitolina, after his family name,
Aelius, and Capitolina, after the Roman god, Jupiter Capitolinus.

"Hadrian also built the main gate into the city that he called the
Neapolis Gate, but these days, it's known as St. Stephen's Gate to
honor the first Christian martyr, Stephen, who was dragged out of the
city through this gate and stoned to death."

As Arria listened, Telemachus spoke with animated confidence.
"According to accounts, the triple-arched gate, which we'll soon
enter, allowed only royalty to pass through the middle, largest arch,
while the flanking gates ushered in the commoners. However, that
custom died away."

"Do you know the reason?"

"Perhaps, over time, the beliefs, commerce, and the flow of
pilgrims made that habit undesirable and antiquated."

Even at a distance, Arria could see the walls adjoining the gate
were topped with decorative statuettes. "The architecture of this
fortress is so exotic and different from what I know. Golden light and
arid heat stretch across the ancient landscape and drench the stone
walls and statuettes in a shimmering luster. It's so beautiful."

"My lady, once we are in Jerusalem, you'll see that the statuettes
only top St. Stephen's Gate. The other gates and city walls boast

strong tooth-like projections, jutting out from the top of the ramparts, complementing the city's beauty even more."

"Thank you. Knowing these details is a most welcome way to enter the city. The history of the Jews and the holy city where Christus walked, of its cultures and peoples and even my ancient ancestors, is fascinating and disquieting. So much glory but so much pain and suffering as well."

Telemachus nodded in agreement. "I gathered just this little from the short time I spent here on the emperor's business. But I think my lady's observation is most accurate. It's truly a city of joys and sorrows."

Arria smiled at him. Her veil fluttered softly in the wind. The sun glared high above them, surrounded by deep blue and tufts of pale-pink clouds. An abrupt and foreboding sense of danger seized her, and she caught her breath. Glancing at the sky, Arria fixed on the clouds for several seconds to push the premonition away. She hoped Telemachus had not noticed a change in her. Looking toward him, she said with a forced brightness, "Well, I've enjoyed learning about Jerusalem. Thank you again."

Telemachus nodded. "My pleasure, Lady Arria."

Arria looked over her shoulder and came to a stop. "Garic and Sam are almost caught up. We'll wait for them here, so we can enter the city together." She watched as Garic led the way, pulling his mule faster. Samuel followed, his animal in no hurry. Arria grinned. From Samuel, she could also learn many things. Still, right now, Telemachus and Justus were unaware that the man they met in Caesarea as Sam, a Frank and Garic's companion in arms, was really a Jew and native to Palaestina.

If all went well, once inside Jerusalem, she could learn more from Samuel about the city, its history, and how it worked. But, their first challenging obstacle lay ahead. They had to sneak a Jew, posing as a Frank, into the city. Failure was not an option.

JERUSALEM: The Olive Tree—The 3rd day of Junius

GARIC

A sense of relief flooded Garic. Once he and Samuel caught up with Arria and Telemachus on the road, Garic thought it wiser that they take lodgings outside the city and inside as well. This plan would allow them flexibility in case of trouble. Everyone had agreed.

The hospitium, called The Olive Tree, stood on a low hill not far from St. Stephen's gate. A brisk walk would bring them to the city's main entrance in less than half an hour. Garic sent Telemachus to rent two of the inn's best rooms. Many hostels existed on the outskirts of the city, but this hospitium, Samuel had informed him, had a reputation for excellent service and a wealthier clientele. Telemachus soon returned, saying their rooms awaited them.

Arria appreciated a comfortable setting, but Garic recognized, she had adjusted to any situation that made their travels easier. She could sleep in a wagon, under a ship's tent, and in small quarters. Only once did she grumble. A night they were forced to sleep on the muddy ground. He had covered the spongy ground with leaves and placed her bedding near the fire. Curling up next to her, they gazed at the stars and fell into their dreams. The next morning, she laughed and admitted that with him beside her, even the hard, wet ground felt better than expected.

He loved her for her resilience and good temper, fortitude, and courage throughout their entire journey, first as lovers, then husband and wife, and now parents and emissaries for the emperor. Garic wanted only the best for Arria, and because she was with child, he was determined she should enjoy the comfort of an uncrowded room.

Garic led them up the hill covered with olive trees. Thick, gnarled pillars shaped from bark and limbs and born from the sloping earth, stretched leaves across their branches. A rich aroma filled the air, and the breeze drifted through grasses and shrubs hugging the ground. He led them to the main door where they dismounted.

"Sam, will you and Telemachus bring the animals to the stables? Arrange to board them for a few days. Arria and I will take our bags and greet the owner. We'll meet you at the rooms. Then to the dining room for a drink and a light meal."

"A glass of wine sounds good," Samuel answered with a broad smile. Telemachus laughed and agreed.

Garic pulled his bedding from his horse and slung the attached strap across his shoulder. "We cannot stay for too long. We must make our entrance into the city and get our approval."

As Telemachus walked the mule to the stable, Samuel held back with the horses to help Arria with her bags.

Garic seized the opportunity and said to him, "The heat of the day, I believe, will be the best time to enter the city. A sleepy guard might allow you in the city easier, but if something happens, I have another plan. So, stand firmly behind me with confidence."

"You know, I will. I trust you in all matters."

Arria interjected, "We have the emperor's approval and scroll. *Samrick* looks the part of a Frank quite nicely. Do you think something may go wrong?"

"I suspect not, but 'Samrick' is not mentioned in the emperor's document. Experience and the few events that have happened along the way make me lean toward caution. As I suggested, we'll find another room to rent inside the old city as well. Just in case, it appears, going back and forth seems risky."

Samuel grabbed the reins. "Caution cannot hurt our cause—or my situation—only help."

Garic slapped him on the back. "If we hurry, we can have two drinks to bolster our courage."

Samuel shook his head but wore a happy expression. Tugging on the reins, he went to find Telemachus to help him unload their things.

Arria gave Garic a hesitant look.

"Mellitula, what is bothering you?"

"An extra wine will not give you the courage you'll need today, only more relaxed confidence, but don't forget, I'll lead and represent us as well." Her eyes narrowed, and she cocked her head in a way that meant she was curious.

"And?" he drawled, somewhat amused. "I believe you have a question."

"What is your second plan?" tumbled from Arria's lips.

Garic, knowing what might happen, hid a grin. "Honoria's medal. It may provide us with important and extra leverage . . . in addition to the official document. Do you remember Honoria giving it to me?" He watched Arria's eyes spark.

"How can I forget." A pout captured the corners of her mouth. "She awarded it to you with brazen admiration and in my eyes, too much flirtation."

"Your jealousy may be the price of our success."

Arria stood on her tiptoes and kissed him. "Not even an emperor's sister can take you from me."

Garic laughed and placed a fallen curl behind her ear. "You're right about that," he said, lifting her off the ground. He gently swung her around and set her down. Taking her in his arms, he kissed her, and added, "Let's settle ourselves, drink some wine, and go find our courage. Our mission is almost at an end. Then back to Licia and home to Gaul."

Arria smiled and grabbed his hand. "And our beautiful farm, Wild Honey, where our child will be born."

XIX

The Hunters and the Hunted

JERUSALEM: St. Stephen's Gate—The 3rd day of Junius, Afternoon

ARRIA

Arria wiped her neck with the border of the green silk scarf draped over her head and then raised the cloth to her forehead. As Garic predicted, the afternoon heat beat down upon their heads with a strange intensity. Fine grains of dust swirled around their ankles. Garic in a tunic, loose-fitting trousers over leather boots, and a sword tucked in his belt walked beside her. Telemachus and Samuel, dressed in similar garb, followed behind them.

Garic carried David's sword, now wrapped in cloth, in a shoulder sack that held a knife, money, a scarf, and Honoria's amulet. Samuel carried the empty silver box along with his belongings in a bag as well. Telemachus had also added a wooden case to his bag to act as another decoy. Their full bags were to confuse anyone who might be watching. Did they possess the weapon, and if so, which of them carried the sword?

A few hundred feet away, outside of St. Stephen's Gate, semi-circular steps led down to a wide plaza made from stone and dirt. According to Telemachus, the area was once a major gathering place. Created centuries before by Emperor Hadrian, the center of the plaza once displayed a pillar in his honor, now, fallen and gone. The plaza ended in front of the gate, where Roman soldiers flanked the entrance. A few feet off the pathway sat a sentry's shelter made of four wooden pillars and a roof covered with palms.

Arria looked at Garic and said, "I'm ready to speak as planned. My official standing should be enough. At least, I hope so. I can't lose this feeling of danger ahead."

"Have faith," he replied, and they walked with confidence through the plaza to the guard's station.

Two Roman soldiers stood beneath the canopy and beside a table holding documents, a carafe of water, and a few glasses. As Arria and the men approached, one of the soldiers, stocky and muscular with dark eyes and bronzed skin, met them. A harsh light bounced off his helmet and glared back at Arria, causing her to wince. She stopped, but quickly collected herself and addressed the guard with confidence. The men stood behind her, Samuel furthest to the rear.

The stocky soldier stared at her. "Do you wish to enter the city?" he barked, glancing at the men.

"We do," answered Arria.

The guard shifted his gaze to her. He looked a bit confused.

"I am Arria Quintia Felix, the emissary for Emperor Marcian, and the daughter of the late Roman senator, Quintus Felix." She held her chin high and stared back at the soldier.

A tiny smirk seized his lips. He squinted and held out his hand. "Then, my lady, please provide the official documents."

Garic shifted feet beside her but maintained his silence. Arria smiled back and turned toward Telemachus. He pulled the document from his bag and placed it in her hand. She gave it to the guard.

The guard looked at the scroll, walked toward the table, and pulled the leather string from the rolled papyrus. With nimble hands, he unraveled the document while the second soldier on duty watched alongside him.

It seemed like an eternity to Arria, but she waited with confidence. There was no question about the authenticity of the emperor's mandate. The only problem would be if Samuel was questioned. The document did state that two royal guards were traveling in plain garb to escort them, but only Telemachus carried the insignia of his status tattooed on his arm. It occurred to her, Samuel did bear the wasp insignia tattooed on his chest from his days in Gaul and initiation into the Wespe fighters, the elite force of Garic's tribe of Franks. But could that explain his role and help him pass as a Frank? A slight unease picked at her.

The stocky soldier returned to them.

"It appears your mission is important, and you carry an artifact of value. Which of these men is your husband?"

Arria gestured toward Garic, who gazed unflinchingly at the soldier.

"And these two men behind you—guards?"

She nodded. "Yes."

"I'm sorry for the inconvenience, but I'll need proof. The city has been plagued recently by subversives and problem-makers. I've orders to thoroughly question all newcomers and pilgrims."

Telemachus stepped forward and lifted the short sleeve of his tunic. On his arm below his shoulder, he had the symbol of the royal guard. The soldier nodded in deference.

Arria began to wave a hand in front of her face. "It's quite warm are we done now?"

The guard smiled but looked past her toward Samuel. "I have yet to see the other soldier's insignia. He is a soldier, isn't he?"

Arria raised her chin. "Samrick is a soldier, but not Roman. Like my husband, he's a Frank. They both bear the insignia of their elite clan, the Wespe. He's been traveling with us but intended to return to Caesarea. Unfortunately, during our journey, Samrick was forced to replace the second royal guard after an incident involving our daughter. She went missing. Thankfully, we found her and decided that the second guard should stay behind and protect her while she waits for us at the Monastery of the Cross." Arria tilted her head with an air of authority. "Now, would you like my husband and his comrade to show you their marks?"

The guard gave her a calculating look and looked at his soldier companion who nodded. "We would my lady."

"Of course," she replied and motioned to Garic. He took a step forward. Towering over the soldier, he looked down. With a firm grin, he tugged the V cut at the neck of his tunic aside. Proudly, he displayed the wasp.

The soldier motioned to Samuel, standing behind Telemachus and Garic. "Step forward and identify yourself," he ordered.

Samuel came forward. "I'm Samrick, a Wespe soldier from Luthgar's tribe of Franks." He lifted his linen shirt and proudly showed the wasp on his breast. Then he dropped the garment and stepped respectfully behind Arria as the legionary nodded.

Without warning, a pungent odor floated over the breeze. A strange mumbling sound came from behind, and a sudden shadow crossed where they stood. An old man with a woven robe and a carved wooden staff staggered beside them. His face showed deep-set lines, and his grey hair and beard were tangled with dirt and dust. He stood there and stared for a moment. Then, he raised a crooked, pointing finger at Samuel and uttered something unintelligible.

Garic stepped in. "Pilgrim, pardon, but we are speaking with the legionaries."

The old man looked past Garic and continued to stare at Samuel. The beggar's voice grew louder, and he uttered more unintelligible words. Bowing his head, his palm reached toward the sky.

Arria glanced quickly at the legionary.

The soldier shifted his gaze back toward Samuel. His eyes narrowed. In a gruff voice, he asked, "Do you know this beggar?"

Samuel shook his head with a mystified expression. Looking away from the old man and toward Garic, he began to speak in Frankish.

The legionary listened attentively to their exchange, but asked Garic with a suspicious tone, "Has your comrade forgotten his Greek or Latin?"

"Samrick speaks some of both but is from Gaul. He feels secure with Frankish, our native tongue. He's puzzled by this man's intrusion," he said confidently.

The legionary pursed his lips and appeared to assess Garic's comment.

Arria held her breath. She could feel the tension in the air, and the seconds march slowly by them as the stocky legionary made a decision.

And then, the Roman guard yelled at the old man grown quiet now and just staring, "Move away or be dragged from the gate and thrown into the road. Go!"

A reluctant frown bloomed on the beggar's face. Hunched and wobbly, he moved away.

Arria quietly exhaled. Once again, she waved a hand across her face. "Are we finished now? I will faint from the heat if I do not get into the shade and drink."

The guard, a scowl on his face, stood rooted as if weighing a decision.

"If it helps," Garic calmly offered, "we also have validation from Rome. Valentinian's sister, Honoria, awarded me her personal medal as a reward and token of her good faith. Here let me show you." Garic pulled it from his bag and rested it in the guard's hand.

Arria watched the soldiers scan and turn the medal over. She could tell by their wide-eyed expressions, they were convinced. Arria and her companions were not imposters with a forged or stolen document, trying to sneak into Jerusalem on nefarious business.

The lead soldier handed the medal back to Garic, who placed it in his bag. "All right, you may pass." He signaled to one of the soldiers flanking the gate, who acknowledged the approval and let them enter.

Arria walked into the city, feeling light-footed and victorious. They had made it into the ancient city and with Samuel, despite the old man's strange intrusion. Perhaps it was a sign that the sword would find its destined home. Still, the beggar's ranting lingered in her mind, and she glanced over her shoulder to ensure all was well.

Once into the market, the bustle of vendors, shoppers, and connecting streets, stalls filled with fruits and vegetables, clothing, and wares, offered them refuge, and they stopped and took a breath. Samuel smiled at Arria and Garic, but said not a word, for fear Telemachus would hear.

Garic put his lips to Arria's ear. "Are you still angry with Honoria? After all, her medallion did help us."

Arria gave him a wry smile and clutched his arm. "I guess I owe her a favor. I'll kiss you when we are alone." Garic laughed and hugged her.

As they walked toward the center of the market, Arria sighed. They were in Jerusalem.

JERUSALEM: A Cellar Wine Bar—Afternoon

CORVUS

A boy carrying a message from Milvus found Corvus and Jax without much trouble, or so he claimed when Corvus asked him.

In a boyish and chatty manner, the messenger informed Corvus that Milvus suggested a few places to search based on what the dealer knew of their habits. Corvus felt annoyed that Milvus might find their habits predictable. After all, he had left Milvus with only the address of their lodgings. A mercenary's reputation for cleverness and secrecy was crucial. According to the boy, Milvus had expressed that they were known for taking an afternoon rest for food and drink at a cellar wine bar where patrons sought escape from the afternoon heat and humidity. Corvus frowned. Possibly, the hunters were also being hunted. The boy dropped the message into his hand and scurried out.

Brooding over this notion, he scowled and opened the note. It stated they should return to the shop as soon as possible. "We've got to go, Jax. Milvus demands our immediate return."

Jax knitted his brows. "Some kind of problem?"

"It doesn't say. Drink up. I'll pay the owner and meet you on the street."

Dry winds barreled through the streets while Corvus and Jax wound their way back to Milvus' shop. A sudden gust rambled over them as they stepped through the doorway. Corvus shrugged off wayward strands fallen over his face. Jax ran a hand across his forehead. The bell announced their arrival. A servant approached, greeted them, and led them to the atrium. As they were about to seat themselves, Milvus and Alexander Kronus appeared. Corvus and Jax remained standing, but Milvus extended a hand toward the chairs, and they all took a seat.

Milvus crossed his legs and sat back comfortably, but Alexander sat closer to the edge of his seat. He had an air of readiness about him, but his blank face showed no indication of trouble or concern. Corvus decided to wait and not be the first to speak. Jax seldom led any discussion.

For a moment, an awkward silence fell over the group, but surprisingly, Alexander spoke up first. Corvus scratched his head and shifted in his chair. Why this urgent demand for their appearance, and why was Alexander taking the lead over Milvus? What news or problem must exist?

"We have information that may assist you in your search," Alexander began, and quickly added, "Another couple is looking for the sword. A Saxon called Nerian and his Egyptian woman, Marcella. They work for Accipiter, also an Egyptian, and a well-known merchant in Jerusalem."

Corvus sat deeper into his chair and folded his arms. "Interesting, but how does this affect us? For a while, we've known that this sword is a valued treasure to more than a few people—and with all due respect—like yourself. We'll just find it before anyone else." He extended his legs a little but did not smile, his mood still sour from the idea of being spied on by Milvus.

Alexander shook his head just a little, and a hint of what Corvus perceived as incredulity, shown on Alexander's face. As if he couldn't believe what he'd just heard.

The Greek merchant's reply was terse. "Your confidence is admirable, but I want you to follow this Nerian and Marcella. They may know things you don't. Up until now, you've had few leads, at least ones that were solid. I met them at Accipiter's shop. After the couple left, Accipiter pulled me aside and assured me they would succeed because he'd been informed by them that they were acquainted, at one time, with this Roman senator's daughter and her barbarian husband. When I pressed Accipiter further, he raised a finger to his lips and said, 'Keep this between us. Nerian and Marcella work for me, and I consider them friends. I'm telling you this, so you'll feel encouraged that they'll succeed. I can say no more.' I thanked him and left and came directly to Milvus. I thought it necessary, you should know."

Corvus couldn't help but narrow his eyes. "How will Goliath take this?"

Milvus jumped in. "Goliath looks only for the end result."

A cloud floating over the open roof dimmed the light shining into the atrium. Alexander sat back in his chair and rested his elbow on the armrest. "I'm obligated to do business with Goliath and not Accipiter, but I followed my own leads and instincts and was led to the Egyptian merchant. As I've been told, you're here for the dirty work. Understand that as a reputable merchant, I like to stay free of any implication of theft. I do not steal. I buy. My hunch is that you'll not be sorry if you follow the Saxon and his woman."

"Do you know where they are staying—what they look like?" Corvus asked, not hiding a smirk.

Alexander's eyes shone with condescension, and he responded stiffly, "I do. I questioned Marcella and Nerian before they left Accipiter's shop. They are at the High Tower Tavern and Inn. She's quite the beauty, and the Saxon is broad and strapping with black hair."

Corvus glanced sideways at Jax. "Got all that?"

Jax nodded with a grin. The space beside his middle tooth, where his incisor had been two days ago before he bit into a lamb bone, gaped back at them.

Corvus heard either Milvus or Alexander snort, but Milvus jumped in. "It's probably best you go now and find the High Tower Inn before dark. Start there."

"Milvus, be assured, we know our job." Corvus stood and gave Alexander only a passing glance. We'll leave now. The next time you see us, I'll be holding the sword. Tell Goliath, we'll be happy to take his coin." Corvus flicked his head at Jax, then walked to the door and out into the street, followed by his loyal companion.

JERUSALEM: Outside the High Tower Tavern and Inn

CORVUS

Corvus watched the entrance to Nerian and Marcella's lodging from across the street. He wiped a bead of sweat trickling from his cheek to his jaw and yawned. He and Jax were perched on a bench, bumped against a shaded wall in a tall, narrow alley that was used by vagrants to escape the afternoon heat. When they first arrived, Jax had pushed the man sleeping there, with an open carafe of stale-smelling wine by his side, out onto the ground. Jax threatened to kick the beggar's ass if he protested or tried to fight him. The man, showing wisdom even in his condition, had stumbled off and disappeared.

An hour had already passed, but there was no sign of them. Before taking their lookout, Corvus had entered the tavern and dropped a few coins in the owner's palm and inquired if the woman and Saxon were in their room. The tavern owner assured him with a discreet nod. He left and found this ideal location to watch the entrance with some semblance of comfort.

Jax lifted a water pouch to his lips and then offered Corvus a drink. He took it, drank with gusto, and then wiped his mouth. At that moment, a tall, black-haired man and a woman came through the entrance and stepped onto the street. A quiver of recognition sparked his memory. This was the same woman he had admired for her beauty at the Thirsty Goat Tavern in Caesarea. He wasn't certain, but he thought the black-haired man had also been her companion that day. In any case, they matched the description given to him by Alexander. Corvus was more than interested now; he was definitely intrigued.

How coincidental that their path had crossed once before with the Egyptian woman and her Saxon companion—most likely her lover. Unless, she felt no interest in the Saxon, but what man could resist her? Corvus would never refuse such a woman. He chuckled to himself. A man could dream.

"Ain't that the peach we saw in that tavern in Caesarea?" Jax asked, in a low voice.

"I believe so. What luck. Our familiarity with their appearance will help keep them in our sights. It appears they are headed in a certain direction and in a hurry. Come, we cannot lose them. They may know where to find the Roman woman and her barbarian husband. The gods may reward us today, Jax."

Jax grunted. "I'll feel better when the sword is in our hands, and we're handing it over to Milvus and Valeria. Piss on Alexander. He's not paying us."

"I don't like him either, my friend, but Goliath can sell it to whomever he wants. Just as long as we get our money."

Corvus was forced to pick up his step with Jax behind him, as usual, when Nerian and Marcella disappeared around a corner. Corvus quickly came around the turn and spotted them not far ahead. "They're moving toward St. Stephen's Gate. Perhaps, they have information. Maybe, the senator's daughter is arriving in the city today. Hurry, Jax!" Corvus said, looking over his shoulder. Jax huffed a bit, but his pace was steady.

They wound through the market up steps and inclines, following the pair, but their course seemed ever bound for the city's main entrance. After a few minutes, Corvus saw an arch and a shaft of light streaming into the city from outside the stone wall. They were almost at St. Stephen's Gate. Nerian and Marcella walked with intention as if they must keep an appointment or meet someone. This pleased Corvus. He suspected that Marcella and Nerian's pace wasn't for a brisk afternoon stroll or to carry out some hasty shopping. He licked his lips and brushed an arm across his brow. His heart beat faster. He and Jax would get this prize. His muscles tightened, and he stepped quickly. What lay ahead?

Nerian suddenly stopped and pulled Marcella with him to the right side of the gate. They stood in a shadow against the wall and looked outside of the entrance. Corvus and Jax swung behind them and followed their gaze. Merchants and native dwellers approached the sentries keeping watch and filed past.

Off the center plaza, near the steps, stood the palm-covered stand where two Roman soldiers handled the business of new arrivals. One looked at a document while the other spoke with a man, pulling a small cart laden with produce. Passing him along, he questioned the next two men in monk's robes, followed by a small group of pilgrims. A third soldier, arms clasped behind his back, stood off to the side, surveying the stream of visitors.

The sun passed its peak, crushed down on the city. Corvus leaned against a sturdy booth that held brass pots. Jax squatted on his heels beside him. When the merchant bellowed, ordering them to find another spot, Corvus tossed him a coin and firmly placed his hand on the hilt of his sword, jutting from his belt. The merchant caught the offering, raised a hand in submission, and looked away. Corvus smirked and swung his eyes back toward Nerian and Marcella.

The Saxon leaned against the wall. Marcella had taken a seat on a granite block beside him. An hour trudged by when the Saxon suddenly stood taller as if alerted. Corvus looked past him, out into the open, and toward the sentry station. At first, he had to look twice. A tall blond barbarian and two men stood in front of the soldier's station.

"Your brow is creased. What do you see?" Jax asked, rising from his sitting position.

Corvus raised a finger toward his companion. "Wait, something is happening." He watched the blond barbarian take a small sidestep. Corvus could see a petite, brown-haired woman standing just in front of the barbarian.

"Jax, I believe we've found the Roman woman and her husband. They're talking to the soldiers. It looks like they're trying to enter the city."

"Are you sure?" Jax craned his neck in the same direction.

"I'd bet my right hand on it," he grinned, "well maybe, my little finger. Need my hand to fight. But, look at Nerian. His posture points like a hunting dog who's found his prey. And the beauty, Marcella, hangs on his shoulder, watching in the direction of the couple as well. This must be the Lady Arria and Garic her Frank husband."

Jax's eyebrows raised. "What will we do now?"

"Hold back and follow. Let Nerian and Marcella take the lead. Their actions will dictate ours, but in the end, we'll seize the sword. I can almost feel it in my hands."

JERUSALEM: St. Stephen's Gate

NERIAN

"I'm going to her," Marcella hissed and rushed forward.

Nerian grabbed her arm and pulled her back. "Think, woman! Your sister and her husband cannot know we're here. Our mission is to possess the sword and not to settle old scores, at least not now." He couldn't allow Marcella's temper to ruin their chances of possessing the sword.

Marcella stopped. Clenching her scarf to her mouth, she let loose a muffled cry into the gathered silk cupped in her hand wrought from pent-up anger.

Nerian squeezed her shoulder. "You'll have time enough to confront her, and I'll help you, but first, we must steal the sword from them and bring it to Accipiter. He'll sell it to the right person, most likely the weapons dealer Alexander, and then we can find Arria and Garic." Nerian knew it wouldn't be wise for Marcella to vent her temper or her desire for revenge before they had the prize.

Nor was it a lie when he said he would help her, but he wasn't sure how far he could or would go. He had fought beside Garic in Constantinople and came to respect the Lady Arria from the little time he spent with them, protecting the Crown of Thorns. What if Marcella wanted a reckoning that included physically harming Arria? Could he choose Arria's safety over his desire and love for Marcella? The thought disturbed him, and he squeezed Marcella's arm tighter to ensure she didn't leave his side. Marcella wrenched it away.

Brooding darkness in her eyes, she answered him, her words loaded with spite. "I hate her. When I see her, my blood screams for revenge. I want to hurt her like she hurt me."

Nerian heard the anguish in her voice, the unresolved nature of her words. He leaned in. "Then calm yourself, or all will be lost. The best vengeance is stealing the sword, a valuable object entrusted to your sister's care by Emperor Marcian. Think, Marcella. If Arria lost the weapon, her humiliation and disgrace would surely allow a stronger satisfaction to fill your bones. Be patient, follow me. The sword can be ours if we keep cool heads and sharp minds."

Marcella looked down a moment. When she looked up, a shiny glimmer welled in her eyes. She sniffed and held back her tears. "As always, your calmer nature rings true. We need the weapon and the money that will spring from it. I can wait, but you must promise me my day, my reckoning with Arria." She stared at him, seeking his assurance.

He nodded. "I promise your day will happen. But all this talk distracts us. For now, we must track Arria and Garic and assess the situation. Where are they headed, and which of them carries the sword? Will they spend the night in the city? Will an opportunity present itself, or must we create one? Our thoughts should be occupied with devising a plan and one which can work. We need success."

At first, a disappointed pout tugged the corners of Marcella's mouth, but then, she sighed. Standing straighter, she flashed him a consenting smile, "What next?" she asked.

Relief washed over Nerian. "Let's move closer to the gate. Watch what unfolds between them and the soldiers. I doubt if we'll be able to hear what is said, but if we do, even better, but we must be ready to follow them and stay out of sight. Secrecy is our weapon." Nerian took Marcella's hand. "We can do this, but we must be smart. Right now, cunning is our best way to the prize." He squeezed her fingers and emphasized, *"Can I trust you on this, Marcella?"*

She closed her fingers tighter around his and nodded. "You can trust me . . . my love," she said, and her brown eyes grew warm.

Nerian winced. A jolting realization of what she said coursed through him. She called him 'my love.' She had declared to him what he felt about her for a while. He smiled back and cupped her cheek. "Our trust and love will make us stronger. Now, let's get that sword," he said with determination. He clutched the back of her neck and kissed her lips. Then turning on his heel, he led the way.

XX

A Conspiracy of Spies

JERUSALEM: St. Stephen's Gate—The 3rd day of Junius,
Afternoon

CORVUS

"**M**y money is on the blond barbarian." Corvus grinned while he stared at the senator's daughter and her companions. "He looks like a Frank, and most likely a noble. They wear their hair long. I'm betting he's the one carrying the sword."

Corvus stood beside Jax. They stared at the three men dressed in barbarian gear and a petite woman wearing a loose-fitting scarf over brown curls. The barbarians and lady stood in front of the sentry station, talking to the soldiers.

Jax asked, "Why choose the long-hair? Why not the shorter one, also resembling a Frank? Or even their companion?"

Corvus exhaled with exasperation and shook his head. "It's obvious to me that the long-hair is the leader. According to Milvus, the blond barbarian is called . . . uhm." Corvus fumbled for a name.

With a broad grin, Jax rushed in with "*Garic.*"

"Whatever it is," Corvus bristled. Jax's smile was too broad for his liking. "We know his woman's name is Arria, and they're working for the emperor. The barbarian, *Garic*, would have to be the keeper of this damn sword." Corvus thought a second. To protect his pride, in case he was wrong, he added, "But if not him, then I'd say it's the other Frank—the scarred one. He seems like a protector and fighter to me."

"I agree. Their companion may be a servant," Jax replied as he looked again toward the group.

"We'll have to follow them. See where they're going first. We can't attack them here. Besides, right now, we're outnumbered." Corvus scratched his head and peered at his fingers, checking for lice. Satisfied all was good, he rubbed his hand on his vest and added, "There are Nerian and Marcella to consider as well. They're also following Arria and Garic in search of the sword. We need some time and a solid plan. We cannot fail."

Jax wiped sweat from his brow and muttered, "Yeah, probably not a good idea, disappointing Goliath."

"Hate to think what might happen if we fail him," Corvus replied, but watched Arria and Garic and their two companions pass under the middle arch and into the market.

Slowly the newly arrived group moved among the shoppers and pilgrims past the stalls and through the streets. Corvus watched as they took in the sites like wayfarers stepped into a new world. They strolled at a steady pace but gazed at clothes, fabrics, ornate lamps, and cured meats, hanging from the shop awnings as they walked the avenue. At times, Arria stopped for a moment and touched the wares. Garic commented as she held a few items or pointed to others, but touching her elbow urged her along.

At a fruit stall, Garic reached into his coin purse and paid the vendor who handed Arria a small sack filled with figs. She quickly gave a few to each man and then bit into one herself as they walked along. While the foursome moved farther into the market, Corvus also kept an eye on Nerian and Marcella, just ahead of them. The couple stalked the foursome, not realizing they were being followed as well.

Corvus watched as Arria and Garic and their two companions passed a few streets off the Cardo Maximus. Then, they turned into a wider lane lined with the western sun. Arria stopped and questioned a merchant who pointed up the street, nodded his head, and smiled as they continued in the direction that he indicated.

Corvus held Jax back in a cool shadow when Nerian and Marcella, also observing Arria's interaction with the man, stopped not far in front of him.

"Careful, Jax," Corvus warned. "Don't want to be discovered. If memory serves me from our scouting trips, this street leads up an incline, a few steps, and ends at a two-story building." Abruptly, Corvus turned away and faced in the other direction, "Turn around swiftly and follow me," he hissed, his voice terse. Jax blinked but followed his order without hesitation.

Corvus knew that after many adventures and their years working together, Jax would respond and never question when commanded that way. Corvus led them behind a few barrels stacked behind an oil stand. "I think Marcella spotted us. She looked right at me, and her brow knitted, and her eyes narrowed. If I recognized her from the tavern in Caesarea, perhaps she had an inkling about me. I don't want them to think they're being followed."

Corvus rested his hand on one of the barrels and deftly looked around its rotund and wooden frame. Marcella and Nerian were moving up the street. He saw Marcella give a furtive look over her shoulder but move on beside Nerian. Glancing back at Jax, he rapidly added, "Anonymity is our first advantage. And our best plan, right now, is to follow Nerian and Marcella—but carefully. Let the Saxon and his woman, following Arria and Garic, lead us to their destination.

MARCELLA

"Do you think we're being followed?" Marcella asked Nerian as they walked along the market street, tracking Arria and Garic and their two companions. The day's heat waxed at its warmest, and Marcella loosened her scarf and tied it around her waist.

Nerian came to a stop. Alarm showed on his face. He squinted as the late afternoon sunlight illuminated his eyes. "What makes you think that?" he asked and glanced around.

Resting a hand on his arm, Marcella leaned in closer. "When Arria stopped and questioned the merchant, and we hid behind a shop's curtain, I turned to view a few baubles. It was then that I saw a tall, dark-haired man near a stall across from us. He was looking in our direction. I was struck; he seemed familiar. But I can't remember where I may have seen him."

Nerian frowned. "Marcella, we pass people every day in this market. Perhaps he's a vendor or a customer of Accipiter. Who would follow us, and why?" Skepticism penetrated his tone. "We have nothing anyone wants. We're the predators . . . not the prey."

A light breeze lifted the ends of Marcella's scarf, and she swiped it to the side. "I've learned to pay attention even when a subtle semblance of doubt or call it an instinct rifles through me. There may be others looking for the sword."

"If this is true, why follow us? We do not have the weapon. We're searching for it, too."

"Precisely," she snapped, but bit her lip and started again. "What if another hunter has learned *we* are looking for the artifact but knows nothing about Arria and Garic? They might think we know more than we do or can lead them to the prize."

Nerian thoughtfully tilted his head. "I suppose it's possible, but I think it unlikely. Accipiter has many connections and sources. Chances are he would know if there was a strong pursuit for the weapon by other individuals. No. I think your imagination is running rampant." Nerian reached for her hand. With the gentlest pressure, he squeezed her fingers. "Hide your fears and come. We cannot let the Frank and your sister get too far ahead, or we'll lose them." His sober glance held affection. "Hurry now. Let's regain them in our sights. We must discover where they're going and their intent."

Marcella pursed her lips, feeling unsure rather than angry. She wanted to change—love again and trust Nerian. She must begin with faith in his opinion. After all, he was the mercenary with years of experience. Perhaps he was right. She'd seen the faces of thousands of men in her life. This particular man may have crossed her path at an earlier time, or he had a face that doubled for many like him and gave the appearance of familiarity. Nonetheless, Nerian was absolutely right about one thing. They needed to move on and track Arria and Garic. Marcella nodded, clasped her free hand over his, holding her fingers, and pecked his lips with a kiss. "I will follow. Lead the way to this treasure and our good fortune."

Nerian spun on his heel, and Marcella set pace behind him.

JERUSALEM: The Cardo Maximus—The 3rd day of Junius, Afternoon

GARIC

The trip through the market was engaging and pleasant, but Garic worried all the same. It proved difficult for him to shed his suspicions, and he kept an eye out for signs of trouble or anything that seemed unusual—a bystander in a shop alcove, or a pedestrian behind him that stopped when they stopped, and then started when they moved forward again. He also asked Samuel to scan the rooftops and instructed Telemachus to guard the rear and occasionally sweep the crowd behind them for any suspicious activity or shifty-looking followers.

Soon, they would reach the offices belonging to the bishop and patriarch. Earlier in the day, before they left The Olive Tree Inn, Arria had sent a message to Bishop Anastasius announcing their arrival and requesting an audience with the most reverend bishop. Through the cleric, a meeting would be arranged with his all-holiness, Juvenal, Patriarch of Jerusalem, to reveal to him the sword and discuss where the relic might be enshrined.

"Arria, perhaps we should have waited for a response from the bishop before coming into the city and seeking his office." His eyes roamed over a few heads while he spoke. Arria kept pace beside him. Aware that his one step equaled two of hers, he slowed himself.

Dropping her shawl from her shoulders into the crooks of her arms and fanning a hand in front of her face, she replied, "We cannot delay. After the theft at the monastery, I am fearful, not only for the sword's safety but ours as well. However, we must hasten and honor the task given to us." Curls danced around Arria's cheeks as her eyes glimmered with resolve. "I long to return to our daughter and then, our home. The letter we carry from the emperor will guarantee an audience with the patriarch. It's just a matter of when and where."

Garic linked his arm with Arria's, pulled her closer, and increased his step. He knew that Telemachus and Samuel behind them would recognize his gesture as a need for some privacy. He leaned toward her ear and lowered his voice, "Even though we are about to meet with these church fathers, have you given any further consideration to Samuel's viewpoint? Are you still convinced the sword should rest in the hands of Christians?" He held her gaze with his. "The sword belonged to a Jewish king. David had it forged, and in its creation, he sought to make amends for his sins. Samuel says that the diamond star, hidden within the pommel, alone carries more symbolic value than material worth. He believes the sword should rest in the hands of the Jewish people."

Arria gave him a sideways glance. "Should we have this discussion now?" she asked but perceived he was intent on speaking about the matter. She sighed. "If so, I empathize with Samuel and what the sword means to his people, but I'm thinking about what the sword can mean to all the pilgrims who come to Jerusalem. Have you forgotten who we represent? I'll not fail the emperor. We must complete the mission he chose us to do." She shook her head and whispered, "No. I cannot return the sword to the Jews."

"Do you fear the emperor's wrath if you defy his request?" Garic was unable to hide his frown.

"The emperor would never harm me; although, he'd be irate. He might order us to return and explain." Arria paused. She seemed to weigh her words. "But, . . . I see the sword in the Church of the Holy Sepulchre. In honor of my father and all people who believe in sacred things. David was a shepherd boy chosen by God to govern his people, and from David's regal roots came Christus, who carried a message of peace and love to the world. An idea we can learn from." Arria's frustration shown through the firm sound in her voice and the weighty delivery in her words.

A prickling heat rushed from Garic's ears to the back of his neck. He stared back at her. "We can speak of this later," he said, fighting to hide his irritation. This wasn't the time or place for a debate. "We've requested an audience. Let's see what comes of our meeting with the bishop."

Arria took a breath, and her tone softened. Her expression warmed, and she rested her hand on his arm. "The sword symbolizes human frailty, faith, and redemption. It deserves to be seen—as an inspiration."

He remained quiet. Perhaps, Arria was right. The relic in Christian hands would be protected and shown for all to admire. And yet, he understood Samuel's feelings. The relic belonged with the Jewish people. It would act as a reminder of their heritage and unity and offer them hope in the face of adversity, Roman oppression, and mistreatment by many. Garic was a Christian, but also a barbarian. He had experienced Roman cruelty and disdain. Just not to the degree and history of the Jewish people as Samuel had shared with him.

A late afternoon breeze began to rise and float through the market. The cooling temperature offered them some relief. This new wave of fresh air made Garic think. He loved Arria and respected her conviction, but he found it difficult to dismiss Samuel's belief and opinion. Perhaps with the right argument, she might change her mind. Still, in the end, he knew it must be Arria's decision. Golden rays of dwindling light dashed between the stalls and painted the pavement. As he gazed at the sandy stones beneath each step, an idea suddenly came to him. If Arria chose to deliver the sword into Christian hands, maybe he could convince her to give David's diamond star of atonement to Samuel. Aside from Arria, Samuel, and himself, no one knew of its existence.

In Garic's view, Samuel would gain for his people the best prize of all. But, would Samuel feel the same? Garic looked over his shoulder behind him. Samuel, about ten feet back, was scanning the rooftops. He noticed Garic's glance and smiled. Garic nodded, grinned back, then turned and looked at Arria. "Let's hurry if we're to find the bishop. I have a feeling all will be well."

A grin tugged the corners of Arria's mouth. She tilted her head and shot him a skeptical look. "Why so confident, my lord?"

Garic grasped her elbow, stepped off the pathway, and brought them to a stop. He grinned back. "I have an idea. We could offer Samuel Bathsheba's star as a compromise."

Arria's happy expression faded. She grew somber and lowered her voice, "My love, I cannot separate the star from the sword. It wouldn't be right." Her green eyes and expectant smile waited for his response.

"Would it make that much of a difference?" He asked, patiently, but pushed his suggestion a bit more. "The star is an icon his people can treasure."

Even though Arria could be outspoken, her momentary silence told Garic she was thinking like a true envoy and carefully choosing her words. She took the fate of the sword seriously.

"I believe the sword and the star belong together as King David intended," she replied. "I want to fulfill our mission, share it with pilgrims, and honor my father's memory. Please, love, will you accept my position regarding the relic?"

Garic looked briefly away, then raised his glance to Arria and nodded. He seldom could refuse her wishes and would respect her feelings and duty as envoy. "Perhaps, you're right, Arria. The star is not ours to give," he said, as Samuel and Telemachus, having caught up to them, waited on the street.

"Thank you," Arria said, and smiling took his hand, then they joined the men.

JERUSALEM: The Offices of the Bishops and Patriarch—The 3rd day of Junius, Afternoon

ARRIA

Arria and Garic proceeded through the market while Samuel and Telemachus followed. With a crisp pace, they turned off the Cardo Maximus, just south of the Church of the Holy Sepulchre, and entered the street leading to the headquarters and offices of the bishops and patriarch. Arria stopped and questioned a merchant, sitting next to a barrel of barley. He pointed ahead, and while the men listened, he informed her that the building she was seeking stood just beyond the Church of St. John the Baptist.

She thanked the vendor, and they quickly moved on. As they passed the church and approached the end of the street, the building loomed before them tall and square. Its two-story stonework matched most of the surrounding buildings—camel brown and covered with a fine dust floating in the wind. The doorway arched below a rooftop with a jagged parapet that offered defense and protection if needed. Four arched, latticed windows, an arm's length apart and carved in Romanesque style, lined the second floor. Two similar windows flanked the filigreed, iron gate below, covering the entrance's black door.

Upon their arrival, Samuel and Telemachus decided to remain outside on the steps leading to the building's entrance, and where a lone merchant sold camel's milk from a small stand. Both men decided to buy a drink and find respite on one of the benches against the building's wall in the shade.

Arria and Garic entered the vestibule greeted by stone walls and shadows in dim light. Small sconces burned along the adjoining hallway, creating a dusky glow and a feeling of sanctioned authority. Farther down the hall, she could see additional doors on each side of the corridor, and at the end, double doors facing them stood open. Inside, rows of chairs and a small altar were visible, indicating a chapel.

To her left—near the outer wall and a tall window—a priest sat at a writing table. On top of the polished surface, a lit candle stood next to a vessel that held ink and a reed pen. A few rolled parchments and a brass stylus also rested nearby. The priest smiled and asked, "May I be of assistance?"

Garic rested a palm on Arria's back, making way for her. She stepped up to the cleric's desk. "Good afternoon. We would like to meet with Bishop Anastasius. We've come from Constantinople on business for Emperor Marcian."

The priest's eyebrows raised, but he replied in a straightforward manner, "I'm afraid, my lady, His Most Reverend Bishop has been called away until tomorrow when he'll return. I am Father Isaac. Do you have an appointment?"

Arria smiled and answered politely, "I sent a messenger early this morning from the inn, where we are rooming. When did the bishop leave?"

Father Isaac rose from behind his desk, not far from a large paneled door with a brass handle. A sign beside the door displayed the title, Offices of the Bishops. "Bishop Anastasius is quite busy, and when he least expects it, often a problem will arise that he must handle immediately. I'm sorry. Perhaps, I can help you."

"In truth, we are really here to see his All-Holiness, Juvenal. As I mentioned, we come in the service of Emperor Marcian. Our mission is of the utmost importance and confidential."

"Oh," the priest replied and knitted his brow. "I'm afraid I've no authority to decide for the bishop who may or may not have an audience with the patriarch. Please, return tomorrow. Would you like to make an appointment now to see the bishop? The afternoon grows late. We're near to sunset and Vespers, and I must close the office." Father Isaac's eyes narrowed, and he waited. His hands rested on a codex, obviously for keeping a record of appointments.

Arria sighed and glanced at Garic.

"We have no choice, Arria. Only the bishop can arrange our meeting, and he's gone. If we get here early in the morning and wait for the bishop, we might be the first people to enlist his time. Being early to meet with the bishop, might also provide us with the opportunity to make an appointment the same day with the patriarch, if he isn't too busy."

Arria sighed and sulked a moment. *If only we had arrived the day before*, she thought, but quickly rebounded. The good news was that they had come ahead without waiting for a reply to their message at the inn. They were here in Jerusalem and would definitely return tomorrow early in the morning. They knew their way to the offices and even who to speak to first, Father Isaac and then Bishop Anastasius. It was only one more day, after weeks and days. "I agree. Tomorrow will have to do."

Garic nodded and hiked his shoulder bag closer. "Let the good father close his office and go to his prayers. We'll find a place for supper that has a reputation for its food, and perhaps its fish."

Arria turned toward the priest. "Thank you, Father Isaac. How early can we see the bishop?"

"You can be his first appointment of the day, but get here early enough so he can see you soon after the morning service. There will be a line of pilgrims and residents who have already arranged to meet with him."

Arria and Garic bowed their heads in a polite farewell and left the building. Once outside, they found Samuel and Telemachus seated on a bench. Garic chose one close by, and placing his bag beside his feet, he sat and stretched his long legs. He ran his fingers through his wheat-colored hair and off his brow, highlighting the v-shaped point in the center of his hairline. He scratched his beard and yawned.

Arria sat beside him and fanned her face a few times with her hand. "I'm afraid it proved harder than expected to gain entrance through the gate. We should spend the night in the city. Besides, the time needed in the morning to get here, from The Olive Tree, will not allow us to be first in line to see the bishop."

"I agree. It's best not to risk getting Samuel out and back in again. And if there were delays or unexpected obstacles from staying at the inn, we might miss another opportunity to meet with Juvenal. The patriarch appears as busy as the pope."

"On this side of the empire, a patriarch has the same status as a pope in the west."

"Your Christian world is complicated. The Franks have our pagan priests, but it's our chief who rules all."

Arria laughed. "Even pagan priests carry a special power that can control chiefs and kings. We did live in Attila's camp and saw the power the shaman and even Basina, who was their healer, wielded."

"True enough, but in the end, it was Attila who ruled," Garic persisted with a smile.

"Yes. Marcian does control the east." Arria snuggled closer to Garic, and with the back of her fingers, she caressed the stubble on his jaw. "And the empire and the church together make for an interesting balance of power," she added sweetly.

Garic grinned. "Kiss me."

Arria felt her body tingle. She suppressed the smile rising to her lips. "My love, people will see. We're in front of the church offices as well."

He placed his hand on her knee and squeezed. "Do you always worry about being proper?" he asked in a husky voice.

The skin on her leg burned beneath her skirt from his touch. "I'm afraid I do—but I have been known to make exceptions." She looked into his blue eyes. They gleamed with excitement.

"Then make one now," he coaxed and pulled her close.

"You're my husband rogue, and I love you," she whispered and kissed him, a bit longer than she intended. Afterward, she placed his hand on her stomach. "I felt our child, perhaps our son, stir inside me when our lips touched."

"See, your lack of propriety was worth it, was it not?"

Arria smiled and hugged him. "I'll always be your temptress—at least, in my heart."

"That's the place to start Arria, in the heart. You'll always have mine, even when I'm a rogue no longer."

Taking his hand in hers, she threaded her fingers through his. "The man I love is more than a rogue, he's a warrior and protector. Our destiny was told by your tribe's priestess. I whispered the words to you after the battle at Catalaunum as you lay in sleep beneath the veil of consciousness. We were meant to be together—in the shadow or the light."

"Our love lives in those words." Garic kissed her fingers and stole another kiss. A presence crossed them, and they looked up.

Samuel and Telemachus stood before them, raising their cups of camel's milk. "To love," they chirped, "but can we go now and find a place to eat?"

Arria and Garic laughed and jumped to their feet. "You two lead the way," Garic barked. "Find us a place to eat—and a place to sleep."

XXI

In the Shadow of Beggars

JERUSALEM: Market Place—St. John's Street, The 3rd day
of Junius, Afternoon

ARRIA

Telemachus took the lead and proceeded down the steps, but Garic called him to stop. Arria drew up beside Samuel. Telemachus, on the last step, turned toward them. Garic sniffed the air. "My nose is sending me in that direction," he said with a grin and pointed down the street toward the Church of St. John the Baptist, where they had passed earlier after leaving the Cardo Maximus. The others raised their noses as well and smiled. The savory scents of garlic and onion and fish frying in oil floated past them.

Everyone laughed, and Samuel added, "Let's hurry before there's a line. Telemachus lead the way."

Telemachus moved at a crisp gate and brought them to the fishmonger's stall. A small line was already forming. Beneath a four-poster awning stood a rimmed table filled with different selections of seafood—Telemachus pointed out several varieties: sturgeon, gray and red mullet, and a cluster of moray eels. Beside the table, an iron kettle perched over a fire banked with bricks. Inside the metal pot, large and small pieces of fish fried in bubbling oil.

"Red mullet, rolled in grain flour and seasoned with salt and thyme is our offering today," announced a short, robust woman with a slotted wooden paddle in her hand. She dipped the utensil into the oil, lifted pieces of the sizzling mullet, and dropped them into several clay bowls, each filled with a hunk of bread, on the nearby counter. "Take what you like and pay my husband. Those few tables and benches behind me are here for your convenience—if you prefer to sit. Kindly leave your dishes in the box behind the tables."

Arria was the first to be served, and the men followed. She was grateful the vendor offered the added hospitality of tables for their customers to rest and enjoy the food. They sat in the shade and found it much more comfortable than a random crate or chest for her to sit on while the men stood.

As they ate, Telemachus related a bit of what he knew about the fishing in Palaestina. Arria watched as Samuel, not wanting to draw suspicion from Telemachus by appearing knowledgeable about the region's commerce, sat silent. He occasionally nodded and mentioned he'd heard in the port town of Caesarea, some of what Telemachus was saying and how the fish came from the Mediterranean, Sea of Galilee, and Gulf of Aqaba. They marveled at the variety they'd seen on the table, the tasty meal of mullet fried in aromatic olive oil, and the warm bread.

The sounds of children running and laughing through the street, and a few vendors hawking their wares, mixed with the heat and light of the day. Arria basked in the smells and actions and peaceful liveliness of it all. She seized and absorbed those seconds, but they fell away when a young woman selling drinks from a tray strapped around her neck, approached their table. She offered them cups of honeyed-wine to wash down their meal. They accepted, and as Garic paid her, she asked in a friendly manner, "Are you pilgrims new to Jerusalem?"

Arria spoke up, "We are."

"Well, if you're looking for lodgings, I know of a place that's clean and safe."

"Our companion," Arria pointed to Telemachus, "mentioned moments before you appeared that he heard of an inn close to David's Tower, not far from here, inside the city wall."

"Oh yes," the wine maid interrupted with enthusiasm. The Red Torch. The owner, Zebedee, runs a proper establishment, which has a reputation for serving hearty meals. Tell him you spoke with Rachel. He'll treat you very well.

"It's nice to meet you, Rachel. Can you direct us?" Garic asked but glanced at Samuel, knowing full well, he most likely knew from his visits on the sanctioned Jewish holy days, where to find the inn. Nevertheless, they needed to maintain the pretense of visiting pilgrims to anyone they encountered.

"Of course. Just go up the street to the bishop's offices and then turn south onto the road that runs along the western wall of Sion. You'll see it shortly after you pass the tower."

When Rachel finished speaking, Arria replied, "Thank you so much for your help."

"And the wine," Garic added. The men nodded.

As the young woman departed, a brash and unexpected wind flew through the awning and rippled their clothes. The cool sensation tingled their skin and raised tendrils off their brows and ears. They finished their last drops of wine, and with reluctance, Garic reminded them that the afternoon was advancing, and the sun would soon set. They needed to find the inn. "We should avoid getting caught on the road at night. The stars are bright, and the moon is full, but better to have clear sight."

They rose from the table and made ready to leave. Arria took a breath. Perhaps ignited by the sudden burst of wind, she felt an overwhelming fear. The same sensation she felt before entering Jerusalem. Now, a warning, running from her chest down to her toes, gripped her body. Dread surrounded her like an avenging demon. *Danger lies ahead* whispered in her thoughts.

She felt a surge of tears and took a breath. She raised her veil and gently shook her head, not letting the men see. *It's only the baby and my protective nature, ruling my emotions. All will be well*, she reassured herself. *We've come this far. We're almost there. Nothing bad will happen.* She moved beside Garic and took his hand. *Nothing bad will happen.*

JERUSALEM: Market Place—St. John's Street, Minutes Earlier

CORVUS

The day's heat faded like spilled wine on soft dirt, but the light in the market still glowed. Corvus watched as Arria, Garic, and their two companions purchased food and seated themselves beneath the fishmonger's awning. The smell of the frying fish made his stomach growl. He licked his lips and toyed with sending Jax to buy some. Why not? They could eat as they watched from several yards away on the corner of a small side street that led to the public latrines.

"Jax. I know it's warm, but raise your hood, to be safe, and get us some of that fish before it's gone."

"They don't know us," Jax said, frowning.

"Remember, Nerian and Marcella are somewhere nearby. I'm pissed that we lost them. But they must be watching the happy diners as well." Corvus shook his head. "No, can't take a chance. They might recognize you—like we recognized them."

Jax grumbled and raised his hood.

"See the wine maid coming our way?"

"*You* buy the wine," Jax replied, his tone sullen. "I could use a drink."

"I'm afraid water will have to do for now. I just had an idea. After I speak to the young woman, follow her to the fish stall, and then, get our fish."

Jax looked puzzled, but before he could speak up, Corvus waved the wine maid over.

She wove her way through a small group of shoppers and walked up to them. "May I help you, sir?" she asked, with a bright smile on her face.

"Indeed," Corvus answered and shot her a robust grin. "Interested in making a few extra coins for yourself today?"

Her eyes narrowed, and her voice sounded wary, "Possibly. What do you want?"

Corvus shook his head and laughed. "It's not what you think. I'm looking for information."

"What kind of information?"

"Go to the fishmonger. Attempt to sell the tall, blond man, the dark-haired woman, and their two companions eating at the table, some wine. But this is important. In your most becoming way—find out where they are going. Once you have this information, return to me, and I'll pay you." Corvus waited a few seconds, bouncing the coin purse in his hand. "Is it a deal?"

The wine girl smiled. "I can certainly try. Will I find you here afterward?"

"Yes. Hopefully, eating fish and awaiting your reply. Remember. Question them without drawing their suspicion."

Now she laughed. "You must be a visitor. I'm Rachel and well-known in Jerusalem for my friendly, persuasive manner and complete discretion. My master has no better servant, and my sales are always at the top."

"Then I'm encouraged," he answered, and tossed his head in the fish stall's direction. "Off with you now, before they leave."

She smirked at him, lifted her chin, and turned on her heel. Corvus watched as she sped toward the fishmonger's stand. He glanced at Jax. "Go now and get us some of that fish. I'm starving."

Corvus plopped the fried mullet fillet in his mouth in one bite. He chewed slowly. It steamed on the inside, but the savory taste was worth the oily heat clinging to the skin. Jax made it back before Rachel. She was still speaking with the Roman woman and her Frank husband. As he and Jax stood there chewing and gulping down water from their pouches, they watched Rachel leave the foursome and walk away. A few minutes later, she circled around and came up the alley where they stood. She had a big grin on her face, and she promptly extended her palm.

"Wait a minute, young miss. You'll be paid, but first, I must hear what you have to say."

Rachel pouted but replied, "They asked me if I knew of an inn near David's Tower. I explained the inn they were seeking is The Red Torch—very clean and hospitable, and safe too. The owner's sons protect the premises."

"Will they go there?"

"I believe so. They were almost done eating when I left."

Corvus looked over Rachel's head and saw from the distance that Garic was standing. He quickly pulled the money from his coin purse and gave it to the girl. "Thank you."

"Anytime, sir," she said and scurried off, collecting empty cups as she went to return them to her master's wine stand.

Corvus leered at her buttocks as she faded into the busy street.

"Well, friends. We meet again."

Corvus jerked around, taken by surprise. Alexander Kronus stood with his arms folded over his chest and with Milvus' annoying messenger boy beside him. "Don't be frightened. I'm here to help," he said, laughing.

"How did you find us?" Corvus snapped, bristling from Alexander's jibe.

"Zoran is an excellent tracker. One of the reasons Milvus bought him. The boy spent his younger years in the cedar forests of Phoenice. I believe his relatives were hunter-warriors who had a falling out with the Romans. "Isn't that right, Zoran?" The boy nodded. "But I'll not bore you with a slave's story—he does what he's told. Have you found the Roman woman, Arria, and her husband?"

"Yes. Just ahead at the fishmonger, eating under the striped awning."

Alexander unfolded his arms and took a coin from a small purse, hanging from his belt, and beside a brightly polished sword. He instructed Zoran, "Buy yourself some fish. When the blond barbarian and those with him leave, climb a nearby crate and wave that red scarf around your neck several times, then return to Milvus." The servant beamed gratefully and ran off toward the fishmonger. After the boy departed, Alexander swung an iron gaze toward Corvus.

Corvus stood taller and met Alexander eye to eye. "No insult intended, but can you fight? Many merchants find it a problem and hire men like Jax and me for jobs that require force, and on occasion, extreme violence. You might hurt your hands." Corvus meant his words but couldn't hide a smirk.

A slight flush rose in Alexander's face, and he grew deadly quiet as he looked down, and then, he raised his eyes. Throwing back his head, he laughed. "You may be a mercenary, but only a fool is quick to judge those he doesn't know. In my years, I've delivered more than a few men to Hade's door. At an early age, I realized that *only I* could truly protect myself—and vowed to become an agile swordsman. My skills were not honed from military life—like many. I found the best teachers who taught me everything I needed to know. You can rest easy. I'm not a hindrance, but rather, an asset. And—I believe— you're out-numbered."

Corvus soaked in Alexander's words. He crossed his arms, rested a hand on his chin, and tapped his foot in thought while Alexander gave him a contemptuous look. If he brought the Greek merchant, and now, it appeared—fighter—with them to steal the sword from three men and a woman, the odds would be more in their favor. After all, they were facing three men with obvious battle skills. Corvus dropped his arms and placed his hands on his hips. He took a breath and glanced at Jax who wide-eyed tilted his head as if to say: *The arrogant bastard has a point.* Corvus kicked at the dirt. Numbers to numbers, it was a smart and rational tactic. Perhaps Alexander would make this venture easier. Corvus balked a bit, but said, "If you're as good as you say you are . . . with a sword . . . it cannot hurt to have you."

"Trust me. I'm confident and very good," Alexander bragged.

"We'll see. Besides, we had Nerian and Marcella in our sights but lost them. They could bring us trouble as well."

Alexander rested his hand on his sword hilt and raised his hood. "That's possible. They do know me if they see me—but might assume you both work for me. This could distract them to our advantage. If not, I guess we'll deal with them, too."

Corvus smiled. "You're a ruthless bastard, after all. We can only win. In the end, Goliath must be satisfied ... and your involvement will ensure you a first bid on the prize."

"I'm planning on it, but no more talk." Alexander pointed in a direction not far from the fishmonger. The servant perched on a crate. "Look. Zoran is waving his scarf. Time to go." Alexander raised his hood. "A little camouflage cannot hurt us," he added and gestured toward their hoods.

Corvus and Jax followed Alexander's suggestion while Corvus wondered if the Greek thought he was leading them now.

Their hoods raised, Alexander looked at them. An odd gleam filled his eyes. "Let's get that sword, and one more thing—never call me bastard again."

JERUSALEM: Market Place—St. John's Street, Earlier

MARCELLA

"My feet hurt, and I'm thirsty," Marcella grumbled, tugging on Nerian's elbow. "I need to rest."

They wove their way through the crowd, anxious to keep Arria and Garic in view.

"Wodan's wolf eat me alive, Marcella," Nerian hissed. "Maybe this will spare me from your complaining. Or better yet, perhaps his sacred raven can peck at my brain and render me senseless, offering me relief from your demands."

Marcella stopped. Her temper at its height, she fumed inwardly. Why couldn't Nerian see that her nature was more sensitive to heat, excessive walking—in the past, she most often used litters and coaches to bring her places—and lack of food and drink. He was a warrior. She'd been raised a concubine. He couldn't expect her to change or become more resilient overnight. "You're unfair. I'm working hard to stay by your side, but at this pace, I feel spent. I'm withering."

An exasperated breath escaped Nerian's pressed lips. "Very well, let's keep Arria and Garic in our sights. If they rest, we will too. If not, I'll buy you food and drink, and I'll go on ahead. You can follow slowly and sit when you need to. When I learn their destination, I can return for you. Does this work?"

Marcella sulked but knew he spoke wisely and nodded. They couldn't lose Arria and Garic. Possessing the sword would provide them wealth and freedom.

"Follow and trust me, Marcella. They'll tire soon, but if we're to rob them, we must know their destination. He grabbed her hand and pulled her through the market street before she could protest or even agree. Within a few minutes, Nerian stopped in front of a vendor who sold satchels, coin purses, and pouches. "There, Marcella. See. The street has ended at—the sign says, 'Offices of the Bishops.' Garic and Arria are entering the building now. Those two men in their company are buying camel's milk from the vendor."

Marcella watched as Garic, his blond hair raised by the breeze, held the door for Arria—*always the princess*, Marcella brooded—to enter first. The two men, holding their drinks, now walked toward a shady bench against the office wall. The one man, who resembled a Frank, struck her in an unexpected way. Something about his stature and black curls appeared familiar. Years had passed since her time spent with Arria in Gaul. So much had happened since the battle at Catalaunum, and her memory evaded her like water through fingers. It tugged at her, but she dismissed her observation in the same way she'd done with the man in the crowd. Marcella sighed. She needed to rest, quench her thirst.

Pretending to inspect a satchel, Nerian looked over his shoulder. "I think now might be a good time to get some refreshment and rest. Arria and Garic must be inquiring about something involving a bishop—perhaps the value of the sword? They might be preoccupied for a while." Nerian smiled at her and returned the satchel to the table as the merchant approached them. He nodded politely but waved the shopkeeper off and turned them down the street, leading them away from the offices. "As we followed them up the street, I saw a small shop selling hot bread and roasted lamb near the church and close by. Let's go there, eat and drink, and then return within the half-hour. Will this help you?"

A sense of relief flooded through Marcella, and she shoved her anger aside. "Oh, yes, that would be wonderful. I'm famished," she answered.

Nerian locked his arm with hers and led her down the street.

Marcella clung to him. She was sure, food, drink, and a place to sit in the shade would help revive her for whatever encounter lay ahead.

Within minutes they arrived at the shop. After finding a small table and bench, a boy, who appeared to be the shop owner's son, came to serve them. He spouted the day's offerings, and they eagerly agreed. Soon the young waiter arrived at the table with a plate heaped with steaming chunks of lamb. Cooked over an open pit near the shop's entrance, it gave off the aroma of cedarwood and succulent, spit-roasted meat. Marcella inhaled the fumes, and they ate with gusto, washing the lamb and pieces of bread down with wine. They ate in silence, each of them lost in their thoughts and hunger. After a bit, Nerian let out a belch, and Marcella laughed. "Not so loud," she scolded. "You'll draw attention to us. We don't want that."

Nerian slapped a fist against his chest and let out a weaker burp.

Marcella rolled her eyes but giggled all the same.

"I will admit," Nerian paused with a sheepish grin, "somewhat reluctantly—you were right, my darling. We needed food and drink, but we must be going. Arria and Garic might be finished with their business. Let us hurry."

For a brief moment, Marcella felt unwilling to leave, but Nerian knew best.

Without further discussion, they rose and left the shop. Nerian leading the way, they mingled with the pedestrians walking west toward the Offices of the Bishops. As they approached, Nerian grabbed Marcella's hand and pulled her to the side and into a lane between two shops. She watched as he scanned the stairs leading to the building, the benches, and the large door. She followed his gaze, as well.

"Shit," he spat, "They're not there." He scratched his head and kicked a small rock near his foot.

Marcella bit her lip. The time spent in the shop, resting and eating, had revived her body and spirit, but now, a pang of unwelcome guilt possessed her. What if they lost the sword because she insisted her needs were met and her desire for comfort was gratified. She closed her eyes, hoping that she'd see Arria and Garic on the steps or seated on a bench when she opened them. But when she raised her lids and looked again, neither they nor their companions were where she and Nerian had last seen them.

"Come with me now," Nerian barked and grabbed her hand. He proceeded down St. John's Street, heading back toward the Cardo. He looked from right to left. "Keep an eye out for them," he said in an impatient tone as he dragged her along. "We'll return to the beginning of St. John's, in case they passed us while we ate. If they've gone onto the Cardo, we could be in trouble, but it's good there are four of them." He moved briskly and stopped merchants and pilgrims along the way, asking if they'd seen a tall blonde man with companions. When he saw a girl at a wine cart filling glasses, he asked her as well.

"I may have seen them," she responded coyly, tilting her head. "Though I'm sure some coin would greatly help my memory."

Marcella peered at Nerian, who glanced at her sideways. The corner of his mouth rose, and he said as smooth as honey, "What's your name, sweet miss?"

She drawled, "Rachel."

"A lovely name."

Marcella watched as Nerian worked his charm.

"Rachel, let me help your memory with this generous offering." He poured several *denarii* from his pouch into her hand. "Here. Now, what can you tell us?"

Rachel, the wine girl, gazed into her hand, and she grinned. "The blond pilgrim travels with his wife and two companions. They asked about lodgings near David's Tower. I told them The Red Torch is the closest inn to the tower and how to get there."

"How long ago was this?"

"Not too long. If you hurry, you might find them finishing their meal at the fishmonger's stand under the awning. Its closer to the Cardo," she said, pointing down the street.

Marcella nudged Nerian, and he plopped another coin on top of the others.

Rachel beamed with delight, and Marcella asked her, "From the fishmonger to The Red Torch, what is the way?"

"Take St. John's to the Offices of the Bishops. Then, travel south and take the path along the western wall of Sion."

"Thank you, Rachel," Nerian replied with his wolfish grin, turned, and pointed Marcella in the direction of the fishmonger. He took a few steps. "We should cover our faces, in case we stumble onto them as they are leaving, but once we find this foursome, it will be easier to follow them, especially since we know their destination."

As Nerian began to mask his face, Marcella pulled him away from the wine stand.

"What are you doing?" He asked brusquely.

"Hear me. We should stay here ahead of them," she suggested firmly. "We'll watch everyone moving west toward the Offices of the Bishops; so, we don't risk missing them or even meeting them head-on."

A pensive shine, housing a bit of shock, reflected from his grey eyes. "Your idea has merit," he replied and considered a moment. "I like it."

Nerian sounded impressed, and she flashed him a proud smile. "I stood on the sidelines of battle at Catalaunum in Gaul along with the camp women. I witnessed and learned a little about clever tactics and the element of surprise, especially if you're not the strongest."

Nerian's brow raised. "I know you mentioned the encounter with Arria and Garic at Catalaunum, but your experience seemed more vengeful than strategic." He grinned. "You do surprise me. And yet, at times, you appear fragile, pampered." He shook his head and smiled. "You're a mysterious woman, Marcella."

"You forget, I'm a woman who's fought my way through a man's world. If you listen, you'll find I have many excellent ideas. So, what do you say? Shall we stay ahead of them—just up there on the higher ground beside those little beggars?" She pointed to a group of children sitting on a mound of dirt laced with a collection of rubble. "We'll wait until Arria and Garic pass and then follow them."

Nerian raised a brow, his gaze sharp. He pulled her toward him and wrapped an arm around her. "I'll never forget anything about you again, I promise." He lifted his scarf over his nose and headed in the direction of the street children, basking in the sun.

Marcella followed suit, and they sat huddled in a shadow behind the beggars. Waiting.

XXII

Old Wounds

JERUSALEM: Market Place—St. John's Street, The 3rd day of Junius, Afternoon

CORVUS

"**T**here you go, Jax. Look over there." Corvus purposely left Alexander, following behind them, out of his instruction. "Next to that nest of beggar children. A man and a woman with scarves over their faces. They just slipped into the crowd behind Arria and Garic."

"It helps that the barbarian is tall and blond. Makes his group easier to track," Alexander commented.

Corvus ignored him but picked up their pace a bit. At times, when they drew too close, they stepped to the side and examined the wares from a line of stalls running through the market. When the street widened, it proved easier to blend into the flow. Soon they approached the church offices at the end of St. John's. Up ahead, they watched as Arria, Garic, and their two companions—then minutes later Nerian and Marcella—turned south onto a stone walkway. It merged with the road leading past David's Tower, uninhabited and unguarded by soldiers.

Corvus came to a quick halt and addressed Alexander and Jax. "They'll pass the tower on the way to the inn. I discovered from a local merchant that the thoroughfare is called David's Road. It narrows where some repairs are being made to the wall near the tower's postern door. This would be a good place to take them by surprise."

"And when they're in the narrow and in front of the tower? What then?" Alexander's question rang with curious skepticism.

Corvus squinted his eyes and cocked his head. Ideas and strategy tossed a moment in his mind. "We run past Nerian and his woman—then we each jump one of the three men. The lady Arria should pose no threat."

"What about Nerian? Won't he pose a threat?" Alexander asked.

Corvus grunted, "I'm betting he'll stay back and let us do the hard work before he tries to get involved, or better yet, he'll see that others—tougher and fiercer—are involved. He and his woman will flee, not wanting to risk their lives for a sword.

"True. They seem calculating and shrewd. They'll find new ways to make money, especially if they're working for Accipiter." Alexander stroked his chin and then added, "And, I prefer not to kill them. They could prove useful to me—us, in the future. Besides, any action against Nerian and Marcella might warn the foursome not that far ahead. We would lose the element of surprise." He flashed an approving smile. "I agree with your plan." He turned to Jax. "What about you?"

"Jax always agrees with me, right, Jax?" Corvus managed a grin but inwardly bristled over Alexander's authoritative manner.

Jax nodded. "Right."

"We all agree then," Corvus said, speaking to both men. "Let's get ready. Only a few hours of light are left. As we draw close to Nerian and Marcella, we'll trot past them. With our hoods raised, they'll be unable to recognize us and may even mistake us for out-of-uniform soldiers in training. As we close in on the foursome, break into a sprint. Attack the first man you encounter. Clear?"

"Clear," Alexander and Jax replied. They left the walkway and moved onto David's road. When Corvus signaled, they began to trot toward the tower, the hunted pilgrims, and the prize.

CORVUS

The western sky melted into streams of orange over blue and cast shadows at their feet. Corvus, Jax, and Alexander trotted up behind Nerian and Marcella. The two hugged the side of the road, looking like an unassuming couple out for a walk or on ordinary business. They wore sun protective scarves draped over their heads and across their faces. The men passed them by without a glance in their direction.

Nerian had either heard or sensed their approach and turned, glancing their way.

"Corvus," Jax said and started to say something.

"Shut up!" Corvus hissed and led Jax and Alexander briskly past them. Did he hear Nerian mumble something? He didn't care. His gaze targeted the back of the first man up ahead, guarding the rear of Arria and Garic's traveling party. He bore the stature of a soldier, more than a mercenary, while the black-haired man beside Arria looked like a Frank. The woman and the Frank were the farthest ahead with the blond barbarian just behind them.

Corvus whispered over his shoulder, "I'll take the rear guard. Fight whoever comes your way. Go now!" he hissed and charged forward.

The soldier turned to look as they pounded up the road. Corvus watched as the soldier instinctively placed his hand over the sword hanging from his belt. As Corvus drew closer, the soldier pulled his weapon and faced him head-on. Corvus heard Arria scream, "Telemachus!" as Corvus brought his sword crashing down on him." Telemachus gritted his teeth, and his eyes blazed with fury. With every blow, Corvus grunted from sheer force of will. Metal rang against metal as Corvus exchanged strikes with hacking downstrokes and jabs. Blood pounded through his veins, and he attacked like a frenzied beast—savage and fierce. His confidence soared, and his focus narrowed. *Tire him, then fake a move—catch him by surprise,* galloped through his mind.

Telemachus, his sword swinging, defended his ground, panting and fading. His breath labored, the soldier shifted his weight. Corvus drew a sharp breath, his nostrils flared. With a forward lunge, they locked weapons. Corvus leaned with a right step into Telemachus, then skillfully raised his left leg and swept Telemachus' leg from under him, a barbarian maneuver learned in his early years as a fighter.

The soldier went down on his back, his arms splayed, and his sword flying out of his hand. Corvus grinned and kicked him in the head. Stepping on his chest, he stabbed him in the gut. The soldier choked a few times. Then a short exhaling breath fell from his lips. Blood oozed from his mouth. Dead and done—Corvus liked it that way. He hated when a dying man lingered.

He wrenched his sword from the soldier's midriff, looked behind himself to be sure no one approached, then checked the bag fallen by the soldier's side. It was stuffed with clothes and nothing of value. He tossed it aside and turned his attention to the fray around him. Just ahead, near a side door to the tower, Nerian stood over Garic. The fallen barbarian clutched his side. Corvus was surprised. Nerian had chosen to fight and not run. Corvus sprinted in their direction. He would kill Nerian and steal Garic's bag. The sword must be there.

NERIAN

Are these soldiers training? Nerian asked himself as three men jogged past them. Hoods hid their faces, but after they passed, he noticed their hands go to their swords. Not too far ahead, Arria and Garic and their companions were reaching the narrow in the road. With the workers gone for the day, timbers and limestone blocks lay stacked beside a gap in the wall near a side door, leading into David's Tower. The square structure stood three stories, almost fifty feet tall. A low protective parapet ran the edge of the roof.

The hair raised on the back of Nerian's neck as the men broke into a run. Something was wrong. *These men could be after the sword. I must go.* He stopped Marcella. "Stay back. There's trouble." Before she could respond, he took off after them, his own sword in hand. He caught up to the men, just as they attacked the group. Nerian heard Arria scream, metal clanging against metal, grunts, and scrambling feet. To his surprise, he came face to face with Garic who came at him hard. Nerian countered the blow and pushed back. Garic came at him again. Strike after strike, each of them held fast. Another blow wielded by Garic toward Nerian's side forced him to lash out, stopping the edge of Garic's sword with his own. Nerian stepped back to circle his opponent.

Garic stared and uttered, "Nerian?"

Nerian's scarf had fallen below his chin, and he answered, "I regret this, my old friend, but I need the sword, more than your friendship."

Garic shook his head in disbelief but continued to circle. "I'm not surprised," he said, sounding bitter. "You're a mercenary, and if Marcella is still by your side, you've learned a lot more about greed."

Bile rose in Nerian's throat. Garic and Arria had been his friends for a short time until Marcella had wrestled his heart away from them.

Could he kill Garic? Was the weapon in Garic's shoulder bag so close and simply for the taking? He frowned.

But an answer to his difficult choice popped into his head. He knew of Garic's weakness, an old wound. After fighting next to the Frank in Constantinople, Nerian had noticed Garic clutch his waist above the hip. Later, while in Egypt, Marcella told him that believing Garic killed her lover, Severus, at the Battle of Catalaunum, she had crept onto the battlefield at the very end and stabbed Garic in his side. After the battle, Marcella learned that Garic had fallen beneath the veil of consciousness, that dark sleep, and would have died, but Arria found a healer to cure him. Still, Garic's wound had rendered his left side weak, causing him pain and making him vulnerable. He gripped his sword tighter. "Money is more than friendship. It buys freedom, comfort—power. Give me the sword and leave."

Garic shook his head. "I took an oath to protect it."

"Even if it means dying?"

"*Ja*, or killing you."

Nerian shook his head and snorted with disbelief. "Not likely, but I'm sorry." As the words tumbled from his mouth, he lunged, thrusting toward Garic with a right jab. Garic swung his sword in an attempt to block him, but Nerian swiftly shifted direction and slid his weapon into Garic's left side.

A soft grunt fell from Garic's lips, and his free hand covered his wound. His right leg buckled, and he went to a knee. Garic gazed at him, but suddenly blurted, "Behind you."

Nerian felt a presence and swiveled on his heel. Grateful for Garic's merciful and unexpected warning, he raised his sword as Corvus rushed him. "Get to the roof," he shouted to Garic, staggering to his feet.

Even in the rush, Nerian could see sweat trickling down Corvus' face and a grimace on his lips. At a disadvantage, Nerian stepped back and back again. His opponent's blade swung past his chin, but he dodged the shiny tip. A slicing sound rang in his ears, and he felt the razor-edged bite of Corvus' sword across his front leg muscle. Nerian stepped back once more, his leg screaming with pain. Corvus heaved forward and sliced his leg again. Nerian winced and licked his lips. He stumbled and watched his hulking enemy tower over him— laughing. A sharp and sudden pinch, a warm sensation, filled his belly. As he reached to stop it, Corvus' boot kicked him in his head.

He fell backward. The breeze brushed his ears and neck, and the back of his skull slammed the stony ground. The light shrank. A shadow passed over him. Darkness.

ARRIA

Thudding feet and a sudden burst of dust alerted Arria and Garic to the attack. Not far from the side door, they turned and watched as a hooded man led and attacked Telemachus ready and facing them.

Arria screamed, "Telemachus!"

Garic shouted at Samuel, "Get Arria into the tower and onto the roof!"

"The sword," Arria demanded from Garic.

He quickly swapped bags with her and dropped hers on the ground as a decoy. "Hurry!" he said. His fiery blue eyes flashed with love and intensity, then he pivoted toward the attackers and raised his sword.

Arria hesitated. She stood rooted, not wanting to leave him.

"We must go now," Samuel insisted, and hurried her up a mound of grass and through the door into the tower.

Inside the empty stone chamber, a flight of stairs led to a second level. They fled up the staircase and stepped onto the landing. More stairs stood before them, but at the very top, they could see a small door that opened onto the roof. Arria tore open the bag. She slid the sword from its scabbard and held it in front of her. Samuel led the way with Arria behind him. In the echo of the block walls, she heard grunting and hurried feet on the steps below her. Samuel, using his shoulder, burst through the door and onto the roof. Arria raised her foot, but a sudden drag on her hem caught her by surprise. She tugged at her skirt and forced herself onto the roof. Behind her, she heard someone yell, "Take the woman, Jax. I'll take the other."

A tall, hooded man shot past her in pursuit of Samuel.

Arria spun around to face her attacker. *This must be Jax*, she thought and raised the sword. A burly man with a missing tooth grinned. "No problem, Alexander," the fool called out.

Arria gripped the sword tighter and steeled herself.

Jax looked at her and laughed, but then his eyes fell on the sword, and his brow wrinkled. He peered closer. "Why don't you hand over that sword like a good lady," he coaxed, "I won't hurt you." He lowered his weapon, a few inches, and extended a hand.

Arria summoned her courage and lifted the sword higher. She shook her head.

Jax lunged like a cat and grabbed her wrist. She punched and kicked at him, but he was stronger. Laughing, he dropped his weapon and wrestled the sword from her hand. Arria clawed at his face. He reddened and frowned—anger shot from his eyes. He raised the sword.

Arria backed up and glanced frantically to her left, then right. Neither Samuel nor the other man was in sight, but behind her, she heard scuffling sounds. Her heart pounding, her panic grew. Would Jax strike her? He stood there and smirked, enjoying her fear. Then, his lop-sided smile vanished. He cocked his head and arched his chest. A shocked expression poured across his face. He raised an arm and tried to reach behind himself, but toppled over like a wounded battle horse. Arria stared down at him. A black dagger protruded from the middle of his back. She raised her eyes toward the doorway.

Marcella stood on the threshold. A dark, hungry look consumed her features. Without a word, she dove for the sword.

Arria leaped toward the weapon as well. She grabbed the handle first, but Marcella fought to wrench it away. "What are you doing here?" Arria demanded, gripping the sword with all her strength.

"The same as you," Marcella hissed, struggling to loosen Arria's grasp. "Winning a prize."

"It's a holy artifact meant for the church. Leave it alone."

"Ha! Always so righteous, but you can afford to be. You're a rich woman."

Like flowers in a storm, they twisted and turned, heads bent, rooted in place. Arria would not let go. Her fingers, wrapped around the handle, burned, and her knuckles turned white. Fighting to keep the sword, she stared with determination into her estranged sister's face.

Marcella, taller and stronger, surged at Arria and pushed, pushed—pushed her back.

Arria leaned in toward Marcella and fought boldly to hold her place. But her right foot slipped, left the ground and stepped into a void. She fell back, losing her grip on the sword. Marcella snatched the weapon away and watched as Arria dropped through the open space of the parapet.

Arria felt her chest, chin, and palms scrape the outer wall. She frantically tried to grasp the top of the roof's edge, a hole, or any crack in the stone blocks. For a second, she found a hold, but it crumbled away. As she slid downward toward the ground, an iron ring meant for banners loomed beside her. With every ounce of her strength, she reached for and clutched the ring with one hand and then the other. Her body twisted and swayed, but she held on. Her arms burned as her muscles tired and desperation overwhelmed her. She looked up.

Marcella stared down, the sword in her hand, and her eyes ablaze. Her face contorted in pain. "What is this object," she screamed. "It burns my hand!" Without another word, Marcella threw down the sword. Arria heard it clang on the stone. Marcella gazed at her palm and shouted, "I should leave you to your death, Arria."

MARCELLA

Arria cried out, "No matter who we are or what we've done, we are *sisters*—and *blood*. Don't let me die, my unborn child die. Please, Marcella," Arria gasped and gripped tighter. "We can be sisters. We'll learn to love each other. I promise."

Marcella stared at her. The wind whipped Marcella's coal-black hair, and in the distance, a bell rang a solemn toll. "Can I kill a child and its mother?" she quietly answered and watched as Arria struggled to hold on, but Marcella hesitated, and her mind raced.

In truth, what wrongs had Arria committed against her? Nerian had asked this question. Greed killed her mother, not Arria. Being born a legitimate child was not Arria's choice but rather her destiny. Arria had even offered to reunite with her as sisters, but still bitter, she had walked away. Now, Arria was offering them another chance—even if only to hold onto her life and the one inside of her. Marcella could finally be recognized as a daughter of Senator Felix and Arria's sister. Arria had given her word. Promised.

An agonizing moan escaped Arria. Her strength and resolve were dying, the searing pain reflected on her face, pushing her to let go.

Marcella glanced at the dying sun, and without a word, she stepped to the edge and fell to her knees. She reached over and extended her hand. Arria clenched her wrist and then Marcella's other arm. With their strength, power, and toughness combined, Arria climbed the wall toward Marcella, who dragged and lifted her onto the roof.

Arria landed on her side and took a deep breath. Her body trembling, she slowly propped herself up on an arm. Marcella sat on her knees before her. Arria wiped sweat and fallen hair from her brow, and then taking another breath, she rose to her knees as well. Without hesitation, she wrapped her arms around Marcella.

As if handling glass, Marcella raised her arms and gently returned her embrace.

Arria hugged her close and whispered, "Today, you are truly my sister."

Marcella's tears brushed Arria's cheek. A slight sob fell from her lips. "I am, Arria, I am," she whispered back.

XXIII

Love Your Enemies

JERUSALEM: David's Tower—The 3rd day of Junius,
Late Afternoon

SAMUEL

Samuel watched in horror as Jax confronted Arria. His name was shouted by a hooded, taller accomplice, ordering him to take the woman. Jax had grinned and yelled, "No problem, Alexander," assuring his partner who came through the door behind him.

Save Arria was the only thought in Samuel's mind. He loved and would protect her to the death. His sword slid easily from its scabbard, and he started in her direction. But the tall one, Alexander, shot past Arria and Jax and stomped toward him.

Samuel's fingers wrapped tightly around his sword's grip, tingled, and his heart raced. He licked his lips and readied his stance. All his Wespe training returned and fell back into the comfort of his limbs. Regardless of this man's name or who he might be, the hooded creature descended on him like *Cacus*, the monster, the fire breathing giant, his eyes furious, his nostrils flaring. Samuel grinned, he felt alive again and stood ready.

A shaft of orange light spread across the roof. A tense silence hung in the shadows that painted the parapet and the gravel floor. Alexander raised his sword. Samuel lowered his point, aiming for the midriff, and thrust, but Alexander deflected the strike with a block. Samuel drew back but moved in and swung his sword down and against the edge of Alexander's blade. The ringing, *clang, clang*, of metal against metal with each blow, reverberated through Samuel's arms, his body, and escaped into the air. Alexander's piercing eyes and dark brows burned into Samuel's mind even as they passed in a flash, and he continued to fight. Advancing to the other's side, each man regarded the other, ready to spring and attack.

Alexander feigned a thrust, then jabbed upward toward Samuel's throat.

Samuel reacted with a quick sidestep, dodged his head to the side, and jumped backward, proving his ability with close combat. He grinned in retaliation.

Alexander grimaced, pushed forward, and lashed out, driving them farther across the roof.

Samuel raised his sword and blocked. A soft breeze circled them as a scraping sound, and a gleaming, silvery light slid beside him and caught the corner of his eye. He knew better, but an impulse forced his glance right toward the object. Without hesitation, Alexander swiped a blow from the left. The distraction cost Samuel. He countered, but his opponent's sword hit hard. Samuel's grip broken, the sword flew from his hand and clattered somewhere behind him. Alexander thrust his sword forward, aiming for the kill. Power surged through Samuel. He nimbly jumped to the side, avoiding the blade, and charged Alexander, pushing him with both arms. His opponent stumbled backward a few feet, and his hood came down. Black curls crowned his head, and a pale, narrow jaw rimmed high cheekbones. His appearance lacked the edge of a mercenary, but it was not the time for Samuel to speculate. He lunged for David's sword resting near his foot, glittering in the day's amber light. As he clutched the weapon, he caught a glimpse of Arria beside the parapet, embracing Marcella—another surprise that must wait—but heard a familiar voice. He spun toward the sound.

Garic faced Alexander, shouting, "Who are you? What do you want?" Blood dripped from Garic's side, his weapon limp in his hand.

Alexander, his balance returned, looked at Garic his sword raised. "Give me the sword, and you can all leave." His menacing look proved he had seen Garic's wound and enjoyed the advantage.

Garic spat, "The sword was entrusted to Lady Arria and me by the emperor. It's our mission and belongs with us."

"I disagree. I've another plan for the sword. Now, give it to me, or I'll take it," Alexander growled.

Samuel rushed to Garic's side and shouted, "Go! Tend to Arria. I must fight him!" His words resonated in the dusky air, and Garic, seeing that Samuel held the sacred weapon, nodded. Throughout their entire journey, Garic had supported Samuel's belief, regarding David's sword. Samuel knew now he must wield the sword—take the risk.

Garic thrust toward Alexander, then nimbly stepped out of the way. Samuel slid in, ready.

Alexander sneered. He attacked and his weapon came crashing down. Samuel blocked the blow. An echoing chime burst from the sword like a sounding trumpet. He winced, taken by surprise, but his wits sharp, he brought Alexander's blow around in an upward motion. This ancient short sword held a disadvantage against the longer *Spatha,* and he had no shield. Yet, his instincts and agility made him stay close to Alexander. He mustn't letup or slacken, despite the pain.

Thrusting and dodging, the two men fought in slower motion. They circled each other for relief. Heat and exhaustion tired their limbs, but gradually Samuel felt an energizing sensation well-up in his hands and through his arms. His chest heaved less, and his legs felt strong, the fatigue in his muscles melted away. With every new clash, the sword sang with a heavenly peal and housed a soft vibration. Strangely, with each step, thrust, and block, the sword owned him. Like an appendage, he felt they were one. Samuel watched his opponent wither. Alexander carried his weapon lower as it grew heavier. His sword thrusts became feeble jabs, and he could barely dodge the blows aimed at him. Sweat poured down the man's face, and his chest moved up and down, signaling his fatigue.

Now was the time. With the strength of a lion, Samuel surged and leaped forward. He slammed his arm into Alexander's body and stabbed his sword into the weakened man's leg. Speed and momentum coursing through his limbs, he struck the sword from Alexander's hand, punched him in the face, and knocked him to the ground. He stood over him and placed the tip of David's sword against his throat. A glossy sheen covered the blade.

"Who are you, and why do you want David's sword? Is it for yourself or others?"

Alexander held out his hands and gasped, "Do not kill me. I seek the sword for my son."

"What does a boy need with a holy artifact?"

A bitter snarl rolled over Alexander's lips. "I desire the sword in remembrance of my son, Joshua, murdered by a crazy Gentile beggar." The words tumbled from his mouth. He hesitated a second, as if catching himself, but quickly continued, "I can pay you a great sum. Perhaps you can understand, you're a Frank, a barbarian.

Romans have shown little mercy to your people as they have to mine."

Samuel stared at him. Was he speaking the truth? "How can you be a Jew? In appearance and dress, you resemble a Greek, and you're here in the city. Jews are not allowed."

A steely expression filled Alexander's face, and his eyes narrowed. "I'm clever—and a wealthy merchant. The combination opens many doors if one tries hard enough." Alexander inched his chin a little higher. "The sword belonged to the Jewish king David and should be protected by a Jew. Have you not heard? The sword carries a warning on its blade—*A curse on the one who wields the sword and not be chosen.* Think. Who can wield it? A mighty warrior, a priest? It implies only a chosen one. Or . . . perhaps, David meant only a Jew, like himself, can fight with it without being cursed. You're a Frank. You fought with the sword and hold it now. You should be afraid."

Samuel laughed over the irony hidden to Alexander. "Your attempt to frighten me will not work" He bent over and rested the sword's tip a little harder against his throat. "This will surprise you. I, too, appear to be something I'm not. It's true. I lived with the Franks and fought with them at Catalaunum, but I was once a slave brought to Rome from Palaestina. I'm also a Jew—Samuel Ben Zachariah. I just fought with the sword, and here I stand and *you*—in jeopardy."

Samuel paused. Never had he felt like this in his life. He could still feel the sword's power running through him. He could barely contain his elation. A realization crept over him, and he took a breath. He had fought with the sword in battle against Alexander and survived. Was he meant to protect the sword? Fear and excitement sped through him at the same time. He quickly gathered himself, before Alexander might think he dropped his caution and brusquely added, "But, I've sworn to help the Lady Arria find the place where *all* can view this ancient and holy artifact, whether it be in Jerusalem or Palaestina. You'll never have it for yourself alone as long as I, Garic, or Arria breathe. So, considering your circumstances, I'll give you a chance to leave. Go back to your home and find another memorial more fitting to an innocent son slain. Do *good* in his name."

Alexander raised his hands slowly in the air. "If you remove the sword from my throat, I will go. Your determination outweighs my desire to die for an artifact that, as I have witnessed, might wish to rest in your hands. Even now, in your palm and away from battle, the Sword of David bears a seductive sheen."

Samuel straightened up and held the sword at his side. Alexander rose to his feet. "My true name is Kalev Ben Jonah," he said, glancing at the minor wound on his leg and then wiping his brow. "My life knows the pain that comes from mistakes and greed. What I witnessed here will follow me all my life. I may not become a poorer or better man. I'm weak and love my comforts. But I see the sword cannot belong to me—not at any price. It should rest—if not with our people—in a place as you have promised, for all to see. If you allow me, and keep my identity secret, I'll leave this tower and return home, where I belong."

Samuel nodded. "I give my word, your secret is safe with me. Gather your weapon. Leave before any others or authorities arrive."

Kalev gave Samuel a grateful bow, then picked up and sheathed his sword. He appeared exhausted, but a grin tugged at the corner of his lips, and he ventured, "You're a smart man, Samuel Ben Zachariah. Tonight, other treasures will arrive through Hezekiah's tunnel. If you need work, money, and care to join me, you may find me there or at Moon Gold Antiquities."

Samuel smiled. "A tempting offer, but I must complete this mission and return to my home in Nazareth." As he spoke, Garic, Arria, and Marcella came beside him. They had quietly watched the duel unfold and would not interfere.

Before Kalev turned to go, Arria spoke up, "Perhaps the sword has chosen, and Samuel is its worthy champion." Her lips pressed together in grim acknowledgment.

Kalev offered a thin smile and sighed. "In time, you may know." He raised his hood and walked out the door.

NERIAN

Nerian's eyes popped open. Something stirred beside him in the thicket where he lay. His mouth parched, he licked his lips and slowly looked at the sky above him. He lay on his back, and somewhere in a tree, a bird warbled short, fragile notes, calling out its dusky tune. Nerian tried to lift his head, but pain shot from the back of his skull toward his brow. He stopped and groaned. His senses growing sharper with his consciousness, he rolled slowly to his right side and used his left arm to push himself to a sitting position. He slumped over his legs, and his head pounded.

He took a breath and then touched the back of his skull. A small amount of blood sat stuck to his matted hair. With a side glance, he saw a flat rock with more of his blood. No wonder his head ached. He remembered his battle with the leader of the hooded men who trotted past him and Marcella on the road. One of the leader's companions had called him, 'Corvus,' but Corvus had quickly ordered him to 'shut up.'

Nerian felt the back of his head again. He was lucky to be alive, but for how long? A new sensation, burning and sharp, filled his awareness. He rushed his hand to his belly and dragged it just above his navel. He gasped and touched the spot where Corvus' sword had entered. Luckily, his leather girdle had kept the sword from running deep. A small trickle of blood covered the belt, and the tunic beneath felt sodden and wet. A sigh of relief tumbled from his lips. The stab, any deeper, would have killed him.

He glanced at his legs. One held two lacerations close together, while the other was a small slice. The second, a deeper slash on his thigh. This had weakened his stance and the reason why he fell and hit his head. His memory still fuzzy, he wondered if hitting his skull and passing out had saved his life.

Throbbing pain and fatigue racked Nerian's body. He stared at the ground and then slowly at his surroundings. A tree stood nearby. Gritting his teeth, he reached behind his back and placed his palms onto the ground. A moan escaped his lips as he heaved and dragged himself over dirt, stones, and gnarling roots. When he reached the tree, he leaned against the trunk, exhaled with a grunt, and licked his lips. If only he had some water.

Untying his scarf, he pulled it from his neck and tied it around his leg. The blood oozed slowly from the wound but must be stopped. It had been his lucky day. No arteries were cut. He turned his head a little to the side and then rested it lightly against the tree. He took another, deeper breath. Where was Marcella? He could only hope she was alive. He wanted to find her but was too weak to move. Just for a minute, he would close his eyes.

CORVUS

Corvus hurried toward David's Tower. While fighting Telemachus, he'd seen people run past them into its side door. Now that Nerian was no longer a threat and the sword nowhere to be seen—nor Jax or Alexander—he figured they must all be there. He crossed the threshold and entered the cool dimness settled on the ancient stones. His eyes adjusting, he looked around and headed toward the stairs. His arms and legs felt heavier than the sword he carried in his hand as he climbed to the second floor. He stepped into an empty room, except for a few wooden racks that once held weapons and bows. Before him, stood a new flight of stairs and at the very top, rectangular light, obviously coming from an open door. Corvus climbed his way slowly to the brightness and tower roof.

As he stepped onto the smooth wooden landing that led to the door, a figure stepped through the entryway, and they were caught face to face. Surprise rippled through Corvus as he gazed at Alexander, and he sputtered his name. Alexander, also startled upon seeing him, just gave him a threatening look and brushed past him. Corvus called out, "Hey!" as Alexander flew down the stairs without a word or backward glance. *What has frightened the braggart?* The question rushed through Corvus as he tried to unravel the actual situation at hand. His nerve shaken, he mustered his courage and told himself to think. Who was on the roof, and what would he find? Jax and the women? Garic and his Frank companion? He turned back to the door and raised his sword higher and proceeded with caution.

His first step into the light, illuminated a cluster of people, partially shaded by the sun's setting glow. Only a few feet ahead of him on the ground lay Jax. A knife stuck in his back. Caught off guard, Corvus gaped with disbelief. He winced and pressed his lips, suppressing a groan. Fury and hate partnered, then barreled through him. Vengeance fueled his heart. He raised his eyes and peered closely at the persons before him. He shouted out, "Which one of you bastards killed him? Come on! Fight me!"

The Frank raised a sword that held a glistening sheen, and the blond barbarian stood beside him. Marcella and the Lady Arria retreated and locked arms near the parapet.

"They call me Samrick, and Garic stands beside me. Your companion threatened the life of Lady Arria, the emperor's envoy. Along with her husband, Garic, they were appointed to protect and deliver the sword to the Church of the Holy Sepulchre."

Corvus stood transfixed, his gaze on the sword. The air seemed to vibrate around it, and a strange shine hugged the metal. Engraved symbols ran down the center, and from what he could tell, the grip appeared made of ivory. He quickly glanced at his own sword. It rested in his hands, plain and mediocre in comparison. Fear slithered down his neck and around his spine like a cold-blooded serpent. He shook his head unable to stop the faint hum, floating on the dying waves of heat. His feet felt rooted, but he wanted to run. The sword must be cursed. Jax was dead and his own bravery, failing. He licked his lips.

Garic stepped forward. "Leave now. Take your friend and bury him," he said, his tone solemn but firm. "There's nothing of value or gain for you here. Only your own misfortune. The sword will not favor anyone determined to steal it for profit."

Samuel added, "But if you are so foolish as to try and take it, we'll fight you to the death." He raised the sword, tip pointing to the sky.

Corvus looked at the women who gazed at him, their chins high. He frowned, pursed his lips, and nodded. Without a word, he slipped his sword into its sheath. He bent over Jax and yanked the knife from his back. Disgust filled him. He scowled and flung it to the side. Corvus watched it clatter across the floor and tilted his head. Which of them had attacked Jax from behind? The men had swords. They said Jax had threatened Arria. Marcella, the dark beauty, looked like she might have the mettle to kill a man. But why would she protect Arria? She desired the sword as well. Yet, here they stood arm in arm.

Corvus placed his hands on his hips. He would never know, and maybe it was better that way. Time to return home and start over. Find another kind of work. Maybe find a woman or go to sea. Standing taller, he scowled one last time. Then he grabbed Jax and hoisted him over his shoulder, turned, and left the roof.

As Corvus lumbered down the stairs, he was overcome by enough. Enough of Goliath, enough of Milvus and Alexander, and enough of the bloody sword. It dripped red with pain and death. His regret—he had chosen not to believe. But now, he did. The sword, for most, was cursed. It killed Jax. A friend worth more than any amount of money that damn sword could buy.

XXIV

Through Chaos, Redemption

JERUSALEM: David's Tower—The 3rd day of Junius,
Early Evening

MARCELLA

As the man called Corvus left the roof, they all watched for a moment in stunned silence. Marcella stood next to Arria, their arms locked together, near the wall a few feet away. Garic was beside Samuel, shaking his head in disbelief. They looked at each other and said a few words. Then, Samuel turned and faced in their direction, clutching David's sword.

The sun sat just above the horizon, and the bright sheen on the blade was gone, its luster waning. Samuel walked a few feet toward the wall, picked up its scabbard, and slid the blade inside. He looked at his hand. A rosy stripe where the grip had rested covered his palm.

"Does it hurt?" Garic asked, as Samuel returned to his side.

"Remarkably, no," Samuel replied. "And your wound?" He pointed to the blood peeking above Garic's thick leather belt.

Arria and Marcella moved closer to the men. Earlier, Marcella had noticed Garic was hurt only when Arria had asked him about his wound. He had quickly assured her he was well, and they had continued to watch Samuel fight. Now, Marcella looked at Garic and worried. She had entered the tower to pursue Arria and left Nerian to fight Garic. Where was Nerian? She wanted to ask but realized it wasn't the time, and biting her lip, she decided to wait.

Garic tucked a thumb into the left side of his thick leather belt. He pulled the strap away from his body. Beneath the belt, a patch of blood-stained the cloth. "Nerian got the best of me."

A low groan escaped Arria's lips as Garic showed Samuel.

Marcella, standing beside Arria, cringed. She had seen wounds far worse, but Nerian was her man, and he had stabbed Garic. This could affect her relationship with Arria. Should she speak and defend him?

"Nerian sought to stop me with a superficial jab, not kill me," Garic added quickly. "I tightened my belt over my tunic and wound. It stopped the bleeding."

Samuel rubbed the side of his neck with a hand, sweat dripped from his temples, and his curls were streaked with dirt raised from the roof's floor in the scuffle. "Despite Nerian's greed and tough Saxon ways—he has a heart. He could've killed you."

Garic snorted. "Maybe half a heart. The wound stings." He nodded toward the sun, and added, "I know we must speak about the sword and the way it shone in your hand, but it's better we leave here first. The sun is almost down."

"I agree, we should go, but I will tell you—the sword came alive in my hand. I'm forever touched and slightly bewildered. I have much to think about."

Garic placed his hand on Samuel's shoulder. "Without question, my friend. Perhaps the sword has chosen its own path."

Marcella felt a nudge. Arria shot her a quick grin and cleared her throat. She gazed at the men and waited.

Garic and Samuel looked their way. Garic glanced from Arria to Marcella and then back to Arria. He scratched his head. Amazement showed on his face, but he managed a smile.

Arria spoke up, "Before we go, there's a matter I wish to share. Today . . . Marcella is my newly born sister." A slight tremble rode the tone in her voice. "She saved my life when she might have let me die. There'll no longer be hatred or ill-will between us. I've promised to accept and love her as my rightful sister. She has promised to accept me as well."

Garic drew a long breath. He opened his mouth as if to speak, but pressed his lips closed, and only nodded instead.

Marcella lifted her chin and looked Garic in the eye. Now was her chance. She would change herself and the circumstances surrounding their animosity. "I hurt you once, Garic. I am sorry. I realized later, I had been tricked into believing you killed Severus. My grief hid the truth from me." She swallowed. Her throat was dry, and her tongue felt heavy, but she knew she must ask. "Can you . . . forgive me for the pain I caused you?"

Arria, standing beside her, smiled proudly and squeezed her elbow, their arms still locked together.

Garic loomed tall as always, his eyes an intense blue. He didn't speak right away. Marcella sensed he might not trust her, and her heart fluttered from fear. If he could not forgive her, would Arria be able to keep her promise and regard her as the sister she so desired to be?

Garic ran his fingers through his hair and let out a breath. "I love my wife more than anyone on this earth. If she loves you as her sister and wants you in her life, I'll accept you as a sister-in-law. I thank you for your apology and accept it."

Marcella uttered a relieved, "Thank you," then shifted her gaze toward Samuel. He looked at her grimly. "Samuel, I have no words for the way I hurt you, and what I took from you. Karas was your wife. But that day at Catalaunum, I was bent on vengeance. Karas was my unintended victim and a terrible accident, I swear. Will you forgive me as well?"

Samuel sighed and glanced up for a moment. It appeared as if he was choking back tears. He looked at Arria and then, back to her. "You have changed, Marcella, and today, I have changed as well. I'll forgive you, but I will ask that you live a better life. Not only for your own redemption but in memory of Karas as well."

Marcella blinked away sudden tears and smiled with relief and gratitude, then nodded.

Arria leaned in with a hug and said, "We'll start fresh and new, Marcella."

Marcella returned Arria's embrace, then stepped back and urgently added, "Sister, there's another situation important to me. It's Nerian. I fear he may be hurt. He would have found his way to the roof by now to find me. But . . . can you and Garic forgive him as well?"

Arria looked at Garic. He directed his words toward Marcella. "In the end, Nerian tried to help me. He's forgiven," Garic answered. "I left him fighting Corvus, who has gone. They fought near the tower's side entrance. I also fear for Telemachus. We'll find them."

Marcella's stomach churned. The possibility that Nerian was wounded, or worse—dead, riddled her with despair. Could she handle the grief of losing another man she loved? "What if Nerian is dead?" she asked bravely. "What will happen? We cannot leave him on the road."

Garic spoke to them all, in a firm but gentle manner. "It pains me to say, if Nerian and Telemachus are dead, we must shelter them in the tower and return tomorrow for their bodies. If they are alive and wounded, I'll go to The Red Torch down the road, and return with a cart and some men. I'll ask the owner to send for a healer—and hopefully, once we reach the inn, they'll recover. This is all we can do for now until tomorrow."

They looked at Garic and nodded their heads in agreement. Arria added, "We must hurry. Time is short, and our mission is not yet finished. But first, let's find our friends."

NERIAN

The sun's corona edged above the black horizon. Among a cluster of bushes and dry brush, Nerian watched the descending rays from the tree his back rested against. His mouth felt dryer than a cracked mudflat, and his head throbbed from lack of water. He knew from military physicians that it was best not to sleep when the head ached, but a drowsy demon tormented him.

With stubborn determination, he listened for any sounds that might bring help and rescue. *Where is Marcella?* Nerian struggled to picture her face above the pain. Sweat dripped from his forehead onto his brows and lashes. He blinked and felt himself slipping, then shut his eyes.

A sharp, loud snap echoed in his ears. He heard voices, and then, a gentle shake to his shoulder roused him. A sweet whisper filled his senses, "Nerian." He looked up. Marcella's face smiled in front of him.

"Marcella," he mumbled.

"Shhh! Just rest. Help is on the way." She lifted her hand to his cheek. "Arria is with me and the one we thought a Frank. His true name is Samuel. Once we saw you were alive but wounded, Garic left for the inn to return with a cart. When he arrives, we'll take you there. A physician will be waiting." She gently wrapped a long strip of cloth she ripped from her torn hem around his leg, and then his head. Lifting his belt, she tucked some fabric from her scarf beneath the leather.

Nerian struggled forward, but Marcella stopped him. "Rest. Right now, you're not bleeding, but any movement you make should be slow and with our assistance. We need to get you into bed—wash and bandage your wounds."

His thirst awoke. "Some water, please," he asked. Then, he saw Arria. She appeared in his vision and knelt beside him.

"Drink," she said and held a water pouch to his lips.

Nerian took a long drink, then licked his lips. Another rustling sound grew closer, and Samuel stepped into view. Nerian overheard Samuel tell Arria, that when he retrieved their bags and grabbed his water pouch, he found Telemachus' cloak. Arria took the woven cape and covered Nerian.

"Garic will arrive soon. Just rest," Arria said.

Marcella grabbed his hand in hers and sat beside him. "Arria and I are sisters now. We've reconciled. I do not want the sword, only you alive, and my sister as well—in my life."

Even in his weakened state, Nerian heard Marcella sound more peaceful than she had in quite a while. He was amazed, and a question tumbled slowly from his lips, "No sword, only a sister—Arria?"

"Yes," Marcella laughed. "When you're well, I'll tell you how and why we've reunited, but for now, no more speaking."

Samuel offered Marcella his cloak while Arria pulled her own from her bag.

"Samuel, take Garic's cloak," Arria said. "He'll surely return with blankets to keep Nerian warm and cover Telemachus."

Samuel agreed.

Marcella leaned toward Nerian and softly explained, "I knew Samuel in Gaul, but so many years have passed, I didn't recognize him. He's forgiven me for the harm I did him as well, and I'm grateful."

They wrapped themselves and sat in silence, surrounded by the soft scent of eucalyptus in the air and twittering nightjars, waking from their sleep. On the horizon, twilight's amber rays spread across the descending night-blue sky. A white disk shone overhead.

After a short time, a low rumble could be heard coming from the direction of the inn and Sion Gate. Samuel stood. "I see a torch," he said. "Wait here. I'll go to the road and see if it's Garic."

"Take the bag with the sword . . . just in case," Arria encouraged, tugging the hem of Samuel's tunic.

Even in the shadows, Nerian saw Samuel nod, pick up a bag from the pile at his feet, and go.

"I pray it's Garic," Arria said. They sat and waited in anxious silence.

Within minutes, the sound of footsteps and male voices filled the air. When they heard Garic's familiar "*Ja*," they all sighed with relief. The light from several torches shone above the bushes. Garic, Samuel, and two other men came into view.

Arria jumped up. Marcella stood as well.

Garic led the way. "Arria," he called as he drew closer. "Zebedee, the owner of The Red Torch, has sent his sons and a cart to transport Telemachus' body and bring Nerian to the inn. On Zebedee's advice, a nearby physician has already been summoned. He should be waiting for us on our arrival."

Marcella knelt back down and wiped Nerian's face with her scarf. "Great news, my love, you'll soon be safe and in good hands."

Nerian licked his lips. "Thank . . . you—all," he murmured.

In the torchlight, Marcella's face glistened a beautiful bronze. "I'll help you rise, help you heal, and never leave your side." She squeezed his arm with both hands.

Nerian offered Marcella a weak, but heartfelt, smile and reached for her hand. He flinched. A hiss wrapped in a snort escaped his nostrils. But he gently tugged her closer so the others wouldn't hear. "My love," he ventured, "if I live . . . will you be my wife?"

Marcella appeared stunned. Several seconds later, a smile spread across her lips. She whispered in his ear, "Yes, I'll be your wife—so, you cannot die." She kissed his cheek, stood and motioned toward Garic and Samuel. Along with Zebedee's sons, they lifted Nerian and carried him to the cart.

JERUSALEM: Shop of the Egyptian merchant, Accipiter—The 8th day of Junius, Morning

ACCIPITER

Marcella and Nerian, smiling and holding hands, stepped into Accipiter's shop. Happy to see them, Accipiter greeted them with arms spread wide. "My friends, welcome. Come join me for some wine."

"You wily rascal. How are you?" Nerian replied, clutching him on the shoulder.

Accipiter laughed. "As good as any day." And you, my friend?" He had heard about the skirmish at David's Tower and noticed that Nerian walked with a slight limp. But a good host would wait before inquiring deeper. First, some polite conversation was in order.

"I'm still here and healing nicely."

"The saints be praised for your survival and good health," Accipiter replied, then reached for and kissed Marcella's hand. "You're as beautiful as ever, but there's a glow of contentment about you." He winked at her. "Does it have anything to do with this gold band on your finger?"

"Most certainly," Marcella cooed. "I'm officially Nerian's wife."

"Then, a celebration is in order—and if you don't mind, a bit of unfinished business." Accipiter grinned and pointed them to the back of his shop.

Accipiter ordered that Babajan provide Nerian with a chair while he and Marcella settled on pillows. Once seated, the servant served them a cup of honey-spiced wine. They spoke about the weather; the beauty of the palms and the way they offered shade from the hot sun, especially in the month of Junius; the flourish of business in the market; the multitude of pilgrims visiting Jerusalem; and buying goods on the Cardo Maximus. After finishing their cups, Accipiter called his servant to fill another. He wanted to hear, as truthfully as possible, the entire adventure surrounding the Sword of David. Although Nerian looked remarkably well, Accipiter knew from informants that Nerian had suffered several wounds in the battle for the relic, but first, he wanted to hear what they both had to say. He had questions he wanted answered, and based on their account, he would decide how to move forward.

"Nerian, have you fully recovered from your wounds? Or maybe I should ask your beautiful new wife, heh?" Accipiter shot Marcella a sly grin.

Marcella laughed, and a blush filled her cheeks that was not from the wine.

"I assure you, my dear host, that Nerian is in robust health." Her eyes danced with merriment, and she gazed at Nerian.

A wry quality filled Nerian's grin. "I have promised my new bride to guard my well-being and health with vigor. I never want to let her down or become a burden. And to answer your question. I'm recovering quickly. An excellent physician met us at the inn. A former army medic, he treated all our wounds with a salve made from honey, salt, and aloe vera. Then he sutured any punctures with catgut thread, that will soon dissolve, and which he covered with woolen bandages soaked in wine. Because of this fine treatment and Marcella's patient care, I have only a few scars to remind me of my stupidity and good luck five days ago."

"Stupid? In what way?" Accipiter's curiosity demanded.

"We trusted Alexander Kronus more than we should have. The man wanted that sword no matter how he got it, but like us—he was changed."

"Changed?"

"Kronus realized that there's something more to that sword than just a relic of a long-dead king. Marcella was a spectator, and so was Kronus. They both witnessed an unusual phenomena or occurrence. Isn't that right, Marcella?" Nerian asked, looking in her direction.

Marcella's eyes grew brighter. "The truth be told, that day on the rooftop of David's Tower, we witnessed an incredible sight, and it changed more than one of us. Samuel, Arria's friend, wielded the sword; it hummed, almost sang, in his hand, and the glow that emanated from the blade and hilt in the orange light appeared magical. It even left a painless mark on his palm. As if it meant to choose and brand him in a holy way."

She took a breath, swallowed a few sips of wine, and continued, "I believe that what they say about the weapon is true. Only a chosen person can wield that sword without a curse. For the seconds I held the sword, it burned my hand, and I was forced to throw it down. I'm so relieved Nerian never touched it. And now, neither would I. Not for all the riches in the world. That's how convinced I am, and you know, I have a fondness for wealth." A coy grin tugged the corners of her lips.

"Who has the sword, and what will happen now?" Accipiter replied.

"Arria and Garic. They'll decide, but I believe it's destined for the Church of the Holy Sepulchre."

"And Kronus gave up on the sword too?" Accipiter interjected, surprised by what he was hearing.

"He did, and wisely so. He fought against Samuel, who got the best of him. I didn't see them fight because Arria and I were engaged in our own battle." A lightness filled Marcella's face, and warmth colored her tone. "That day, I desired not only the prize but revenge for the resentments I felt my entire life toward my half-sister, Arria. We struggled hand to hand, and I pushed her over the parapet. I can't explain, but in the moment, I saw her hanging from the roof, grasping desperately onto that iron ring, I thought my hatred complete, full circle. She would fall to the ground, broken and dead. An end, she deserved for just being Arria—born to a Roman soldier and senator who loved and acknowledged her and called her daughter. For being fortunate.

"As I looked down on her, and she pleaded not just for her life but for the life she carried, a chill ran through me. I heard her call me sister and swear she would love me as her own blood. I looked at my hand—the burn was gone. An impulse compelled me to reach out and grab her arm, and with all my strength, I pulled her to safety. Seconds later, we embraced for the first time in our lives."

Marcella felt the need to pause and absorb the gravity of her statement and what it meant to her after all the years of her conflict with Arria and now behind them. "Arria did not lie. She has accepted me as her sister and helped Nerian heal. Her husband, Garic, has forgiven me for trying to take his life years ago on the battlefield at Catalaunum and has accepted me as well. I've never felt so full and alive—happy."

Marcella smiled at Nerian and then gazed back at Accipiter, who nodded. In his estimation, they both appeared at peace and perhaps resolute about their future. He asked, "What's next for you both?"

Nerian answered, "Marcella asked Arria if we might travel with them after this affair with the sword is over and their mission completed. Marcella wants to be with Arria when her child is born. Afterward, we'll decide on our future and where we might go. We're both adventurous, but we do long for a home and a family. Maybe, when our wanderlust is complete, we'll settle down near Garic's farm."

"We're excited to visit Wild Honey," Marcella added. "Arria claims it's quite beautiful."

Accipiter sat a little deeper into his pillow and crossed his arms. "Amazing," was all he said, but then, he added. "I guess this will leave me with Alexander Kronus to contend with."

"How so?" Nerian asked, showing some surprise.

"I received a letter from him a few days ago. He explained only that things had gone badly regarding the weapon. He apologized for playing two sides in his attempt to procure the sword. He wrote that he no longer desired to own it, and he would not interfere in any more attempts I might make to possess the artifact. However, like a sharp and shrewd businessman, he mentioned that if I was interested in buying or selling any other items, artifacts, or weapons, he'd be pleased to work with me. I could inquire discreetly through Milvus at Moon Gold Antiquities, and his sister, Valeria, his Constantinople liaison. They're aware of what transpired with the sword and have no interest in it as well. He also assured me he had an excellent pipeline into Jerusalem with a high rate of guarantee." Accipiter laughed. "See, not all is lost."

Marcella grinned, nodding her head, and Nerian raised his cup. "To new ventures," he toasted.

"Yes, to new ventures—especially now that the sword is lost to us," Accipiter added with a small pout.

They laughed, drank, and Accipiter called out, "Babajan! Another cup to toast the newlyweds!"

XXV

Child of Mine

JERUSALEM: The Red Torch Inn—The 8th day of Junius,
Early Morning

GARIC

Garic raised his head from the pillow. The bed felt warm, where Arria had slept beside him, but she was gone. Most likely to bring him food to break his fast. He sat up slowly. His wound itched beneath his bandage, but he resisted the urge to scratch the fresh scar and only pressed on the woolen strip. Days earlier, the physician checked the catgut stitches that were naturally absorbed and announced all was well. Garic's wound was healing, and he insisted that Garic move about, but not too strenuously. Being a good patient, Garic had obeyed. He heard from Arria that Nerian, in a neighboring room, was recovering nicely and doing the same. Unlike poor Telemachus, Garic and the Saxon mercenary had survived the ambush and altercation.

The door opened, and Arria swept in, holding a basket covered with a linen cloth. "Good morning, my love," Arria said, her manner bright.

"Good morning," Garic answered as he slipped on trousers, lying at the end of the bed, and stood, pulling them to his waist and carefully over his bandage. In his bare feet, he padded over to a small table and two chairs as Arria pulled, one by one, a round, crusty loaf of freshly baked bread, its aroma strong and sweet, a jar of dark honey, and a wine flask from the basket and set them on the table.

Garic wrapped his arms around her waist, and his kiss lingered on her neck, then her lips.

Arria dropped the basket onto the floor and tenderly returned his embrace. Afterward, she whispered, "I'm happy you're feeling yourself again."

"*Ja*," he replied, with a half-grin, but added, "I'm eager to finish this mission, so we can return to Licia and go home. But forgive me.

In all this turmoil, I've been concerned with my own health. I've neglected to ask about you and how you are feeling."

"I'm well, despite what happened at the tower, and thankfully, this time, there has been very little morning sickness. Instead, my craving for figs and honey has grown, especially in the afternoon, oh, and now water. I'm thirsty for water." Arria started to laugh, reached toward the floor, and pulled a water pouch from the basket. "This child, I suspect, will own a sweet disposition, but I'm calling him my water baby."

"Him?" Garic asked, taken by surprise and amused curiosity.

"Well, only the Lord knows, but my intuition hints a boy. But perhaps the child will be a bold girl like Licia."

"Either boy or girl will bring me joy, and we shall pray the child is born healthy." Garic paused, then pursed his lips. His sentiment spun into another, and he added, "Arria, we must end this mission as quickly as possible and return to Licia and Brother Bruno. I want to take you home where you can safely birth this child."

A small sob escaped Arria, and the sudden tears welling in her eyes dissolved her sunny disposition. "I agree," she said, wiping several drops from her cheeks. "These last few days have been filled with emotion, pain, fear—and death. I never imagined when we left Constantinople, we would encounter so much conflict." She shook her head. "Even now, we missed our appointment with the bishop and must return to meet with the patriarch. But has the danger passed? Others may still seek the sword."

Garic clutched her elbow. "True. We can be sure of nothing, and possibly, we'll face more danger. I'm certain the bishop, upon his return, heard about us from Father Isaac. They may be wondering where we are, even though you sent them word about the reason for our delay. They might have sent a scout into the city to investigate our claims and whereabouts. We should return later this morning to the Offices of the Bishops and insist on seeing a bishop, or even Patriarch Juvenal, right away. If no one will meet with us and make us a priority, then I say we give the sword to Samuel."

A grim expression, doubtful but mildly resolute, covered Arria's face. "And if later, we are confronted by officials looking for the sword, what will we say? We lost it?"

Garic watched the emotion beneath Arria's chest rise. He shook his head and leaned closer. "We can say it was taken from us, and the man escaped."

"But that's not true."

"It would be if the man who took it was Samuel. We would just hold back . . . that we know the culprit." Garic's eyebrow raised, and he slipped in a grin.

Arria avoided his gaze and frowned. "It's unlike you to suggest such an idea. I find that risky and would fear for Samuel's safety. Besides, I still believe that all pilgrims should have the opportunity to safely and easily view this prize in the most logical setting—in my estimation—the Church of the Holy Sepulchre."

Garic sighed, swept a hand through his hair, and sat on the chair. He grabbed the bread, ripped off a chunk, and reached for the honey jar. "I'm hungry. We should eat," he said with a resigned expression, but quickly added, "You're right, I wouldn't want Samuel in any danger. I promised to complete this mission with you and for the emperor. You know what I think, but the final choice is yours." He pointed to the other chair. "Come, sit and share this bread with me, and afterward, we'll go to the Offices of the Bishop and urgently request an audience. Hopefully, the bishop or patriarch will meet with us and help bring this mission to an end."

The bread's aroma filled the room, and the stream of sunlight across the table made the bee nectar glow. A tiny pout lined Arria's lips, but she came and sat across from him. Garic handed her a chunk of bread and slid the honey jar across the table in her direction.

"My frustration will not outweigh my determination," she replied, cupping the morsel in her hand. "I agree. After we eat, we'll ready ourselves and bring the sword to these holy fathers. In the name of Emperor Marcian, I'll request an assurance that the relic is enshrined at Holy Sepulchre. Once they confirm our petition, I'll place the Sword of David in their hands. We'll be free to return to Constantinople for a final meeting with the emperor and then to Gaul and Wild Honey. I promise."

Garic reached for Arria's slender fingers and wrapped his warrior hand around them. They were warm to the touch, and his heart beat faster. "I trust your sense of loyalty and the honor you feel that's tied to this quest. I also believe in your promise. We'll get this done, and with your sister, Nerian, Licia, and Bruno in tow, we'll return home. *I promise you*." He kissed the tips of her fingers. Arria's eyes grew warm, and her beautiful smile made Garic smile, too.

JERUSALEM: The Streets—The 8th day of Junius, Mid-Morning

HE

(Nemesis)

He pulled the petite girl along by her little hand, and the brother, called Bruno, walked beside her. They had been silly doves, easy to fool. Odd how people, especially children, the elderly, and religious folks, trusted. He knew better—learned early. He had promised himself to never trust another living soul, not even the dead. He had trusted his mother a long time ago, but now her spirit plagued him. Many nights, he woke covered in sweat. She had come to him saying: *You are good, my son, not evil.* Even now, he heard her words echoing in his mind, but hers was the biggest betrayal of all. He was not good.

He hated himself for it, but an unexplainable, almost supreme power within him had grown greater than his self-loathing. This power spiraled upward and through him, catching his imagination, whispering in his head—*You're a victor, the rightful owner of your father's land, an avenger*—and commanding that he walk this path, the way to his ultimate goal—his ultimate happiness. The first sword he stole had been a fake. Arria and Garic would pay for his humiliation and defeat. *The little girl will be the price.* This time, he must possess the *real* Sword of David—then sell the weapon for every piece of gold he deserved.

He tugged a little harder on Licia's hand. Her feet tripped along, trying to keep pace, and Bruno wheezed behind him. The streets of Jerusalem hummed. Mid-morning shoppers, pilgrims, and merchants, beckoning to passersby to enter their stores, crowded the streets. They had left the monastery for Jerusalem earlier in the day. Convincing Bruno to bring Licia and come with him was not difficult. He simply told the child's monastic caretakers, and the old monk, that the Lady Arria had enlisted him to escort them quickly to Jerusalem where they would reunite and celebrate Licia's birthday the next day. Nemesis chuckled to himself. Almost too easy.

After the day in Milvus' shop, when he discovered that the weapon he possessed was a fake, a poor replica, his humiliation, despair, and rage had forced him to slip backward. He wanted to dull his pain with the poppy, that euphoric elixir. His craving, but lack of coin, demanded he find an easy source. He realized that the best, quickest route to the drug was to return to Brother Evander at the Monastery of the Cross.

It was on the short trip back to find Evander and the poppy that images of the girl child and Brother Bruno took shape in his mind. With them, he would rise up again like the phoenix, the bird of the old story that rose reborn from the ashes of fire and destruction. He would hold them as willing captives and trade them for David's sword that the Lady Arria and her husband possessed. How could a mother and father refuse?

Before leaving Jerusalem, he heard from an arms dealer with a shady reputation, and to whom he hoped to sell the weapon, a fight over an *ancient artifact* had ensued at the Tower of David. Dead and wounded men were brought to The Red Torch, an inn, situated between Sion and David's Gates. Had others in pursuit of the sword managed to get ahead of him? Now that he was back in the city, he must start at the inn. But first, he would stop and buy his little dove and the old man some food.

Licia tugged on his sleeve and looked at him with big blue eyes. "When will we see Mama?"

"Are you hungry, little bird?" Nemesis stopped, ignoring her question and smiled.

"Yes."

Bruno came to a halt as well, but with a few panting breaths.

Licia looked at the brother and asked, "We are going to see Mama and Papa soon, aren't we?"

Brother Bruno smiled at her. "Of course, my child. We'll be with them shortly."

Bruno glanced at Nemesis. He nodded his assurance and rested his gaze on Licia. "Now then, I shall get you and Brother Bruno something to eat before we find your mother."

They followed the Cardo south, then turned west on a small street that brought them onto David's Road. Nemesis learned from a merchant that they were just south of the inn. He led them to a food stall beside the road near the wall. Crates were piled on one another filled with a variety of fruits and vegetables. Beside the boxes, a table held several baskets filled with wheat bread, and one longer basket held smoked fish. Nemesis chose two fishes, a pomegranate, a cluster of grapes, and a small loaf of bread.

After he paid the merchant, he addressed Brother Bruno, "There are mulberry trees here to give us shade. You can rest. I won't tire you and the girl out. While you eat, I'll jog down the road and look for the inn where Lady Arria told me she's staying. If she's there, I'll return for you and bring you both to her."

"And if she's not there?" Bruno questioned, his brow wrinkled. Black tufts of his hair and the folds in the robe draped over his lean frame lifted in the breeze.

"I'll return, and we'll continue our search."

Bruno appeared weary and looked relieved to be able to sit. He nodded, and Licia bobbed her head in her childlike manner.

"Here, take this water." He handed Bruno a leather pouch. "The day is hot. Drink. Make sure the girl drinks as well."

Bruno nodded. "How long will you be gone?"

"The inn is not so far. I expect to return within the half-hour or less."

"Very well. Licia and I will wait for you here. I hope you find them."

Nemesis gave the monk a wide grin. "I hope I do, too."

JERUSALEM: The Red Torch Inn—The 8th day of Junius, Mid-Morning

ARRIA

Arria entered The Red Torch's dining area and looked for the innkeeper. The tall, squarely built manager with a grizzled beard was sweeping the floor near a window. The shining light streaming onto the floor promised a bright, summer day just outside the door. As Arria approached him, her soft linen gown swished against her legs, and she lifted her light shawl higher over her shoulders.

The innkeeper had a tough look about him but owned a heart of gold. He had been so kind and helpful on their chaotic arrival and most willing to accommodate any of their needs. Arria smiled at him, wishing him a good day, and inquired about Marcella and Nerian. She had knocked on their bedroom door, but no one answered.

"My lady, the mistress, and her new husband just returned from the church, but have gone out again."

"Husband?"

"Yes, they were married early this morning. Thinking that I might see you, she asked me to give you this note and say that they would see you later this evening." The innkeeper handed her a small rolled parchment.

Garic came down the stairs into the dining room and joined them. Overhearing their conversation, he asked, "Who is married?" His gentle hand caressed her hair clasped with a silver brooch at the nape of her neck.

Several curls fell loose over Arria's cheek as she shook her head. "My sister, I suspect, will remain forever impulsive," she replied, pushing the wayward strands behind her ear.

He smirked. "I know someone just as impulsive as Marcella. They're related."

"Whoever do you mean?" Arria piped back, offering him a pretty scowl. She unrolled the note and explained while she read. "Marcella says that she and Nerian decided days ago that they would marry once he was able. The morning's sultry heat, the scent of blossoms in the air, and golden light, lured them to this day." Arria glanced at Garic and added, "There is a poetic touch to her writing." Then she returned to the note. "She asks our forgiveness for not telling us sooner, but after what we all went through, they felt their marriage should be a private ritual. They hope later, once we're away from Jerusalem and arrive in Constantinople, we can celebrate as a family together. After the ceremony, they plan on seeking out Nerian's friend Accipiter, the Egyptian merchant, to set things right with him."

"That's interesting. What do we know of this merchant?" Garic asked, looking uncertain.

"I only know that Marcella, Nerian, and Accipiter were working together to get the sword and became also involved with those awful men at the tower: Alexander, but really Kalev, Corvus, and that frightening but unfortunate man, Jax. Marcella has admitted feeling some remorse over killing Jax, but driven by her hatred and desire to confront me herself, she felt justified. She also explained, as we waited while the doctor treated you and Nerian, how she and Nerian had come to know these men."

"Hmm. Do you believe the worst is behind us? And Marcella has changed?"

"I want to believe in Marcella, and so, I will. If I'm wrong, we will find out soon enough."

"But at our peril?"

"Have faith. We can all learn new truths and, in the process, grow. Which is—change. Is it not?"

Garic took Arria in his arms and held her tight. "And you tell me I'm the wise one." He held her chin and kissed her mouth, then lightly on her forehead. "If today goes well, tonight, I'll love you like a bridegroom as well."

A lusty laugh escaped her lips, and Arria hugged him closer. His neck smelled from the honey soap he used to wash and shave his face to just a fine stubble. "Then, let's leave now and deliver this demanding sword."

Garic clasped her tighter, then stepped back. "I just remembered, where's Samuel? I thought we'd find him here huddled over a bowl of barley stew. More than once, these last few days, he's expressed a great fondness for the dish."

She held Garic's hands now. "I can appreciate why. It's quite delicious, and in the last few weeks, not all our meals have filled us or tasted so good."

"Perhaps he's at the stable, helping the innkeeper's sons build the coffin for Telemachus. The innkeeper and his wife's kindnesses, from calling the physician to preparing Telemachus' body for burial, have been without measure."

Arria tilted her chin. "Actually, he left early this morning. We met as he was going out, and I was coming in from the market with our morning meal. He's gone with the eldest son to transport Telemachus' corpse to the cemetery now that his body is prepared and dressed for burial. I have sent word of his death to the emperor with the details for the benefit of Telemachus' family. Through Samuel, I've arranged for our friend and soldier's funeral service to be held customarily at sundown. Once we finish the business of the sword, we'll return to the inn and collect Nerian and Marcella and proceed to the cemetery.

My heart aches for Telemachus and this tragic outcome. He was a good man and too young to die now."

"Mellitula, a soldier's life is unpredictable, but his death saddens me as well."

Arria felt a lump in her throat, "We won't forget him."

"And after the burial?" Garic asked, looping his arm through hers while they walked out the door to the warmth and sunlight.

"Let us spend another night here in the city. Then in the morning, we'll return to The Olive Tree Inn, collect all our belongings, horses and mule, and leave right away for the monastery. I'm anxious to see Licia and celebrate her birthday. The following day, we can begin planning and packing for our trip to Constantinople."

Garic nodded his agreement and said, "Wait here, Arria. I'll go to the room and fetch the sword." He gave her a loving look and reaching for her hand, he kissed her fingers.

Arria crossed one end of her scarf over her shoulder as Garic went inside, then she looked out over the day.

When Garic returned, he held the shoulder sack and his own sword tucked into the scabbard on his belt. "Are you ready, Mellitula, to bring this mission to an end?"

"Krieger, my love, I've never been more ready. Today, we keep our promise to Emperor Marcian. I only hope Patriarch Juvenal agrees."

HE

(Nemesis)

He couldn't believe his eyes. There they stood. Garic kissing Arria's fingers. Having an intimate conversation. He froze. The tenderness exchanged between the husband and wife brought a cynical chill to his bones. *What shit.* A twitch gripped the corner of his mouth, and his eyes narrowed in the fleeting memory of his father beating his mother. The bastard's drunken shouts—her bleating cries made from her knees, bruised hands covering her head. He grunted. *They'll be there one day,* he thought, with a twisted smile. Pulling a flask from his shoulder bag, he gulped down some wine. He felt the pain nag louder. He needed more poppy. The amount Evander had given him was weakening, but his chance to get the sword and take his revenge was unfolding now. He must act.

Nemesis wiped the sweat streaming down his face with the back of his hand and watched Garic enter the inn while Arria waited. What was happening? He kept his eye on her. She was the most elegant creature he'd ever seen. Chestnut flowing curls, beautiful green eyes, and her shape so graceful and feminine. Why not capture her? A tingling of desire ebbed through his body. His eyes widened. Over time, his mistress, poppy, had numbed his feelings of lust. He looked again at Arria with a sharper vision. Should he add her to his bevy of doves? *Take the mother over the child* popped into his mind. Nemesis watched Garic return with a bag. Most likely, the sword rested inside the woolen sack. The couple started down David's road headed to St. John's Street.

Within seconds, he was running back to the mulberry tree to gather up Bruno and baby dove. He would force Arria and Garic onto a side street just off the road before they reached St. John's. His heart beat faster with every footfall. Exhilaration coursed through his blood and filled him to the brim with determination. He would take the sword and his revenge. He would win.

XXVI

What We Seem and Who We Are

JERUSALEM: An Alley—The 8th day of Junius, Mid-Morning

HE

(Nemesis)

"Come, little one, we must leave right now!" Nemesis huffed as he ran up to Licia and Brother Bruno beneath the tree on a mound of grass. Bruno sat munching on the grapes, but Licia had risen to her feet when she saw him coming. She appeared anxious to hear what he would say. He came to a full stop in front of them and took a few deep breaths.

"Did you find, Mama? Are we going to meet her?" Licia asked.

Bruno pushed to his knees and then to his feet. Yanking the long strips of his cord belt, sagging from his lean waist to the side, he dusted grass from his robe. His short, wavy strands of hair, circling his tonsured scalp, appeared damp and wilted in the heat. "Did you talk to them? Are they well?" he asked.

"The Lady Arria and Garic are expecting us but have gone on ahead. They've important business concerning the sword and wish to make arrangements for the girl's birthday celebration tomorrow. I've been instructed to collect you both and catch up to them."

Bruno picked up his bag with a lopsided grin, ready. The girl stood waiting and chattered how excited she was to see her *Mama* and *Papa*. Nemesis grabbed Licia's hand and led them down the road at almost a trot. In the distance, he could see the bend in the path and the faint figures of Arria and Garic. He knew from his earlier trip to the city that just around the curve, a small alley off the road led to a garbage heap, and farther up, David's Road ran into St. John's Street. It was crucial to time things just right.

"Hurry!" Nemesis yelled as he dragged the girl along faster. Bruno still didn't understand what was happening and followed. "Is that the lady and her husband in the distance?" was all he said.

Nemesis glanced over his shoulder at the monk and only nodded.

Arria and Garic's figures were growing bigger as they began to round the bend. Nemesis pushed harder. Licia's feet began to trip and drag. "Hurry!" he yelled at her and pulled her along harder. Several whimpers fell from her mouth.

Nemesis felt for the sword at his side and his knife beside it with his free hand. The lady and noble were gone and out of sight, the curve in the road hiding them. This was almost the moment he'd been waiting for. He licked his lips and turned to the girl and shouted, "Run, if you want to see your mama and papa." He glanced at Bruno and barked, "You too, run."

The brother, huffing and puffing, furrowed his brow but obeyed.

They made the bend in the road, and off to his left sat the entrance to the alley. A little farther down the road and in hearing distance, Arria and Garic walked with their backs to them. Nemesis pulled Licia to the alley's entrance. He ignored Bruno, who stopped to catch his breath, looking confused.

Nemesis pulled his knife. "Hey! Hey!" he screamed and yanked Licia from behind and held her in front of him. His one hand clenched her shoulder, and the other held the blade at her throat.

Bruno gasped, stunned by what he saw, and ran shouting, waving his hands at Arria and Garic, who turned around. They walked at first, and then, raced their way.

He dragged the little dove deeper into the narrow alley toward a back wall. The foul odor of rotting food, excrement, and decaying animals buried in a mountain of garbage forced him to wince. The girl started to cry, but he squeezed her jaw. "Shut up, or I'll kill your papa, then your mama, and then you, or maybe I'll keep you as my pet."

The dove shivered from head to toe as he returned his grip to her shoulder. Sniffling, she stifled a sob.

Thundering footsteps and the figures of Arria, Garic, and Bruno entered the alley. Garic led, with Bruno and Arria behind him. They halted, side by side, ten feet in front of him. Garic held an axe and his sword sheathed on his belt. Arria's chest heaved; Bruno wiped his brow, looking grim.

"Justus?" Arria sounded surprised. Despite small gaps in her breath, she demanded, "What is the meaning of this?"

Garic, a fierce look on his face and axe raised, interjected, "Why are you here in Jerusalem—this alley—holding Licia hostage?"

His hidden self revealed and no longer Nemesis, Justus answered, "Where should I begin?" Unable to suppress a biting sneer, he added, "I came for my prize. The one you tried to cheat me out of with your fake sword."

Arria raised a pacifying hand, looked at Licia, and then him. "Please, let her go. With the knife pressed against her throat, you might kill her. Please, she's just a little girl and did you no harm."

The girl whimpered again, but he tapped her cheek in a warning and hissed, "Not until I get what I came for. Slashing her throat would mean nothing to me. Not after everything I've suffered. Without the truth, my vengeance is not complete."

"Justus, you're the emperor's soldier." Garic's brow furrowed, and his tone expressed disbelief, "What has happened?"

"Are you surprised?" he snapped, finding it hard to contain himself. "We stand here for a reason. The sword and its value—is owed to *me*. I'm entitled. I grew up the son of a Pannonian landowner. My brother and I toiled beside our father to farm the land. But all the years of Roman occupation, heavy taxes, and the government stealing crops for the passing armies made my father angry and bitter. He drank and inflicted cruelties on us. On the outside, we were nobles and free, but in truth, we were poor and broken."

Arria quickly responded, "But you rose through the ranks to the elite guard. Aren't you proud and content with that?" She shifted her eyes to her little bird.

"Ha! Even the military proved painful," Justus spat. "My younger brother, Seneca, and I joined the army when he came of age. We were close." He stopped. Taking a sharp breath, he swallowed, then set his jaw. "Over time, our nobility and hard work helped us to advance. But I rose higher and faster. I became a tribune and went into the emperor's guard. Seneca didn't live long enough to rise past centurion. He never adapted as well as I, and after his fallout with Lucius Marcian . . ."

"Lucius Marcian?" Arria echoed. Garic frowned and growled, *Marcian?*

"What?" he laughed. "Surprised again? When I got to court, I made the acquaintance of a *merchant-sailor* and court informant.

Paolino. Remember him? For a price, he shared information with me that might benefit the emperor. On the side, he traded in contraband and drugs.

"One night, Paolino, in a poppy stupor, told me about an ancient sword belonging to King David. He claimed it was owned by Emperor Marcian's son, Lucius. Paolino had heard, from a soldier under Lucius Marcian's command, that the soldiers believed the weapon was cursed. Especially, after the drunken fight involving the sword and two of Marcian's soldiers, one called Leo and the other— Seneca, my brother." His temples throbbed. A cavern of pain lived within him; he must speak. They should know why they would pay the price with their daughter's life.

"The story of the sword's curse spread among the ranks after Leo was crippled and Seneca, sent by Marcian on a dangerous mission . . . was killed in a barbarian ambush." Justus licked his lips, his throat parched and dry. "Rage consumed me. Knowing the precise details of my brother's death tore my heart to shreds. Lucius Marcian knew that Seneca wouldn't survive the mission. He sent my brother to his death." Justus spat on the ground. "He murdered my brother—my best friend."

Licia whimpered once more, and Justus swept his hand from her shoulder and squeezed her chin.

Arria took a slight step but stopped. "Shh . . . Licia. Mama's here. Don't cry," she said and shot him a steely look.

Justus gazed at Arria. "When I heard your husband was mortally wounded while wielding the sword, I was overcome with joy." He smirked as his inner demon gloated, and smoothed the hair on Licia's head. She sniffled but remained still, looking at her mother. "My army service is at an end. With the money from the weapon, I can return home, buy-back and rebuild our farm, but before that happens, I'll need the sword . . . and retribution. I cannot rest or truly breathe without it."

Garic tilted his head and stared at him.

Justus detected a calm and predatory expression in his gaze. He arched his back and stood ready.

"Lower your knife, and I'll lower my axe," the blond barbarian offered. "Perhaps we can find a better solution. We'll trade you the sword for our daughter's life and let you leave peacefully, but first, we must know how a noble soldier arrived at such an end."

Anger fired through him and rested on his lips. "This is not my end—only my beginning," he snarled.

Arria stretched out a hand in a gentle manner. "Please. Just lower the knife for a moment."

The demon silent now, the dove's voice, soft and kind, resonated in him. Justus let the knife drop a few inches, and Garic did the same with the axe.

Brother Bruno shifted, shuffling his feet, and wiped his brow.

Justus shot him a warning look and quickly raised the knife against the girl's throat.

Arria took a step forward.

"Stop right there, or I'll cut her throat," Justus commanded. "Now, get me the sword."

ARRIA

"Tell me first what I must know, then the sword will be yours, and we'll not stop you," Arria answered in her dulcet tone. All her life, she'd been told that her voice held a warmth, pleasing to the ear. She tried using it now to persuade and buy time. She believed and knew Garic understood once Justus had the sword, he planned to kill Licia, his final act of revenge. They needed more time. If Justus let down his guard, Garic would strike. She was sure of it.

Justus stared at her. "Get on with it then, my patience is dying."

"Did you kill Paolino aboard the ship?"

"I saw Paolino before he saw me. I couldn't risk him exposing me in front of everyone. I needed to protect my identity. When I saw the squall approaching, I lured him to the stern behind a stack of open crates holding cords of rope. Before he could say a word, I stabbed him in the heart, tied him with rope, and tied the other end to a cleat. I carved a sword on his forehead—you mistook it for a cross—to seal my promise for revenge. Then, I hung him over the side for all to witness."

"And Leo? You killed him as well?" Arria quickly added, seeing that Licia's legs were quivering from fatigue.

Justus grimaced. "Leo enlisted Seneca in his scheme to take the sword that led them to fighting and dire consequences. He deserved blame for my brother's death as much as Marcian. But Leo was on the ship. Two kills would have been difficult, so I knew I could wait. Leo didn't know me, and he was always drunk. Easy prey."

"And the *star* carved on his forehead?"

An impatient expression crossed his face, and he sighed. "David's star showed my gratification, and like Paolino, was meant as a warning."

As Justus spoke, Arria secretly touched Garic's leg, she felt him tense and knew he was ready, just waiting for an opportunity.

When the soldier finished speaking, Arria raised her palms up and took a small step forward. She watched Justus stiffen, but she extended her arms outward. "Let Licia go. Take me as your hostage, even after we give you the sword. Garic or any authorities will not pursue you if I'm your willing prisoner. If later you choose to release me, then we'll all have what we want—you will own the sword, and Licia will be free."

Justus tilted his head, and his gaze showed a longing that may have filled the heart of an innocent boy. For a moment, he appeared vulnerable and answered, "All right, we can trade." Then without warning, the fragile young man in him vanished. His face twisted into a dark glare, and he barked, "But let me see the sword first!"

"Brother Bruno," Arria responded softly. "Bring the bag forward and remove the sword, so Justus may see."

The monk obeyed and retrieved the sack. With trembling fingers, he opened the bag and lifted up the sword. The gems in the pommel, and the metal scabbard, gleamed in the sunlight.

Justus stared, transfixed by the beauty of the sword. His hand, holding the knife against Licia's throat, unintentionally lowered.

Arria shot a rapid glance toward Garic. His eyes shone with determination, and a readiness beamed through him. Then suddenly, in slow horror, Arria watched Licia. Stricken with fear and weakened by the heat, she began to faint, and her knees buckled. As their daughter wilted and fell, her body pulled the lunatic soldier, gripping her arm forward.

Garic ran toward Justus. Like a wolf, he lunged and threw his axe. It whirled through the static air, struck Justus on the edge of his shoulder, and glanced off, clattering on the ground. Garic drew his sword.

Taken by surprise, Justus dropped his knife. He reached across his chest and touched the small gash on his shoulder.

Brother Bruno bolted to Licia and dragged her away as Arria ran up and guided them to safety beside a low wall.

Justus quickly rebounded. His eyes spitting fire, he jumped back and drew his sword. The afternoon light bounced off his vertically held blade. Garic rushed him and, with two hands, brought his sword down on an angle. The force of metal clashing against metal sounded through the stifling heat around them. Justus blocked Garic's blows, then leaned in, pushed him away, and pulled back. They circled one another. Sweat poured down their faces, and they wiped the perspiration from their eyes.

Garic maintained his distance but stepped close enough to tap Justus' sword. Justus swung his weapon down, then slid sideways, dust circling his ankles. Garic jumped in and tapped the soldier's sword once more. Justus swung his weapon again. He tried to deflect Garic's, but Garic dropped his sword under his and attacked from the other side. He cut Justus' leg. Justus jumped back. A dark-red surge spread across Justus' tunic as he swung his sword up and over and struck against Garic's waiting blade. Like hawks, their silvery talons raised, they clashed.

Arria pressed her hands against her cheeks. She wanted to cover her ears—to protect herself against the *clang, clang, clang,* of crashing metal. Garic's breath was labored, and his eyes narrowed, showing his pain. Arria's heart raced, and a lump filled her throat. Could his wound, newly healed, bear the slashing blows?

Very slowly, a low hum like a bee's song and a sudden vibration crept its way into the battle happening before her. Arria tore her eyes away from the men and looked around. Licia sat next to Brother Bruno in a spot shaded by a larger heap of trash, with the monk's arm wrapped around her. Not far from her feet, the bag holding David's sword lay open, the grip and its hilt in view. Arria looked back toward the men. Justus hacked step after step while Garic parried every blow.

Justus screamed, "Bastard," and crossing swords, he pushed and wrestled Garic to the ground. He leaped up and stood over him. A victorious bellow poured from his lips. He raised the grip with both hands, the tip pointing toward Garic's chest.

"You *will not* kill my husband!" Arria's angry shout rang through the air.

Justus spun toward her voice, just behind his shoulder.

Arria lunged and stabbed him above his belt. The sword glided deep into his stomach, and his flesh skimmed across the inscription carved in David's blade—up to the glittering hilt.

Justus crumpled to the ground. The sword slid from his body and stood proudly in Arria's hand. He lay on his back and stared up at her. Garic, to his knee now, watched her too. The faint hum rode the breeze, and the sun broke free from the passing clouds, making the day brighter and beautiful.

Justus fixed his frantic gaze on Arria, and tears welled in his eyes. "A dove has killed me," he whispered, the sad irony reflected in his tone.

Arria knelt beside him with the sword nestled in her hand. She looked at Justus and shook her head. Her voice was soft, but her tone steely, "I'm not a dove—I'm a raven."

XXVII

The Truth Be Told

JERUSALEM: An Alley—The 8th day of Junius, Almost Noon

ARRIA

Justus closed his eyes, his chest fell, and a final gasp left him.

Arria rose. She opened her hand and lifted the grip. A red stripe rested across her palm. She stared at it a moment, then went to Garic and knelt beside him. She laid the sword—quiet now, the bright sheen faded—on the ground beside them.

He grasped the back of her head, and crushing her curls in his fingers, he rested his forehead against hers.

"I've killed a man," she whispered. "Justus—someone we thought we knew. I had no choice. I couldn't risk him killing you, and maybe later, Licia, to complete his revenge."

"Arria, I heard what you said to Justus. You're the bravest woman I've ever known. The first day I saw you, I knew there could be no other love for me. We proved the prophecy. We are each other's destiny." Arria and Garic rose together, and he held her in his arms. "You saved my life and our daughter's. Let me see your hand," he said and gently opened her fingers. He gazed at the mark across her palm. "Your heart is stronger than a sword among ravens. I suspect only a few can wield the blade. The weapon chose you and Samuel. A great honor among the living and the dead."

Arria rested her head against his chest. She felt changed. Was the sword meant to be revered only by pilgrims or returned to the source and people of its creation? Samuel and Garic were right. "The sword belongs to Israel, its home," she said, and Garic nodded.

Arria turned toward Licia, who now ran to her. The monk walked toward them, relief on his face. Garic stepped beside her, and together they hugged Licia, who wrapped her slender arms around Arria's hips and held her tightly.

"Are you all right, my sweet?" Arria asked, bending toward Licia, stroking her hair.

Licia nodded and hugged her again.

A sudden cloud of dust and horse's hooves alerted them to an approaching rider. Samuel rode up and jumped from his mount. "What has happened here?" He looked over at Justus' body and then the sword, laying on the ground.

Arria sighed. "It was Justus who killed Paolino and Leo—stole the replica sword. His actions were revenge for his brother's death. He blamed my dead husband, Lucius, and Leo. The informant, Paolino, got in his way. He tried to steal the sword from us and would have killed Licia, but Garic fought him and saved her."

"In the end, Arria saved me," Garic added, and glanced at her with admiration. "She wielded the sword and killed Justus. See her hand," he said, pointing to her palm.

Arria raised it for Samuel to see.

Samuel stared. Lightly taking her hand, he lifted it higher. "My dear, brave friend, you're like a sister to me. I cannot say I understand what has happened to us, but without question, we've been chosen and blessed." A wave of emotion passed over him, and it could be heard in the heartfelt tone of his voice. "I must confess that I've had a change of heart. This magnificent sword, containing a strange and wondrous power, deserves more than isolation and solitude in the hands of aging rabbis and patriarchs. It should reside in the Church of the Holy Sepulchre, where it will be kept safe, viewed, and admired by many—perhaps even by my people, if only on our holy day. And hopefully, one day, Jews will be allowed to enter our city again freely. Maybe the presence of King David's Sword is the beginning and sign we need."

Arria glanced at Garic, and they both smiled. "Oh, Samuel," she said, "just before you arrived, I conceded to Garic that I would give you the sword as you wished. What now?"

Garic placed his hands on his hips in a waiting posture.

Samuel lifted tender brown eyes to her and pursed his lips, but a sweet grin seeped into the corners of his mouth. "Arria, your love and loyalty have always given me hope and been a source of strength. You bought me my freedom, and I know your heart better than you may realize. I'll not change my mind. The sword is yours." He hesitated, and his eyes grew round. "But, last night, an idea came to me as I settled down to sleep that perhaps . . . you might gift me

Bathsheba's star with its diamond, and let it rest in the hands of my Jewish brethren."

Arria shot Garic a quick glance, who shook his head. "I never said a word of this to him."

Samuel swung his gaze between them. His brow wrinkled, and he appeared baffled, but asked, "Will you give us the star?"

Arria stepped forward and hugged him. "You're the best of men, Samuel Ben Zachariah. I believe the sword has spoken. The star will go to the people of a chosen one. Guard it well, and let it live through the generations. David's love, his sin, and redemption have come full circle. Its mission is complete."

Garic spoke up, "You've both made the right decision." He picked up the sword and handed it to Arria. "And we must go. Time grows short. We must see the Patriarch about the sword, and bury Telemachus . . . and now, Justus. Brother Bruno, please bring Licia back to the inn and wait for us there. Samuel, we'll use your mount to carry the body."

The brother took Licia by the hand after Arria kissed her, and Samuel went to gather his horse while Garic walked toward Justus.

Arria stood there. She looked at the sun high in the sky. She rested her free hand on her belly. She had said the words and taken an action that now defined her in a new way. She would fight and do anything to protect those she loved.

On this mission, a sword had risen among them all, foretelling the end of anyone foolish or brave enough to wield it. Along the way, she witnessed Marcella's hatred turned to love; Justus' anger and sorrow turn to destruction; Samuel grow even greater as a man; Licia, awakening in Arria a mother's drive to protect her child. And Garic, as always, her reason for living—her partner of the soul.

Arria felt a sudden movement within her belly. They would go home now and welcome their land, family, friends, and the peace all would provide. She patted her stomach and smiled. Tonight, they would say farewell to Telemachus, a soldier and friend, gone from the world. Tomorrow, they would celebrate Licia's birthday and write a new page in their story. The sun golden bright, Arria gripped the sword tighter and walked toward its scabbard, shining on the ground.

Wilder Honig, beautiful Wild Honey—we're coming home.

Epilogue

Home

CONSTANTINOPLE: The Emperor's Palace—The End of Junius

ARRIA

Arria reached for her water pouch and took a drink. The breeze gliding through the palace's open corridors had little effect on the humid heat clinging to her skin. Besides, as time moved along, her craving for water only grew stronger. She felt like a fish or a mermaid, the sea creature that Licia so loved to talk about. Garic had begun routinely bringing her rotating pouches to keep her happy. She was showing now, but she still felt agile and able to perform her daily tasks. The palace physicians determined she was three and a half to four months along. This seemed reasonable to her, and she was relieved and ready to leave for Gaul. She wanted to have the baby at Garic's farm, Wild Honey.

In Jerusalem, Arria and Garic had finally met with Patriarch Juvenal, who heard their story and was more than eager to attain the sword as a relic for pilgrims to venerate. After leaving the sword safely with the church, they started their journey back to the Great City. Reuniting with the emperor and reporting the success of their mission had proved rewarding for them all. Emperor Marcian felt an immense sense of relief to know the Sword of David rested in the Church of the Holy Sepulchre, but he found the news of Telemachus' death and Justus' betrayal surprising and sad. He also took on the task of informing any family Telemachus might have and offering relocation of his body if they desired.

Arria walked onto the veranda and found a seat on a marble bench. The view from the hill on which the palace sat overlooked the city and a broad blue sky. She tried to spend as much time with the emperor as she could, and he with her. They knew their farewell might be their last. Time together with her former father-in-law was precious. He'd always treated her with kindness, affection, and respect. His son, her first husband and love, had been so much like his father. A piece of her heart would always be with Lucius Marcian.

In two days, she and Garic, Licia, Catalina, and Brother Bruno would leave for Brundisium on the east coast of Italia and then make their way again across the Via Appia to Rome. From there, they would go to her villa in Tuscia and then, after a few weeks, on to Gaul. A most exciting part of this trip would be the new companions joining them, Marcella and Nerian. Her sister had asked to come and spend time with them in Tuscia. Arria had agreed. She wanted the opportunity to get to know her sister and her new husband. Sometimes, when she looked at Marcella or watched the way she expressed herself, Arria saw hints of her father, Quintus Arrius Felix, a great senator and loving father.

The one person she found hardest to leave was Samuel. He had traveled with them back to the monastery and from there returned to Angelus in Nazareth. He carried Bathsheba's star in a silver box and showed excitement over being able to share it with his family, temple, and community. He hugged Arria for a long time. "I'll come and find you again," he had promised. "When Angelus is older and a stronger man. My life would have been spent as a slave, if not for you, Arria. I can never repay you."

They had walked in the monastery gardens that morning before he left. Upon hearing his feelings of gratitude, she had stopped and reassured him. "Samuel, you owe me nothing but your friendship. Over the years, I learned many things from you, and by your side, I always felt protected, even when those drunken soldiers, so many years ago, beat you for the misunderstood act of helping me. We may not be brother and sister in blood, but we are in spirit. I'll miss you so much." Arria kissed his cheeks, and they hugged once more. Samuel said his goodbyes to Garic and Brother Bruno, Licia, and Catalina, too. Then he mounted his horse and rode off, leaving them waving their farewell.

Thinking of Samuel and the new course they would soon take made Arria's eyes well with tears. As she wiped the corners of her eyes, Garic came onto the veranda. "Mellitula, why are you crying. You should be happy. All is well."

"I'm not sad, just a bit melancholy. I really hope we can see Samuel again one day, but the distance between us is so far."

Garic sat beside her on the bench and wrapped his arm around her shoulder, he clutched her tighter. "I have a feeling that he'll make the journey very soon. He loves Gaul, and some of his best memories live there."

She smiled. "That would be wonderful. I'll pray that day comes soon."

He nodded, then shyly ventured, "You know what else would be wonderful?" A playful spark lit in his deep blue eyes.

Her eyebrow raised along with her suspicion. "Hmm. Does it have anything to do with an afternoon nap while Licia is playing with friends?"

Garic brought his lips to her ear and murmured, "*Ja*," and kissed her neck.

"Well, my lord, then . . .," Arria jumped up, and shot him an impish grin, "I'll race you to our room," she cried, and ran toward the hallway.

Garic waited a moment. He wanted to relish the capture. Then as quick as lightning, he bolted up and chased after her. Tomorrow he would bring Arria home.

GAUL: Wild Honey Farm, Harvest Time

Garic sat beside Arria and wiped damp curls from her brow. She smiled at him and looked down at the baby sleeping in her arms.

"I can't believe we have a son, Arria. He arrived with such a hearty cry. He'll be strong."

"Strong and handsome with blue eyes like his papa," Arria said, touching the baby's cheek.

Garic touched his son's fingers. "Welcome little . . ." He quickly glanced at Arria to be sure.

"Kai, son of Garic—as we agreed," she replied and kissed the top of Kai's head.

ACKNOWLEDGEMENTS

This third book took me on an adventure deeper into the mystery, suspense, and thriller genres, which I feel most at home with as an author. However, love is the heart of Arria and Garic's relationship, and so, threads of their romance weave through the novel. Once again, I must credit the story and muses for leading me through old and new characters and historical details that fell naturally into place.

However, the real work comes in the revision process, and my novel group writers, Janet Souter, Tamara Tabel, and Carol Cosman, helped me through it. We have spent years together, editing, critiquing, enriching, and polishing one another's manuscripts. Thank you so much for being part of my journey.

Also, my most sincere thanks to: My husband, Greg, for supporting my writing goals and acting as a sounding board when I need it; My publisher Angela Hoy and her team at Book Locker Inc., and Cathy Helms at Avalon Graphics; My Beta readers, Linda Hlavacek, India Edghill, and Sheila Bunnell; and the night writers at the Barrington Writers Workshop.

All the experts who have helped me through their written works—especially the histories, *Rome and Jerusalem* by Martin Goodman; *Jerusalem: The Biography* by Simon Montefiore; and *Jerusalem in History* by K.J. Asali. And also, through online sites and forums with direction, suggestions, and quality information, most notably, UNRV Roman Empire Forum; the Jewish Theological Seminary librarians, Deborah Schranz and Ina Cohen; my friend and expert Hebrew character contributor, Marty Kander; Father Nicholas Spencer, Quarr Abbey, Ryde, Isle of Wight; Helen King, Professor Emerita, Classical Studies The Open University.

Omnia ad Dei gloriam: All for the glory of God.

Cynthia Ripley Miller

Thank you for reading my novel. I hope you'll consider leaving a review on the site where you purchased it. I would also love to hear from you and can be reached at: cynthia@cynthiaripleymiller.com

Cynthia Ripley Miller is a first generation Italian-American writer with a love for history, languages, and books. She has lived, worked, and traveled in Europe, Africa, North America, and the Caribbean. She holds two degrees and has taught history and English. Her short fiction has appeared in the anthology *Summer Tapestry*, at *Orchard Press Mysteries.com* and *The Scriptor*. A Ring of Honor: Circle of Books Award winner, and Chanticleer International Chatelaine Award finalist for her novel, *On the Edge of Sunrise*, she has reviewed for *UNRV Roman History*, and blogs at *Historical Happenings and Oddities: A Distant Focus* and on her website:

www.cynthiaripleymiller.com.

Cynthia lives in a suburb of Chicago with her husband, and their cat, Romulus. Her books are set in Late Ancient Rome, France, and Jerusalem.

The Long-Hair Saga series:
On the Edge of Sunrise, The Quest for the Crown of Thorns, A Sword Among Ravens

Also connect with Cynthia on: Twitter:@CRipleyMiller
Facebook: https://www.facebook.com/cynthiaripleymiller/

3 1125 01133 5252

CPSIA information can be obtained
at www.ICGtesting.com
Printed in the USA
LVHW110757190121
676854LV00003B/162